City of Silver

City of
Silver

Annamaria Alfieri

FELONY & MAYHEM PRESS • NEW YORK

CITY OF SILVER

A Felony & Mayhem mystery

PRINTING HISTORY
First edition (St. Martin's): 2009
Felony & Mayhem edition: 2011

ISBN: 978-1-934609-73-6

Manufactured in the United States of America

Printed on 100% recycled paper

Library of Congress Cataloging-in-Publication Data

Alfieri, Annamaria.
City of silver / Annamaria Alfieri. -- Felony & Mayhem ed.
    p. cm.
ISBN 978-1-934609-73-6
1. Nuns--Peru--Fiction. 2. Murder--Investigation--Fiction. 3. Silver mines
and mining--Peru (Viceroyalty)--History--17th century--Fiction. 4. Potosí
(Bolivia)--History--17th century--Fiction. 5. Peru (Viceroyalty)--History--
Fiction. I. Title.
PS3601.L3597C57 2011
813'.6--dc22
                                    2011003695

For David

Other "Historical" titles from

FELONY&MAYHEM

TIMOTHY BROADBENT
The Smoke
Spectres in the Smoke

DAVID STUART DAVIES
Forests of the Night

ANTON GILL
City of the Horizon
City of Dreams
City of the Dead

KEITH HELLER
Man's Illegal Life

PETER LOVESEY
Bertie and the Seven Bodies
Bertie and the Crime of Passion

FIDELIS MORGAN
Unnatural Fire

KATE ROSS
Cut to the Quick

CATHERINE SHAW
The Library Paradox
The Riddle of the River

DAVID WISHART
Ovid
Germanicus

ACKNOWLEDGMENTS

THANK YOU TO:
Toni Plummer, my editor, and Nancy Love, my agent, for making this happen, Robert Knightly, the best writing buddy ever, Katherine Hogan Probst, Ph.D., life-long friend and Latin scholar, and especially Steve Strobach and Naty Reyes, who took me to Potosí.

HISTORICAL NOTE

Though the characters and plot of this story are fictional, the background history and the city of Potosí are real. In 1650, as part of the Spanish Viceroyalty of Perú, it was the largest city in the Western Hemisphere, with a population equal to that of London. In 1987, UNESCO declared Potosí a Patrimonio de la Humanidad (Patrimony of Humanity). Its glorious architectural masterpieces, which are the scenes of this novel, still exist. Many of them have been lovingly restored and can be visited in this, the world's highest city, at an altitude of more than 4,000 meters (13,000 feet), in what is now Bolivia.

Potosí
Alto Perú
1650

DRAMATIS PERSONAE

THE CITY OFFICIALS OF POTOSÍ

Francisco Rojas de la Morada, *Alcalde Municipal, head of
the Cabildo (City Council)*
Ana, *his wife*
Inez, *his daughter*
Gemita, *his daughter*
Felipe Ramirez, *Tester of the Currency*
Jerónimo Antonio Taboada, *member of the Cabildo, ally
of Morada*
Juan Téllez, *member of the Cabildo, ally of Morada*

THE FAMILY TOVAR

Antonio de Bermeo y de Novarra Tovar, *Captain of the
Corpus Christi Mine*
Pilar, *his wife*
Beatriz, *his daughter*
Domingo Barco, *Mayordomo of the Ingenio Tovar (mine
and smelting works)*
Santiago Yana, *miner in Tovar's employ*
Rosa, *his wife, cook in the Tovar household*

IN THE CONVENT OF SANTA ISABELLA DE LOS SANTOS MILAGROS

Mother Maria Santa Hilda, *Abbess*
Sor Olga, *Mistress of Novices*
Sor Monica, *Sister Herbalist*
Sor Eustacia, *Sister of the Order*
Hippolyta de Escobedo, *postulant*
Juana, *a maid*

THE MEN OF THE CHURCH

Don Fray Faustino Piñelo de Ondegardo de León, *Bishop
of Potosí*
Fray Ubaldo DaTriesta, *local Commissioner of the Holy
Tribunal of the Inquisition*
Fray Pedro de la Gasca, *Grand Inquisitor for New Spain*

THE KING'S EMISSARY

Doctor Francisco de Nestares, *President of the Charcas,
Visitador General*

Those who think it is not easy for a woman to succeed in whatever she attempts are mistaken, for many women have surpassed men in valor, in use of arms, and in knowledge.

A man who has acquired great wealth through excessive greed, taking advantage of the sweat of the poor, might better have met his obligations.

Peace is the offspring of Justice, and one cannot obtain where the other is not meted out.

—Bartolomé Arzáns de Orsúa y Vela
Potosí, 1676-1736

City of Silver

CHAPTER

1

Santiago Yana approached the mine by night. He had climbed the steep, winding path worn smooth over a hundred years by the hooves of llamas and mules and the barely shod feet of thousands of Indians like himself. Up the Cerro Rico in the weak gray light of the waning moon. His barrel chest heaved. He gulped the icy, rarefied air. Below, the great stone-and-stucco city of Potosí sprawled out at the base of this silver mountain, like the train on a Spanish woman's gown. On the near side of the river, an occasional torch flickered in the yards of the refineries. Across, in the grid of streets surrounding the central plaza, dull candle-light glowed in the windows of the many rich houses. Spaniards burned wax as if it were cheap as stones.

Santiago paused at the mouth of the mine. Always before, he had gone down in daylight, with his comrades. Standing shoulder to shoulder among them, he sensed himself as part of one large animal, a beast courageous enough to descend the deep main shaft. At the bottom, he became a digit on that powerful creature's hand, making it possible for him to thread himself through the tight, dusty tunnels and, in the gloom and the din of iron banging on stone, to tear away chunks of silver to be refined and sent to the King of Spain.

Alone here in the night, he was riveted, bound by terror to the entrance. Dank air rose from the main shaft and froze his back and legs.

He blessed himself thirteen times and whispered a prayer to the Virgin of Candelaria. He drew from his pocket a wad of coca leaves and lime and chewed them reverently as he prayed.

He stepped out of the wind onto the top *barbacoa*, the wooden platform at the mine's entrance. As he struck his flint to light a candle, his callused hands trembled, and it took four tries to get the flame. How the other miners would tease him if they could see him frightened like a child, like a white woman. When the candle was finally lit, it cast grotesque shadows against the rocks. He placed it in its holder on his black felt hat and grasped the ladder's heavy ropes of twisted hide. With his foot, he felt for the first wooden rung and immediately slipped. "Madre de Dios!" He had forgotten to take off his sandals. He scrambled back up and left them. He repeated his prayers and began again the descent.

When the captain first gave Santiago the package for safe-keeping, he promised that if Santiago would hide it where no one would find it and return it when asked, he would give Santiago ten pesos, equal to a month's wages. The mine was the only place Santiago Yana knew where surely no one would find the package.

He reached the bottom of the first ladder—ten *estados* down—the height of eleven men. There were seventeen more. He prayed again and descended.

Ten days ago, when he had hidden the canvas-covered package in the mine, he had expected—when it was called for—to bring it up at the end of his next shift. But tonight the captain had demanded to have it before dawn.

As Santiago descended, the air grew even colder and sudden currents made the candle flicker. He felt in his pocket to make sure he had his flint. "*Dios mío.*" He had left it at the entrance.

Too far to go back. He moved more cautiously, trying to keep his head still so the candle attached to his hat would stay steady. If it went out, blackness would envelop him.

This mine was cursed. Every Indian knew the story. Their ancestors had found silver here before the Spanish came, but when the Indian people tried to take the silver from the mountain, a great god voice had boomed out from within, "Stop. This silver is not for you. It is for someone else." Some miners believed the gods had been keeping the silver for the Spanish, but some said it belonged to the gods themselves and that it was sacrilege for any mortal—even a Spaniard—to take it.

Santiago shuddered as he descended from the twelfth *barbacoa*. It was no darker in the mine at night than during the day, yet he felt the blackness more. Water dripped. Strange rumbling noises echoed in the stones. "Pachamama." He spoke the name of the old Indian goddess. Her image and the image of the Virgin converged in his mind. Both protectors. But Pachamama could also be cruel. He concentrated on the Virgin. The priest said she was more powerful than Pachamama and never cruel.

At the bottom of the last ladder, his lone candle gave him only a small circle of light. Traces of silver glinted in the reddish brown walls of the tunnel. Santiago longed for his comrades, even for the brusque orders of his Spanish masters, anything not to face this darkness alone.

Rubble left by the mining slid beneath his feet. He crashed into a pile of hammers and picks that awaited the next shift. "Mierda!" They clattered, and the noise echoed off the stones. He held his breath for a moment. The sound died.

He limped to the back of the tunnel, past the filthy place where the men relieved themselves, and held his breath until his chest ached. He inhaled and wanted to retch. At the end of the tunnel, where the stench was worst, the sloping ceiling forced him to stoop more and more until he was snaking along on his belly. There, under rocks he had carefully arranged to look as if they had fallen, he groped and grasped the packet.

He scampered back to the ladder and bound the packet to his leg with a leather thong, as he would have bound heavy sacks of ore if this had been a work shift. In his daily climbs with the ore tied to his legs, he paced himself to be able to bear the weight to the top. Without the burden, he was as light as smoke.

Tonight, climbing was like dancing. What worries the ten pesos would remove. Debts weighed on him as heavily as twenty bags of ore. With the money from hiding the packet, he would pay them all and still have enough to buy maize, potatoes, *charqui*, chilies, maybe even a bit of fresh meat for the feast of Easter, if Rosa would allow such an extravagance.

Rosa did not believe in the religion of the Conquistadores. She said no one should believe in a religion that required people to fast during the harvest. Santiago had asked the priest about this strange rule. The priest had explained that in his country it was the end of winter now, not the end of summer. What a magical place that must be, that it could exchange the seasons. But the priest also said the fast was not about making sure there was enough food, but to prepare the soul to celebrate the Resurrection of Christ. Rosa did not believe a man could come back from the dead.

By the fifth *barbacoa*, Santiago's chest constricted. Every breath hurt. He had climbed much too fast. A pain in his side doubled him over. He lay back on the wooden platform to rest. Then it happened. His hat! His candle! He felt them go, grabbed for them. He yelled as he watched the light stream away until the candle went out and the glow of the wick died completely. He groaned. The darkness was total.

He lay trembling so violently that he thought the spasms would throw him off the platform to his death. In the thunder of his thudding heart and the creaking of the mountain, he heard Pachamama laugh.

"*Madre de Dios*," he whispered over and over. "Help me."

He groped for the ladder leading up. "Oh, Virgin Maria, please. My children. My wife. Please."

He scrambled onto the next *barbacoa* on his belly and slithered across until his hands found the next ladder. Disoriented in the dark, he could hardly tell which way was up. Water rushed somewhere near, coming to wash him away. He panted and struggled to grasp the leather ropes with his sweaty palms. Air. He felt a current of air. Oh, gods, be merciful. The top! The entrance must be near. He scrambled up to the next platform. But there was another. And another.

He had lost track of how many were left. When he worked, he always counted as he climbed, always knew exactly how far he was from the air.

Now he began to weep. What shame he would feel if his comrades could see him.

Before bringing the package to the mine, he had let Rosa convince him to look at the contents, even though the captain had warned him not to. He had scolded her for being too nosy, but he was curious, too. She carefully removed the thick blue thread that had bound it, keeping it in one piece and laying it across his knee. He had been disappointed. The parcel contained only papers, with writing they could not read. She had sewn it back up again with the blue thread, stitching the canvas in the same holes, pushing the needle in backward for the last stitch because the thread was so short. No one would ever know they had opened it.

At the next level, a weak shaft of milky moonlight floated before his eyes. He blinked, bit down again on the wad of coca leaves in his mouth. Yes. Yes. He scrambled up the ladder now, panting, wheezing.

He arrived, covered with sweat, at the mouth of the mine. A blast of frigid wind froze his skin but gladdened his heart. He untied the packet from his leg, slipped his feet into his sandals, and began to grope around for his flint.

He smelled the horse before he heard the man approaching. The captain must have become impatient waiting at the inn.

"Señor, I have the package here," Santiago said to the figure in the black cape who approached him in the gloom. He held out the packet and his palm, waiting for the feel of the coins.

The man snatched the package from him and stuffed it into a bag. He laughed. A familiar laugh. But this was not—

The man grabbed him, lifted him as easily as a baby. The world spun. "No. *No!*" Santiago cried.

With a grunt, the man flung him down the mine shaft.

Santiago Yana did not even hear his own scream of terror as he fell to his death.

Around midnight that same night, Inez de la Morada prepared to go out to collect the packet of papers that would bring her heart's desire. She had no fear of being discovered by her father, Francisco—the Alcalde, head of the City Council and the richest, most powerful man in Potosí. He had left the house at eleven, as he had done every night for many weeks, to oversee the departure of a mule train. Many believed that Francisco de la Morada was, little by little, sending his enormous fortune out of Potosí to hide it in the vast, desolate high plain that surrounded the city.

Friends and enemies alike speculated on the reason for the removal of his wealth. Some said he expected another war—like the one fought between the Basques and the other Spaniards twenty-five years ago. Others said he foresaw that the dams, which held water in lagoons above the city, would break again and that the ruination would be even worse than the last time. The rational laughed at these fears. How could anyone, even one as powerful as the Alcalde, predict such events?

His daughter Inez knew the reason and the false impressions behind the mule trains. But tonight she would take possession of her own fate, and what her father did or desired would mean nothing.

The first time Inez stole out of her parents' house at night, her heart had nearly stopped with fear. She wished she could slip out unnoticed as effortlessly as she would brush an errant dark curl from her forehead, but tonight her breathing fluttered once again. On this second Sunday in Lent, she was leaving this place forever.

She dressed in heavy velvet clothes and light slippers that made not a sound as she walked through the darkness. She glided down the wide corridor and entered her father's study. In the flickering orange light from the torches in the courtyard outside, she opened a secret drawer in the tall desk near the window. She withdrew a bag of silver and hefted it. More than enough. The papers she was about to reclaim would bring her all she longed for. Until then, these coins would pay for what she needed.

Silver, she had learned from infancy, was the most powerful substance there was. Everything in Potosí depended on it. The city's whole existence, the importance of its citizens individually and collectively, stemmed from silver and only silver.

Her father had taught her this, as he had taught her so many things. She felt a small pang for him. She had loved him so when she was a little girl. But seeing him through her mother's eyes, she had grown to scorn him. Briefly, when she was thirteen or so, she had openly mocked his pretentious manners, his vanity about his clothes, the lumbering way he walked. Rather than evoking his ire, her barbs wounded him. She learned then that she could get whatever she wanted by giving and withholding her love. His weakness for her only made her despise him more. By now, she had pretended to love him so often that sometimes she almost did.

She made her way noiselessly back down the corridor, dragging her fingertips along the smooth plaster wall until she felt the jamb of her mother's bedroom door.

She hated her mother. Only for a few months—when she had been threatened by a fever—had she cared anything for her. But she was not worth a daughter's notice. Even the servants mocked her. Not when they knew their mistress was listening, of course. In her presence, they feigned respect. Away from her, in their own language, they freely criticized their weak, self-indulgent *padrona* in front of the smiling little girl they thought did not understand. Everything they said was true. Her mother was a pig. She had been so drunk once that she had vomited in the central plaza, in front of half the nobility of the town. Inez could not walk in the Calle de los Mercaderes with her without seeing the other shoppers whispering behind their hands. Never again. Tonight Inez would collect that packet of documents, her passport to freedom.

Holding her breath, Inez gently turned the latch of her mother's door, entered, and in a flash exited again by the servants' door opposite. The stairway led her quickly through the kitchen and out to the silent, stone-paved street.

Behind the draperies of her disarrayed bed, Ana Rojas de la Morada smiled. Her daughter probably assumed she was asleep when she stole through the room. But Ana waited each night to see if she would hear the faint click of the latch and to sense, not quite to hear, her daughter moving through the room, to revel in this betrayal her husband so deserved.

Husband and daughter both despised her. And she had learned to despise them in return.

She giggled, like the lovely, lively girl she had been when her bankrupt noble father gave her to Francisco Morada in marriage. Morada, the commoner who dragged her from her elegant, benign Lima to this money-grubbing Gomorrah with its intolerable society and unbreathable air. From the first, she had loathed her boorish clown of a lowborn husband—his coarse speech, his rough manners—everything about him, except his sex. On her wedding night, Francisco had taken his pleasure of her without regard to hers. But even as a girl she had learned to find her own satisfaction alone behind the curtains of her virgin bed. With him, she discovered that the same fantasies that had served her before their marriage brought her to ecstasy as he moved within her. Each night, when she lay down and drew the finely embroidered marriage linen over her, she welcomed the only part of him that interested her—what he thrust through the slit in the sheet.

He was intense. He believed that true vigor in their coupling would give him a son. To her enormous gratification, he had kept at it nightly for almost a year before he impregnated her.

She brought forth Inez.

When he returned to her bed three months after the birth, he came with increased energy and stamina. For more than two years, she did not conceive, but she had him nightly, giving her pleasure beyond her imagining and, as was seemly, completely without his knowledge.

When she gave him Gemita, another daughter, in return, he gave up.

At first she had tried to persuade him to return to her, reminded him that it was their duty to procreate as God had ordained. She had even said she wanted to give him a noble son. *Noble* was a word that she thought would entice him, since noble was what she was and what he longed to be. But that common worm of a social pretender had had the gall to reject her.

"I want no other child but Inez," he had said, as if the second dainty pink infant in the cot were nothing to him. Inez was then barely four years old, yet father and daughter were bound in a potent rapport that was to grow and blossom and make Inez dearer to him than any son could be. Or any wife.

Ana grinned. Weakling that he was under all his bluster, he adored his daughter. He thought he knew her.

The mother rose and glanced through the shutters at the shadowy figure disappearing down the deserted street. When he discovered Inez had gone out into the night, it would wound him worse than the knife Ana dreamed of plunging again and again and again into his flesh.

Just before dawn the next morning as she rose to go to the chapel to chant Matins and Lauds, Mother Maria Santa Hilda, Abbess of the Convent of Santa Isabella de los Santos Milagros, was called urgently to the door of her cloistered abbey. There she found Inez de la Morada begging in a shaky voice to be let in.

The Abbess sent the Sister Porter to the chapel to ask the Mistress of Novices to lead the morning prayers. Then she led Inez into the refectory, lit a candle, and sat beside the girl.

Inez's beautiful oval face was pale, her blue eyes wary and red-rimmed. She had the face of a Madonna, except that she often betrayed emotions stronger than those ever portrayed in representations of Our Lady. "What is it, my child?" the Abbess asked.

The girl paused and then began to sob. "I have seen the error of my ways, Mother Maria. I want to enter here and atone for the sins of the world." She reached out and gripped the Abbess's hand.

Maria Santa Hilda held the girl's small white fingers. Inez was seventeen, an age at which the self-sacrifice of the cloister held a romantic allure, when what seemed like a call to God's service could be real or just a beautiful but superficial dream. And an age when fathers sought to choose husbands for their daughters and when some daughters preferred a life with God to submission to a man they found odious.

The look in the girl's eyes was fear, the Abbess thought. "Why today, at this hour, Inez? You are distraught."

The girl's mouth opened and closed. She was struggling with the truth, it was clear.

"Is it something your father wants you to do? Someone he wants you to marry?"

Inez's eyes brightened for a second, as if the Abbess had hit upon that which she did not want to admit. But they clouded again. She put down her head and wept quietly.

The Abbess's heart trembled like the girl's lips. If defiance of her father, the Alcalde, was the girl's purpose, aiding her could be dangerous. Francisco Morada would not tolerate anyone interfering with his wishes, especially if it meant coming between him and his daughter.

The Abbess let go of Inez's hand and groped for the rosary that hung at her waist. Several of the sisters in this convent had been put here by fathers who had failed to bend their daughters to their wills. But Morada was no ordinary case. He was the Alcalde—the Mayor of Potosí—and he loved Inez and indulged her beyond what most fathers allowed. Also, he was the convent's greatest supporter. For the past three years, out of his own purse, he had supplied food and medicine for the hospital the sisters ran for Indian children. If the Abbess helped his daughter defy him, his beneficence might well evaporate.

She reached out and lifted the girl's chin. "Tell me the truth," she demanded.

"Please, Mother Maria," Inez pleaded. "I must stay here. It is the only place I will be safe."

"Safe?" the Abbess said. "From what?"

"From sin."

That same morning, across the canal in the private quarters of one of the huge *ingenios* that comprised both the silver refineries and the villas of miners, Pilar, the wife of mining captain Antonio de Bermeo y de Novarra Tovar, sat waiting on her stone balcony carved with exotic vines and images of the planets. Her maid Rosa was late bringing her morning maté. The bright sunshine on Pilar's back warmed her bones but not her disconsolate heart. She missed her daughter, Beatriz, and cast about in her mind for a way to bring the stubborn, silly girl back home.

An uproar intruded from the other side of the wall that separated the smelting works from the family's mansion. The door to the work yard flew open, and the noise grew louder.

Pilar stood and peered across the inner patio. To her complete astonishment, two *pongos* carried in something wrapped in a muddy gray blanket. They laid down their bundle on the stone pavement near the fountain. One of them hurried into the ground-floor kitchen.

In seconds, wailing and screaming streamed out the kitchen door, and slight and wiry Rosa Yana emerged, black braids flying, and threw herself on the bundle. She tore back the blanket.

"Dear Mother Mary," Pilar gasped, and blessed herself over and over. The mangled body of Rosa's husband, Santiago Yana, one of the miners who toiled in the Tovar lode, lay with limbs askew, in positions one could not imagine on a living person.

Rosa shook the corpse and shouted at it in Aymara. Ascensia, the scullery maid, stood in the kitchen doorway, her hands over her open mouth.

Pilar grasped her skirts to keep from tripping on them and sped down the broad stone steps. She took Rosa by the shoulders and tried to lift her away from the pale, crumpled body that used to be her husband.

"Wake him. Bring him back!" Rosa shouted at her. "Your Jesus came back from the dead. Call your priest. Make him bring back my Santiago. Call the priest."

"Rosa. Oh, Rosa. I am so sorry." Pilar turned and commanded Ascensia, "Get her some maté."

"I don't want tea. I want my Santiago." Rosa turned finally and faced Pilar. "Mistress, I beg you. You believe, you told me you did, that your God brought Jesus back from the dead." Her black eyes defied Pilar to deny it.

"Yes," Pilar whispered.

"Then make him bring back my Santiago. Jesus had no wife, no children. Santiago has us. We need him." She gripped Pilar's hands and kissed them. "Please, please. Call the priest."

"The priest cannot resurrect him."

"You said you believed!" Rosa pulled away her hands and raised her fists. Pilar stepped back, away from blows that looked certain to come.

"Stop this!" Antonio's voice boomed from the doorway to the *ingenio* yard.

At the approach of the master, Rosa crumpled to the ground in a heap of sobs. Under his red-plumed cavalier's hat, Antonio's elegant face was grim. He strode to the body of his *barretero* and looked down on him but said nothing.

Rosa rose to her knees and scuttled over to Antonio's feet. She wrapped her arms around his ankles and wailed, "Capitán, I beg you. Call the priest. Make him come and bring Santiago back."

Pilar moved closer to her husband and pleaded with him with her eyes. Through the passive expression he feigned, she saw his grief and anger. He peeled Rosa's arms from around his legs and stood her up as easily as if she had been a child of three. "Santiago should not have been in the mine at night," he said, as much to Pilar as to Rosa. "This kind of accident befalls people who did what he did."

Rosa stiffened. "He did not fall by accident. He was murdered, I am sure of it."

Pilar doubted her. "Who would do such a thing?"

"And why?" Antonio asked.

"Because of the letters he carried." As soon as the words were out of her mouth, Rosa's fingers flew to her lips. "It was a secret."

"What letters?" Antonio demanded.

"We could not read them, but they were dangerous. Santiago said the person who gave them to him said they could kill a man."

"Who gave them to him?" Pilar asked.

Antonio raised an eyebrow. "If you could not read them, how could you know what they were?"

Pilar put an arm around Rosa's thin shoulders. It was no sin not to be able to read. She could not read. Her father, like Spaniards of his day, had considered it unseemly for a woman to read.

"The captain who gave Santiago the papers told him to hide them where they would never be found. That they were dangerous enough to cost a man his life. This is all I know."

"Who gave them to him?"

"I do not know."

Antonio crossed his arms over his embroidered doublet. "We found no papers on Santiago."

"He went to the mine to get them last night." Rosa's face was set in defiance. "He was killed for them."

Antonio's face softened, then hardened again. "How can you know such a thing?" He spread his hands in a gesture of finality and turned to cover Santiago's body. He instructed the *pongos* to take it to the chapel at the back of the *ingenio*. "Send for the padre to bless his body," he said to Pilar.

"What can be done?" she said.

"The death of one Indian will garner no attention." He wanted to seem as if he didn't care, but she heard the pity in his voice.

"Someone should suffer for this," Pilar said to him quietly. "Suppose what she says is true?"

"How can we ever know that?" Antonio said. "I will suffer. We will all suffer. The workers are already saying that Santiago died because the mine is cursed." He drew his black alpaca cloak around him and followed the body out through the door to the *ingenio* yard.

Rosa took Pilar's hand and kissed it over and over. "Please, señora, justice. Please, justice."

Pilar took her chin and raised her head. The pleading in Rosa's expression tore at her soul. She shook her head. Antonio was right. Justice over such a thing seemed as remote as the planets out in the ether. "I will try." She patted Rosa's shoulder in a vain attempt to comfort her. "I will talk to Padre Junipero. He cannot bring your Santiago back to life, but he may be able to bring his killer to some form of justice."

"Promise me," Rosa demanded.

"I promise." Pilar could not resist saying it, though she knew it was impossible.

CHAPTER

2

hree weeks later, early on Holy Thursday morning, a powerful black horse stamped impatiently against the cobblestones outside the Convent of Santa Isabella de los Santos Milagros. He snorted a stream of white steam, which clouded around his elegant head. A rider in a black cape slid from the richly adorned leather-and-silver saddle and approached the carved stone portal of the convent.

From behind the heavy jalousies of her cell window, Mother Maria Santa Hilda recognized the short, stout rider carrying the canvas-wrapped parcel—Don Felipe Ramirez, an official of the city government. The Abbess knew immediately what he wanted and sent the sturdy maid Juana to meet him. More silver for the convent's depository. The safekeeping of silver for wealthy families was just another responsibility that weighed on the Abbess.

She turned from the window and knelt before the huge crucifix that was the only adornment of her spartan room. The patrician face she turned up in supplication revealed desperation and confusion. "Dearest Lord," she murmured. In years of silence imposed by the rules of her contemplative order, she had developed the unconscious habit of speaking aloud her private prayers. "What am I to do? I want to do Your will." But how could she know God's will? So many times in her life she heard others call something God's will when she saw it was really their own.

Her present dilemma was of her own making. She had always overindulged Inez de la Morada, who as a spirited seven-year-old first came to the convent with other daughters of rich families to learn comportment and needlework. Her tiny feet danced more than walked. Her speech filled the rooms with music and laughter. She seemed a prize, and the Abbess had sought to win her. By the time she was ten, whenever she wanted something—an extra helping of sweetmeats or another girl to let her win in a game—her worldly-wise, large blue eyes would go blank just for a second. And the next thing she said would be disarmingly charming. In those moments, the girl was more like an enchanted doll than one of God's creatures. Yet when Inez protested her love or her innocence, it was impossible not to believe her.

"Dearest Lord, forgive me," Maria Santa Hilda whispered up to the passive countenance under the crown of thorns. "If you had granted me marriage and family, instead of a religious vocation, Inez is the daughter I would have wanted."

Now, she found herself between God and the girl's father.

She crossed herself and gripped her hands together. A vein of envy shot through her admiration for Alcalde Morada's love of his daughter. It was exactly the sort of love she had sought but failed to win from her own father. Whatever the cause of this rift, the Alcalde and Inez must be reunited. But first, the Abbess had to secure the salvation of the girl's soul. Doing that meant holding out for a while longer against the Alcalde's demand to have his daughter back. "If I send Inez home now," Maria Santa Hilda said to the impassive statue, "she threatens to defy her father in another way, become a wanton. Surely this is only a tactic. But she is desperate, and her very soul is at stake."

Despite her resolve, the Abbess of Los Milagros knew she must tread as if on spikes. If she offended the Alcalde, he would withdraw his support for the poor. "Must I choose between Inez's soul and the lives of the poor children in Contumarca and Caricari?" Maria Santa Hilda demanded of the statue on the cross.

Twice already, she had managed, even in the face of the Bishop's intervention, to stave off the Alcalde's commands. Now Morada had grown desperate and the Bishop surly. His Grace had summoned the Abbess for the third time. This morning, he would not be put off. Would the Abbess have the courage to refuse the Bishop yet again? She was afraid. And afraid of being afraid.

She rose from her knees and prepared to go out into the bone-chilling autumn morning. The wind whipped this bleak land whose reversed seasons made a mockery of the beautiful imagery in the hymns she and her sisters practiced each day in anticipation of Easter. They sang of fields and trees reawakening with the Resurrection of Christ. So it had been in the Spain of her birth. The Spain she longed for but had left when the convent that had been her refuge began to feel like a prison. She had professed to her superiors a calling to do God's work in New Spain. She admitted only to her confessor that she came to Potosí to give her sterile life some meaning. The guiltiest part of her guilty heart knew she had come not to save souls, but to find employment for her prideful intelligence, an outlet for her passions—for adventure and a taste of the exotic New World.

The work of saving souls had pursued her across the wide ocean to this place of forbidding beauty and desolation. Here, after four months of grueling travel, she had found a large and well-organized city so like the Spanish city she had left behind in Europe, it seemed a gossamer vision. Dozens of churches, plazas, stone-paved streets with Spanish names, white stucco houses with red-tiled roofs, haciendas surrounding tranquil patios, gurgling fountains, carved stone portals surmounted by coats of arms. Then, just as she had begun to accept that it was

Spanish, it surprised her again. The carvings around the door-
ways of houses and churches were not the expected garlands of
grapevines or roses with cherubs. The motifs portrayed instead
strange little forest creatures with almost human faces, leaves
and vines of the New World, and the faces of Indians with rings
in their ears. The work was skillful, and the effect mystical. She
knew at once that when she built her convent, she would have it
decorated by those artisans. And she had. For fifteen years now,
she and the sisters who had come with her and the new sisters
born in this far land had prayed and constructed a true Catholic
and Spanish holy place, but one of this world, not the old. Yet for
all that she had accomplished, saving Inez's soul could turn out
to be the hardest labor of all.

The Abbess put on her mantle of black vicuña and placed
over it a stole of brown alpaca fur to protect her from the brutal
weather. Touching the foot of Christ on the crucifix, she whispered, "Give me courage, Lord."

She crossed the front cloister and knocked at the door of
Sor Olga, the Mistress of Novices. A chair scraped against the
brick floor of Sor Olga's private chapel, and the wiry old nun's
searching dark eyes appeared behind the iron grille in the door.
"Mother Abbess, I thought—"

"I decided to go out early. The crier called out that they
will read an urgent proclamation in the Plaza Mayor at nine this
morning. On our way to our audience with the Bishop, we must
pass there to hear the news."

Sor Olga's eyes disappeared, leaving a whiff of disapproval.
Sor Olga disliked the Abbess's curiosity about events in the
outside world. Sor Olga disliked a great many things.

In seconds she came out of her cell, mute and bundled
against the cold. They bowed to the Sister Porter, who unbolted
the heavy front door and let them out to the street.

Indian women bread sellers behind tall baskets, haughty
noblemen wearing metal breastplates and plumed hats, and
smiling Mestizo tradesmen all saluted them as they passed along
the Calle Real in an ever thickening, wind-whipped throng

heading for the main square. The nuns nodded in response to the greetings but spoke to no one, not even one another. Their silence was born of habit from their years in a contemplative order, but also of a tension between them. Both knew there was bitter disagreement, maybe even animosity, hovering and ready to pounce if too many words were spoken.

The Abbess searched her heart for a spot of tenderness toward the small, hard nun at her side. Underneath Sor Olga's armor of rigid piety there must be a real human story—like the stories of the convent's other women, young and old.

There were those—and many—who entered for the pure joy of doing nothing but loving God. Sor Olga had none of the serenity of such a one. Nor had she the heat of passion for Christ that infused the women whose eyes flamed as they gazed at the raised host during Mass. Something else had brought Sor Olga to the religious life. The Abbess was sure she would never know what had wounded this tiny, unyielding woman so long ago.

As befitted their lineage, the two nuns took their places with the nobles on the steps of the cathedral, which the locals called La Matriz—the Womb. The leading citizens near them were typical of Potosí's elite, Spaniards, richly and fashionably dressed. Men stood proudly, as if posing for a painter's brush, head to toe in severe black with white high collars, their capes and doublets embroidered in silver and gold. Ladies, whose thick and elaborate brocade gowns could not protect them from the cold, huddled in plush fur cloaks, their hands plunged deep into muffs of white and gray. They bore their gold-and-diamond necklaces like princesses, stepping daintily across cobbles in slippers sewn with pearls and precious stones. Even their maids wore gold on their chests and pearls embroidered on their sleeves. The women of Potosí had so much to spend on beautiful dresses that they displayed them on their servants as well as themselves. Wealth was the reason for this city's existence, and its citizens flaunted all they had.

In every skin tone from the smooth ebony of the statuesque African slaves to the bronze of the Andean Indian ore carriers to the pallor of the Spanish nuns who stood in silence on the steps of the cathedral, the chilled faces of the crowd revealed a certain apprehension about the nature of the news they were about to receive, but also a smugness born of living in the largest, richest city in the Western Hemisphere, of knowing they participated, in their various ways, in the most important activity in Christendom. They believed in the power of Potosí. Their city had dominated the economic life of the planet for nearly a century.

They faced the elegant, cut-stone façade of the Alcaldía Municipal—the headquarters of the city government—across the plaza. From the railing of the second-floor balcony, the city's multihued coat of arms, given a hundred years ago by King Carlos, the Holy Roman Emperor, rippled in the wind between bright banners of red and gold. "I am rich Potosí," it proclaimed, "treasure of the world, the king of mountains, and the envy of kings." The head of the city government—the Alcalde Mayor, Francisco Rojas de la Morada—would soon emerge to read a proclamation.

Maria Santa Hilda reached for the rosary that hung from her sash and fingered the beads. The news could be bad. It might further sour the Bishop for their discussion. Though her position as Abbess gave her clear jurisdiction over matters inside her convent, she could not defy the Alcalde *and* the Bishop forever.

Long ago and far away, she had gone to the convent searching for peace. That naïve novice soon became a woman burning with ambition. Sor Maria Santa Hilda rose rapidly in the estimation of her superiors and in the responsibilities they bestowed. Just days after her thirtieth birthday—only fifteen years after she had put on the ring and married Christ forever—the Mother General of the Order appointed her to cross the ocean and found the Convent of Santa Isabella. Since her arrival in Potosí, while she was immersed in the euphoric work of building, her energy and the inspiration of God's love had glowed within her. Now, the convent was built and its great church almost completed. Instead of simple stones and mortar, she had to deal with conflicts that plagued her conscience and responsibilities that weighed like boulders. For the noble women and girls of her community, she stood in the place of Christ—unworthy though she was. She had to decide for them, and many of those decisions—like the problem of Inez—gave her no clear choice between good and evil. She prayed to the Holy Spirit to inspire her, but so far she had prayed in vain.

In his mansion only a few yards away, from behind the heavy Neapolitan silk draperies of his upstairs sitting room, the Bishop Don Fray Faustino Piñelo de Ondegardo de León scanned the plaza and the hundreds of whitewashed brick-and-stone buildings beyond. His stern eyes narrowed. Would that the life of Potosí were as orderly as the grid pattern of its streets. The souls of its inhabitants ought to be as clean as the whitewash on its buildings. Their faith should shine as brilliantly as the sun in this clear, rarefied air. But the behavior of the citizens resembled more the uneven ground on which the city was built—high ideals and religious fervor in some quarters, low lawlessness, enslavement to flesh and violence elsewhere. The riches of the mine had spawned this great city, but everywhere, the turbulent mining camp of its past showed through its veneer of elegance.

The Bishop let the curtain drop. How he longed to be in Sevilla or Andalusia. Almost any warm city in Spain that offered small compensations for the sacrifices of the priesthood—a decent wine, a fresh peach—that was all he wished for. But for the circumstances of his birth, he would have the life he wanted. Instead, fate had forced him to accept what was offered—a perilous voyage amid unspeakable shipboard conditions—filth and crowding beyond description. Two months from Spain to Panama. Across the isthmus by mule. Another stench ridden ship south to Lima. Then that tedious trek up the endless mountains. He saw the barren Altiplano as a remnant of the earth before God created Eden—earth separated from sky, but nothing else. Here he lived, fourteen thousand feet above the sea. Why had God put that mountain of silver in this miserable place?

Because of that silver, remote and desolate as it was, Potosí's citizens felt themselves at the center of the universe. Fools. They may as well have been buried at the bottom of the deepest ocean.

The Bishop turned again to look out. He sighed deeply. The city gave only one consolation. The quantity of its riches and suddenness of its citizens' good fortune made them generous with God's representative. His own fortune grew. He had already enough money to erect, one day, a chapel that would hold his earthly remains—one to rival the glorious tombs of the popes in Rome, of the same marble, sculpted by the finest artists. If his mother had been a different person, he might have aspired to be Pope. As it was, perhaps, if his fortune grew large enough and the King's coffers required it, he might even purchase the Viceroyalty itself. Other lesser offices had been for sale to the highest bidder for some time. Why not the highest office in this land?

Rumors troubled him. Talk of problems with the currency— problems that could threaten his own wealth. The men in the plaza spoke of counterfeit coins, made not of pure silver but adulterated with baser metals. If this turned out to be so, the coins of Potosí would not be trusted. The King might even devalue the pesos stamped in Potosí. The Bishop shuddered to think that soon his eight hundred thousand might be worth only half that.

A sharp rap at the door halted the descent of the Bishop's thoughts.

"Come," the now deeply annoyed Bishop called across the room. Only one person would have the temerity to disturb him at this moment.

Juan-Baptiste, the porter, entered, went down on one knee, and predictably announced Fray Ubaldo DaTriesta, the local Commissioner of the Holy Tribunal of the Inquisition.

The tall priest, thin and dry, entered from the hall and bowed. "Good morning, my lord Bishop," he said in his lowborn Spanish.

Eyes still lowered to the floor, the porter said, "This parcel arrived this morning, my lord." He placed a canvas-wrapped package on the inlaid marble table near the door. He folded his hands in an attitude of prayer, bowed from the waist, and backed out the door, which he closed without a sound.

DaTriesta glanced at the parcel and raised his eyebrows questioningly. This local representative of the Inquisition was nothing if not inquisitive.

The Bishop refused to indulge him with an answer. The package was a private matter. The plebeian Commissioner's pretensions at intimacy stuck in the Bishop's craw, little gravels of annoyance, like the pebbles in a turkey's gullet. But DaTriesta's power was not to be trifled with. The Bishop suppressed a snide remark about the priest's shiny, grease-stained cassock. He unlatched the window and wrinkled his nose instead at a whiff of acrid smoke from the llama-dung fires in the Indian section to the south, on the slope of the Cerro.

"Look. I see some movement behind the balcony doors of the Alcaldía. Perhaps Alcalde Morada is ready to read the announcement."

DaTriesta crossed the room. "The talk in the plaza is of Inez de la Morada. The whole city knows the Abbess Maria Santa Hilda is defying the Alcalde by keeping his daughter in the convent. And they all know that you have asked the Abbess more than once to send the girl home."

The Bishop fingered the fine green silk of his draperies and hid his rage. "I should think the citizens would be more interested in the proclamation they are gathered to hear. The words come from their King. Do you think it will be about the currency? There have been so many reports of false money."

"Smugglers' rumors." DaTriesta waved a skinny hand as if to shoo a gnat. Again, he swiveled his narrow head and eyed the canvas-covered parcel near the door. "Problems with silver are the things of Caesar. Your concern must be the Church. You are the Bishop of a hundred and sixty thousand in this city. You cannot be seen to allow the Abbess to defy you. You have the means to control her if you are willing to use them."

The Bishop stroked his ecclesiastical ring. He hated DaTriesta when he was right.

The Commissioner went on. "I've heard also about a heretical Indian woman who demanded that her husband be brought back from the dead."

The Bishop turned to the window. "Just an overly emotional woman—like all of them."

Across the plaza, the door to the balcony opened and three members of the Cabildo—the City Council—filed out. The Alcalde's powerful form paused on the threshold. The Bishop opened his window wider. Wind ruffled his lank gray hair as he cocked his head to hear.

Before going out to read the proclamation, the Alcalde Francisco Rojas de la Morada took pen and paper and scratched out a single sentence. He dropped the quill on the long oak table, lifted the page, and blew on it before folding it and handing it to a liveried footman by the door. "Take this to the Abbess of the Convent of Los Milagros. She is standing on the steps of the cathedral," he whispered, though the members of the Cabildo were unlikely to overhear him. They filled the room with chatter.

He turned his face away and struggled to gain control of himself.

Pellets of grief burned in his heart. For these past three weeks, he had been unable to still his own mind and soothe his hurt. He gulped rich pastries at dinner every night despite the Lenten fast. He went over and over his accounts, tallying his wealth three or four times a day. He changed his clothes every few hours, wearing more and more elaborate dress until his friends began to taunt him to reveal the name of his new mistress. In fact, not even Doña Laura's beauty and skill could distract him.

On the afternoon before Inez disappeared into the convent, she had sat with him in his study at home, as she so often had. It was a place ordinarily forbidden to women, but he had welcomed her there from the time she was four years old. At first to sit on his lap and tickle him with his quill. In those days, she had often stood on the chair behind him while he worked on his accounts. Many times she had fallen asleep with her arms around his neck and her head on his shoulder. He would reach behind and hold her to him and walk her gently and deposit her, still sleeping, into the arms of her nurse.

As the years passed, she sat across from him, her bright eyes shining with intelligence and understanding as he explained to her the workings of his affairs. But on the afternoon before she ran away, those blue eyes shone instead with challenge and resolve. Her persistence had shocked and angered him. Suddenly, they were battling, and she was defying him.

Regret overwhelmed him. He was right not to have given in to Inez, but he should have held his temper, reasoned with her. She responded to logic. In this way, she was like a man.

He had no son of his dreams, tall and deadly with a sword. He always consoled himself with the thought that no son could have been more fearless and clever than his Inez, and a son might one day grow to challenge him. He had not expected a daughter to do such a thing. But now that Inez had, even this seemed only natural for a creature like her. She was female, but strong-willed like him, and despite the weakness of her sex, a girl of her quality of mind would have her own ideas.

"I will go to Buenos Aires," she had said. "I will establish myself there. It will give us a foothold in another place. That way—"

"Are you insane?" he had shouted.

She remained cool. Her blue eyes looked upon him as if he were her little sister who needed to be cajoled into playing a game Inez's way. "Father, you still think of Potosí as the center of the universe, but given what you have told me about the currency, it will not always be that way. If I go to Buenos Aires—"

"Buenos Aires! It is backwater. Nothing of importance happens there. And how can you go there without your family?"

"I am—"

"You are stupid. Exactly like your mother!" His breath quickened. No words could have injured her more.

She glared at him.

He kept his countenance stern, but he felt his heart tumble down a mountain.

He had thought she would shout. She looked as if she might slap him. But then her gaze left his face. She rose and said calmly, "Very well, Father."

That evening and the next morning, it was as if the argument had never happened. Then that night, she disappeared into the convent, where she had been ever since.

Why had he let his blood flare? He should have charmed her. She was a girl, after all. Daughters were hardly worth the notice of a man like him. Now, for three weeks, he had suffered without her. No one but Inez could be a comfort to him in his home. Certainly not his droning wife or that silly little Gemita. He got nothing out of those boring, frivolous females.

His noble wife, Ana, had brought him social position and a dowry of twenty-five thousand pesos. He had cultivated those seeds into a vast fortune—the greatest in the city. His wife took and spent the wealth he bestowed on her without one thought to the intelligence, determination, and fearlessness it took to amass it. Only his Inez understood, as well as any son would have, that his fortune was more than a mere means to luxurious ends. It was the measure of him as a man. Inez delighted in the details of his work, offered her own clever suggestions, some of which had paid off handsomely. She admired him. Why had she suddenly decided on this ridiculous scheme of leaving Potosí?

It must have been the influence of the Abbess, who meant well enough, or that meddling priest. Who was that sanctimonious Jesuit to preach about money and how it was gotten? He and his fellow men of the Compañia de Jesus prayed in a golden church.

The burning pain under the Alcalde's heart flared again. There had been moments when he had looked into Inez's eyes and caught— What? A fleeting glimpse of something that seemed to belie her love. It never lasted long enough to see, just to sense. He dismissed the thought, as he would an unworthy supplicant begging in his patio. How had he become so enthralled to the love of a daughter? It was unseemly for a man of power. Yet he saw clearly how bleak his days would be if Inez never returned.

Morada approached the stained-glass window, where, unobserved from outside, he could survey the dense crowd in the plaza. The women's bright silk mantles stood out like jewels against the deep black of the men's attire. His friends and supporters stood fast together near the massive brick-and-stone bulk of the Mint, every man proud and stoic. Among the group of overdressed Creoles who lingered near them were five or six old campaigners, with sun-burnished skin and masses of gray hair that made them look like statuary carved from the rocks of the Cerro. Even their hats were the color of earth— tan vicuña—the headgear that had identified their side in the bloody civil war. Morada had fought beside them in his youth against the Basque bastards who still controlled more than their share of the city's wealth and power.

On the other side of the sloping plaza, between the Mother Church and the ornate façade of the theater, the opposition Basques held the highest ground. In the center, Antonio de Bermeo y de Navarra Tovar, that snob who gave himself such airs because of his noble lineage. Morada did not have a famous bloodline like Tovar's, but his father, Juan de la Morada, had fought with Pizarro. The son of a Conquistador was as good as any son of a womanish old *conde* who had stayed behind in Spain.

The Alcalde de la Morada allowed himself a sad smirk. That Basque Tovar had willingly sent his daughter, Beatriz, to the convent. Put her in that prison on purpose. It was an oddly comforting thought: that his chief rival's only child was with his and that Tovar also was without the bright eyes and animated conversation of his daughter at his dinner table.

If the proclamation Morada was about to read delivered the hardships it threatened, his great consolation would be that it would harm his enemies as much as it harmed him. More, since his own wealth was in pure silver ingots and very well hidden. Seven million pesos. A huge fortune. He had sent a train of Indian porters into the country every night for the past month. Everyone suspected they carried silver, but no one knew where they went. Only his most trusted supporters—men he owned body and soul—knew where his fortune lay.

Felipe Ramirez, the Assayer of the Mint, touched Morada's arm. "It is time," he said. Ramirez was short and stout, but no one would be better at one's side in a fierce fight.

Morada straightened his cloak and carefully folded back the right side to reveal the golden silk of its lining and the gold-and-silver embroidery of his doublet. The work had been done in Genoa and the garment tailored to his measurements in Lima by the Viceroy's own tailor.

"I am ready," he said. He followed Ramirez to the door. He paused until the crowd in the plaza focused completely on him. Then he took up the proclamation that had arrived from Lima yesterday and stepped out on the breezy balcony.

He held the parchment aloft and then read: "By the hand of Don García Sarmiento y Sotomayor, Count of Salvatierra, sixteenth Viceroy of Perú. His most Gracious and Roman Catholic Majesty Felipe the Fourth sends greetings to his subjects in the city we are pleased to call our Villa Imperial of Potosí. Know ye that for some time we have had the wish and determination to settle many matters of disturbance to our city, by reason of its great importance to the service of God and the increase of our Holy Catholic faith and to the welfare of all our subjects, especially those resident there in the Villa Imperial. False coins, coins of alloy, yet stamped with the royal seal and minted in Potosí, are abroad in the world. This is an affront to the Royal Person of the King as well as a threat to the holy work of His Majesty in defending our Holy Faith. His Royal Majesty has therefore appointed Doctor Francisco de Nestares, President of the Charcas, as Visitador General, to exhaust all means which may appear conducive to find and prosecute the bandits with no respect for God or royal justice, to ensure the peace and tranquillity of the Villa Imperial, and to prevent interference with the King's revenues.

"Visitador Nestares will immediately begin to inform himself in minute detail what aspects of the silver industry are not being carried out in conformity with royal orders, and in all that he finds make correction, giving rules and instructions by which the mining and refining and minting of silver are in the future to be governed, to that end, without injury to the silver industry, the correction of all abuses which may have grown up in its management. The King has deemed it convenient to his royal service that Visitador Nestares shall arrive in Potosí no later than the Monday following Easter in the year of Our Lord 1650. I, the King."

The crowd stood in stunned silence for a few heartbeats and then erupted in a hundred exclamations. "Can it be true, then, that our money is false?" "It is what the Portuguese from Brazil have been saying." "Oh, dear Lord, we will be ruined." "So soon?" "Monday?" "That's only four days from now." "Why did we not have more warning?" "How can he arrive so soon?"

Morada knew the answer to the last question. Though ordinarily they would know months or at least weeks in advance of the arrival of a royal Commissioner, this time they were given only four days' warning. The Viceroy and the Crown hoped to catch the citizens of Potosí off guard.

The Alcalde held up both his hands until he could again be heard. "To welcome the King's emissary, we will have two weeks of celebration." The city was world famous for the extravagance and beauty of its festivities—banquets, masked balls, bullfights, processions. Everyone in the plaza prayed they would be able to mount a welcome lavish enough to turn the head of Visitador Nestares. Or he would certainly ruin them.

Morada grasped the hilt of his sword and, feigning a complete absence of emotion, strode inside.

A harquebus shot's distance away, in the corner of the square beyond the massive whitewashed granite hulk of the Mint, which more than the cathedral dominated the aspect of the city, Father Junipero Pimentel watched from in front of the rose-colored stone monastery where he lived—the Compañia de Jesus. The slight, tense Jesuit understood the exclamations of the crowd both in lilting, excited Spanish and in worried, staccato Aymara.

They talked only of silver. They craved it like a drug. Even the Indians. This great city existed only because of the ore torn from the hellish mountain with the blood of God's poorest creatures, brought to the mills across the canal where more forced laborers extracted the silver, which was then carried under guard here to the Mint. Behind these four-foot-thick walls, the silver was formed into ingots or stamped into irregular coins marked with the coat of arms of the King of Spain: reales, pieces of eight, the pirates called them.

Llamas and mules carried one-fifth of the coins, the tribute due King Philip, over the Andes to the coast, where they were loaded onto galleons and shipped to Panama. Thence across the isthmus to the Caribbean, and on to Spain. That is, if English or Dutch pirates did not take the ships on their way.

A hundred years ago, Indians and Spaniards both got rich from the mines. Some wealthy citizens of this city were descended from those first, fortunate Indians. But Spanish greed had triumphed. Now, armed soldiers walked the roof of the Mint to ensure that no silver went into the pockets of the workers, who more likely than not would die in the course of their labors.

The conscripted, more like slaves than workers, walked under guard to Potosí in columns from villages hundreds of miles away, where their relatives played funeral marches for them as they left. Conventional wisdom said that without their forced labor—the *mita*, as the system of recruitment was called—Potosí would fall; and without Potosí, Perú would fall; and without Perú, Spain would fall; and without Spain, the Catholic Church would fall. Protestants would rule the world. A terrifying thought. Would God allow such a calamity? Or was this theory just a sanctimonious rationalization to support greed that wanted cheap labor?

The people of Potosí were capable both of passionate devotion to the Holy Mother Church and of enormous greed. They competed in their devotion and especially in their extravagance. Don Jerónimo Andrade dressed himself and his bodyguard of eighteen in capes so laden with silver embroidery that they could barely walk. Don Juan Sarmiento once gave a party for three hundred that lasted the entire forty days from Easter until Ascension Thursday. Don Bartolomé Alameda trumped them all when he paid ten thousand pesos, the price of a hacienda in Spain, for a single fresh fig.

They tolerated violence, mayhem, drunkenness, and debauchery. Every day, irritable young men fought duels over the most trivial points of honor. Murders and rapes were constant occurrences. Yet Potosinos had built some of the most beautiful churches in Christendom. They gave dowries to poor maidens. Some achieved a religious mysticism that in its most extreme seemed to the priest, God forgive him, indistinguishable from madness. Others gave alms with abandon. A beggar in the right place at the right time might receive ten thousand or even twenty thousand pesos. A white beggar, that is, with nothing to recommend him but his white face. Yet the city's pillars of generosity paid their *mita* Indian workers only ten pesos a month, barely enough for food. From these meager wages they had to buy their own tools, even the candles they carried in the mine. Nothing was left to feed their families.

A rock of disgust weighed in the priest's stomach. Sins piled up like the slag beside the mine openings in this miserable and wonderful city.

As the agitated crowd in the plaza dispersed, Pilar Tovar approached him. He whispered a prayer he knew would be in vain that she would not raise again her pleas for justice for that dead miner.

He greeted her warmly and received her greetings. Just as she began making her demands, Mother Maria Santa Hilda and Sor Olga descended the steps of the cathedral and also approached. He interrupted Pilar's words with a greeting to the sisters. Of the two difficult tasks these women asked of him, the Tovar woman's was by far the more frustrating. He had made an effort to find out from the workers in the Corpus Christi lode any word about these mysterious documents that Santiago Yana had supposedly hidden in the mine, but the Indian's fellow *barreteros* denied any knowledge. And since none of them were literate, it seemed impossible they could have understood what the papers, if they existed, could have meant. And where would he go with suspicions that Yana had been murdered? The powerful men in the city were not likely to redress the grievance of an Indian's widow.

He much preferred to leave off this subject and speak to the Abbess about Inez de la Morada. He stood by while the sisters and Pilar exchanged pleasantries and Doña Tovar withdrew.

As Inez's confessor, he was responsible for the well-being of her soul. Beyond that, he had great hopes for her. He saw in the spirited girl a powerful intelligence and an irresistible energy of character that were the makings of greatness. If he could mold these gifts, he might guide her toward a spirituality that one day might rival even Maria Santa Hilda's. If this was ever to be so, Inez needed to remain—as she was now—removed from her father's influence. No doubt Alcalde Morada loved his daughter, but he treated her too much like a son, involved her in worldly pursuits. If she was going to turn her considerable talents to godly interests, she must remain in the sphere of the holy women of Los Milagros.

A few minutes ago, he had seen Alcalde Morada's footman hand the Abbess a note. It must concern Inez. The padre was curious to know its contents.

"What do you think of the proclamation?" the aristocratic Abbess asked immediately.

"If the money is devalued, it will ruin this city. If Potosí's coins are rejected, we are nothing but an imitation Spanish city in the most desolate spot on earth." A sigh he would have preferred to suppress escaped him. "The poor will suffer far, far more than the rich."

The wizened Sor Olga gave a knowing grin. "You are always thinking of your Incas."

He forced a smile in response to hers. She was just an old woman. She did not mean to be unpleasant. She just enjoyed sparring with him. But it annoyed him that she called the Indians Incas and trivialized the distinctions among their tribes. And that she called them his, not only because he defended them, but because he was a Criollo—a person born on this side of the Atlantic. He did not bother to remind her that despite the location of his birth, he was not a Mestizo. His mother was not an Indian. Though she lived in Hispaniola, she was as Spanish as Sor Olga's mother in Andalusia had been. It irked him that she ignored his pure Spanish blood, and it pained him that he was so proud of it.

"The King himself has decreed the Indians are human beings and must not be enslaved. Yet we treat them no better than pack animals. Doña Tovar and I were just speaking about the death of one that will in all likelihood go unpunished, no matter how hard I try to help his widow." The rock in his stomach pressed on his guts. He had again let her draw him into this same old argument.

"You will try to get justice for him? My dear padre, you might as well try to get justice for a mule that dies at the treadmill in the Mint." The old nun's face glowed with the thrill of verbal battle.

"The Indians are human. The Vatican established that over a hundred years ago," he said with all priestly sanctimony.

"There are those who believe that the natural state in which our countrymen found the Indians was life as God intended it to be."

She gave him a look of genuine shock. "Father! That they should live without the Holy Faith? If they are human, I am sure God did not intend that. Besides, you yourself have reminded me that there was a great civilization here: weavers, potters, builders of massive buildings. Not simple men living in nature." The corners of her mouth curled again in that smug smile.

He refused to acknowledge her triumph. She could best him in these little debates, but she was wrong in her heart. He would give her extra penance at her next confession. He forced away the thought as petty and sinful in itself. Pride and vengeance in one conversation. How did this holy old woman bring out the worst in him?

He turned to the Abbess. "The proclamation the Alcalde read did not tell the whole story."

"What more is there?" The Abbess's brown eyes showed more fear than curiosity. Hidden information always meant danger in the Byzantine world of the colonial government.

He lowered his chin and whispered, "The Grand Inquisitor is coming, too. There will be an investigation into more than just the currency." DaTriesta, the local Commissioner of the Inquisition, had bragged to him about it, though it was supposed to be a secret.

Sor Olga folded her thin, reptilian hands in an attitude of prayer. "May God speed their holy work. What would be the point of controlling the purity of our coins if we did not also control the purity of souls?"

The fear in the Abbess's eyes turned to annoyance. "Reforms are sorely needed, but we are unlikely to get the ones we most desire."

He knew she referred to the Bishop and his money-grubbing practices. "Be very careful, Mother Abbess," he said. "The Bishop feigns carelessness, but he is a formidable enemy. And you have something he wants."

"Inez."

"More than the return of the girl herself, I think he wants to be seen to have you in his command."

The Abbess's eyes flitted sideways toward her companion and back to him. A warning not to be so open in Sor Olga's presence. "He is the Bishop," the Abbess said lightly. "He is infinitely more powerful than I."

The sisters went off then, toward the Bishop's door, without telling the padre what Morada had written to the Abbess.

Maria Santa Hilda entered the Bishop's drawing room just as his Dutch clock chimed the quarter hour. She shuddered to find the local Commissioner of the Inquisition in the room. The combination of the proud and opulent Bishop and the pious and cruel DaTriesta boded no good for her. Apprehension stiffened her neck. She and Sor Olga crossed the room to kiss the Bishop's ring. His fleshy fingers were warm. "Good morning, my lord." In a city where the air was so thin as to be hardly breathable, the atmosphere in this sitting room was oppressively heavy.

"God be with you, my daughters," the Bishop said. "Please forgive me if I come right to the point. I have to be in the cathedral in a few moments to say the Holy Thursday Mass. I am afraid I must order you, in no uncertain terms, to return Inez de la Morada to her father."

Maria Santa Hilda suppressed a smile and reached into her pocket for the Alcalde's note. "My lord, I have—"

"His Lordship here has told me that you harbor some strange ideas about protecting young women from their duty to their fathers," Commissioner DaTriesta interrupted her.

Fear, like the footfalls of a spider, crept across the Abbess's shoulders. DaTriesta was sniffing for heresy. She bristled at the threat. Showing him the note would stop him, but she was tempted to let him stumble into a losing fight. She withdrew her hand from her pocket. "We live in a licentious and quarrelsome city, Father Commissioner," she said with forced humility. "My sisters and I devote our lives to prayer that we may be a wellspring of grace to serve God's people."

"Is it true, as I have heard," DaTriesta said, "that you harbor opinions about women that are very liberal—almost Protestant?"

The Abbess looked to the Bishop for some defense. He suppressed a belch and turned to the Commissioner. "Come now. The Lady Abbess…" His voice trailed off, as if he could offer nothing but her nobility to credit her.

"I think the Lady Abbess should answer my question," DaTriesta said, and licked his thick, dry lower lip.

Sor Olga's face worked. She looked as if her tongue were scraping something off the roof of her mouth. Her eyes gloated that her repeated warnings to the Abbess had come to pass.

An excess of temper forced the truth from the Abbess. "I merely reminded His Grace that it often falls to convents to take problem women off the hands of the wealthy." She refrained from saying such as poor wretched girls who had lost their virginity and were no longer marriageable. The insane. The deformed. The merely ugly. Women considered useless because they would make no nobleman a desirable wife.

"Be careful of pride, my daughter," DaTriesta said.

"May I respectfully remind you, Father, that I am answerable only to the head of my order in Madrid." She looked to the Bishop, but his small, round eyes deferred to DaTriesta.

The Commissioner held back his haughty head. "If you are thinking of appealing to your Mother House, remember it will take six months for your letter to cross the ocean and a reply to return. Much can transpire in such a time."

She met DaTriesta's gaze and struggled to hide her disdain.

"Shall I tell Captain de la Morada that he may come and get his daughter?" the Bishop asked.

She withdrew the paper from her pocket. "In fact, my lord, he writes me that he has relinquished her to the convent. He begs only that I keep her safe and to pray for both of them."

The Bishop took the paper and read. His mouth opened and closed in shock. He fell silent.

The Abbess took back the letter. "Perhaps Captain Morada has seen that in this regard, it is best to allow his daughter some time in my convent to come to peace within herself." Mother Maria did her best to hide the triumph in her voice. "I will seek to restore Inez's former attachment to her father, the Alcalde. However, if she comes to believe that her soul's salvation lies in a life of contemplation, I will welcome her as my Sister."

The Bishop's pale lips drooped in a dyspeptic frown. "With Inez de la Morada and Beatriz, the daughter of the mining Captain Tovar, your convent may soon be collecting two very large dowries."

"Be careful, Lady Abbess," DaTriesta said evenly. "With all that wealth, your convent will become the envy of other religious orders in the city."

The Bishop nodded in agreement.

She bowed to him. "Perhaps, Your Grace, but I think Beatriz Tovar may soon leave us."

CHAPTER 3

In her cell at the Convent of Santa Isabella de los Santos Milagros, Beatriz Tovar sat listening to the brooding silence of the cloistered garden, where the last leaves and one forgotten shriveled apple clung to the branches of a lone tree. Fear shone in her dark eyes. Two possible fates awaited her: endless days as empty as this in the convent or, if she gave in to her father, a life at the beck and call of some odious man chosen because he had money and connections. Both choices filled her with dread. The rock of fear in her heart flamed into molten anger. She would not give in to her father, a life at the beck and call of some odious man chosen because he had money and connections. Both choices filled her with dread. The rock of fear in her heart flamed into molten anger. She would not give her body to anyone but Domingo Barco. If she could not have him, she would be the bride of Christ. She would never submit to a husb—

Her heart went cold again. Her breath faltered. This wish might come true. Her stubbornness might condemn her to spend the rest of her life here, with nothing but her woolen habit and God to keep her warm.

God was supposed to be enough. Sor Olga, the Mistress of Novices, said so. To be a worthy person, she must leave off her selfishness and take on the cross of humility. She was willful. Her prescribed penance—a flail—lay on the table beside her narrow bed. She should mortify herself as Christ was tortured—loosen her novice's habit, expose her back, take the silver handle, and swing the chains so that the barbs on the ends bit into her skin. Punish herself for her pride.

She fell to her knees before the crucifix on the wall and begged Jesus to forgive her unwillingness to use the flail.

Her father would want to see her whip herself. "Marry Rodrigo or I will put you in the convent," he had said. He had commanded her in a harsher tone than he used with his Indian miners.

"Then I choose the convent." How could she answer otherwise? She would never marry this Rodrigo, whom she had never met. She was in love with Domingo Barco. But she could never tell her father because Domingo was Mestizo—half Spanish, half Indian. And he had no money. But he was good, not at all as people described others of his ilk—as wastrels who cared about nothing but clothes and gambling and fighting duels. Domingo was the *mayordomo* of the *ingenio*—her father trusted him to command the men of his mine and refinery. Why, then, could she not marry him? He worked hard. He was so handsome and forceful. She had no brothers or sisters. As her husband, Domingo could one day take the place of her father as Captain of the mine. Like her noble father, he knew how to fight with a sword. When she was ten, he had taught her to do it, secretly, when her father and mother were away. That was when she fell in love with him. He took off his doublet and stood in the patio in his shirt, his straight black hair gleaming in the sunlight, and showed her how to hold a sword, how to parry, and laughed when she said she wished she could grow up to be a knight in the King's service. Domingo's teeth were so beautiful. His laugh so deep and heavy.

So what if he was half Indian? It was evil of her father to hate him for that. Padre Junipero as much as said so.

And Domingo loved her. He always brought her sweetmeats when he went to the market on Wednesdays. And he saluted her when he saw her watching him from her window as he oversaw the work in the *ingenio* yard. The best proof came when her father dragged her to this place. Domingo had insisted on coming with them. She saw him blinking back tears as he looked up at the convent's stout stone walls. That profound sadness in his eyes was what kept her resolve. Domingo loved her so much, he wept at the thought of her being swallowed up here. As long as Domingo loved her, she could hold out against her father.

She went to her small, unglazed window and looked out at the belfry—as high again as the building itself. Her thoughts twisted like the carved stone columns running up its sides.

Her sister novice Inez de la Morada claimed she really wanted to live in this prison. She said she intended to stay forever. Beatriz could not believe it. Live a life of prayer and repentance? Naughty Inez?

Since they found themselves together in the convent, Inez had made surprising overtures of friendship, even told Beatriz secrets. In the past, they had quarreled because their fathers were enemies. The convent was all they had in common. They had learned music and needlework together here when they had been too young to know about their fathers' war. They used to talk about how romantic it would be one day to take the veil, to lie facedown, arms outstretched on the floor of the chapel, and take Christ as their bridegroom. An act of heroism and beauty. Beatriz tried now to summon the swell of love for God that had moved her so when she was ten. Now her chest contained only the stone-cold fear that she would be lost forever in profound silence and solitude, would never go again with her sweet mother to the Calle de los Mercaderes to order silk for dresses. Never eat Rosa Yana's bread, hot and crusty from the oven. Never see Domingo's hair gleaming in the sunlight or the love in his dark, serious eyes.

She went and poked the fire in the brazier. These rooms were so cold. When she was finished with the novitiate, would they let her have her cozy fur cape? She thought about her beautiful dresses. Her mother may have already given them away, even her blue Calabrian silk with the silver embroidery and Venetian lace. To prove her resolve, she had told her mother to give it to Inez's little sister, Gemita, but Gemita would never look so well in it.

After vespers that evening, Beatriz walked the silent corridor softly, as she had been taught, her hands tucked into the sleeves of her novice's habit, staying close to the wall with her head bowed to show humility. She entered Mother Maria Santa Hilda's office, curtsied, and took the small oak stool as the Abbess's gesture indicated. She struggled to imitate the saintly expression of the Virgin in the painting on the wall behind Mother Maria's head.

The Abbess's mouth was stern, but her eyes were as kind as ever. "A vocation is a serious matter, Beatriz." Her voice held a hint of reluctance that frightened the girl. Punishment was coming.

"Entering the convent requires a pure act of love for God." Mother Maria Santa Hilda also commanded her emotions not to show. The words she was about to say came dangerously close to a lie. Beatriz—alert, inquisitive, but frivolous—had a simple problem, but one not easily solved. She was a rosy, dimpled girl, but her soft exterior hid a core of steel. This valuable tenacity could turn to stubbornness if she was not handled well. "My daughter," the Abbess said with purposeful gentleness, "life here can be very beautiful—peaceful, without the sharp conflicts of family life, but—"

An insistent tapping at the door stopped the Abbess's thought. "Enter," she called impatiently.

The door opened to reveal the small, intense face of Sor Monica, the Sister Herbalist who looked after the sick. Her large, tender dark eyes were wide with fear. "Mother. You must come at once."

"Is it Sor Elena?" asked the Abbess, referring to the old nun who lay wasting away in the infirmary.

"No, Mother. It is Inez. When she didn't come to chapel for Vespers, Sor Olga and I went to her cell to see if she was ill."

"And?"

"You had better come."

Maria Santa Hilda leapt to her feet and made for the door.

Beatriz considered that she ought to wait here for the Abbess to return but quickly abandoned the thought and followed. They rushed across the stone-paved courtyard, passed the refectory, and sped down the corridor toward the rear cloister and the cells of the nuns and novices. Sor Olga, the Mistress of Novices, and chubby Hippolyta, another postulant, stood before the door to Inez's room. Sor Olga was tapping on the door and calling insistently, "Inez. I command you to answer me... Inez!" Between her commands, the dark silence of the cloister descended. When Mother Maria Santa Hilda approached, the others backed away.

"If she has fallen into a faint..." Sor Monica, the Sister Herbalist began.

Mother Maria held up her index finger and shook her head to silence her. Sor Monica held out her hands in capitulation.

Beatriz read the emotional eloquence behind the hand signals. Women in contemplative orders communicated this way to minimize the amount of talking they had to do. Mother Maria's long, aristocratic fingers commanded. Sor Monica's soft, tiny hands accepted without question.

"Inez, come out," Mother Maria called in her sternest voice. "At once." Without waiting for a reply, she stretched up to look through the grate in the door.

"It is covered with a black cloth," Sor Olga whispered. "And it is locked." The second sentence carried the high pitch of shock and indignation. Cells were never locked. Never.

Mother Maria stuck her long fingers through the wrought-iron bars and tugged at the black cloth. It did not budge. "Inez. Open *now*!"

In forbidden curiosity, several pairs of eyes appeared behind the grates of doors along the cloister.

Beatriz stepped back and caught the glance of Hippolyta, a girl her own age, and made a face. The two new postulants, who had sinned many times by breaking silence while scrubbing the floor of the refectory side by side, passed immediately a silent message: "Inez is really in trouble now." Beatriz thought she detected gloating in Hippolyta's blue eyes.

Mother Maria again grasped the black cloth, this time with both hands. She pulled with all her strength and managed to tear it out through the grate. *"Inez!"* There was a tinge of fear in her voice. She peered into the cell, stood on tiptoe, moved her head up, down, left, right. "I can't see her." She turned to Sor Olga. "How is the door locked?" There were no locks on the cells in the Convent of Santa Isabella de los Santos Milagros.

The Novice Mistress's old wrinkled hands opened in front of her in a gesture of futility.

Beatriz gulped.

"Inez..." Mother Maria turned the round wrought-iron latch and pushed on the door. It moved a fraction of an inch, but no farther. The Abbess pushed harder. Again and again.

Now eyes stared from grates around the entire cloister. Hippolyta looked again at Beatriz, whose hands went to her mouth. Silence, Beatriz thought. I am supposed to maintain silence.

Mother Maria turned back to Sor Olga and Sor Monica. "This door is barred, but I cannot see how."

"I know, Mother." Beatriz's voice was barely audible to her own ears. All eyes turned to her. She looked away from the expectation and disapproval in their faces. "There is a plank. It is wedged behind the *armario* and behind the bed." She glanced up again. "Inez told me she had it."

Sor Olga came forward and grabbed Beatriz's hand and squeezed it in her hard, bony grip. "And you said nothing?"

Beatriz bit her lip against the pain. "I told her if she did not give it up, I would report it in chapel on Friday at the Convocation for the Holy Rule." That odious weekly meeting when each novice prostrated herself in front of the whole convent and revealed all the ways she had broken the rules of the order. "I told her it was wrong to—"

Mother Maria held up her hand. "Leave that. We must open this door."

The strongest of the sisters took a long log brought in from the walled field behind the convent and used it as a battering ram. They shattered completely the peace and silence of the cloister. After many bashes against the door, they managed to push it open far enough so that Sor Eustacia could slip her hands in and lift the plank that barred it.

Mother Maria Santa Hilda and Sor Monica, the tiny Sister Herbalist, were the first to enter.

Inez Rojas de la Morada lay facedown on the tile floor, completely naked. Her abundant dark hair lay loose, covering her shoulders to her waist. Sor Monica turned her gently and put an ear to the girl's chest, touched her temples. The Sister Herbalist looked up at her Abbess and shook her head. Mother Maria Santa Hilda averted her eyes from the nakedness at her feet, opened the *armario*, and grabbed a blanket to cover the body.

Inez's novice's habit and her undershift lay thrown haphazardly on the narrow, hard cot, which was still made up with its linen sheets and pale brown vicuña wool blanket, as the maid would have left it that morning while Inez was in chapel for Matins. The plain wooden table that should have stood beside the cot was upset, probably by Inez's fall to the floor. Next to the body lay the things that would have been on that table—her rosary, her flail, a miniature painting of Santa Isabella, the patron saint of the convent, the leather-bound breviary that contained the holy office—the prayers for every time of day and every season—and a smashed crockery water carafe. A fallen drinking cup and a small puddle of Inez's drinking water lay next to her left hand, which was as pale and immobile as the ivory hands nailed to the crucifix that hung on the opposite wall. The girl's lips and the tip of her nose were blue.

Without allowing herself to show her shock, Mother Maria went to the door and looked into the expectant faces of the sisters. "Take the entire community to the chapel," she said to tall, somber Sor Eustacia, who had thought to get the battering ram. "Sing a responsory for the repose of Inez's soul." Given the apparent gravity of the sins Inez had sought to hide, Mother Maria wondered if her soul would ever reach God.

A boy came at sunset to call Padre Junipero, the spiritual guardian, to the Convent of Santa Isabella de los Santos Milagros to administer extreme unction, the sacrament of the dying. The padre whispered a prayer of thanks, assuming saintly old Sor Elena was finally to be released from her long suffering. He followed the boy out to the Calle Real and took the opportunity to instruct the child on the value of offering up one's pain for the sins of the world.

Juanito was a typical Mestizo—born of an Indian mother and a Spanish father—with dark olive skin and lustrous coal black hair. He earned a few pesos a week by waiting in the plaza near the convent for small commissions from the sisters. His fine-featured young face was grave. The priest put a hand on his thin shoulder. "Do not be afraid," he said. "Death comes to take Sor Elena to heaven. She has borne—"

"It is not Sor Elena, Padre," the boy said. "It is the Alcalde's daughter. And Luisa, the maid who sent me for you, said she was already dead."

In shock, the priest quickened his step. Then he broke into a run. It could not be. A young woman in the bloom of good health? So suddenly dead? He had heard her confession each week since she entered the convent. The sensation came back to him. That even in the confessional, the girl had been holding something back. She had confessed that she had talked back to her mother, that she had purposely made her little sister cry—the small sins of girls her age. But the way she spoke them, as if by rote, made his skin prickle with apprehension that her confessions obscured more than they revealed of her inner soul. Deep inside him lurked the conviction that no one, not even her confessor, would ever know all the secrets of her heart. Sweat broke out on the priest's back.

He slid to a halt at the convent door and jerked on the bell cord until Sor Diogene, the Sister Porter, arrived. He demanded confirmation of the news young Juanito had given him.

The lashes of the nun's round gray eyes fluttered in dismay. Her hands came together. "Lord have mercy on her soul."

Tears and anger boiled within the priest like some plume of steam that had escaped a volcano in the depths of the ocean. He turned away and pressed his fists to his mouth lest his emotions break the surface.

He dismissed the boy with a coin and unlocked the thick, arched vestry door of the church attached to the convent. The iron hinges squealed.

Without stopping to light a candle, he quickly donned a stole and surplice and took the holy oils of the last sacrament from their gold-and-silver cabinet. Through the gloomy, silent halls of the convent, he followed Sor Diogene to the infirmary. There lay the body of Inez Rojas de la Morada, clothed not in the fine silks and brocades she had worn all her life, but in the plain wool habit she had so recently taken.

As ordinary Church practice permitted, Padre Junipero administered the sacrament to the already lifeless girl. He anointed her body, cool but not cold. Perhaps, though breath and heartbeat had stopped, her soul lingered within and would hear and benefit. The nuns chanted in the chapel across the cloister.

The priest laid hands on the veil that covered Inez's soft brown hair—still long because she had not yet professed even temporary vows. He commanded his hands to be quick and businesslike, but they lingered in spite of him. *"In nomine Patris, et Filii, et Spiritus Sancti…"*

When he finished his prayers, he capped the holy oils and went out to find Mother Maria Santa Hilda, Sor Olga, and Sor Monica in the dim cloister. The chanting voices from the chapel were louder out here and rang in the chill, still air like tens of perfectly tuned silver bells. The three holy women stood together in silence under the stone arcade carved with scrolls and leaves. In its center was a square patch of grass surrounding a fountain made of marble shaped like the Star of David with a cross rising from it.

"What happened to her?"

The Abbess suppressed any look of disapproval at the priest's New World lack of good manners. A true son of Spain would have greeted aristocratic women with queries about their health and protestations of sympathy at their loss.

Sor Monica covered his gaffe with her answer. "I hope she is with God."

Mother Maria Santa Hilda spread her hands in a gesture of permission. She needed them both to help her find the answer to the padre's question. The priest would have to help them understand what had happened, and the tiny Sister Herbalist had the finest medical mind in the city, regardless of what the bloodletting doctors thought of their fancy European studies.

Sor Monica's huge eyes glanced into hers, looking for assurance. "Go ahead. Tell him," the Abbess said.

Monica's next words were so soft and tentative, they might have been the rustling blades of grass on the cloister lawn. "We think she might have taken her own life."

The priest jerked his head as if he'd been slapped. "Suicide?" He gave the Abbess a look as much accusatory as shocked.

A pang of guilt hit her gut. Well he should he accuse her.

Inez had been in her care. If Inez had indeed taken her own life, the soul they had both most sought to save would be condemned to hell for all eternity. The girl would not even be permitted burial in Christian ground.

"What could make you think such a thing?" he demanded hotly.

Maria Santa Hilda turned away from his tormented eyes and scanned the shadows of the distant hills of the Altiplano, just visible over the convent's roof. She wanted an answer that would soothe him and her both. She might as well seek rosebuds in the barren mountains. Or escape from this tragedy. She dragged her eyes back to his. "I do not accept the idea of her self-destruction. Inez showed no signs of despair. Nothing in her manner or speech led any of us to imagine she had lost all hope..." Her voice faded.

"Surely there is another explanation. I cannot think Inez's soul is lost to God forever." The priest was as desperate as she was. Inez was one of the great spiritual links between them. They saw her the same way—troubled, but holding such great potential. Like the city they both loved so passionately, she had the capacity to become as beautiful in her soul as she was in her physical presence. The Abbess looked into the priest's eyes and saw his pain and his resolve, both matching hers. "Tell me the circumstances of her death," he said.

"She had locked herself in her cell," Mother Maria began.

"Locked?" the padre interrupted. He glanced along at the row of identical heavy oak doors. Each was fitted with a simple iron latch.

"Only the vault where we store the deposited silver and the street doors have locks," the Abbess said, "but Inez had managed to wedge a plank of wood behind the bed and the *armario* so that the door was barred. There is no other way in or out of the room. The only window is high and narrow and covered with bars. No one could have gone in or out once she barred that door." The Abbess had gone over it and over it in her mind for the last hour, like the repetitions of the prayers she should have been saying.

"Could there have been someone hidden in the room with her?"

Sor Olga shot him a shocked and disapproving look. "She was completely alone."

"You mentioned an *armario*," the priest offered.

"I opened it to take out a blanket to cover her," Maria Santa Hilda said. "There was no one there." She paused and lowered her voice to a faint whisper. "I think you should know she was unclothed."

"I see," the padre said blankly. His eyelids fluttered as if he were trying to clear his mind's eye.

The Abbess went on talking. "Sor Monica and I have gone over all possibilities. It was not noxious gases from the coal in the brazier. There was no fire." Such gases had killed many inhabitants of this bleak place, who built their rooms small and practically windowless to keep out the chill and had nothing to burn on the treeless mountaintop but poisonous coal.

"Her death was sudden," Sor Monica said. "Her lips were blue, as if she had been suffocated."

This surprised Mother Maria. "There was nothing covering her face." She turned to the Sister Herbalist. "Could it have been her heart?" Her mind raced for some way to wipe out the image of Inez taking her own life, destroying herself before the Abbess found a way to help her unburden her sins.

"I cannot say for sure," Sor Monica said, though her voice sounded completely decided. "I only know that vigorous, otherwise healthy young women do not drop dead of heart failure. Nor had she any fever or infection or complaint of any sort. Except for a certain intensity when she spoke, her humors seemed completely in balance. She ate her dinner in seemingly perfect health."

"A spider? A poisonous snake?" The priest was grasping at straws.

"Father, there are none such at this altitude." Sor Monica clenched her hands together in an attitude of desperate prayer. "We have examined her and tried to posit every explanation. We have none, except that there was a carafe of water and a glass on the floor next to her. She could have made herself a draft of something."

"Where would she have gotten such a mixture?" he demanded.

Sor Olga was indignant. Sor Monica chewed her bottom lip and looked at the Abbess's feet.

Mother Maria folded her hands into her wide sleeves. "Outside substances do come in. The maids come and go and…" She did not finish. A sigh escaped her and betrayed her exasperation, her fear, her frustration.

Sor Monica reached into her own sleeve and drew out a glass vial. "I have collected the water left in the carafe and from the floor. I put one drop on my tongue." She glanced into the Abbess's eyes. "I made a perfect act of contrition first."

The Abbess could not help but smile. "And?"

"It tastes like plain water. I…"

"Yes. Yes. Go on." The Abbess saw that the priest disapproved the sharpness her voice betrayed, but he did not have to put up daily with the Sister Herbalist's excesses of humility.

"I do not like to endanger one of God's creatures, but I had thought to feed this to the cat, to see if it had any effect."

"You must!" the padre replied vehemently. "You must prove that it is not poison, that she did not take her own life." Meeting the Abbess's glance, he modulated his voice. "The scandal of a suicide could hurt your convent, Mother."

"How well I know that," Mother Maria responded, "but unfortunately, showing the water is not poison will prove nothing."

Sor Olga seized this. "She might have eaten something of which she left no sign. Considering the circumstances of her death, we must assume she destroyed herself."

"No!" The Abbess clenched her jaw. "We will assume no such thing."

"If she did not plan to commit some sin, why did she lock herself in?" Sor Olga demanded.

The Abbess saw Sor Monica and the priest look to her for

an answer. "There could be any number of reasons," she said, though she could think of none that would help Inez's soul before God. "Even if the water is poisoned, that does not mean that she killed herself. Someone else could have put poison there."

"Mother!" Sor Monica said in shock. "Who in this convent would take another's life?"

"Who indeed?" Sor Olga demanded. "The girl took her own. She must have."

The Abbess held up her commanding fingers. "Stop. It is not our place to accuse Inez of suicide when we have no proof. If the water is not poison, we must assume that she died of some unknown natural cause."

"The Bishop and Fray DaTriesta will take a great interest in this," Sor Olga said quietly.

Mother Maria looked up into the sooty clouds that surrounded the pale, rising moon. "Suicide or murder, either way it bodes no good for this convent." The Abbess saw how this grim scenario might unfold. How the Alcalde might respond. "We will bury Inez here in the choir, with our sisters who have gone before her. We will not accept the idea that her soul is lost."

The priest nodded in agreement. "Then we must try to establish to the Bishop's and Fray DaTriesta's satisfaction that she did not kill herself."

Sor Monica shook her head. "They will be hard to satisfy."

"Perhaps not," the Abbess said. "I am sure the Bishop would prefer to avoid any scandal, especially with the Grand Inquisitor and Visitador General Nestares both coming."

The priest agreed that they must give the girl a proper burial, but the Abbess's heart held no optimism about what would happen if they were accused of breaking Church law by burying a suicide in a sacred place. "We will be ready if we are challenged. We must find out all we can. Padre, you will look for information outside these walls. Sor Monica and I will determine all we can within them."

"Is it permitted to make such an investigation during Holy Week?" It was, of course, Sor Olga who reminded her that these were the holiest days of the year and should be given over to prayer and repentance.

"Grave accusations can be made against the Abbess unless we can defend our decision with facts," the priest said. "Besides, discovering the truth *is* God's work."

"And the Inquisition, the auto-da-fé... We must never..." Sor Monica reached out impetuously and grasped her Abbess's hand.

Maria Santa Hilda drew back from the gesture and from the danger she knew to be real. "You are letting your imagination run away with you, Sister."

"Perhaps," the priest said, "but we must prepare to protect you, Lady Abbess."

"Sor Monica, you will examine the body again for any sign," the Abbess commanded.

Sor Monica's hands went to her chest. "I am not as well trained as the physicians in these matters."

Sor Olga's dark eyes narrowed. "We cannot let a man examine her body."

"No, of course not," the Abbess said, "but I am sure your examination will tell us as much as any surgeon's, Sor Monica. We will establish Inez's innocence of suicide, and we will allow no scandal to besmirch this convent or to threaten any of us."

A maid came along the corridor with a lit torch, placed it in a bracket near them, then disappeared into the gloom beyond the chapel.

"Will you tell her parents, Father?" The Abbess regretted having to ask him.

His shoulders sagged, but he said, "I will do it."

Across the cloister, a door banged, and a figure in black darted into the shadows.

Sor Monica gasped, and Sor Olga's eyes widened in fright.

The Abbess hesitated a second, then grabbed the torch from its bracket and made quickly along the round-arched arcade. Padre Junipero followed, with the others trailing at a safe distance.

At the corner, where a statue of St. Jerome looked down from a niche, they met Beatriz Tovar running toward them.

"Beatriz!" the Mistress of Novices scolded. "What are you doing here? You are supposed to be in the chapel."

Beatriz halted and stared down at the stone pavement. "I'm sorry, Sister," she said breathlessly, "but I had something—

"Sor Olga's bony fingers grasped Beatriz's elbow. "Return to the chapel at once. This is an outrage."

A whimper escaped the girl. "But, Sister, you have to…" Her big, round eyes pleaded with the Abbess.

Mother Maria stepped forward and extended an arm between Sor Olga and the girl. "What is it, Beatriz?"

"I have to show you," Beatriz said defiantly.

"Show us what?" Maria Santa Hilda demanded impatiently.

The girl drew a crumpled piece of paper from her sleeve and gave it to the Abbess, who read it aloud by the flickering torchlight: " 'Bea, please come to my room after Vespers and stay the night with me. I am plagued by secret knowledge, and I fear for my life. I need help. Please come. Inez.' "

"I thought she was exaggerating," Beatriz said plaintively. "You know how she was."

Mother Maria put a steadying hand on the girl's shoulder.

"It must mean someone was threatening Inez's life," Sor Monica said. "Someone who feared this secret knowledge. It proves she did not commit…" Her voice trailed off.

Sor Olga gave the Sister Herbalist a look of patronizing indulgence. "You are letting your hopes get in the way of your judgment. Inez's words could just as easily mean she was afraid of what she might do to herself."

"I refuse to believe that," the priest said softly.

"Then we must find irrefutable proof that you are right," the Abbess said. "Before the Inquisitor arrives with the Visitador General, we must know exactly who or what took Inez's life."

"In just four days," Sor Monica whispered.

An hour before the padre delivered the dreadful news to the house of Francisco Rojas de la Morada in the Calle Linares, word of Inez's death had already crossed the canal to one of the huge *ingenios.*

On her stone balcony, Pilar Tovar sat as she did every evening, waiting for the work of the refinery to stop at eight and for her husband to return to the house. She pondered and prayed for a way to relieve the grief of her maid Rosa over the murder of Santiago. Murder she was sure it was, but no one cared about the stalwart Santiago's death three weeks ago. Pilar longed to discuss the problem with Beatriz, who had a New World sensibility and would see a way to solve the problem. Pilar's heart ached in the absence of Beatriz.

She gazed out on the interior patio below her and saw in her mind's eye a thousand images of her daughter. Beatriz as a baby, taking her first marionette-like steps, her chubby arms held out stiffly. As a little girl with a crown of white feathers, dancing in her first satin shoes. At thirteen, bowing demurely to the Bishop when he came to bless her the morning before her confirmation. And the desperate young woman shouting and screaming the day her father told her of the man he had chosen to be her husband.

Pilar had no memories of other children. Only the infant ghost. The son. She turned away haunting thoughts—calculations that would tell her how old he would be now. What he might look like. But sadness and loneliness beat in her heart like the pounding of the waterwheel beyond the wall, where the Indians broke down the ore from the mine and prepared it for refining.

At the very beginning of her first pregnancy, her husband had insisted that she go down into the valley of Tarapaya until the birth, but she had been afraid to have her baby alone. She had longed to be in Spain with her mother or Luz, who had nursed her from infancy. Bad enough to give birth without them in this remote place, but to go away even from Antonio?

He could not leave the mine at that time. They had a new overseer, one he was not sure he could trust. As if one could trust anyone with the temptation of all this wealth. Pilar had insisted on staying in Potosí, desperate to have at least Antonio at her side. She dismissed his and the doctor's predictions as exaggerations meant to convince her to go. What did men know of childbirth? So, their son had been born in this house and had died within two weeks. She found out only later—when she became close enough to other wives to discuss pregnancy—that no European babies survived longer than a month in the thin air of Potosí.

She chewed her knuckles. Pain and remorse gripped her still. She had confessed the sin over and over. Padre Junipero had told her for years that it was a greater sin to hold on to guilt after God had forgiven her.

In fact, God had shown her His forgiveness and meted out His punishment. The gift of forgiveness was Beatriz, whom Pilar had gone down to the benign green valley to have and to raise for the first year of life. The punishment was infection, the crucible of pain that blessedly passed but left her as barren as the Altiplano—useless to give Antonio a son with whom he could face his responsibilities.

She rang the small silver bell she kept in her pocket—three rings to alert poor, bereft Rosa that she needed more of the green Indian tea for her headache, the pain that ebbed and flowed but never completely went away in this thin, unbreathable air.

Antonio, the middle son of a noble but impoverished father, had come to the New World to seek his fortune. There had never been a better place on earth to do so than in Potosí. Pilar had followed him on his great adventure, but today she would trade half of her possessions to live away from the constant pounding of the mill that throbbed in her head. Where was Rosa? If Rosa could not come, then Sagrada or Ascensia should. The hot water was supposed to be always ready. All Rosa had to do was pour it over the leaves. Pilar rang again and, before the icy pinging faded, again.

Sagrada's small brown face appeared below in the patio at the kitchen doorway. She crossed and stood under the balcony, looking up at her mistress. Fear showed in her dark eyes, but greater fear than of having been late with the tea. Fear for Pilar, not of her.

"What is it?" Pilar demanded.

"Rosa says—" She broke off her sentence, as she always did when speaking Spanish. "A boy was walking with the priest... Rosa was coming from the Plazuela Arche with the meat—"

"What did she say?" The throbbing in Pilar's head put a sharp edge on her voice.

"She heard a boy tell Padre Junipero that Alcalde Morada's daughter Inez is dead."

Pilar gasped. "Dead? Is she sure?" It could not be.

"Yes," Sagrada said. "They saw Padre Junipero running toward the convent."

God forgive her, Pilar gave no thought to Inez. The shock of the news flamed into terror. Beatriz! A plague! If some disease was in the convent, it could kill Beatriz. She thought to send Sagrada to fetch Antonio, but she ran herself. Her cousin, her sister-in-law, and three nephews had died the year before in a plague in Spain. Suppose it had come here? She sped down the stairs to the door that led to the mill, a door she never passed through because it was considered unseemly for a woman to show herself in such a place. She flung it open.

What she saw in the gray light of that dusk was what she had seen many times through the jalousies of her window above, but never in twenty years at eye level. Indian men, their heads bowed with fatigue, arriving from the mine with donkeys and llamas laden with leather bags of ore. Pilar picked her way among them. Their astonished faces looked away from the Spanish woman who wore not even a shawl over her hair.

Domingo Barco—the handsome, always so polite and

deferential overseer—came and blocked her way. "My lady!" he exclaimed. "What can I do? Please go back into your house. I will help you if you have any errand here."

"I must speak to the Captain immediately." She was breathless from the small exertion in the rarefied air.

Barco grabbed an Indian by the shoulder. "Go and bring Captain Tovar here at once." Then he raised an arm to block Pilar's path and indicated the door with his other hand. "If you will only return to the house, Doña Tovar, I will send the Capitán to you at once."

She stood there, unwilling to push past her husband's overseer but unwilling to obey him, either. In the awkward silence between them, the braying of the mules and the bursts of Quechua and Aymara spoken by the Indians hung in the air.

"Please, my lady—" Barco began.

"I heard you," she said. They were the words and the tone her daughter used when she meant to defy her. Barco did not press her further.

They both saw Antonio, the red plume on his hat blowing in the wind, striding across the yard. His approach made further argument unnecessary.

He accepted the greetings of the workers, grinned at the children, showing white, even teeth and a glint of mischief in his eyes that had stirred her sex when she first saw him and still did whenever he entered her bed. Theirs had not been a marriage of dutiful coupling through a slit in the sheet, as her mother had taught her to expect. In the daylight, they never spoke of the passion of their nights, but it buoyed all that passed between them.

Nevertheless, Antonio's winning smile disappeared when he saw her standing there in the *ingenio* yard behind Barco, who still posed, arms outstretched, like an actor declaiming a verse in a play on the feast of Corpus Christi.

"Captain," she addressed her husband, her lover, "I must speak with you most urgently."

Without a word, Antonio swung his black alpaca cape off

his shoulders and used it to cover her. He dismissed Barco with a look and hurried her through the door back to the patio of the house. "What is the meaning of such behavior? Do not tell me this has something to do with your notions about the supposed murder of Santiago Yana."

"Inez de la Morada is dead." She watched his face.

A cloud of fear passed his eyes before the heat of anger returned. "How can you know such a thing?"

"The maids."

He accepted her answer immediately, as she knew he would. The maids knew everything. And they were never wrong.

He raised his hand to stop her next words, ushered her into his study, and sat her in the carved wood and tooled leather chair where Domingo usually sat when they discussed men's affairs.

"What do you know about how the Morada girl died?" he asked her. His face revealed consternation but little sadness over the death. He and Morada had been enemies too long for him to mourn even such an event. Morada had killed his brother in the vicuña war, shortly after Pilar arrived from Spain, on that awful day when the men of Potosí, the Basques against the other Spaniards, went out—like knights in some pageant, plumes bobbing and armor shining—to the field of San Clemente to fight the battle that had decided nothing but at least exhausted them into an uneasy peace. Jorge, Antonio's younger brother, wounded and knocked to the ground by Morada, had begged not to be finished off until a priest heard his confession. Priests had been running back and forth on the field of battle, trying to reach the dying, anointing, praying. The weeping Antonio had found one and brought him to Jorge, but too late. The brother Antonio had sworn to his parents he would protect died without confessing. Antonio had attacked Morada in revenge, but Morada protested he had not slain the unshriven man, that Jorge had died of the blow already inflicted in battle. Later, however, when they prepared Jorge's body for burial, they found two wounds on it. Hatred had festered between Morada and Antonio forever after.

"My husband," Pilar said, "I am afraid there could be a plague in the convent."

Antonio dismissed the idea with the back of his hand. "One dead girl does not constitute a plague."

"Let me bring Beatriz home. Please, Antonio." She never called him by his given name except in their bed, when the curtains were drawn. "Please tell her she does not have to marry Rodrigo. Let her come home."

He paced in front of the painting that hung behind his desk—the Virgin de Cerro, the Madonna whose robes took on the conical shape of the mountain of silver to the south of the city. The picture had disturbed Pilar since he had first brought it into the house. To her, it symbolized a confusion of love of God's Mother and faith in silver. Antonio called his refinery Ingenio de Corpus Christi. Was his devotion divided between God and Mammon? Or were they one in his mind?

"Do you remember when I awoke shouting from my sleep last night?" she asked.

He stopped moving and turned to her. "Yes," he said softly. He had taken her in his arms and soothed her until her heart stopped palpitating from the fear. Then he had made it beat even harder with passion.

"I dreamt of two dead girls. One must have been Inez. I am terrified the other will be Beatriz. I cannot lose her." She stood and grasped the side of the heavy table between them. "You must relent. You must."

"You are becoming overwrought." He came to her, touched her shoulders, and pressed her back into the chair. "When Easter week and the celebrations for the arrival of Visitador General Nestares are over, you must go to Miraflores and stay in the valley for a rest."

Anger flared in her. She fought it down. She defied him in as sweet a voice as she could muster. "I will not leave, and I will not let you change the subject. I do not need a trip to the lake. I need my daughter. I will not see her perish in a plague." Tears welled, unwanted, in her eyes.

He sat next to her and took her hand. There were splatters of reddish brown water on his white hose. "Then persuade her to marry Rodrigo de Villanueva y Silva. You have not even tried. If you supported the match, she would have accepted it by now." His voice was soft, but he held his shoulders stiffly in that way he always did when he was completely determined.

"You are unfair, my husband. I did urge her, in my own way. You credit me with having more control over her than I do." She did not admit that her efforts had been halfhearted. She did not know this Rodrigo. She was not at all sure he was the kind of man for her daughter.

He raised one eyebrow and gave her a sardonic smile. "It is your own fault that Beatriz is so willful. You insisted that we send her to learn to read and write."

"All the modern girls learn those things. I wanted her to have what they have."

"Yes, and now she is beyond the control even of her father. She is seventeen. This is the year she should become betrothed. And yet she defies me. I cannot even talk to her without her flying off into a tantrum."

"You do not approach her the right way."

He leapt to his feet. "Are you questioning me? Do you criticize me, woman? Does a father have to follow a protocol when he speaks to his own child?"

She put up her hand, wanting to touch and soothe him, but she knew he would not accept that. He never understood his daughter's emotions. He tried to reason with her, as if the choice of a man to marry were some engineering problem or an equation about how much mercury to put with the ore to extract the silver. It was always like that when their daughter became distressed. Beatriz would be sobbing in desolation, like a person vomiting, and he would try to talk practicalities to her and end up upsetting her even more. And Pilar would watch and weep and wonder why anyone would try to reason with someone who was vomiting.

She had to make him see that this recent defiance was more

than a girl's stubbornness. Should she betray Beatriz's secret? She must. A betrayal would be better than allowing her to perish of some plague in that convent. "She is in love with Domingo Barco. She says she will not marry anyone but him." Pilar bit her lips and hoped she had not misspoken.

Antonio's jaw dropped. "Are you crazy? He is completely unsuitable for her."

Pilar twisted the yellow ribbons that hung from the waist of her brocade dress. Her husband would never be able to understand what their daughter found attractive in Barco. But she did. "Beatriz does not see him the way you do. And he cares for her, too. Have you not seen how sad he is since you took her away?"

He threw back his head and groaned. "Have you lost your mind?" He went to the window, unglazed but shuttered against the wind. He fumed, "This is completely wrong. You do not know what this means. What makes you think you could have an opinion? There are issues at stake of which you know nothing."

She stood, too, in defiance of him. "I know nothing because you keep me in ignorance."

"I protect you from knowledge that would trouble you." He was shouting now.

"I do not want such protection. You think I should devote myself to prayer and poetry, spend my days writing little notes to the other Basque wives, asking if they slept well or if the baby has cut his teeth. I cannot be so trivial. I am alone. I want Beatriz back, and I am willing to do whatever it takes to get her."

"Not if it means she will marry Barco. That is absurd. He is a Mestizo. He has nothing but what I pay him." He turned and glared at her. "Never even entertain this idea. Do you hear me?"

Her hands went to her hips. She forced them behind her. "I will entertain whatever thought I wish. I am a woman, but I am still God's child. He gave me a mind to think with."

"You should be thinking about Him instead of Beatriz marrying Barco. She will marry whom I say or she will rot in the convent."

The thought doubled her over. Now her hands clutched

her stomach. She went down on her knees. "I beg you, Antonio. Do not do this. I traveled here and risked death. I said good-bye to my mother forever. For you, Antonio. But I will give you up before I give up my daughter." The words, meant to shock him, shocked her, too.

"Please, Pilar, do not say such things." His voice was gentle but shook, with fear or anger she could not tell. He came and lifted her from the floor, led her back to the chair. She let him do it. She knew his soul—its smallness as well as its depth, his pride and stubbornness, his secretive nature as well as his honesty and generosity. He was always the fairest of the *azogueros*, caring about his workers, magnanimous with their families. He had given a large stipend to Santiago Yana's widow and children when the *barretero* was found dead at the bottom of the mine, even though Antonio insisted that they could never prove anything about the mysterious documents, that the man had probably gone down at night to steal ore to sell on the black market. Why, Antonio asked over and over, would anyone give valuable documents to Santiago Yana?

He took her hands again. "Have I not been a good husband to you? Do you regret following me here?" He watched her eyes. "I think you do, don't you."

She laid her hand on the side of his beautiful face. "No, Antonio. No, I do not regret it. It is my love for Beatriz that propels me, not any remorse over marrying you."

"Have I not treated you well?"

"You have. In this place where so many temptations exist, you have been more loyal to me than most." Other women had husbands who gambled, went with courtesans, drank to excess. Antonio spent every night in her bed.

He looked away, but he held her hand. "Completely loyal. No one could move me as you do."

She drew his fingers to her lips.

He straightened up and affected a pose of relaxed command, the way he stood when she watched him from her window, giving orders to the *pongos* and *barreteros* in the refinery yard. "If you love me and Beatriz, how can you even imagine that marriage to Barco could be good for her? How can you help her defy me?"

"I know how happy a woman can be when the lover who pleases her is also her husband."

He fell silent. They did not speak of these things.

"I followed the custom today," she said softly. "I visited seven churches to pray on Holy Thursday. In every one of them, I asked God and His Blessed Mother for only one thing. To return my daughter to me. Perhaps Barco would not be a suitable husband for Beatriz in Spain, but here things are different." Daring speculators came to Potosí, not conventional Spanish aristocrats. They vied with one another in making and wasting fortunes, and they had a great tolerance for departures from what was considered correct in Spain.

"It is impossible!" His voice was harsh again. "The needs of our family forbid it."

"Needs of our family?" She shocked herself by shouting at him. Her hand went to her mouth.

"Yes. Needs," he boomed back at her. At that moment, the thudding hammers of the mill stopped, signaling the end of the workday. In the stunning, sudden silence, other sounds quietly emerged—the trickle of water in the patio fountain, Sagrada in the kitchen, singing while she cooked.

"Explain it to me so I can understand, Antonio," she pleaded with him. "You know I am a woman who can accept what she understands." Though nothing could make her accept her separation from her child.

"It is complicated. It has to do with the mine."

"Yes, of course." She could not keep her impatience out of her voice. "Tell me. I will understand. Other women are given responsibilities by their husbands. Doña Clara Pastells is the administrator of Don Francisco's estate. Doña Immaculada manages the mine when Don Bartolomé goes to La Plata for the Audencia." Her voice rose with each example. "Isabella the Queen ruled with King Ferdinand." She was half out of her chair.

He raised that ironic eyebrow. "The Queen?

"She smiled at her own grandiose thoughts. "Yes. The Queen. I may not be a monarch, but I am not asking to rule a country. Only to understand my own family's business."

He looked at her long and hard and finally sank into the chair behind his writing table and ran his hand over the inlaid pattern of the sun and moon on its surface. "I am in debt, Pilar."

"In debt?" When he took so much silver from the mountain? When he did not gamble like other men?

"Yes. Deeply in debt." Shame twisted his features as pain might contort the faces of tormented souls in a painting of damnation.

She waited, wrestling with her fear.

"Our mighty river of silver is down to a trickle."

"Ours?"

"Not just ours. All the mines of Potosí."

She did not understand, but she held her tongue, waiting for him to make it clear.

"The mine has been worked for a hundred years. They took the best ore at the beginning. Now we have to work much harder to take out ore of poorer quality."

"But it still contains silver?"

"Yes, but hardly enough to cover our expenses."

"Surely we can live more simply. Eat plainer meals, buy fewer—"

He chuckled, but his eyes remained sad. "We cannot save what we need by giving up a few dresses."

"But where did such a debt come from?"

"I spent money—all the *azogueros* did—to build the lagoons and the aqueducts that store and bring the water to the city to run the waterwheels. When the dam broke at Caricari, we had to pay to rebuild the destroyed property."

The devastating flood had happened the year after Antonio's brother Jorge was killed in the war. People still feared another deluge from the reservoirs above the city. At the time, she and the women of the city were concerned with the dead and the dispossessed. "That was so long ago."

He leaned forward, spoke in earnest. "Debts continue until they are paid. And there are other problems. You know we must have quicksilver to process the ore."

"Mercury. It comes from Huancavelica on the mules."

"Exactly. The King controls its price. To get the mercury, we must buy on credit, then we pay with the silver it extracts."

"So when the silver is gotten, it is already owed." She surprised herself by understanding quickly how that worked.

"Having enough silver left over to make a profit depends on the number of *mita* Indian workers we get. But there are fewer and fewer of them. Many Indians died of the pox. So we have to pay the local Indians more than the forced laborers. Our costs go up."

"Padre Junipero says there are not enough *mita* workers because they die of overwork." Again her sympathies for Rosa Yana surged through her, but she held that diversion at bay. If she was going to convince Antonio to let Beatriz come home, she would have to understand what troubled him.

"Workers do not die in my mine."

"Santiago Yana died," she let slip.

He turned away from her. "I have had to pay for that, too. Since Yana died, the workers are frightened. Local Indians do not want to come to work for me. I have to pay them more and more. They use their superstitions to extract more pay from me."

She gave him an ironic smile. "We have our methods for extracting silver from the mine, and the Indians have their ways of extracting it from us."

He reached for her hand and smiled, too. "And they do not have to pay the King exorbitant prices for mercury." He patted her hand and let it go. "There is more."

"Go on."

"You know that Don Francisco Nestares, the Visitador General, is coming. Do you know why?"

"Something about false money. I really don't know what it means."

"All over the city, men have found their fortunes dwindling because the mining is harder. To maintain their wealth, some apparently have cheated by making coins that are not real silver, but tainted with copper and lead." He rose again and bunched his fists at his sides. "I do not see how they thought they could get away with it. The rest of the world was bound to find out."

A small sun rose in her brain. Its light pained her already throbbing head. "If the world does not trust our money, we cannot use it to pay our debts."

"And we will all be ruined." His eyes held respect for her understanding as well as defeat over the very idea of such ruination. "If Nestares should declare that our money is worth one-third less than before, instead of owing the King sixty thousand pesos, I will owe him eighty. And I cannot pay the sixty."

"What about the silver we put in the convent for safekeeping?"

"It is already gone."

She gripped her chair. "And the ingots you hid in our bed?"

"They are Beatriz's dowry."

"Barco would not require a dowry."

He blew out an exasperated breath. "I told you not to even speak of that," he growled. "Beatriz must marry Rodrigo. It is our only hope."

"Because he is rich? Can he save us?"

"He is not only rich. He is the Viceroy's nephew. He can protect me from prosecution."

"Prosecution?" Alarm tightened her grip on her chair.

"For the debt I owe the King. You don't understand, Pilar. They are saying Nestares is coming to investigate the false money, but he will be much more powerful than that. He comes as Visitador General. He will be able to have anyone thrown into jail, even executed, simply by shouting an order from his balcony."

"Why would he want to do such a thing to you? What have you done?" She was rigid with fear.

Antonio came and knelt at her side. "I have done nothing.

But times are turning even more dangerous and nasty than before, Pilar. Nestares will have to show that he is controlling the problem. He will be a very dangerous man. And the Inquisitor is coming, too. Both of them arriving together means the King is doing the utmost to show his power and exert complete control over Potosí."

"You once told me miners had royal protection from such things."

"Not anymore."

"And how will Rodrigo save us from Nestares if he is in Lima?" It was one of the reasons she had not supported his suit. She did not want Beatriz to live so far away.

"Rodrigo is here right now," Antonio said. "He arrived two days ago with dispatches from the Viceroy." He put an arm around her in a gesture he had never made before in daylight. "May I introduce him to you? Will you convince Beatriz of the importance of this match?"

She laid her hand on the embroidered breast of his doublet. "Let me meet him." She prayed to the God whose houses she had visited all morning not to force her to choose between Beatriz's future happiness and Antonio's.

CHAPTER 5

Fray Ubaldo DaTriesta saluted Padre Junipero Pimentel cordially as they passed each other in the Plaza Mayor. The local Commissioner of the Inquisition pretended not to notice the grief in the eyes of the Jesuit who hurried toward the Calle Linares. DaTriesta needed no explanation for the priest's pained expression. Word of Inez's death had come to him almost immediately from his source within the convent. He thanked his God that the Jesuit, not he, carried the dreadful news to Alcalde Morada.

In gratitude to his God, and under His gaze, the pious Commissioner of the Holy Tribunal dropped small coins into the outstretched hands of two beggars on the cathedral steps— Doña Clara, the ragged former courtesan, and the nameless mad, bearded hermit who mumbled to a human skull he had been carrying through the streets of Potosí for twenty years. It was edifying for the populace to see this poor creature constantly contemplating mortality. The Commissioner placed an extra coin in the hermit's filthy hand. "Yes, my son," he said.

"Keep your soul always ready for God's judgment and continue to remind other sinners of death's ever-present threat."

From an Indian woman who sat impassive with her dirty children on the doorstep, DaTriesta bought a candle decorated with red-and-green scrolls and a cross of silver foil. He swung open the thick oak door of the cathedral. The beauty and grandeur of the Mother Church immediately enveloped and soothed him. The sweet scent of incense and a hundred burning beeswax candles. Mellow chanting of monks reverberated in the vault of the nave. The faithful murmured the Stations of the Cross in the side aisles. Soft, warm light glowed on the gold-leafed altars and pure silver candelabra. The red sanctuary lamp guarded the presence of the Holy Sacrament in the tabernacle. Serene faces gazed down on him from statues and paintings of the saints and God's Holy Mother. In this perfectly ordered world, joy swelled his heart. Unlike the sinkhole of chaos and depravity that surrounded it, God's house was all beauty and tranquillity.

He took holy water from the font near the door and blessed himself. Kneeling before the painting of Saint Anne, the mother of the Blessed Virgin, he lit and placed his candle in the wrought-iron stand. He spoke in his heart to his own mother in heaven, one of those few chosen women who had the grace to rise above her sex. Unlike the hypocrites who called themselves ladies and looked down their noses at her, she attained, poor woman that she was, the true nobility of saintliness. Uncomplaining in her suffering, she instilled in him the faith and devotion that were the mainstays of his life. I will not fail you, Mother, he whispered to her in his heart. After touching again the candle as he wished he could touch her dear hand, he stood and bowed and turned away.

At the front of the church, he genuflected as he passed the main altar. He continued through a side door into the vestry, where he expected to find the Bishop preparing for the benediction service. Instead, three young priests, four altar boys in miniature clerical garb, and a gaggle of musicians carrying guitars, mandolins, and flutes awaited the Bishop's arrival.

"Finally," José, the tall, skinny sacristan grumbled from the door to the street.

DaTriesta looked out. The Bishop's gilded carriage, with the Villaumbrosa coat of arms on the door, came clattering down the paving stones. It was one of His Grace's most annoying affectations that except for solemn processions, he would not walk through the streets. He always rode in his coach, even the few steps from the door of his residence around the corner to here. What would the Bishop's father, the Duque de Villaumbrosa, think of this scene? The coach that bore his insignia and his illegitimate son was pulled not by four handsome horses, but by mules, which though inelegant had the stamina to survive such heavy work in this rarefied climate. The Duque's bastard emerged and strode majestically into the building. "Forgive me, Brothers," he said without a hint of regret, "I was unavoidably detained." He scowled at DaTriesta and deposited his cloak on the long arm of the long-suffering sacristan.

"A brief word, my lord Bishop," DaTriesta whispered.

The Bishop gave him an exasperated look but demurred.

DaTriesta drew him out of earshot of the others. "Padre Junipero is at this moment taking shocking news to Morada."

The Bishop raised a gray, unruly eyebrow.

"Inez de la Morada is dead." The Commissioner paused while the Bishop blinked and sucked air in surprise. "She took her own life."

The Bishop's eyes glazed over with shock. "How do you know this?"

"She was found dead in her cell with the door barred." He did not add that the disgusting little virago was naked at the time.

His Grace remained stupefied. "How do you know this?"

"God is all-seeing, Your Excellency, and we servants of His Holy Tribunal, in our efforts to be God-like, seek also to be all-seeing."

The Bishop curled his lip and moved to open an ornately carved wardrobe door and began to don the vestments for the service. "This is dreadful news," he said mechanically as he pulled an alb of rich Venetian lace over his head and tied a silk cord at his thick waist.

"Dreadful, yes," the Commissioner said softly, "the loss of a soul—always painful, very painful. But—" He paused to make sure he had the Bishop's full attention.

"Go on," the Bishop said impatiently. He drew a long, narrow silk stole from a shelf, kissed the cross embroidered in its center, and placed it around his neck.

"Maria Santa Hilda intends to give the Morada girl a Christian burial despite her apparent suicide. This may be the opening we need to rid our city of the meddlesome Abbess once and for all."

The Bishop donned the chasuble and over it swung a heavily brocaded cope, which he fastened at his neck. He pulled DaTriesta farther into the corner. "Are we sure the girl took her own life? Are we sure about the burial?"

"Reasonably. More information will come out. They will, of course, inter the body as quickly as possible, and if the Abbess errs in this matter, we have her."

The Bishop looked intrigued but hesitant. "If we know she is about to err, is not our first duty to prevent the sin rather than stand by and watch her commit it so we can punish her for it?"

DaTriesta could not believe his weakness. "She is a very dangerous woman. You yourself have told me about her questionable opinions. Remember how she instigated those women to ostracize Don Fulgencio when he took the life of his wayward daughter and her lover. The man was within his rights. Our Holy Roman Catholic Majesty's kingdom is vast and cumbersome. Here on the outskirts of the empire, where there are more dancing schools and gambling houses than churches, we must be doubly vigilant against wrong thinking such as Maria Santa Hilda's. When Satan worms his way into the empire, he will choose just such a vulnerable place as this. The purity of the Faith is paramount."

The Bishop put on a magnificent cross encrusted with diamonds, rubies, and emeralds. He handed DaTriesta his miter and bowed while the Commissioner placed it on his large but apparently empty gray head. "That does not mean we must abandon civilized behavior," the smug Bishop said. "I insist you go and speak to the Abbess tomorrow, before the burial." Crowned with the miter, the Bishop had let his voice become annoyingly authoritative.

DaTriesta did not have to obey. He was answerable only to the Grand Inquisitor in Lima, not to this noble son born on the wrong side of the sheets. The Bishop was not debauched and riotous like so many who gratified their desires through an ecclesiastical career far from the seat of power, but he was idle, worldly, and self-indulgent. DaTriesta bowed to him. "And if I warn the Abbess and still she goes ahead? Then will you cooperate in her prosecution?"

"Maria Santa Hilda has the highest pedigree of anyone in Perú. She is first cousin to the Marqués of Catera, to the Count of Villafranca, and also to Juan Ponce de León, a distant relative of my own. We must be careful with one who is so powerfully allied."

"She will never use those connections. She has severed those ties forever. You know that."

The Bishop moved toward the others waiting near the arch leading to the sanctuary. "Speak to her tomorrow morning. I insist. If our paternal warnings do not dissuade her, we shall be obliged to put the yellow robes of the heretic on her." He gave the signal, and a young man holding a tall gold and silver crucifix opened the small door to the main church. The musicians fell into line and struck their instruments. Somber music filled the small vestry and opened to a huge echo as the players exited under the stone arch. The altar boys swung their censers; clouds of sweet, pungent blue smoke billowed forth. The Bishop adjusted his miter, firmly grasped the golden shepherd's crook that was the symbol of his authority, and followed the deacons into the cathedral.

DaTriesta went out and took a place in the first pew and prayed. He basked in the glory of the ritual, forcing himself to separate the holy ceremony from the unworthy man who performed it. Eventually, sentences he would have to say to Mother Maria Santa Hilda began to form in his mind and interrupted his thoughts of God.

Padre Junipero prayed unceasingly as he made his way to the Casa de la Morada in the Calle Linares. He had lingered too long on his knees before the statue of Santa Isabella in the dark, deserted convent church, listening to the muffled chanting of the nuns, struggling to banish from his mind the powerful image of Inez's corpse. Finally, totally unprepared to break the news to the Alcalde but driven to escape the scene of Inez's strange, troublesome death, he had set out on his grievous mission.

His pace slowed as he rounded the corner of the Calle Zarate, where he met a train of llamas carrying the last silver to the Mint. Work would stop now for the Easter holiday and for the festival in honor of Visitador Nestares.

Each beast bore up to two hundred pounds, yet they stepped gracefully along between their flanking guards. Would that he could bear his own burden so lightly. But unlike the Lord's beasts, men must endure the pain of consciousness and conscience.

The Alcalde, who had always respected the padre, had been angry and vindictive the last time they had talked. He had blamed Padre Junipero for Inez's flight to the convent. Evidently, she had told her father that the priest urged her to live her life at the highest level, but Padre Junipero had not urged Inez into the convent. In fact, it had never occurred to him that she would contemplate such a move. He had been as surprised as anyone when the girl had presented herself there. In fact, Inez had never discussed her intentions with him, not even in confession. Until the Abbess told him Inez was in the convent, he would have doubted the girl's commitment to a spiritual life. He had sensed a wrestling within Inez's soul. He never succeeded in learning what it was she struggled with, but whatever it was, she was settling it now before the Almighty.

Had the girl perhaps taken her own life? Sor Olga was right—Inez's note could be interpreted either way. But that seemed impossible. The taboo against such an act was so strong. Besides, when she had confessed after entering Los Milagros, she had told him that she wanted to repent for the sins of the world. Her eyes were clear and earnest, her countenance luminous with the peace of true contrition. She would never have committed the ultimate sin. The passion of her dedication burned away any doubt.

"Is there more you want to tell Our Lord?" he had asked her in that last confession.

He had seen her shy smile in the dim light of the confessional. "Not if you must hear it, too, Padre."

"The impression you make on God's poor servant is nothing. What is important is the impression you make on Him. Make a good confession, my child."

"Give me penance as if I had committed the worst sin you can think of," she had said. "Perhaps the grace I receive from it will give me the courage to tell you everything the next time."

He had given her passages from the scriptures to contemplate and admonished her to mortify her flesh as was seemly during the holy season of Lent. He had felt safe in the knowledge that she was intelligent and serious. Whatever troubled her would come out, and he would help her rid her soul of it. Now, it was too late. He had failed her in the most important task she had asked of anyone.

By the time he reached the Casa de la Morada at the angle of the Calle Linares and the Calle de la Paz, his pace had slowed to a funeral march.

A man leaving the Alcalde's house greeted him, and distraught as he was, the priest responded without recognition until the man had mounted his mule and ridden off. Only then did Padre Junipero realize it had been Domingo Barco, the *mayordomo* of Tovar's refinery. Strange that he was at Morada's.

Morada and Beatriz's father were sworn enemies. And Barco was a Mestizo—a group Morada was well-known to despise.

The priest approached the Alcalde's enormous wooden door. It was studded with bronze nails and framed in stone carved with rosettes and garlands, with a coat of arms on the lintel. Though Morada lacked noble blood, like many of his rich compatriots in this city, he had invented this insignia over his portal to give an aristocratic air to the house. In truth, an ancient coat of arms was the only thing the Alcalde's lordly mansion lacked.

Nothing grew or was manufactured in Potosí. The city produced only silver, but for a hundred years it had done so in such quantities that all other products flowed in, making its market the best supplied in the Americas. Stuffs arrived by mule and llama pack either through Lima as the law allowed or smuggled through the back door from the Atlantic ports in Brazil or Buenos Aires. Men like Morada, who had the cleverness to bring in goods, earned a return of as much as a thousand percent and made themselves richer even than the miners. It would be easy to condemn such a man for his well-known vanity, but the priest who entered under the red shield, which bore a Maltese cross and two lions, held nothing but pity for the coming grief of the rich commoner who pretended to nobility.

Immediately inside was a torchlit entrance patio, a kind of waiting area for petitioners who came to beg favors or entreat justice from the Alcalde. Four Indian men and a woman sat on benches, hoping for an audience. The woman wore a battered cavalier's hat and had fallen asleep with her chin on her chest.

The square space open to the sky, the brick paving overlooked by shuttered windows, reminded the priest of another such place and brought him a new measure of pain. "Give me penance as if I had committed the worst sin you can think of," Inez had said. He himself had committed the worst sin he could think of, and he had done so in a place very like this, in Spain. The young men with him had laughed and enjoyed their sport. Fear had filled him. But he had proven his manhood. "Dear Lord," he whispered up to the cold, dark sky over Morada's patio, "accept the painful act I must now perform as penance for that crime."

At the far end of the entrance court, before a second portal, stood one of Morada's armored guardsmen. "I must speak to the Alcalde urgently," the priest told the burly man.

"He is busy, but I will take you inside to wait, Father."

"Thank you. Please send word to him that I come on a matter of the greatest importance." The priest fought to keep his grief from showing.

The footman drew an enormous key from behind his breast-plate and turned it in a complicated pattern in three different keyholes to open the inner door. He motioned for the priest to enter and then bolted the door behind them. They crossed the interior patio. Great balconies projected over it like the prows of ancient warships, each supported by humanlike figures—too ugly to be angels, not horrible enough to be devils. Like Inez's soul? Like his own?

The guard showed him into a spacious side room where the only light came from a meager fire in a brazier. On a stand in the corner was a saddle and a cloth embroidered with gold and encrusted with pearls and diamonds; above it perched the Alcalde's ceremonial helmet, sporting varicolored plumes.

The priest ran his fingers over the cloth. In Inez, the Alcalde had lost his most precious jewel. Perhaps somehow Morada already knew. News traveled fast in this city. Suppose the boy Juanito had thought to come here, to beg a few pesos in exchange for important information about the family? Perhaps the Alcalde was already over the shock.

This was wishful thinking. Junipero knew he would be the one to inflict the wound. And what could he offer the girl's father by way of an explanation? The priest had long feared the girl bore some heavy guilt she wished to conceal from her father. Did the Alcalde suspect anything? The priest could not imagine a sin Morada would not forgive her.

And who on earth might have wished Inez harm? Her contemporaries disliked her, but that was just jealousy—

because she was more gifted, prettier, richer than they. The Abbess did not believe Inez had a true vocation. She had wanted to reunite the girl with her father as soon as Inez was ready. Perhaps the great Abbess herself felt threatened by the girl, feared that one day Inez would outshine her. The priest's own thoughts annoyed him. How absurd to think the Abbess would do anyone harm. She was a beacon of profound grace. Though he, as chaplain to her convent, was supposed to be her spiritual guide, she was often his. Not that she preached to him. Quite the opposite. More than a few times, in the midst of a philosophical discussion, she had asked him a question so subtle and pertinent that it had illuminated vistas of knowledge of God's ways and the world's.

The door opened. A different guard entered and eyed the priest's fingers on the bejeweled cloth.

The padre jerked his hand away. "Remarkable work, this," he said lightly.

The guard squinted over the priest's shoulder, as if he suspected the padre had prized loose and pocketed an emerald or two. When he was satisfied to the contrary, he escorted Junipero back across the interior patio to a brightly lit room where Morada and several other men who served on the Cabildo—the City Council—sat at a long table laid with a fine linen cloth and laden with fruits, nuts, and sweet cakes on golden plates.

The Alcalde stood. "Tell the watch," he said to the guard, "the Cabildo is offering five hundred pesos reward for a certain Sebastián de Castillo. If they find him, he should be flogged and then brought to me here."

The guard nodded curtly and left.

"Good evening, Father." Morada stood to greet the padre. He still had on the fancy clothing he had worn when he had read the Viceroy's letter that morning—a red sash embroidered with precious stones, a tunic of brocade the color of mother-of-pearl. Two gold chains around his neck held a medallion in the shape of the sun. He showed none of the anger he had heaped on the priest at their last meeting. Perhaps he preferred to hide those feelings from his guests. Or he might feel a little sheepish about serving such a fancy spread during the last days of Lent. "We are just finishing our main meal of the day, Padre," he said. "Please take a seat." He indicated a chair next to Don Felipe Ramirez, the Tester of the Currency. "Will you take something to eat, some maté?"

Junipero remained standing. "No, thank you. Nothing."

"We have been planning the festivities to welcome Dr. Nestares. We have a great deal of work to do to be ready for Monday."

"I have something very urgent that I must tell you in private," the priest told Morada quietly.

Morada eyed him with a hint of suspicion. "Please step into the next room. We are almost finished here. I will join you in a moment." He pointed to a door that led to a small antechamber. The priest went in, and Morada closed the door behind him.

The room was interior—without a window—and lit by a single candle on a desk that nearly filled the space. There was no source of heat. The padre drew his cloak around him. It was always like winter in this godforsaken city.

He made out muffled voices from the next room and then clearly: "Buenos Aires is a backwater. Here in Potosí, we are at the center of life in this hemisphere." The accent was Estremaduran, but the padre could not tell who had said it or what he meant by it.

"We must convince Visitador Nestares that drastic measures against Potosí would be a disaster for the King as well as for the city." That was the voice of Ramirez, deep and resonant, carrying authority despite his short stature.

Others chimed in, but the priest could not make out their words. His eyes had gotten used to the dark. There was a prie-dieu against the wall and over it, on a plain wooden shelf, a remarkable statue of the Virgin. Her serene face and praying hands were of ivory; her wimple, robe, and cape were of gorgeous gold-brocaded cloth. She wore a silver crown of graceful delicacy. The priest sank to his knees before her and rehearsed again, as he had in the convent church, the words he would say to Morada. "Your daughter is…" "I have awful news…" "God has seen fit to take…" His eyes burned and his throat ached.

He did not know how long he had been there when the door burst open, letting in a shaft of bright light. "Isn't the statue beautiful?" Morada's voice retained its earlier friendliness. He turned and bade good night to his companions, who were leaving by the opposite door. Morada turned back to the statue and touched its garments. "The face and hands came from China on the Manila galleon."

The priest rose, reached around the Alcalde, and pulled the door closed, even though the outer room was now empty.

Morada's expression turned suspicious. He studied the padre's eyes. Holding Morada's gaze, letting the Alcalde see his fear, was excruciating. "What is it?" Morada demanded.

The padre could not speak, only whisper another prayer in his heart. A tear escaped him.

"What is it?" Now Morada's voice took on an edge of panic.

"Inez—" He choked.

Morada was on him in a second, taller, stronger, gripping his shoulders. "What?" he barked.

"Dead," he said, no louder than the tick of a clock.

Morada shook him, sent a searing pain down his spine. "What?"

The padre grasped Morada's forearms and tried to force them away. "She is dead, Alcalde. I am sorry. She is dead."

Morada let him go and staggered back as if the priest had punched him in the face. Padre Junipero tried to support him, but he fell against the desk and upset it. Its contents crashed to the floor. The padre reached out to help him to his feet, but Morada leapt up on his own, slapping away the priest's hands. A small painted writing cabinet had fallen off the desk. The priest bent to pick it up, but Morada snatched it, grasped it to his breast, and sank back into a broad chair in the corner. He hunched over the *escritorio* and moaned.

Padre Junipero righted the desk and mumbled, "I'm sorry. I'm sorry."

The Alcalde looked up. The pain in his face was impossible to behold. The padre looked away to the serene face of the ivory Virgin.

"No!" the Alcalde shouted. "No. You are sure of this? I don't believe you. You—"

The priest backed against the wall. "I anointed her body myself. She is gone."

"How? How could such a thing have happened?"

"We don't know. They found her dead in her cell."

"*Don't know?* How could you not know? Was she ill? Had she a fever? What happened to my daughter?"

"Mother Maria Santa Hilda and Sor Monica, the Herbalist, are trying to figure that out. As far as they know, she had not been ill." He could not bring himself to tell Morada that there was even a hint of suspicion that Inez may have taken her own life. He did not accept that himself. They would find the proper cause, and the Alcalde would never have to know they had suspected Inez's soul was lost.

Suddenly, Morada came at him, got him by the throat. He choked, fought back in vain. "Murderer!" Morada shouted. "Murderer!"

The priest struggled to pry the fingers loose from his neck. He sputtered, gasped, got no air. Just as he thought he would black out, Morada threw him against the wall. He crumpled to the floor, panting. His intestines trembled, and for a moment he thought he would soil himself. He despised his own weakness, yet he had chosen to be weak, to be sure he would never hurt another person again. He cowered. He deserved this.

Morada hovered, took the heavy, rustic writing cabinet that had fallen again to the floor, and for a moment the padre thought Morada would bash him with it, but he replaced it on the desk. When he turned toward the priest, his handsome face was rigid with calm, terrifying hate. "This is your fault. You did this. You killed her."

"No, Alcalde," the padre protested. "No, I did not."

"Yes, you did," he cried. "If it weren't for you, she would never have gone into that convent. You. You turned her against me." He raised his fist.

The priest lifted an arm to block the blow, but it did not come. "I did not turn her against you, Alcalde. How could I have done such a thing?"

Morada gained control of himself, lowered his arm, and sank back into the chair, sobbing. "You taught her to hate me."

"I—I—I urged her to God to—"

"You drove her to that tomb of a convent in defiance of me." The hate in Morada's voice struck the priest harder than a blow. The Alcalde's tears glistened in the dull candlelight.

The padre waited. His own grief would not let him speak.

Morada took a shuddering breath and fixed the priest with a desperate, hard stare. "What do you know about how she died? You are hiding something."

"As I said," the priest answered guiltily, "I do not know what killed her. Do you know of anyone who would have been a threat to her?"

Puzzlement softened Morada's rock-hard features. "What do you mean?"

"Did she have any enemies?"

Morada glared at him. "An innocent girl like that?"

"Yes, I know," the padre said, "but she died so suddenly of no apparent cause."

Realization of what the priest was saying dawned in his eyes. "I cannot believe that. I will not believe anyone would take the life of my angel."

"I do not want to believe it either, Alcalde, but I prefer to believe that than to accept the possibility of..."

"Of what?" His voice was a dagger.

"Nothing," Padre Junipero said. "Mother Maria is investigating. I will help her. We will find out how this tragedy happened." He reached out his hand. He would have liked to touch Morada's arm to comfort him, but he didn't dare. "We have to think about the interment. The Abbess wants to put Inez in the vaults in the convent choir."

"In the convent?"

"Yes," the priest said gently.

"No," Morada said, "she must be put in a tomb in the cathedral. With Mass said by the Bishop. I will erect a gorgeous monument."

How could the padre explain the need to bury Inez without fanfare unless he spoke openly of the question of the suicide? "The cathedral would be difficult at this time. With the Holy Week services."

Morada looked doubtful. He was too powerful to consider impediments to what he wanted.

"If we let her stay in the convent," the priest said, "the sisters will pray for the repose of her soul forever. Or at least as long as there is a Potosí."

Morada sighed. "The sisters would pray for her every single day." It was half statement, half question.

"They would. And as I said, with Holy Week, the cathedral probably is not possible."

Morada strode back and forth in the tiny room. "Money would speak to the Bishop."

"Yes," the priest said, "but the arrival of Nestares— We do not want to involve him in any inquiry. He might—" Padre Junipero let the thought hang in the air.

Morada sighed. "I will make an endowment to the convent. Her full dowry."

The priest nodded. "I say my daily Mass in the convent church. I myself will remember her every day."

Morada paused, pensive for a moment. "I agree, then. Can the burial be tomorrow?"

"Yes, but it will have to be quiet."

"So be it," Morada said. Then he bent forward and put his head in his hands. He was a man defeated. "Inez," he whispered over and over, and sobbed uncontrollably.

The padre held his breath and bit his lip against his own pain until he tasted salt.

After too long a time, the Alcalde gained enough control to look up at the priest and say, "Leave me. Go to her mother. Go."

Doña Ana! Padre Junipero had been so intent on the grief of the Alcalde, he had not given a thought to that strange, sad, remote lady. How would he ever tell her that her firstborn child was no more?

CHAPTER 6

An African servant girl with a seductive walk shocked
Padre Junipero by ushering him directly into the bedchamber of
Doña Ana. Normally, ladies of the aristocracy met priests, or any
guest, for that matter, on their patios or in their receiving rooms.
He entered their private quarters only to bring Viaticum to the
dying.

Though the lady was not ill, Doña Ana's chamber carried
the odor of a sickroom—of a place too long closed up and a
person too long unbathed. The room itself was of the Moorish
style, typical of ladies' bedrooms fashionable in Sevilla when he
had studied there—when such places had not been unknown to
him, as they were now supposed to be. The whitewashed walls
were covered with tapestries fashioned like Turkish carpets but
made by local Indians. Under the windows ran a raised platform—about six inches above the floor—covered with carpets
and velvet cushions. On this *estrado* lay the remnant of a beautiful woman. Her heavy cosmetics camouflaged neither her
pallor nor the black signatures of dissipation under her dark,

glassy eyes. She sipped *chicha* from a cup and fed sweetmeats to a little red Chinese dog. She seemed not to notice the oddity of a man entering this room that, like a seraglio, was meant to be sacrosanct.

"Padre," she said languidly, through the dullness and distraction induced by the strong drink. Her hair was almost as dark and straight as an Indian's. It fell awry around her shoulders. "Bring his chair near me, Bernardina," she ordered the maid.

The stately African carried from a gloomy corner a chair covered with painted leather. The presence—in an alcove—of a huge gilt bed with lace-trimmed sheets and pillows in disarray made him sit stiffly and greet the lady as formally as he could. There was a silver chamber pot in the corner.

Without sitting up, Doña Ana handed the dog to the maid, who carried him out. The pillow behind the lady's head was embroidered with a double bird—the Indian symbol of fertility— and the words *Sonreír y Besar*. The tragic eyes of the woman told the priest that little smiling and no kissing took place here.

"Have you come to hear my confession, Padre?" Her thin, pale hands swiped at the wrinkles in her rumpled blue silk gown.

"I am not here for that purpose, but—" He despaired at ever finding the wisdom to discharge his duty with her any more mercifully than he had with her poor, grief-crazed husband.

She was, like the padre himself, a white Creole, the daughter of a wealthy *encomendero*—a rancher who had been brother in arms to Morada's father in Pizarro's army, reportedly a stern, silent man who was as frugal as Morada was extravagant.

"Will you take some maté? Some *chicha*?" The offers were diffident, from a person whose offers were never accepted.

"It is the climate, the cold, the thin air, that has reduced me to this." She spoke distractedly, half talking to herself. Everyone in Potosí bore these hardships, but women of her class seemed more susceptible to their ravages than the men or the Indians. The priest questioned the wisdom of bringing white ladies to this altitude. Out of self-interest, the Crown encouraged Spaniards to marry and settle in the territories, but the King and the Council of the Indies gave little thought to the fate of Spanish women at the frontier.

Out the window, across the courtyard, the moon lit the barren, ocher-colored hills. This was hell for a delicate nature such as Doña Ana's. She was more isolated behind the locked doors of this house than any nun in a convent. She had nothing to do all day except sit with her daughters and sew clothing for gaudy religious statues. Like the dolls of a child, a collection of them lined shelves over the windows. Those and her dresses and her jewels were supposed to sustain her. Her only role was to bear the children of the master of the house—not even to care for them after their birth—and to be a testimonial to his manliness, a sparkling bauble that adorned him like the pearls embroidered on his ceremonial saddlecloth. Few women maintained their sanity in such a life, especially in Potosí, a city dominated by Venus and Libra, where venery and the pursuit of riches were the preferred proofs of manhood.

"My husband never comes to my bed," she said, as if she had read the padre's thoughts. "He has told me to my face he is bored with my love." She sipped again from her *chicha* cup.

To such laments, a priest was supposed to answer that she must accept her husband's infidelities without complaint, that she should strive for the virtues of patience, humility, and obedience. How could he mouth such advice tonight? Besides, God help him, Padre Junipero saw in her slovenliness Morada's excuse. Who would desire such a woman?

"I know you are thinking how unattractive I am."

He jumped at the accuracy of her guess.

She laughed a laugh of bitterness and desperation. "You are looking at the effect of his neglect, Padre. Not the cause."

His skin itched with fear of such insight. He had always imagined that Inez inherited only her beauty from her mother—that her intelligence came from her father. Now, he saw that this ruined lady was astute. Could she not then see that he had brought her a terrible sack of woe?

"You may wonder why I care," she said languidly, "about the

attentions of a smuggler and social climber." She raised herself up enough to look him in the eye. "He is, you know. Since he married me, he pretends to be of the aristocracy. But he is common. He has raised dealing in contraband to a high art. He does not even hide it. My father used to pretend he was going hunting when he was really going out to bring in goods. Francisco Morada does not even pretend—" She broke off and looked at the padre quizzically for a second. "Why are you here?" Her eyes challenged him, and she waited.

He could not bear to speak. He stared, riveted by her pain. Through the window came the barely audible voices of Holy Week hymn singers walking in procession in the street below.

"I suppose you mean to mollify me in some way. You think I should be satisfied that I have more dresses than the Princess of Asturias." Her voice was thick with drink and self-pity.

He let his reticence torment him.

"You are here because you want to talk about Inez. Captain Morada told me he has relinquished her to the convent." Doña Ana seemed to enjoy this fact. He knew she was waiting for him to speak, but he could not.

Their silence was a third presence in the room.

Doña Ana gave in first. "Inez must have told you in confession that she did not honor me. She shouted at me in the street. I am sure it was the talk of Potosí. This city is so filled with gossip. I have never been able to control her. It is my own fault. I let an Indian wet-nurse her. Inez drank in savage ways with the mil—" She broke off. "Ah, but then you are the great defender of the Indians, so now you too will hate me."

He did not blame the milk Inez drank as an infant for the defects of her character. What the girl had lacked was a proper mother.

"She hates me," Doña Ana moaned.

"No, she does not," the priest protested. Inez no longer hated anyone.

"Yes, she does. I can feel that you are here to tell me that she never wants to see me again."

"That is not it," he said softly, "but I do have bad news."

"What?"He hesitated, lost in her accusing eyes.

She rose, knocking her *chicha* cup to the floor. It was empty. "What? I cannot have bad news. I do not allow a single knot in the house. I burn incense to the Virgin every day." She came to him and grabbed his hands.

He looked directly into her glazed eyes. They suddenly read his heart and fired with recognition. Her face contorted.

"Bernardina!" she screeched.

The maid was in the room and on her knees near to the door before the sound of Doña Ana's scream faded.

The trembling lady never let go of his fingers, never took her eyes off his. "Coca. Bring the gum from that tree. *Now!* And tobacco. *Now. Now.*"

The maid hurried out. He said nothing. Then, Doña Ana began to beat on his chest with an energy her wasted body had seemed incapable of. Beating and shouting, "There is not one knot in the house. I tell you I never had one dream. No. You are lying. You are a liar. All Jesuits are liars."

He caught her as she fell back, his heart shredded by anguish.

She fought him off and fell to the floor. She pounded it with her fists. "I did it," she wailed. "I killed my own daughter. I did it. I killed her."

CHAPTER

7

The next morning, a frosty Good Friday dawned and fear gripped all but the drunkest, most debauched, most addle-brained Potosinos. Many had spent a strange Holy Thursday scrambling to prepare a suitable welcome for Doctor Nestares, who held their fate in his hands. Others had anesthetized themselves with the drug of acquisition. Panicked that the power of their silver coins would soon diminish, they sought to buy while they could. Goods disappeared from the shops. Prices spiraled upward as shopkeepers realized that their products would hold value even if the currency did not. Late on the night of Holy Thursday, the weary merchants had finally turned out their clamoring customers and closed shop for the holiest days of the year. Dazed citizens trudged home through the stone-paved streets, quaking with an unnamable terror that the center of their existence would not hold.

When morning came, they turned to God. A desperation for His mercy intensified the usual Good Friday outpouring of penance. Even the most materialistic and impious joined those burning with genuine remorse in an attempt to stay their Maker's wrath. Beginning at dawn, processions of penitents formed and wound through the streets, calling at all the churches.

On his way to the Convent of Santa Isabella de los Santos Milagros, Fray DaTriesta, the local Commissioner of the Inquisition, stopped to watch a huge parade pour out of the great stone Church of San Lorenzo and make its way along the Calle Zarate toward the Church of Jerusalén. Before his approving countenance passed children wearing only white tunics and dragging heavy fetters. Their heads were covered with ashes, and they chanted, "*Lava quod est sordidum.*"

Yes, thought DaTriesta, wash what is defiled.

A group of noblemen wearing hair shirts followed. Don Juan de Armuña whipped himself. Blood ran on his back. Don Francisco Casteñeda, his hands bound, wore an iron gag fastened with a heavy lock that clanked as the old man hobbled along. Twenty or so men in black hoods with eyes cut out bore huge crosses on their shoulders. Others dragged heavy logs with outstretched arms. The men of the Cabildo in white robes of rough cloth carried litters with statues of San Pedro and the Pietà. A group of Indian men bore a weighty silver litter that held an image of Our Lady. Indian women wearing crowns of thorns recited the rosary in chorus with their children. Noblewomen dressed in mourning, wearing ashes on their heads, carried candles in the gathering daylight. Doña Niña de Figueroa caught Fray DaTriesta's eye, folded her hands, and bowed her head. The Commissioner raised his right hand to bless her, but his heart was not in an absolving mood. Sinful as this city was, not even such outpourings of repentance were guaranteed to repulse God's anger.

DaTriesta turned his reluctant steps toward the convent to warn that troublesome Abbess not to commit the sin that would finally deliver her into his power.

At that moment, inside the convent in her tiny private chapel, the Abbess knelt in prayer before the oval image of the Virgin of Carmen with the Christ Child. "My conscience is clear," she said to God's beautiful Mother. "It is right to bury Inez here in the convent. I am sure of it," she told the boy Jesus, who held a globe and red rose. "The girl came here for sanctuary, and I must keep her here. And I must confront whatever secrets lie in my convent." The possibility of scandal made her stomach tremble. The threatened flames of the auto-da-fé made her sweat. "I came here to serve You, Lord. I will do what is right by Inez. After that, I put my future in Your hands."

Even as she spoke these words, she understood that although her life was in God's hands, the plans she had been formulating in her mind all night were the key to saving her from the Inquisition. There were still unknowns—questions that would not emerge until the first facts came to light. She had instructed Sor Monica and Padre Junipero on what they were to try to learn. Sor Monica must determine what exactly had killed Inez. The priest, because he could move freely about the city, was to find out the meaning behind Inez's pleading note to Beatriz Tovar, why Inez felt threatened, what was the secret that frightened her, the knowledge of which may have taken her life. Their discoveries would light her way to safety.

She herself meant to uncover any information Inez might have shared with her sister, Gemita, a sweet, bland girl who had never much attracted the Abbess's notice. Now, she needed Gemita's trust, but she did not have it.

"How could I have known that I would need her?"

The pretty, benign faces in the painting remained impassive to her pleas for help. She would have to find her own way. Nothing in her education had prepared her for this. She smiled ruefully at her own naïveté. She used to imagine that life in a cloistered convent would bring her a peaceful existence.

Even as a child, she had wanted the convent—at first as her only escape from the strife she found at home. But she grew to love and desire her beautiful vision of tranquillity and a simple life of prayer. She did not even speak to her father of her wish. Girls of her breeding and station had only one duty—to marry the man of their fathers' choosing, to seal alliances, to secure property.

Then that happened which made marriage impossible and sealed the fate she so willingly embraced. She buried her screams and accepted the notorious crime as God's way of sending her to the life He intended for her. She found the peace she sought. For a while.

On the day she professed, the Cardinal Archbishop had smiled benignly down on her in the lofty stone church of the Mother House. "What do you request, my daughter?" he had asked.

"I ask for the blessing of God and for the favor to be received into this congregation," she had answered. "I offer Our Lord my liberty and my family, and I ask only for His love and Holy Grace."

The Cardinal had placed his hand on her head. She had kept her eyes closed. She easily offered God what was left of her family. Her mother was dead and her dear brother, Juan, gone off to the court in Madrid. At that point, a husband was impossible for her, but she wanted none anyway. She had seen in her father and in her brother-in-law, Luis, what husbands were. In place of children of her own, she took God's. The babies of the poor, and the girls who came to the convent to learn. The willful Inez, who might have been the daughter of her heart, who had come so close to confiding in her.

"Are you resolved to despise the honors, the riches, and all the vain pleasures of the world in order to pursue a closer union with God?" the Archbishop had asked at her investiture.

"I am so resolved." She had heard the determination in her own firm, clear young voice. But now she possessed what she had promised to sacrifice. Honors in her position as Abbess, and riches, too—at least as much material comfort as she ever needed. Vain pleasures? She used to think they were dresses and pretty jewels. Vain pleasure was really the exercise of her will. A will about to break under the strain of having to choose between evils. She straightened her back. No. She would not admit defeat. She bore her weight on her knees.

"*Veni Creator Spiritus,*" the choir of nuns had sung at her investiture. Come, Holy Spirit. Never in her life had she so required inspiration as she did on this Good Friday in Potosí.

Creaking shoes in the passage outside warned her that one

of the sisters approached. She blessed herself and, still lacking the answer to her prayers, went out to find the Sister Porter, who kept watch at the convent's door. "The Commissioner of the Holy Tribunal asks to speak with you, Mother Abbess."

"You may show him into my office."

The Sister Porter folded her arms into her sleeves and bowed her head. "He wishes you to come to the locutory," she said apologetically.

"Yes, of course." Maria Santa Hilda knew well Fray DaTriesta's distaste for the company of women. Whenever they occupied the same room outside the convent—as they had yesterday in the Bishop's mansion—he never looked her in the face. He cleaved to the conviction of many priests—that women were the source of all evil. It was true, she thought petulantly, if you considered that women were the source of all men.

She went to the entrance of the convent, to the place where the nuns received visitors who could not or would not come inside. She entered the box—like a confessional with a heavy grille—and lowered her black veil over her face. Actually, it suited her to speak with DaTriesta here, where he could not read her thoughts in her eyes. She, on the other hand, saw him very well. She had had this part of the convent constructed so that the visitor's compartment contained a window facing north that threw maximum light on his face.

The dry, waspish Commissioner had the kind of severe and ugly looks—a high forehead, little hair, a pointed nose, a big pale mouth—that made him seem much older than his years. He was probably not more than thirty, and the energy of his relative youth gave him a threatening air of being always on the verge of a violent fit of temper.

The Abbess leaned toward the heavy iron grille. "God be with you, Father," she said, wishing with all her might that the Lord's grace would soften DaTriesta's heart but despairing that it was possible.

"And with you." There was a sarcastic edge to his thin, tinny voice.

She waited for him to tell her what business had brought him to her portal, but he did not speak for such a long time that it became impossible to bear the silence. "How can I serve God in your person this day?" The sharpness of her voice outmatched the disdain she had heard in his.

"I come to condole with you over the death of your sister de la Morada."Behind the veil and the grille, she allowed herself a wry smile. "Thank you for your kind sympathy, Father."

Silence fell again. She realized he wanted information about how Inez had died, but she was determined to make him work for it. She closed her eyes and counted the piercing seconds.

"I understand there were irregularities in the way she died," he said finally.

Maria Santa Hilda started. How could he know that? Padre Junipero was the only one outside the convent who could have told him, and he never would have. She twisted her fingers in her lap and blessed the veil that hid her fear. "We do not know what took her from us, but we are sure her soul is with God."

"From what I know, we must assume that she took her own life."

The Abbess forced her breath to stay calm. "No, Father. We need make no such assumption."

His sparse eyebrows rose. "Have you then determined what killed her when she was locked alone in her cell? Pray tell me what it was."

"We have evidence that she locked her door because she feared for her life."

"Do you mean you harbor a murderer, Sister?"

"You have no jurisdiction in my convent." The sharp words flew out of her mouth. She regretted the wrath they would incur.

His pale lips curled in a smile. "You have a weakness for intemperate speech, my daughter." When she encountered him face-to-face, he always averted his small, dark, hard eyes. Here, herself hidden, she saw them clearly. They were brilliant with hate.

She fought to compose herself. The Grand Inquisitor was coming in three days. If DaTriesta accused her, his superiors could order her to Lima. The convent would have to pay the cost of her journey and the expense of her jailing. Worse, the order would never recover from the disgrace. If the Tribunal decided against her, they could excommunicate her. Nobody on earth could remove the interdiction but them. Without the Holy Sacraments, her very soul would be in danger. "I have done nothing to warrant the wrath of the Holy Tribunal." She tried to say it simply, but her voice shook.

"Nothing definitive yet, but I already have several pages on you in the Sumaria, Lady Abbess."

Indignation stiffened her spine. "What is it that I have done that so interests you?"

"I guard this corner of our Holy Empire against Satan's encroachment."

"Satan? What could I possibly want from him? There is nothing he can tempt me with." She knew the words were proud and a sin of themselves. "What could I ask? Prowess in battle? To win at cards?" Freedom from the likes of you, she thought. She made the sign of the cross on the back of her hand with her thumb. She did not want him to see her bless herself against the sins he drove her to.

His nostrils narrowed, as if he caught the scent of a decaying animal. "What do I know about what a woman wants from the devil. Perhaps health. The intelligence of a man."

"I already have those." Pride again, but she could not help it.

"How do I know where you got them?"

"From the same place you got your gifts, Fray DaTriesta. From Almighty God." It was folly to defy him, but impossible to forgo her own defense.

Noise intruded, of a procession approaching to visit the church attached to the convent. Moans of penitents. Children and women reciting the rosary. Their presence gave the Abbess an opportunity to change the direction of the interview. "Perhaps we should not be thinking of these things on this holy day?"

DaTriesta turned away, as if he had caught a glimpse of her face and could not bear to look on it. "Every day is the right day to preserve the integrity of the Holy Faith."

"To be sure," she said. He put her in mind of those thugs who fought in gangs on the hill of Munaypata—bloodthirsty out of reason. She held up her hands, folded as in prayer. "Individualism, materialism, violence. These are the real evils of our city, Father Commissioner. Can we not fight these together?"

"Those are the faults of men, Lady Abbess. I do not see how you can fight them."

"With prayer, Father." She lowered her voice and spoke with the false sanctity that marked his every word. It came out sounding like a mockery of his voice. She flinched at the gravity of having given such an insult.

His seething anger boiled to the surface. "Beware. You have brought our notice on yourself by teaching women to read and write, by putting ideas of independence in their young heads. You would do better to support the feminine virtues: modesty, seclusion, chastity, fidelity." He named them as if they were mountain peaks no woman could properly climb. "You put your very soul in danger. I do not threaten you lightly."

She gripped her arms to her sides and hoped he did not see the chill of fear shake her. "Inez de la Morada came here to repent and serve God. I believe she died in the state of grace. I intend to give her a Christian burial."

"I will require you to prove she deserves it. We men of the Inquisition are trained to look for facts. If you cannot substantiate your claims, you will be subject to our censure."

She knew what that meant. Once they got her, they would find a way to keep her. Only her selfish and dissolute father would be able to save her. And she would never give him the satisfaction of asking.

DaTriesta smirked as if her silence meant his victory. "Go to your cell, Lady Abbess. Betake yourself to prayer. You still have time to mend your ways."

"I will struggle to be holy," she said.

"A struggle that goes on forever," he said sanctimoniously. "Like all struggles between good and evil."

Sor Monica had never threatened a living thing. She regretted having suggested to the Abbess this experiment with the cat. Now her Mother Superior, whom she had vowed to obey, who was also the person she most loved and admired in this world, had asked her to feed the cat the water from Inez's carafe. And she would have to do it.

In her bones, her blood, she still remembered when, as a young child, she had sat up on the top of her father's carriage with Pedro, the driver, on the way to Sevilla. It was forbidden for the noble little girl to sit there. She was supposed to ride inside as befitted a child of the aristocracy, but on the country roads, with no mother or father present to enforce the rule, Gelvira, her nurse, had given her a treat. The little girl saw the world as a bird might have seen it, flying above the ground. Then suddenly a rabbit darted from the ditch beside the road and ran under the wheels. *Thud! Thud!* The heavy carriage rolled over it. She stood and turned and saw it lying in the dust. Brown and white and bloody in the searing Spanish sunshine. It seemed to her it was her fault.

"Stop," she had cried. She wanted to go back, to fix the rabbit. She sobbed so long and hard that Gelvira had to lie to her mother that she had a cold. Her mother wept and worried that she would die. They kept her in bed for many days and made her drink nasty-tasting things the doctor prescribed. One sin of disobedience and so much turmoil.

She had prayed to St. Francis to make the rabbit well. Sometimes she imagined it had gotten up and scampered away. The older she became, the more certain she was that no such miracle could have occurred. She still felt that childish guilt. Now, she was about to feed what might be poison to the cat. He might expire in her hands.

Death did not frighten her. She had seen people die. Old nuns, mostly, like Sor Elena, who lay now over on the cot near the window. Death would come as a relief for that old woman's pain. When one of them was dying, Sor Monica was able to ease her sister's suffering until she passed peacefully into the arms of Jesus. Human beings had immortal souls that lived on after death. But when animals died, they were completely obliterated. Forever.

She crossed the cluttered infirmary to Sor Elena. The pale gray light of that Good Friday dawn shone on the old woman's already ghostly face. Sor Monica broke silence and confessed her fears about the cat. "Even if the cat dies, I still will not know if Inez took poison on purpose or if someone else put it in her water. I am sorry I thought to do this test. I do not want to destroy one of God's creatures."

"You should give the water to me to drink." Sor Elena's voice was weak but determined. "If it sends me more quickly to my Maker, I will be glad."

Sor Monica blessed herself and whispered, "Do not say such things, my sister," but her heart knew what a relief it would be to speed Sor Elena on her journey and spare her the waves of torment she suffered more and more often. The Sister Herbalist felt herself a sinful woman to think such a thought.

"In a way, the cat belongs to Juana, the maid," Sor Elena said. "She brought it here as a kitten. Ask her permission. Perhaps that will put your conscience at ease."

"Juana would certainly say yes," Vitallina, Sor Monica's assistant, called from across the room. The big African woman, who had come to them from Brazil, had ears that could hear a straw break in the next street.

"Go and fetch Juana to me, please, Vitallina, and bring the cat also. It is probably sleeping in the corner of the postulants' refectory."

The stately Negress bowed gracefully and left the room. She was the most gifted person with medicines Sor Monica had ever met, but she was also the most superstitious. She had carried many pagan beliefs from Africa and learned many new ones from the Indians of the Amazon where she had lived. Now she was incorporating the beliefs of the Andeans into her weird cosmography. But she practiced no black arts.

"Will you make me a yerba maté to calm my stomach?" Sor Elena asked.

"Certainly." Sor Monica took a gourd from the shelf and spooned in some Paraguayan tea. Then, using her apron to grasp the ladle, she poured in water from the cauldron boiling over the fire. After a moment to let the tea cool, Monica held the gourd so that Sor Elena could drink from the silver straw.

"You are my angel of mercy," the old nun whispered.

Sor Monica's mouth hardened against embarrassment. "I am only God's instrument. I can do nothing until He lifts me up."

Sor Eustacia, who had so boldly directed the sisters who broke open Inez's cell, appeared at the doorway. Her nose was red and her eyes a little glazed, as if she might be starting a fever. She touched her lips, a signal the sisters used to gain permission to speak. Her normally square shoulders sagged. Her cheeks were flushed.

"Sister," Sor Monica asked, "are you ill?"

Before Sor Eustacia could answer, Sor Olga, the Mistress of Novices, came into the room and demanded to know what information the cat experiment had yielded.

Monica resented Olga's imperious tone. In a certain sense, the Mistress of Novices was her superior and would certainly be the next Abbess if anything happened to Mother Maria Santa Hilda. That in itself was a strong reason to protect Mother Maria. The Sister Herbalist prayed for compassion and holy patience. "We have not done our experiment yet," she said humbly. "We will, in a few minutes."

She turned back and placed her cheek against Sor Eustacia's forehead. "You have a fever, Sister. I will give you something. You must steam yourself and stay in bed all day."

"But, Sister," Sor Eustacia protested, "it is Good Friday. I must be in chapel."

"Indeed!" Sor Olga interjected.

"Nevertheless," Sor Monica insisted, "you cannot allow yourself to become cold and damp." She searched the jars on the shelf. Balsam of Tolu. Ipecac. Jalop. Guaiacum. Here it was—cinchona. It came from the bark of a tree. Vitallina had gotten it from the Indian herbalists in the market in the Plaza de la Fruta. Potosí's European doctors thought the Indian medicines useless, savage, and so never bothered to investigate them. Sor Monica had found many that were beneficial. "Stir a spoon of this in water mixed with the juice of a quince and drink it every time the chapel bell rings. It will take away your fever. If you need more, Vitallina will bring it to you. She will come to see you every few hours." She shook some white powder onto a bit of clean linen and rolled it up.

Sor Eustacia took the packet, bowed, and left. She was one of those naturally silent people for whom the sacrifice of talk seemed no hardship.

Sor Monica busied herself replacing the jar and rearranging her stock of herbs. Though normally no plants grew at this altitude, she and Mother Maria had managed, in the shelter of the cloister wall, to plant a single apple tree and an herb garden. They had recently begun to harvest their patch. The jars were full, and more bunches of their produce hung drying from the colorfully painted rafters.

She returned to give Sor Elena more tea.

"Kantuta flowers. You have some?" Sor Elena asked.

"Yes, but not from our garden. They are plentiful in the market." The Andeans believed they restored balance to the body.

"There is a beautiful story," Sor Elena declared. She was off in a minute, telling the Indian myth of the beautiful Incan princess who had fallen in love with a handsome commoner. The girl ran away from her father, the King, on a moonless night. Near her lover's house, she slipped and fell into a ravine. The kantuta flowers supposedly took their scarlet color from drops of her blood. Sor Elena told the story at least once a day. She talked nearly constantly, as if now at the end of her life, she was compelled to speak all the words she had held inside for the nearly fifty years she had lived in silence.

"I don't understand why you and the Abbess prefer to believe there has been a murder in this convent," said Sor Olga, the Novice Mistress. When her final day came, she would not have as many pent-up words as Sor Elena.

Sor Monica tapped her fist on her breast in the signal of apology, pretending to be sorry for rejecting conversation, even though they were bound by the rule of their order to avoid talk. "I must prepare some medicine for Sor Elena," she whispered.

She busied herself cutting precious melon and grapes into tiny pieces, but she thought about what Sor Olga had said. Murder. It was the first time Sor Monica realized that the Abbess had asked her to help investigate a murder. She had examined Inez's body in minute detail. There was not the slightest sign of any illness. Poison was the most logical answer. If Inez had not killed herself, who in the convent would have and how and why? Inez was just a girl. A willful one, certainly, but what enemies wanted her dead? Were there people in this small community who harbored such evil in their hearts? There was a bit of strife, as there would be in any group of God's imperfect creatures. The Abbess inspired some envy. She was powerful and highly aristocratic, too well loved by the many. A few of the sisters and several people of the town resented her. The Bishop and Fray DaTriesta had long been looking for an excuse to depose her. But Sor Monica could not believe they would murder Inez just to rid themselves of the Abbess. Perhaps the poison was meant for the Abbess and went to Inez by mistake.

Sor Elena began to cough. The Sister Herbalist hurried to her side. The old woman's fevered dark eyes pleaded with her. She begged for relief. But there was only one escape from her pain.

After a few minutes, the terrifying coughing subsided. "Don't worry," Sor Elena choked out. "I will survive today. I am not worthy to die on the day Christ died."

Sor Monica stayed for a while and held her hand. It was small and brown. Sor Elena was of the holy type called Beata—

women who had visions, ecstasies, some even had the stigmata, though Sor Elena never bore Christ's wounds.

In the past few weeks, she had told a fantastic story that she swore was true, and the brownness of her skin attested to it. She was born, she had said, at the mouth of the Ganges and was taken as a child by half-caste Portuguese pirates, who baptized her and sold her into slavery to the Viceroy of the Philippines. He, in turn, had sent her, dressed as a boy to protect her virginity, on the Manila galleon, an arduous seven-month trip across the Pacific as a gift to the Viceroy of Mexico. But riots in Acapulco had prevented the ship from landing. She eventually entered the convent in Lima and then came to Potosí with the much younger Mother Maria when she founded Los Milagros.

Sor Elena was asleep. Sor Monica got up to prepare a *mistela* of wine, water, sugar, and precious cinnamon for when she awoke.

"It snowed in the hills overnight," Sor Olga said casually, startling Sor Monica, who had forgotten her presence. Olga was the one who taught the novices the rule of silence, and she was silent only in front of them and the Abbess.

Vitallina returned carrying the cat. "Juana is away from the convent," she said. "They say she went to help her brother, but I would wager she went to spend her money. It is what they are all doing, you know. Everyone says that the worth of the money will be cut in half. So they want to spend it now, while it still buys them something."

"What can you expect in a city like this, that lacks any restraint of civilized life?" Sor Olga said dryly.

"Perhaps Juana did go to help her brother," Sor Monica said. "He is trying to get excused from *mita* labor." She snipped a piece of sugar from a cone and ground it in a mortar.

Vitallina stroked the cat. "Juana has told me she fears her brother will die if he goes into the mines. He has had problems of the lung all his life."

Sor Monica prepared coca to include in Elena's drink. It would open her pores and warm her body. "I have seen many sickened with lung disease by their work in the mine. One with that weakness would not last long. They say that in the Indian villages when they march the *mita* workers away, they play funeral music."

"The Indians die of other ailments just as easily," Sor Olga said. "Smallpox and measles."

Sor Monica set aside the elixir and considered the cat. Its fur was brown and white, like the dead rabbit's in the road. She went to the cupboard and drew out the jar where she had stored the water from Inez's carafe. She prayed.

"I will apologize to him for you," Vitallina said. She buried her face in the cat's neck and whispered to it in a strange language.

Sor Olga glared as if she were witnessing a satanic ritual.

When Vitallina finished, Sor Monica took the cat. It squirmed in her hands, clawed at her, hissed, and bit her fingers. Vitallina grabbed it back, and almost immediately it became calm again. Sor Monica sucked at the stinging wounds on her hands.

Vitallina placed the cat on the counter and unclenched its jaw with her powerful fingers, forcing open its mouth. The animal did not protest. "Juana will not mind our using this cat," Vitallina said. "She was very fond of Señorita Inez." She flicked the cover off the jar and poured some of the water into the cat. It sputtered when she finished. She stroked its throat until it swallowed. Then it let her pick it up again and hold it.

They waited in silence. Nothing happened. The cat began to purr.

"Maybe God smote Inez for her sacrilege," Sor Olga said.

"What sacrilege was that?" Vitallina asked. Sor Olga did not answer. It was not the kind of question a Mistress of Novices would answer. Sor Monica wondered herself. She knew Inez was headstrong and seemed too worldly-wise for a novice, but she knew of no actual desecration of anything sacred.

"It was just a manner of speaking," Sor Olga said at last.

"The devil could as well have taken her," Vitallina said. "She was the kind of girl who could go either way. Strong for God or strong for the Evil One."

Sor Monica blessed herself in horror at the thought. "Mother Abbess believes she was truly repentant," she said, "and so do I. That the cat lives shows us the water was not poison." She said it as if it proved something, but she knew it did not.

"Perhaps the poison will take a little longer to—" Sor Olga was interrupted by a moan from Sor Elena—a moan that turned to a scream of anguish.

"Quick, Vitallina, get the tree sap from the blue bottle." Sor Monica took the coca-and-wine infusion to the old nun. She held it to the writhing old woman's lips. "Drink. Drink it all."

Sor Elena gulped the medicine. Vitallina thrust under her nose a gummy brown paste that Sor Elena inhaled. They had to treat the substance with great care. Even a whiff of the aroma inhaled while handling it made a person woozy. "Breathe," Vitallina cooed. "Breathe."

In a minute, Sor Elena fell back on the bed. She moaned again, but not in pain this time.

"The substance brings on vivid dreams," Sor Monica explained to Sor Olga.

"Do not let them take her to the stake!" Sor Elena suddenly shouted with a firmness and energy of which she was incapable when not under the influence of the drug. "Our Abbess. Our Abbess is in danger!" she continued to shout.

"How does she know this?" Sor Olga demanded. "What have you told her to disturb her final days with such worries?"

"Nothing," Sor Monica replied, stupefied. "I never spoke of the Abbess's danger to anyone except with Padre Junipero last night after—

"Sor Elena cried out again. "They want to walk her through the streets naked to the waist—to humiliate her."

Sor Olga's dark eyes widened with alarm. "This poor old woman has become a succubus to the devil."

"Or the gods," Vitallina said.

"She is just delirious from the drug," Sor Monica said, and prayed it was the truth.

Sor Elena's body pitched with a strength it had not shown

in years. "They will drag her the seven hundred leagues to Lima. They have a secret prison there. We will never see her again. Tell her to confess if they try to burn her. Tell her to let them strangle her before the flames reach her. God will forgive her for lying."

The shriek of the old nun's voice, the terror of her visions, curdled their blood.

"I will not listen to this." Sor Olga sped from the room.

As if her leaving calmed the hallucinations, Sor Elena suddenly opened her eyes. "The Tribunal protects its own," she said in a calm voice. "They are corrupt. They find ways to prosecute the wealthy, so they can collect fines and confiscate property, which they use for themselves."

Sor Monica blessed herself and glanced at the door through which Sor Olga had just exited. "Please, Sister, do not say such things. It is dangerous."

"What will they do? Kill me?" Sor Elena laughed merrily, as if she had just discovered herself safely in heaven.

"Still," Sor Monica said. Sor Elena was safe from the Inquisition, but no one else was. Not even the Viceroy. Certainly not Mother Maria Santa Hilda.

"The cat," Vitallina said. She and Sor Monica turned to look for it. They did not find it anywhere in the infirmary, but while they were searching, on that day of Christ's passion, Sor Elena quietly died.

"Search for the cat. You must find it. Perhaps it has gone off to some corner to die." Maria Santa Hilda knew that Sor Monica would obey her. But she also doubted that the cat had died. From what Monica had observed, Inez's death had been instantaneous. If poison had been in the water, would it not have killed as small a creature as a cat as quickly as it had a grown girl? Maria Santa Hilda had no idea if the inner workings of a cat bore any resemblance to the inner workings of a young woman.

"Oh, and Sor Monica, please ask Beatriz Tovar to come to me."

There were things she needed to know that Beatriz might be able to find out. Beatriz, she had remembered, was friendlier with Inez's sister, Gemita, than Inez herself had been. Gemita might know something that would explain her sister's death, and she might reveal Inez's secrets to Beatriz.

And if Beatriz could be persuaded to go home, she might then act as a suitable messenger to carry information between the Abbess and Padre Junipero.

A note lay on Maria Santa Hilda's desk from the priest, warning her that the Grand Inquisitor was arriving soon from Lima and that DaTriesta was making inquiries about the town of people known to resent the Abbess of Los Milagros. There were those. She had often been courted by new arrivals who thought to form a bond with her. Whenever she suspected that their interest was in her noble blood rather than the nobility of her work, she snubbed them. She had been harsh with many silly men who wanted only to gratify their pride by bragging about their lofty connections. She had been wrong to be so rash. Eventually, she had learned to entertain their pretensions and to try to turn their vanity into true passion for good works. But some of the wounds she had inflicted in the distant past still festered. DaTriesta was building his case with those who bore them. The Abbess and her supporters must tread with great care and complete secrecy.

While she waited for Beatriz, the Abbess took up her pen to respond to the padre.

Later that gloomy morning, in the pale light filtering in from the clerestory windows above, Beatriz followed the turnings of the corridor to the convent chapel where Inez's body lay. "Comfort Gemita. That is the most important thing you must do. But if you can, try to also find out if she knows any secrets that would explain why Inez died." This was the task Mother Maria asked of her. Beatriz knew how to pry secrets out of Gemita. What she did not know was how to comfort her. She had no idea what it was like to have had a living sister who then died. Her mother had told her so many times about the dead baby, her older brother, as if she were supposed to mourn him. But he had died long before she was born. She could feel nothing for him. She tried to feel sympathy for her mother. Sometimes she did, but most of the time she just felt lost, as if her mother cared more for the lost baby than she did for her living daughter. But it was not as if her mother did not love her. Sometimes her mother loved her too much. Needed her too much.

Inez's poor little sister had practically no mother at all. And no father. All the girls knew that the Alcalde doted on Inez and ignored his sad younger daughter.

Beatriz carried a cross of guilt with her to the chapel. Inez had asked for help, and Beatriz had ignored her. But how could she have known that Inez was serious? Inez always lied. And teased. When she had asked Beatriz to come and stay with her that night, she might even have been setting a trap to get Beatriz into trouble.

Now Inez was dead.

Beatriz's steps slowed as she neared the chapel door. Her neck tingled in anticipation. She was afraid. Never had she seen a dead body. Suppose Inez were to sit up in her coffin and accuse Beatriz of abandoning her in her hour of need? Beatriz blessed herself and told herself that no such thing was possible. Then she blessed herself again and forced herself to walk on. She would not let fear overcome her. She was a Potosina. She would be brave, like the Cid she had read about in her father's book. A book girls were not supposed to read, but that her mother allowed her. For her mother wanted her to be modern.

She pushed open the chapel door just enough to peer in and see Gemita kneeling with her arms crossed on the bench in front of her, her head down. She wore a beautiful dress. A silk petticoat trimmed with silver lace and broad double ribbons the color of the green leaves of the trees at Lake Tarapaya in the spring. Her waistcoat and girdle were embroidered with pearls and cunning little knots of gold. A white lace mantilla covered her dark hair. Her body was so still, she might have been asleep. Or dead.

Beatriz gulped and pushed the door farther. The hinge squeaked. Gemita lifted her head and turned and gave Beatriz a wan smile. Her eyes and nose were red. Her sweet round face wore a puzzled, questioning expression, as if she had a fateful decision to make and didn't know how to choose.

Beatriz genuflected and knelt between Gemita and the bier. The cedar coffin was surrounded by huge silver candelabra, but it was plain—as befitted a nun, rather than a wealthy Spanish girl. There was not one silver ornament on it. Inez was dressed in her novice's habit. A rosary was wound in her pale hands.

That was as far as Beatriz's eyes would go. She blessed herself and closed them and bowed her head long enough to say an *Ave.* Then she forced her eyes open and looked right into Inez's face.

There was nothing frightening about it. It was peaceful. And beautiful. That wide mouth that had laughed so uproariously was closed and calm. The skin of her cheeks was whiter, but as flawless in death as it had been in life. She looked as holy as she had said—in these past few weeks—she wanted to be. "Are you all right?" Beatriz whispered to Gemita without taking her eyes off Inez.

"I am an unworthy person." Gemita's voice was a little hoarse.

Beatriz took her chubby hand. "You aren't."

"I am," Gemita insisted. "I am here keeping watch with my dead sister and all I can think about is myself. Do you want to know what I was thinking when you came in?"

Beatriz did, but she did not say so.

"I was thinking how my father always sent Inez to church in his calash, but he sent me here in a lowly sedan chair. He has never cared for me. I was thinking that now that Inez is dead, maybe he will learn to love me the way he did her. Maybe I will get to ride to church in the calash. Is that not an awful thing to think?"

"No," Beatriz lied. "I think you are just too upset."

"I am not upset enough. I should feel bad for Inez, but do you know what I have been wondering? I have been thinking that if my father died, too, I would have half his money and be very rich. Then I could go to Spain and live like a princess."

Beatriz squeezed Gemita's hand tighter and thought, If I

had all that money, I would take Domingo Barco out of that sad little house where he lives with its rough furniture and its dirt floor. I would bring him to live with me in a mansion. Then she bit her lip and asked God to forgive her, because she did not want her father or her mother to die.

"My father loved her because he thought she was good," Gemita whispered. "But she was bad. I am good, but he has never loved me because I have no arts to make him. Is it a sin for me to want my father to love me as much as he loved her?"

"No." The sin was in Beatriz's own heart, because she could think only what freedom it would give a girl if her parents did not love her so much.

"My mother has been crying since she heard the news last night. She could not come because she is so ill. Not even her medicine helps her. She once cursed Inez in public. Did you know?"

"I heard." All of Potosí had heard the story.

"My mother keeps screaming that she is responsible for Inez's death. I think it is because of that curse she made."

"She just feels bad. It is her grief. Inez is with God now. We must remember that and not be sad." The last words came automatically, and Beatriz wondered if she believed them.

A nervous shadow crossed Gemita's face. "Do you think she died in a state of grace?"

Beatriz quickly crossed herself. "She told me that she would spend the rest of her life in penance, in mortifying her flesh."

"But she was very bad," Gemita whispered, and turned conspiratorially. "She read forbidden books. And she knew about things she shouldn't know. Hidden papers that she said would protect me if I was in danger. I think they must contain the words to forbidden Indian spells. Do you think she is in hell?"

Beatriz looked again at the peaceful face of the girl in the coffin. "She repented. God can forgive anything to the soul who repents." Padre Junípero told them this often. But suppose what Gemita suspected was true—that Inez had truck with Indian sorcerers? She would spend a long time in purgatory.

"She went out at night." Gemita's voice took on an insistence, as if she wanted to believe that Inez was in hell.

"She did?" A drop of jealousy tinted Beatriz's shock.

Gemita nodded vigorously and then straightened her mantilla. "She had a lover."

"No!" Beatriz's shout echoed in the silence. The candle nearest her sputtered. She stared at Gemita in utter disbelief.

"She told me herself. He is an actor. Before she came here to the convent, she said she wanted to run away with him."

Beatriz's jaw sagged. She could not speak, only stare into the serene face of what remained of Inez.

"I don't know how she did it," Gemita moaned. "I wish I did. I would do it, too."

"Do what? Leave the house to meet a man?" Gemita was only thirteen, still a baby to have such a thought.

Tears streamed from her eyes. "To make my father love me as much as he loved her."

Beatriz put her arm around Gemita, who sobbed and sobbed into her shoulder.

Later that morning, despite the Commissioner's dire warnings, the funeral of Inez de la Morada took place in the convent church of Santa Isabella de los Santos Milagros. The Abbess would have been hard-pressed to stop it without a major scandal.

After Beatriz told her about Inez's lover, the Abbess had considered postponing the interment. This new information made her wonder if her conclusion had been right. Perhaps Inez had gotten pregnant. Lesser girls had taken their own lives to hide such a sin.

The Abbess had consulted Sor Monica. "No," the Sister Herbalist had said. "I examined her body thoroughly. She was not..." Her voice faded. "She was no longer as she—"

The Abbess suppressed her impatience and provided the words the shy Monica could not utter. "She was no longer a virgin."

Monica nodded and grimaced. "But she was not pregnant. The womb was not at all swollen."

"Perhaps he threw her over, and she had a broken heart."

"It would have shown in her humors. She was not out of balance. I had never once in these three weeks seen a sad expression on her face."

So the Abbess did what her heart had dictated from the first. She let the burial go on, especially in the face of what had transpired out in the town.

The Alcalde Francisco Rojas de la Morada had accepted Padre Junipero's advice—urged on him also in Mother Maria Santa Hilda's letter of heartfelt condolence—to accept his daughter's death as God's will. Given the season and the promise of daily prayers for the repose of her soul, he relented and agreed to bury his beloved Inez quietly in the vaults beneath the floor of the choir loft of the convent, along with the saintly Sor Elena.

The Alcalde told only his closest associates the tragic news and instructed them that he wished to forgo the pomp ordinarily accorded the deceased of such an important family. His devoted followers—Don Felipe Ramirez, and Don Antonio Cerón and the members of his guard—took him at his word. But many others—Don Juan Pasquier, Don Luis de Vila, the Treasurer of the Cabildo, and Don Melchior de Escobedo, the *contador*—saw the Alcalde's request as an indication of the depth of his grief and an opportunity to demonstrate their sympathy and loyalty to the most powerful leader among them. Working through the night, they organized a procession to escort him to his daughter's funeral.

When the Alcalde and his nearly prostrate wife—supported by her African maid, Bernardina—left their *palacio* that morning, they found a grand funeral procession ready to follow their carriage to the church: First came the Indian guard, known as the King's Yancanas, wrapped in black wool blankets and wearing black armbands. Several non-Basque mine owners wearing mourning caps were accompanied by their Indian workers, who wore their typical black hats but with the brims turned down. Then artisans of the city, wearing black woolen shirts and high-crowned hats; they carried bows and arrows at their backs and trailed the flags of their guilds along the paving stones. The *caciques*—Indian leaders—of Potosí and many of the surrounding towns, dressed in Spanish-style mourning, dragged their black woolen mantles along the ground, holding on to the corners with their left hands. A company of harquebusiers, dressed in black taffeta with their weapons reversed, their drum heads loosened, and their flags trailing, was followed by a company of musketeers, who wore black bands on the arms of their dark silk uniforms. All of the King's non-Basque officers and the non-Basque members of the Cabildo marched slowly to the sad drum in single file. Even the Father Provincial of the Franciscans was in the train. White wax candles burned in the windows and on the balconies of Morada's supporters.

Confused passersby, having heard no public announcement of a nobleman's death, wondered at the elegance of the procession.

The Alcalde's carriage at the head—draped with crepe and accompanied by his guard on horseback—alerted the populace that this was not just another group of Holy Week penitents. Rumors spread. That the Alcalde's beautiful and dissolute wife had succumbed to one of the many drugs she was known to take. That in anger at his daughter's committing herself to the convent, the Alcalde was staging a mock funeral for the girl, though no one could think what priest would officiate at such a ceremony. Seeing the elaborate outpouring of sympathy, some even believed that the Alcalde himself was dead. Whether this last opinion was caused by the widespread anxiety over the currency, no one could say.

Many citizens ran ahead of the procession to the *plazuela*

outside the church of the Convent of Santa Isabella de los Milagros, where a bonfire warmed the damp, overcast day. Those who managed to catch a glimpse saw the Alcalde alight and himself give a hand to his suffering wife. They and his guard and four or five others, including Doña Margarita de la Torre, a widow who was rumored to be the Alcalde's mistress, entered the church. The doors were then closed, leaving the hundreds who had marched in the cortege locked out and Don Juan Pasquier, who had spearheaded the arrangements, stupefied.

Once inside the church, the Alcalde and his men repaired to a small room left at his disposal as the church and convent's main benefactor. After they stored their cloaks and swords, the men returned to the main church and marched silently with the ladies up the center aisle. The Alcalde's younger daughter, who had spent the night in vigil at the convent, prayed near her sister's casket. In every corner, more than a thousand candles burned. Their light dazzled off gold-leafed altars and beams and the golden decoration on the richly colored paintings of the Virgin and the saints.

Up in the choir behind a rood screen, only two small candles stood watch at the coffin of Sor Elena. The church and the convent were built side by side and shared a common wall, but the only communication between them was through an arched opening to the second-floor choir room, where the nuns went to attend Mass and other services in the church. Otherwise, the sisters used the chapel within the convent for their private community devotions.

Wearing their black veils over their faces, the Sisters of Santa Isabella chanted a piercingly sad requiem for the deceased.

"Populus ejus et oves pascuae ejus."

Sor Olga's lips chanted the words. She knelt erect and proud. She was one of God's people and a lamb of His pasture, but she was dignified before God. Not some poor blasphemous servant who resented her master. She was clear on the object of her indignation. Maria Santa Hilda chanted distractedly at her side, nearest the remains of their blessed sister. Sor Olga seethed that Sor Elena's holy memory was being polluted by joining her requiem with that of the damned soul whose body was down in the main church. Elena, who had spent nearly fifty years of her life in the order, was one of the first to come to Potosí. Olga remembered her face, luminous in prayer, inspiring them all in the daunting task of imploring grace and mercy from their Creator for this venal, violent city. Sor Elena deserved a Mass of her own. Deserved to have the whole city turn out to honor her holy life. Instead, all she had was this shambles—second place to the unworthy daughter of a worthy father. A daughter aided in defying her father by the proud Abbess who was every bit as willful as her young protégée.

The bell at the vestry door rang out. Father Junipero, two of his brother Jesuits, and two Indian altar boys entered the sanctuary of the main church. The sweet aroma of incense wafted up to the nuns in the choir, who intoned the *Introit* of the Mass for the Dead. Sor Olga prayed that God's judgment of the Abbess, sure to come at some point, would arrive with due speed.

Turmoil roiled beneath the calm exterior of the Abbess. Compelled to bury Inez here by an irresistible conviction of the girl's innocence, at least of the crime of suicide, she had committed an act the Bishop and Fray DaTriesta were sure to call defiance. The power of Inez's personality, even in death, had seduced her into endangering herself and the reputation of her convent.

A force that she could not withstand had taken possession of her. Something that had nothing to do with her orderly life of carefully planned steps taken to achieve ends of obvious merit. Something outside herself, or so deep within that it seemed outside. Like the sexual passion of sinners. Or the ecstasy of the saints.

She chanted the mellifluous phrases of the requiem and,

by slow, quiet concentration of her will, absorbed their peace and beauty until they calmed her spirit and surrounded—but did not soften—the steel resolve within her.

After the coffins were placed in the vaults beneath the choir floor, she stayed behind while the other sisters went off to their cells to contemplate their loss in private. When she was sure she was alone, she took a lit candle from in front of the painting of Santa Barbara and stood in the center arch that overlooked the church. This was the prearranged signal— made necessary by the certain presence in her convent of a spy for the Inquisition. Her talk with DaTriesta had confirmed this. But still this clandestine act made her feel soiled, as if she were arranging a sexual assignation.

Three loud raps on the sanctuary door in the church below answered her. She blew out the candle, slipped behind the tapestry on the wall to her right, turned a hidden lever, and opened a secret door that only she knew existed. She had had the builders put it here because she had imagined they might one day need to take some innocent who claimed sanctuary in the church to safety in the convent. Now she was using the door to go in the opposite direction.

She closed it behind her and silently descended a musty, narrow stone staircase leading to another concealed door that from the church looked like nothing more than a painting of San Juan Batista. She opened it and stood immobile, waiting for him to approach, heart beating as she imagined a girl's heart would beat at the approach of a lover.

Long ago she had expunged all thoughts of physical love, turning her mind to the grief such weakness brought to women. Instead she had used her energies to relieve the misery of children brought into the world by indulging those appetites. In her current state of uncertainty and fear, those longings had perversely returned.

A door latch clicked and a shadowy figure passed under the painting of San Casimiro in his opulent red-and-blue robes. "Mother?" a voice whispered.

She grinned in the gloom. It was not the name a lover would have called. "Here, Padre." She stepped down the last step into the church. "Have you found out anything?"

"I could not bring myself to ask the Alcalde probing questions at such a grievous moment. The only thing..." Padre Junipero's voice trailed off.

"What?"

"Nothing important, really. Doña Ana collapsed at the news. She began to shriek that she had killed Inez. She was distraught, and I don't think she would have shouted it out if she had actually done it."

The Abbess reached her hands toward him, then pulled them back before they touched. "Yes, but she might have done it and then become overwhelmed with grief. Sinners do repent."

"A mother kill her own child!"

The innocent priest seemed really to believe that no mother could harm her own child. The Abbess knew better. The histories of the children who had passed through her care told her full well how much malevolence could live in a mother's heart. "I would think that Doña Ana is too weak to accomplish much at all, good or evil, but we must not eliminate any possibility until we are sure."

"How could she have managed it? Did she come here yesterday to visit Inez?"

"No," the Abbess said. "At least not that I know of. But she could also have employed an accomplice within the convent walls," she said. The words uttered her most secret fear.

"You have, then, considered the idea that one of your sisters—"

"I intend to ferret out whatever evil may lie within my walls," she said.

"Has anyone come forward with any information?"

"Only Beatrice Tovar. You saw the note she had."

"She is a good girl."

"And so full of silly notions—romantic enough to fall in love with her father's *mayordomo*."

"Is she?"

"So she says. She came to me after a conversation with Gemita. She has several theories of how Inez might have died, all of them highly imaginative. I sincerely doubt the veracity of any of them, but to be absolutely sure, we must not dismiss any notion before we have investigated it."

"Does Beatriz suspect someone in particular?"

The Abbess smiled at him, not sure he could see her expression in the dark. "She said she thought Gemita stood to gain a great deal by Inez's death."

"Was she really accusing that poor child?"

"I don't think she realized what she was saying. I told her I thought the notion that Gemita would actually harm Inez was absurd. So she came forward with an even more unbelievable theory —that Sor Olga had murdered Inez to get me into trouble with the Inquisition, so she could succeed me as Abbess."

The priest snorted.

"When I pointed out that Sor Olga could not have been sure Inez's death would accomplish such a thing, she said perhaps Sor Olga intended to poison me and that somehow the substance was mistakenly consumed by Inez."

"Preposterous," the priest said, but without much conviction.

"Yes," said the Abbess. "But there is a worse story. One I fear is true. Inez was not exactly the person we hoped she was. Gemita told Beatriz about an actor."

The Bishop, who shepherded a flock of 160,000 in Potosí, was forced to forgo the quiet contemplation of Christ's passion on that Good Friday morning. He ought to have been preparing his soul to conduct the three-hour-long service that was to begin at noon, but while the wind howled and shook his shutters, he bore as best he could the constant interruptions to his meditations.

Ocampo, the cook, wanted approval of the menu for Monday's luncheon in honor of Visitador Nestares. Ham, smoked sausage, blood pudding, stuffed suckling pig. "And let us give him some Peruvian specialties," the Bishop told Ocampo. "Onions and chilies pickled in vinegar. Potatoes roasted in embers. And that delicious thin bread of maize." The Bishop's Lenten-starved taste buds watered at the thought. For the moment, he had to satisfy himself with stimulating but bitter Paraguayan tea while he pictured the sumptuous banquet table less than three days away. He wished he had fine porcelain plates to lay out. He had only silver, which in Spain would be a sign of great wealth, but here everyone had them.

Bustling workers and several penitential processions dogged the streets beneath his windows. The noise of their comings and goings invaded his already discomfited thoughts. He had tried to get the Abbess to give up Inez, hoping his good offices would ally him with the Alcalde. Such a rich man could prove a great patron for projects of the Holy See. Look what he had done for the convent—the expansion of the building, the erection of the great church attached to it, to say nothing of the missions in Caricari and Contumarca. They said the Alcalde had given Los Milagros more than five hundred thousand reales—an amount greater than the Bishop's total fortune, but only a fraction of what Morada possessed. Pack trains had gone into the country every night for a month. Everyone knew they carried away Morada's silver, now concealed somewhere out on the craggy Altiplano. Now, with the girl dead, de la Morada was slipping through his fingers just when an alliance was so critical to his future.

As an appointee of the Crown, he, like all bishops, had civil as well as ecclesiastical responsibilities. Certainly His Majesty the King would approve of close cooperation between the most powerful temporal power in the city and the local head of the Church. Just as certainly, DaTriesta's obsession with prosecuting the Abbess would spoil any chance of such an alliance. How could anyone hope to endear himself to the Alcalde by accusing his dead daughter of suicide?

The Bishop might win Morada's support by siding with the Abbess against DaTriesta, but he had to be careful there, too. The local Commissioner of the Holy Tribunal kept detailed records of all he knew. Charges could always be trumped up, even against a bishop. His Grace had heard of a man who, viewing the heavens on a clear Andean night, said there were too many stars. The Inquisition brought him up on charges of blasphemy because he implied that God had erred in His creation. Once he was accused by the Holy Tribunal, even a bishop's reputation would be tainted forever. His chances of an appointment to the Viceroyalty would be ruined, no matter how much silver he could pay into the King's coffers. He dismissed a niggling doubt that the circumstances of his birth had already negated his chances. He was noble. After his belated ordination, he had been appointed directly to the Bishopric of the most powerful city in the Western Hemisphere. The King favored him. He did not doubt that. His Majesty could even legitimize his birth if he wanted to.

Such a dilemma. A chance to ally himself with local power and to profit thereby, or the slimmer chance for far, far greater riches by remaining out of DaTriesta's clutches and in favor with the King. As his Dutch clock chimed eleven, His Excellency reached for the bell and rang for a small early lunch. Even on Good Friday, the denial of the flesh need not be complete. But before the silver pinging faded, a sharp rap at the door told him the irksome Commissioner was here to torture him anew. He sighed, offered up the anticipated annoyance for the souls in purgatory, and called out, "Come."

DaTriesta made a curt greeting and rubbed his thin, hairy hands together before the fire in the brazier. "Workers are running every which way, preparing for the arrival of Nestares. The sinners clog the streets, making a show of their great penance when we all know they will be back to gambling and whoring before their Easter soup is cold."

"Yes, yes. Daring and unscrupulous people are always drawn to a place like this." The Bishop let his voice show the distaste he felt. DaTriesta would think it was for the sins of his flock and not for the Commissioner himself. "Who would come here but greedy adventurers and their camp followers?"

DaTriesta eyed him askance. "Who indeed?"

The Bishop turned away. What gall! Dealing with this worm was like having to drink the putrid water on the galleons that crossed the ocean. One did it to stay alive, but it turned the stomach of a sensitive man.

Without invitation, DaTriesta took the wide oak-and-leather chair opposite the Bishop's. "We have seen many bloody battles in the streets, corruption, revolting sexual crimes. We must put a stop to them, Your Excellency. We must strive for the triumph of true Spanish traits—honor, piety, the supremacy of the spiritual over the material." DaTriesta tented his hands and nodded as if to show agreement with his own words.

The Bishop nodded, too, although he was sure that stamping out materialism at the world's richest silver mine was about as possible as banishing the burning sun at noon or the piercing cold at midnight.

"The Abbess has put the condemned girl in the vaults with the other nuns," DaTriesta said triumphantly. "If this is not blasphemy, I do not know what is."

A savior of an idea glimmered in the Bishop's mind. There might be a way to appease DaTriesta, get rid of the overly independent Abbess, and leave the door open to a friendship with the Alcalde. "Blasphemy would only put the Abbess in prison. Perhaps we should come up with a more serious charge." He rummaged in his mind for the best one. "Possession by the devil, for instance."

DaTriesta waved his long, skinny hand. "Too difficult to prove. Half the time the proofs are the same as those for sainthood. Besides, we have no evidence."

"Witchcraft, then. It is very easy to prove."

DaTriesta's pale, irritable mouth worked, as if he were tasting wine and not sure if it had turned. "Such a charge might involve a number of the nuns."

He was warming to the idea. The Bishop nudged him forward. "Exactly. They took in that Negress slave from Brazil. We all know that Rio de Janeiro is crawling with Jews."

"You are right that blasphemy would mean only prison. Witchcraft could bring her to the auto-da-fé." The Commissioner's eyes glowed, as if he looked upon a plate of food he wanted to devour.

"Precisely!"

"With a charge of witchcraft, we could close the convent. Their coca plantation at Cochabamba, their vineyard at Pelaya, the cattle ranches in Tucumán, these would all revert to the Church. That is, to your control."

The Bishop held his breath. DaTriesta saw even more benefit in it than he did.

The Commissioner's expression suddenly soured, as if the food and wine of victory had turned indigestible. "No. I am sorry. I can see why you would favor such an approach, but I remind you, I am a university-trained lawyer. I cannot bring false charges against the Abbess."

What? Was he giving up the meal entirely?

"No," DaTriesta said with specious sympathy. "I am afraid we must charge her with the sin she has committed. Defiance of Church law by burying a suicide in a sacred place. This blasphemy can also bring her to the stake."

For the first time in her life, Mother Maria Santa Hilda could not even pray. She sat on the hard oak chair in the corner of her tiny private chapel, her breviary open on her lap, looked up into the faces of the expensive paintings on her walls, and despised herself.

Several of her sisters had come to counsel or console her. She was too fearful or proud to take their words into her heart. Sor Olga had accused her of flouting Church law and insulting the memory of their dead sisters by interring Inez among them. Sor Monica feared for her Abbess, not because of the burial of Inez, but because on Good Friday they should think about no other death but Christ's. Mother Maria knew Monica was right. She should give up this idea of investigating Inez's death. She should let the Bishop and DaTriesta do their worst and submit to whatever judgment the Holy Tribunal would impose on her. The pious thing to do would be to accept their accusations as one of life's tests to destroy her love of self. If she were striving for virtue as she ought, she would remain passive, as befitted the role of a woman who had given herself as a bride of Christ.

But her old pride welled up in her, and she could not put it down. The Bishop and DaTriesta were so like her father and her brother-in-law—so sure of themselves, so certain of their rights to dictate to all women. Her mother had died because of her father's selfishness. She would not let herself die or even be disgraced because the Commissioner and the Bishop thought her insolent.

She had always counted herself fortunate, to live at a time when passengers regularly crossed the great ocean and to have crossed it herself. Now she felt isolated among the whitewashed stone buildings huddled on this vast, desolate plateau. She had made a life for herself here, but that life was threatened. She could be banished from her beautiful convent. Her carved and painted beams, wainscoting of oak, stone from Panama, wood from Guayaquil, red ebony from the islands of the Main. This tiny chapel, her pride and joy, a retreat where she could come and meditate or play on her small foot-pedal organ the beautiful music of Bocanegra. To study and write. These simple joys. And the complex satisfactions of command of the convent, the hospital, the missions.

In Spain, she might have been able to save herself by appealing to her father. He would entreat the King. But only after he gloated at her having to humble herself before him. She had told him she would never forgive him. And she would not. That was twenty-five years ago, when she was fourteen. The day after her mother's funeral.

The doctor had told her father another pregnancy would kill her mother, but he had indulged his appetites—gotten the poor, weak woman with child for the tenth time. Both the woman and baby, like six of its predecessors, had died. Her father was a pig. He deserved no humble petition from his daughter, though she be threatened by the Inquisition. Besides, any letter of appeal to him would take three months to cross the ocean. His reply would take a minimum of six months. By then, the Abbess of Los Milagros would be dead.

She was more and more afraid.

Christ had been afraid, too. In the garden of Gethsemane, He had prayed to be spared. Like Him, she—

What was she thinking? How could she compare herself to the Lord?

She rose and went out. She rang the bell and gathered all the sisters to the common room. She stood before them and watched their somber faces. Perhaps one of them would give a sign of discomfort, betray a guilty conscience. "My daughters," she said, "we must face the serious fact that one of our number has died mysteriously. Sor Monica has fed the water from Inez's carafe to the cat, yet the animal lives. If not by poison, how did Inez die? Even if there were an easy answer, we would still have some explaining to do. Inez was barred in her room by means of a plank. How did she come to possess such a thing?"

At that moment, young Beatriz bowed her head. The Abbess watched her for a moment, but the postulant did not look up. Did she know more than her harebrained theories revealed? The Abbess went on. "Sisters, I am reluctant to say this—my heart does not want it to be true. But Inez's death reveals the certain existence of secrets among us. Secrets that must be uncovered."

Young Hippolyta, standing near Beatriz, stared straight ahead, her eyes filled with terror and her pudgy hands gripped so tightly together that the skin on her fingers was mottled. What could these young women have learned in a few weeks that the Abbess of the convent did not know?

"We are a community," Maria Santa Hilda continued. "We must be able to trust one another." Even as she said this, she knew she had been hiding from herself all these years the knowledge that this convent, like the Mother House in Madrid, like every convent or monastery, like every family's home, held secrets, animosities, small or large depravities. Even in God's strongholds, wherever humans entered, sin entered also.

"First of all, I will speak to each of you to try to piece together what led up to this tragic event. Before our Creator, I call on each of you to come forward with the truth." Young Hippolyta's gripping hands tightened. "Everyone here has sanctuary under the protection of this convent. No matter what you have to confess, it will never bring anyone here to temporal punishment. I assure you of this. Go to the chapel and pray silently. I will call you to me one by one. I will begin with the maids and then with the sisters who have been here longest."

She led them across the outer cloister to the chapel and left them in the stalls along the walls. She went to the postulants' refectory, next to the chapel, taking Clara, the youngest maid, with her.

The plainness of the room befitted the exercise she would perform here. Rough wooden tables, ordinary pottery, white walls, a plank floor unadorned by carpets. These stark surroundings were supposed to teach humility to the girls who entered the order. The only adornment in the room was a gruesome painting from Cuzco of Christ at the pillar, bloody, in agony, enduring the Roman soldier's lash. Appropriate for the season and for the painful exercise the Abbess was to perform.

She faced young, shy Clara across the table. The girl stood behind the chair the Abbess had placed for those who would come to speak to her. Girls of Clara's station never sat in the presence of noblewomen or lifted their eyes to meet the glance of their mistresses. How was one to judge their veracity without seeing into their souls? To encourage the girl, the Abbess addressed her questions in Aymara, the Indian language. The girl squeaked out answers. Had she noticed anything particular about Inez de la Morada on the day she died? No. Had the postulant seemed ill? No. Had Clara herself entered Inez's room that day to clean? No. Clara knew nothing. Or at least admitted nothing. The Abbess asked the girl to send in the next youngest maid, the garrulous, lazy Luisa, who for reasons the Abbess could not fathom hated her fellow maid Juana and always found excuses to accuse her.

Before the Abbess was able to formulate a proper question in Aymara, Luisa interrupted. "You should be asking questions of Juana, not of me."

"But Juana was gone from the convent well before Inez's death," Maria Santa Hilda reminded Luisa. "She went to help her brother."

"Yes," Luisa whined, "and she is still not back. She always gets special privileges. She always has some excuse. She has to be away because her Mestizo nephew has joined a gang of thugs and been hurt in a fight. She has to go to her sister's wedding. I never get so many privileges. And it is only because I don't have so many relatives. Is that my fault?" Her voice had reached the shrill pitch of locusts.

"Do you know anything that bears upon Inez's death?"

"I know that Juana usually cleaned the postulants' rooms. She could have put the poison in Inez's water."

"There was no poison in Inez's water. If there had been, it would have killed the cat."

"Inez could have drunk the poison part and left only the pure water."

Maria Santa Hilda sent the ignorant woman away.

The questioning went on for two hours. The maids undoubtedly knew the most but admitted the least. The nuns were not much more helpful. Sor Olga preached, which strained the Abbess's nerves and added nothing to her knowledge. Sor Dolores had heard strange sounds in the wee hours of the night before Inez died but eventually admitted she had heard the same noises many times before. Always overly cautious to speak only the truth, she would not speculate about what the noises were. They could have been rapists or shutters banging in the wind; if Sor Dolores did not see it with her own eyes, she would not say which she thought it was.

The Abbess spoke in turn to all the sisters—except Sor Eustacia, who was in bed with a cold—and then moved on to the postulants. She had chosen the order of questioning to give Beatriz and Hippolyta maximum time to mull over the knowledge that had disturbed them earlier in the common room. The more uncomfortable the girls became, the easier it would be to get them to confess.

Earnest and comical Beatriz Tovar began with her bizarre theories about who might have benefited from killing Inez.

The Abbess interrupted her wild musings. "I think you know something, something that bears on this matter, that you are not telling me."

Beatriz's eyes met Maria Santa Hilda's and then found the gold-leaf frame of the painting on the wall infinitely more interesting.

The Abbess switched her attack. "You have been astute enough to conclude that Inez was murdered." She leaned forward in an intentionally conspiratorial pose. "I agree with you on this point. My very life depends on my learning the facts to prove our theory." This playacting was calculated to appeal to the girl's romantic heart, but with a shudder, the Abbess realized that what she offered as drama was actually true.

"I will do anything to help you find the murderer, Mother Abbess," Beatriz declared passionately.

"Then tell me what you know."

The girl looked her full in the face and seemed genuinely puzzled. "I have already told you."

"Something disturbed you when I spoke to the sisters in the common room."

Beatriz's eyes flickered. "I...I..."

"Tell me, my child," the Abbess coaxed.

"I should have gone to stay with her. I could have saved her." She raised her eyes, and they were full of searing remorse. "I thought locking her door would be enough."

"Was it your idea to lock the door? Did you give her the plank?"

"Juana," the girl said softly. Then quickly, "But I don't want to get Juana into trouble. She is so nice to us. She is the only one who makes us feel at home here."

"What exactly did she do for Inez?"

"She gave us the plank and showed Inez how she could use it to lock herself in." The girl's face pleaded with the Abbess. "She was just trying to help. She wanted to protect Inez."

"Do you know against whom or what?"

"No, Mother. Inez said it would be dangerous for me to know." She crossed her arms over her chest. "I was never sure any of it was real. You know how she was. Making herself the center of attention and then teasing. Always trying to make another girl the goat."

"Was she?" The Abbess hadn't known, but she was not surprised. Inez was...what? María Santa Hilda had always been compelled to admire her, though hardly anything she did was admirable in itself. There was something in Inez that did that. Made her more important than anyone around her. The more the Abbess learned, the more her love and hopes for Inez now seemed a baseless fantasy. "No, Beatriz," the Abbess said finally. "You must not blame yourself for anything that happened. If you want to redeem your conscience, I ask that you stand ready to help me. There may be things I cannot do that I will need your help with. In the meantime, tell no one what you have told me."

Beatriz stood, her face aglow with determination. "I will help you find the murderer, Mother. Remember we are Spaniards, and there is nothing a Spaniard cannot do."

It was a line right out of the history of the Cid. The Abbess did not remind the girl that she was born here—not in Spain. Nor did she remonstrate with her for having read a secular book, for how could the Abbess do that without admitting that she knew the book herself? "You can do one thing for me right now, Beatriz."

"Anything, Mother. Anything. Just command me." No young lieutenant in Cortez's army could have been more zealous.

"Go back into the chapel and send me Hippolyta," the Abbess said with a wry smile.

Downcast and disappointed, Beatriz left the room.

Sounds from the street penetrated—hammering and scraping of tools. Indian workmen were out there erecting floats for the vain parade in honor of Nestares. Nestares, who approached with the Grand Inquisitor in his entourage. The Abbess's smile died.

Hippolyta entered and, without raising her eyes from the floor, took the chair opposite the Abbess. The girl was young and sullen and beginning to take on the weight of her condition. She had been so closely guarded by her family that scarcely anyone knew of her existence. Until she came to the convent, she had never even heard Mass outside the oratory in her own home. Yet she was with child. Her outraged father had publicly accused and slain his young Mestizo page for the crime and sent the girl here to have her baby and to spend the rest of her days doing penance for her sin. When the baby came, one of the maids would place it in a basket and carry it to the steps of the Convent of Santa Teresa on the other side of the city. The Abbess there would keep the child in her orphanage, just as Maria Santa Hilda accepted babies left before her portal and sent them to be cared for in Caricari.

"My daughter," Maria Santa Hilda said to the child who was with child, "I will not dissimulate. I saw your fear in the common room this morning. It told me you know something that bears on Inez's death. Please reveal all you know."

Again the girl's pudgy hands grasped each other. They went to her forehead in supplication. She said nothing.

"Look at me, Hippolyta."

"I cannot, Mother."

"What are you afraid of?"

"Of harming the person who has been nicest to me of any person in the world."

That had to be Inez. They had arrived, as it had happened, on the very same day. Maria Santa Hilda noticed a special bond forming between them as the strong and confident Inez took a protective attitude toward her shy sister postulant.

"You cannot hurt Inez now."

Hippolyta burst into tears. "I know I am not supposed to weep about her, Mother. I know she is better off with God than she ever was in this world, but I cannot help it. She was my friend."

The Abbess moved to a chair near the girl and handed her a handkerchief.

The tense hands unclasped to take it. She stroked the Venetian lace around the edge. "This is nice—" She sobbed and blew her nose.

"Tell me," the Abbess said firmly.

"I have an even better friend here who will be hurt if I do." She sniffed and offered to return the handkerchief.

The Abbess raised her hand. "You can return it to me another time." She reached out and lifted the girl's chin.

Hippolyta's eyes were large and soft—like the great, sad eyes of the llamas in the pack trains. There was desperation in them. "I promise you no harm will come to anyone because of what you tell me." The Abbess considered explaining to the girl the dangers the coming Inquisition threatened, but she did not want to test the girl's loyalty. Instead, she took Hippolyta's hand and waited.

The Indian workmen in the plaza shouted to one another in quick, staccato Aymara. Something about nails.

Hippolyta sighed. "No harm?"

"None."

"How can that be? If she has done something evil." The llama eyes searched the Abbess's face.

"If someone in this convent has done something evil, she will have to answer to God's judgment, child. But she belongs here. She will have sanctuary here from prosecution. I myself will pray for the remission of her sins."

A final sob shook the girl's chest. "Must I betray the only person who has truly understood me?"

The Abbess's heart twisted with guilt. Whose life would she ruin to save her own? "You must say." She looked gently into Hippolyta's anguished face.

"Sor Eustacia," the girl wailed as if she had found her mother dead. "Sor Eustacia is the only one who could have killed Inez."

The Abbess reeled in shock. "How can you say such a thing?" she demanded in a voice harsher than she intended. Not Eustacia. Never Eustacia—her strongest, most stalwart ally. She had to force her hands not to take the child and shake her. "Tell me," she commanded as calmly as she could manage.

"Sor Eustacia must have killed Inez. Because Inez knew a horrible secret about her."

CHAPTER 10

In a remote corner of the darkened Mint, the Alcalde drained his *chicha* cup. The liquor burned his throat but did nothing for his spirits. "Enough. I'm tired. I buried my daughter just this morning." He pushed back from the rough wooden table and stood.

A candle tottered, and Felipe Ramirez caught it and set it upright. He was quick, Ramirez. The very man to have at one's side when danger approached.

Jerónimo Antonio Taboada and Juan Téllez, who with Ramirez were Morada's closest allies on the Cabildo, stood as well. Taboada grasped the Alcalde's shoulders and said, "Again, let me say how sincerely my heart and that of Doña Manuela are with you and Doña Ana in this hour."

Morada embraced his friend who spoke of hearts. There used to be a heart beating in his own breast. But it was gone now. Ripped from him by his loss. But it ached still, as they said the hand of a man would if it was cut off. "It is God's will," he said, scarcely believing it

Téllez embraced him. "We will take responsibility for the fiesta. Leave everything to us. Everyone knows Potosí's processions are grander, our bullfights bigger, our banquets more lavish than anywhere else. We will not fail to impress the Visitador General."

Morada could only nod. His poor naïve friends actually believed their festivities could stay the consequences of the debased currency. He knew better. He encouraged them to go through the motions, but he had seen it coming for some time. Their hospitality would never win over Nestares.

He watched the short, stocky Ramirez take a shovel full of ashes from the scuttle near the brazier and smother the charcoal fire. It was what the devaluation would do, smother the life force of the city, set them all back a hundred years. Their isolation on this windswept plateau gave them the illusion of independence, but Madrid ruled the earth, no less here than in Sevilla or Manila or Naples. They had been arguing for hours in secret, criticizing the shortsighted Viceroy, who stayed in Lima coddling his collection of ragtag aristocracy in a mockery of the royal court. Every Potosino worth his salt was sick of the faraway central government's interference in their affairs. Even the Basque bastards hated sending their tribute to a monkish King who left their fate in the hands of the Council of the Indies—a womanly lot too invested in their own jealousies to see what they ruined here. But these thoughts were treason. And given the least provocation, that clique of Basques would string up everyone not of their brotherhood. The Council of the Indies knew of the civil rivalry in Potosí. Probably approved of it. As long as the city's Basques fought with the other Spaniards, neither group would challenge the Crown.

There was a glimmer of a solution in these traitorous thoughts. Morada's absent heart ached anew. He longed to talk over the problem with Inez. Sometimes just speaking his thoughts to her made them clearer to him. "Enough!" he said, more to himself than to his companions. He flung open the door.

Outside, his guardsmen awaited him with torches. The Vesper bell had rung only a few moments ago, but it was already dark. "Home," he said to his captain, and followed his men through the gloomy, eerily quiet Mint, closed for Holy Week. No smelting fires burned, no hammers clanged, the giant wheels of the mill did not creak. Only their footsteps echoed in the silent, arched brick vaults.

In the torchlit outer courtyard, workers had stored floats for the Visitador General's entrance parade. Ramirez, Taboada, and Téllez paused to admire an image of the King fashioned by Indians completely out of feathers.

Morada drew his cloak around him against the penetrating cold. "Adios."

His friends saluted him, and he followed his guard, past some drunken, devil-worshipping Mestizos who were sleeping it off under the monumental carved stone portal. A sow and three piglets rooted through garbage in the gutter. Morada, surrounded by his guard, turned uphill, toward the Calle Linares and his cheerless mansion. In his pocket, he fingered a gold chain he had bought. Perhaps it would awaken some feeling in his distant younger daughter. She would never be as clever as her sister. But she was all he had left.

Morada's friends lingered before the cunning image of their sovereign until the Alcalde was well out of earshot. "I wish there were a way to console him," whispered the elderly Taboada.

Téllez leaned close to his compatriots. Their faces were grim in the flickering torchlight. "Does anyone know how the girl died?"

Taboada shook his head gravely. "I have heard a rumor of suicide."

Téllez drew a sharp breath. "But she was buried in the convent."

Ramirez grasped each of them by the forearm. "Through the door, on the night he learned of her death, I heard him accuse Padre Junipero of killing her."

"If that is so," Téllez murmured, "her death must be avenged."

After Lauds at daybreak on Holy Saturday, a day when the tabernacle was left open and empty and the sanctuary lamp extinguished to signify the entombment of Christ, the two remaining postulants in the Convent of Santa Isabella de los Santos Milagros set about their task of dusting and polishing the choir overlooking the church. Like all the noblewomen who entered the order, neither Beatriz Tovar nor Hippolyta de Escobedo had ever cleaned anything in their lives—not even their own feet—before they entered the convent. It was their lesson in humility that they learn to scrub.

Beatriz always began the task in earnest but soon lost herself in daydreaming. She polished over and over the same spot on the same gleaming silver candlestick. The church below was empty and dark. All the statues and pictures were covered with purple cloths, as was the custom on Good Friday and Holy Saturday. The silence of the convent and its church was dense and liquid, and Beatriz felt herself drowning in it.

For reasons she could not fathom, her companion—the squat, sad Hippolyta—had lifted the purple cloth over the great crucifix on the wall and was dusting the carved skull on which the cross rested, poking a rag into the eye sockets. She caught Beatriz looking at her.

They were not supposed to speak.

Beatriz dipped her cleaning cloth into a bowl of vinegar and then in salt and rubbed again the silver candlestick in which she could already see her own distorted image. "My mother came to see me between None and Vespers yesterday," she whispered. "She has met this awful Rodrigo my father wants me to marry. She says he is lovely, but I don't believe her. She agrees with my father that I must marry him. I am without hope if even she is against me."

Hippolyta put her hand on her stomach. "You should obey your parents," she said.

Beatriz turned away in distaste. Who was Hippolyta to give advice? Pregnant by her father's page. She was a Castillian. Like the Estremadurans, enemy to the Basques. When it suited her, Inez de la Morada had ignored the old rivalry of their fathers, but Hippolyta made frequent references to Beatriz's Basque ancestry.

Continuing to polish the skull, Hippolyta said softly, "Inez will look like this soon."

Beatriz shuddered. "I don't want to think about that."

Hippolyta looked around at the door and tiptoed over to Beatriz. "I am not afraid of death. I am afraid of something worse."

Beatriz nodded. "Spending the rest of your life in this place."

Hippolyta looked confused. "I have no choice about that."

Beatriz's fingers flew to her lips. "I'm sorry! I didn't mean—"

Hippolyta's fat little hands grasped Beatriz's arms. "I am afraid of something I did. I think the Abbess despises me for it."

Beatriz was shocked and intrigued.

"The Abbess reminds me of my mother," Hippolyta said.

"She is very kind," Beatriz said, hoping Hippolyta would tell her a secret.

"Oh, I don't mean that. I mean there are things going on under her own roof that she knows nothing about."

Beatriz thought about Hippolyta making love with her father's page and blushed. "You didn't say that to her?"

Hippolyta's grip tightened on Beatriz's arm. "I did. And I told her worse."

"What?" Beatriz demanded.

"Something very, very bad. I am so ashamed." A tear rolled from her big, frightened eyes. "I have destroyed the life of my best friend in the world."

"Inez?" Could harmless little Hippolyta have murdered Inez?

"*No!* Sor Eustacia."

"Sor Eustacia?" What had the tall, kindly nun to do with anything?

"Yes. More than anyone else I have ever met, she cares about me. And I betrayed her."

"Betrayed?"

Hippolyta nodded gravely. "I will confess it this afternoon when the padre comes, but I don't think God can ever forgive me. I told the Abbess that Sor Eustacia was in love with Inez."

"What?"

"That Sor Eustacia and Inez had an unnatural friendship."

"A what?"

"I saw them. I went to Sor Eustacia's room in the night a few days ago. I found Inez in her bed."

"What? But they are two women! That's not possible."

"You don't know anything," Hippolyta said.

Beatriz blushed. "Oh, of course, I know all about that." But she didn't, and she couldn't figure out how this child knew so much more than she did.

"It was Inez's fault, not Sor Eustacia's. I am sure Inez must have been the one to start it." Hippolyta put her hand on her belly again. "I know how it happens."

CHAPTER

11

The Abbess once again stood terrified before the sisters gathered in the community room. She held her body in a posture of command that belied the fear boiling in her belly. She did not want the knowledge she was compelled to search out.

All her life—she now realized—she had kept certain kinds of thinking at bay. She had muffled her doubts with carpets of the silence in which she lived, blanketed all strong emotions under layers of solitude, drowned out niggling suspicions with torrents of chanted prayer.

She breathed in and made her words strong. "I intend to search this entire building for an explanation of Inez's death. Sor Olga, Sor Monica, and Sor Eustacia, you will join me. Except for Padre Junipero and Fray DaTriesta at the locutory, no one has entered or left the convent since Inez died. If any clue remains, we will find it." She signaled to Monica, Olga, and Eustacia to come to her side. The tall, serious Eustacia immediately stepped forward. She was not quite recovered from her cold, but she would not keep to her bed, preferring to see to her prayers and her duties. The Abbess refused to believe the rantings of the over-wrought Hippolyta that Sor Eustacia had been in love with Inez. Eustacia was the most loyal and sensible sister in the convent. If it came to it, she had sworn, she would go to the stake in her Abbess's stead.

Sor Olga stood, head high and hands together, one over the other, as if she held a trapped bird between them. This was her pose of command—a position that today seemed to sit much more comfortably on the Mistress of Novices than it did on Maria Santa Hilda. That Sor Olga had urged the Abbess to be more authoritarian made such an approach the more distasteful—as if disliking Olga meant rejecting all her advice, however wise. Now the older, cynical woman's counsel could not be avoided.

"Go to your cells and remain there," the Abbess said sternly to the sisters of her community. "The maids too must go to their dormitory and wait. In an hour, Padre Junipero will hear our confessions. Spend the intervening time examining your consciences." She raised her hands, signaling the sisters to stand and be dismissed. The community scattered. Only the whisper of their swishing skirts and the creaking of their shoes broke the silence.

When they were gone, the Abbess turned toward the three women who had gathered around her. "We will begin with my quarters."

They made their way around the front cloister to the street end of the building and Maria Santa Hilda's suite of rooms. Their search of her office was thorough, unsurprising to her companions, and painless to the Abbess.

But in her tiny personal chapel, to her mortification, Sor Eustacia rifled through the music on her small foot-pump organ and found Maria Santa Hilda's mediocre compositions. Eustacia was a good enough musician to see at a glance how simple and uninteresting the songs were. The Abbess held up her head and bore the younger woman's wide, quizzical glance.

Eustacia, like everyone else in the convent, was becoming an enigma to the Abbess, whose heart refused any suspicion of this steady, intelligent, and devout sister—the dearest of the few Maria Santa Hilda felt she could count on as friends. Maria Santa Hilda's mind saw, however, that she could not dismiss the information Hippolyta had so painfully and reluctantly given up. The Abbess's duty was to take the child's revelation seriously, and when she did, she saw the possibility that it was true. Passions of the soul and body often resided in the same person. Eustacia possessed the one. Why not the other? Maria Santa Hilda knew too well that the body's longing for love did not cease with vows, and a soul's loneliness grew in the silence of the convent. The Abbess lacked the moral indignation she was supposed to feel. She felt only sorrow that she must torment her younger sister with questions. God give her strength, she prayed, Eustacia's secret life was just another misery to be faced.

Sor Olga, who read no music, glanced at the manuscripts and disapproved out of habit.

In the Abbess's cell, where no one but the maids ever entered, Maria Santa Hilda barely endured their discovery of her secular books—Acosta's *Natural and Moral History of the Indies* and the story of the Cid. They were not scandalous, but they revealed her love of adventure that she had hidden from the world as if it were a sin.

Sor Monica searched the *armario* without disturbing a single fold of the neatly stacked underlinens. When she was finished she went and stood by the door, her face red with an embarrassment equal to what the Abbess felt but concealed.

Noises from the plaza intruded and gave urgency to their search. Out there, Indian workers hastily sawed boards and mixed plaster for some construction to honor the arrival of Nestares—who would bring the Inquisitor with him.

"If you are satisfied, Sisters, that there is nothing suspicious here, we shall go next to Sor Olga's quarters." She took perverse joy in the Novice Mistress's shock and indignation and her silent—for a change—and stony submission. Of course, they found nothing to incriminate Sor Olga. In fact, they found nothing at all. The older woman's cell contained her clothing, her breviary, her devotional articles, and not a single other thing—not a book, no ink or quills, not even a scrap of paper.

In the main chapel, they searched even behind the ebony-and-gold frame that held the jewel-encrusted Madonna before which the community prayed six times a day. Aristocratic ladies often came to the convent to petition the sisters to pray for special favors—the recovery of a sick child, the safe return of a husband who had to cross the sea to Spain, the rescue of a loved one trapped by a cave-in at the mine. If their prayers were answered, they gave a precious stone, pearls, or gold to adorn the Madonna. Over the decades, the artisans in the Calle de los Mercaderes had attached the jewels to the image, creating the splendid Madonna of Los Milagros. On Holy Saturday in the year of Our Lord 1650, the opulent Virgin looked down serenely on the Sisters of Santa Isabella. She concealed no secrets behind her exquisite frame.

The searchers went next to the vault that abutted the church. Wealthy Potosinos often deposited their valuables in convents and monasteries for safekeeping. Each religious order kept a secure place such as this to store jewels and silver. On a table in the counting room, the sisters found a canvas-wrapped parcel. "Dear Lord, forgive me," the Abbess exclaimed. She had neglected her duty here. Captain Ramirez, the Tester of the Currency, had brought in some silver two days ago. She had sent Juana, the sturdy maid, to take the deposit. Then that evening, in the confusion following Inez's death, the Abbess had forgotten to come and lock it away in the vault.

While the others searched in the counting room cupboards, she unwrapped and weighed Ramirez's ingot and entered the amount in her account book. She took a key only she possessed and opened the fortified door to the adjoining vault. In the dank interior, she caught an odd whiff of candle wax and found a sprinkling of sand on the floor. This had not been here the last time she had come in. Under her wimple, her scalp went cold. A theft as well as a murder? Had someone penetrated the vault? She looked around quickly and saw nothing amiss. Yet something had happened here. Was there anyone she could trust? Instinct told her not to reveal this to the others. She would say nothing as yet to her sisters. She put down Ramirez's silver, left the vault, and locked the door.

She focused on her search of the convent. In the kitchen storeroom, they found nothing untoward among the sacks of maize and barley and boxes of salted fish that had been their sustenance during the fasting season. And nothing among the *vihuelas*, guitars, and mandolins in the room where they taught the girls music.

In the refectory, Sor Eustacia searched even the bowl of ashes kept on a table by the door as a reminder of the dust they would all one day become.

By the time they reached the rear cloister and the living quarters, the silent sisters were filing out in answer to the bell that called them to confession. The Abbess and her sisters searched the cells and found many things that outraged Sor Olga—a stash of coca leaves here, a gold bracelet, the memento of a former life, there, quite a few hidden sweetmeats, even during Lent, and a number of forbidden secular books and diaries—but nothing that connected anyone to Inez's death.

They passed to the upper floor, to the dormitory of the maids, whom Maria Santa Hilda dismissed. They went to prepare the noon meal while the sisters rifled through their meager possessions.

Like the others, Juana, the missing maid, kept her belongings in a wooden box under her bed. Among her things, they found religious pictures in frames marvelously carved with motifs of the sun, the moon, and mermaids playing guitars. "These are beautiful," the Abbess said.

Sor Eustacia fingered the fine carving. "Sculpted by her brother, the one she is trying to save from the *mita*."

"I thought he was illiterate," the Abbess declared. "Evidently he has found another way to express his thoughts."

"It looks very pagan to me," was Sor Olga's predictable response.

From the bottom of the box, Sor Monica pulled a rough *pañete* sack. In it was an animal horn containing ground lime and coca leaf wrapped in a rag, and under it a glass vial. Monica held the vial up to the light from the window. "It is some sort of dark resin." She pulled the cork and sniffed. "Very aromatic. It might be some drug the Indians inhale—like the one Vitallina found in the Plaza de la Fruta that relieves pain." She wet her little finger on her tongue, thrust it into the vial, and moved to taste the stuff.

"No," Sor Eustacia cried out. "It might be poison."

Maria Santa Hilda stayed Monica's hand. "You must not risk it. Feed it to the cat."

Sor Monica recorked the vial and put it in her pocket. She put back the horn with the coca in it. Sor Olga snatched it up. "We must destroy this."

"I don't—" Sor Monica began to object, but in the face of Olga's grim determination, she demurred.

"Leave the coca," the Abbess commanded. Whatever it was to the Europeans, it was more like a tonic or elixir to the Indians.

Sor Olga dropped it into the box and pushed the box back under the bed with her foot. Wrinkles of resentment stood out around her lips.

"We are finished with this search," the Abbess said. "Sor Monica, please try this new substance on the cat and report to me what happens. Sor Eustacia, I must speak with you in my office after Vespers." She knew they would follow her orders—they had vowed to obey—but neither showed enthusiasm. "For now, Padre Junipero awaits our confessions."

They walked together in silence across the rear cloister, but then the Abbess broke off from the others. She indicated with a hand signal that they should go on without her. She doubled back to the counting room.

When she unlocked the vault, Ramirez's silver ingot was where she had left it. She lifted it onto the proper shelf. Then she felt along the wall that separated the vault from the church.

Above the sand on the floor, she found a loose brick, and when she pulled it out, several others came away with it, opening a hole large enough for a person to crawl through. On the other side of the wall was the otherwise locked *guardarropa* where Morada and his bodyguard left their swords and cloaks when they attended Mass in the church each morning. The Abbess put her head through the opening. Except for a bit of red plume that must have fallen off a ceremonial helmet, the room was empty.

She replaced the bricks, took a candle, and checked the bags and boxes of silver on the shelves. They all seemed in order. The obvious had not occurred. No silver had been stolen from the convent's vault.

On a hunch, she lifted the carpet near the door, found loose floorboards and, under them, a huge excavation filled with silver. Bars, ingots, bags of coins. It struck her dumb how much silver was hidden here. A vast fortune. And in a flash, she knew what it was. Those caravans of Indians that everyone said went out each night into the surrounding plain did not carry Morada's silver, as rumor had it. Bit by bit, every day for many months, perhaps years, he and his guard had, on entering the church for daily Mass, carried his fortune here.

The enormity of this shook her breath. She was the unwitting guardian of a king's ransom. Men would kill for far less.

Her mind froze on a thought: Inez's death must have something to do with this. Any other theory was unthinkable.

The Abbess put everything back as she had found it and re-locked the vault and counting room doors. Crossing the cloister, listening to the deep silence of the convent within the vast silence of the mountains, she gazed up at the Cerro Rico. The barren rocks and earth of the mountain shone green, orange, gray, yellow, and red in the pale autumn sunlight. The Cerro dominated the city, like a pagan goddess of good and evil. The cross at its summit seemed too small in the face of its power.

She went to wait her turn for the confessional. Her mind swam in a sea of doubt and speculation. She prayed that this spiritual exercise would somehow prepare her to confront Eustacia, as she knew she must. That would be the most difficult conversation of her life.

When her turn came, she looked into Padre Junipero's quizzical face. His eyes had a perpetual wariness, as if he held some inner guilt and feared it might be read.

Maria Santa Hilda made the sign of the cross. "Bless me, Father, for I have sinned."

Padre Junipero heard the troubled Abbess's confession of her failings and doubts. She whispered to him of the weakness of her faith, of her pride, failings that seemed to the priest to have nothing to do with the woman before him. Words of guilt poured forth from her, but the intensity of her feelings did not match her words. Before giving her absolution, he hesitated. "Mother Maria, I sense there is some trouble you are not confessing."

She did something at that moment that he never expected to see her do. She burst into tears.

Unable to think of a single comforting word, he could do nothing but wait for her to recover herself. Blessedly she did, quickly.

"I forgot myself," was the only explanation she offered. "I have an idea of why someone might have murdered Inez. I believe it has something to do with her father's fortune. Please, go and find out if there is anyone she talked to before she came here that night. Find out what she said, what she knew. Find out if she knew the real hiding place."

"It would help if you told me more about what you suspect."

"Not yet, Father. I do not want to give you this knowledge if knowing it killed Inez."

"Do you know where the silver is? I sense you are afraid of something."

She paused and averted her eyes. "I am upset over something about Sor Eustacia."

"Does she know where the silver is? Did she—" He could not finish the sentence, but the Abbess knew what he meant.

"No," she said distractedly, "Eustacia did not kill Inez." Then, "No," too definitely.

"Lady Abbess," he said, "Beatriz Tovar just told me—"

"Stop," she almost shouted. "Padre, you cannot betray the seal of the confessional."

He was insulted that she would even think such a thing. "What I am going to say is not a sin of her own that she revealed. It is information about someone else."

"Oh, Father, I have heard Beatriz's suspicions. She is a good girl at heart, but she lets her imagination run amok. Please spare me hearing her wild speculations."

"I suppose," he said. "She is overly romantic."

He absolved the Abbess and gave her a small penance. They agreed to meet and exchange information early the next morning, after Mass.

"Don't forget," she said. "You must find the people Inez spoke to before she came here."

"I will," he said. Having blessed her with God's forgiveness, he watched her leave the confessional obviously as troubled as she had been when she entered. I have failed her, he thought. But I will save her. I will.

He hurried from the convent, along the Calle Real toward the theater.

In this very street only yesterday, he had joined his fellow Jesuits in a penitential procession of more than two hundred Potosinos. Dressed in prickly hair shirts, they had performed harsh acts of self-discipline—lashing themselves savagely with metal-tipped scourges. Marching behind banners bearing the images of San Ignacio, the Apostle of the Indies, he and his brother priests wore ashes on their heads and crowns of long thorns. His temples still bore the wounds of the barbs; his shoulders still ached from the heavy cross he had carried. Such penance was supposed to remind him of the pain of Christ's suffering, to cleanse him. It had only deepened his guilt. The procession had seemed just another form of masculine excess. Men could go too easily out of control with self-abnegation or to the opposite extreme with sex and violence.

His mind tumbled, like the rock slides one heard from time to time echoing across the Altiplano. He feared for the Abbess's life, for his own, and for his city's future. Like the war between the Basques and the Vicuñas twenty-five years ago and the bursting of the Caricari dam that had once flooded the city and killed so many, the coming devaluation would devastate the city, cause enormous suffering among the rich and even more among the poor. The most destitute might starve to death. In Potosí, the richest city on earth. City of churches glistening with gold and silver, of underfed Indians, of ladies of easy virtue and holy women in ecstasy before the martyred Christ, of smugglers toiling ceaselessly in pursuit of fortune, Mestizos fuddled by coca, artists who carved stone into patterns as delicate as lace. Magnificent music in the cathedral; snide, satiric verses posted on the street corners. Children squealing with delight as they played—or dragging themselves home at night after a day of work that would exhaust an adult. Potosí had a Spanish soul: proud, greedy, cruel, and noble. It had beauty. Grandeur. Chaos. The rhythm of Potosí was the rhythm of his heart, which swelled with love of all of it. Each time he extended his arms in the form of the cross at his daily Mass, he wanted to embrace the whole city—the lowest and the highest. The impossibly blue sky, the filthy beggars, the covetous, jealous, and zealous. He loved them all. And they were all threatened. And none more than the Abbess.

He knew where to find the person he was sure was the last to see Inez before she went to Los Milagros and her death.

The façade of the theater was one of the city's wonders. Under its soaring arch were three stories of graduated columns, built and decorated in the Baroque style but carved with Indian and Mestizo motifs. Instead of the fruits and flowers and baby angels one saw on buildings in Rome, here were Inca figures and leaves and vines found in the jungles of coastal Perú. Near the red-wood brass-studded doors, a hand-painted sign read, "Antonio Encenas and Francisco Hurtado present Troupe Astilla in Mareto's *Trampa Adelante*, staged in honor of the arrival of Doctor Francisco de Nestares, Visitador General. Admission: fifty pesos." Fifty pesos! Such a price. A man could buy three or four shirts for less.

Padre Junipero swung the thick knocker and after a few moments was let in by a statuesque African who wore a red-and-gold silk turban and doublet of the same fine fabric. This resplendent porter showed him into the auditorium, where a rehearsal was in progress under the proscenium. At the rear of the hall, painters decorated a canvas. The odor of their paint brought back a powerful, deeply buried image of a soft, shapely young actress sprawled naked on a couch. The priest banished the memory.

The African, who evidently was more than a porter, climbed onto the stage. In the seats for the audience, a group of barbers and hairdressers watched the proceedings and General Juan Velarde Treviño, a knight of the Order of Calatrava and a former magistrate of the city, lounged with two blowsy farceuses of the company.

Padre Junipero excused himself and called out for Sebastián Vázquez. The actors stopped reciting and scowled at him. A woman in a bright red wig sitting with General Velarde raised her index finger to her lips and waved him toward a door that led backstage.

The priest went through, up a few steps, and along a musty hall. At the end of the corridor, he found a room with the door ajar. Inside, a strikingly handsome blond man sat on a packing crate and ate from a plate he held in one hand. He was left-handed. The aroma of beef told the priest the man was not keeping the fast. This one would not be intimidated by priestly robes. He was studying a book propped up on a bench before him.

"Excuse me, sir," Padre Junipero said. "I am looking for Sebastián Vázquez."

The man leapt to his feet, hurriedly set aside the plate, and bowed graciously. "At your service, Padre." He was graceful and lithe and spoke with a perfect Castillian accent. His elegant black doublet might have been a costume, but it fit him too well. This was no theatrical roustabout. It was easy to see he was a nobleman. A great many such men wandered Perú—men whose fortunes had run out and who could no longer live in Spain. But one did not usually find them in acting troupes.

Vázquez pushed a sack onto the dusty floor and offered the priest a rough bench. "I am sorry we have no fire. The impresarios are afraid of burning down the theater." He pulled his cloak around him. "Why is it always so cold here? Why didn't they build the city on the southern slope of the mountain?"

"You forget," the priest said, "that you have crossed the equator. Here the north side is the warmer." He sat and studied the young man's steady dark eyes. "Are you the Sebastian Vázquez who knew Inez Rojas de la Morada?"

Wariness and fear crossed the man's classic features. "I don't believe I have ever heard the name."

The priest raised an eyebrow. "Your expression has already betrayed you. I would have thought an actor could better conceal his feelings."

The man laughed heartily. "You are a smart one, Father." He stood and paced to the wall. "If the truth were known, I have spent more time in the prompter's box than on the boards." He glanced at his image in a mirror. He had the vanity if not the proper skills for his profession. He was also unnerved.

"Please sit down, my son, and speak to me," the priest said softly.

The actor paused for a moment, gazing at the crate as if he were assessing its ability to hold his weight. He sighed and sat. He leaned forward with his elbows on his thighs. His dark eyes were resigned and a little bored, as if he knew what the questions would be. "What do you want of me?"

"First of all, tell me who you are. Your accent and your mannerisms betray a certain lineage."

Sebastian smiled in surrender. "I am the son of a Castillian nobleman, but alas, my mother was not his wife. My father took a liking to my blond locks and deigned to educate me, but that only made my life more frustrating—to know so well what I could not have."

The priest thought he saw the type of young man he was dealing with. "Did you then do something to incur your father's wrath, so that he cut off your allowance?" The actor's beauty and grace were the obvious attractions he held for Inez. Now, the priest understood that along with her beauty and charm, her father's enormous fortune would be a powerful inducement for this man.

"My father died." Vázquez's sadness seemed authentic. "My brothers—his legitimate sons—did not see fit to continue his generosity. In Spain, I worked as secretary to a *conde* for a while, but I decided to try my fortune in the New World, where I had heard the cobblers eat off silver and the common people live much at their ease and have their soup year-round, as only the richest do in Spain."

"How did you cross the ocean?" Everyone, even priests, required a license to take passage on a Spanish ship. The House of Trade scrutinized credentials.

The actor shifted the crate and leaned against the wall behind him. "In the usual way of men like me, by bribing the ship's officers to transport me under the guise of a personal servant. Are you going to report me to the authorities? Condemn me to rot in their jails?"

The question displayed no fear, as if he already knew this priest would never do such a thing. "No," the priest said. "Not on that count. How did you meet Inez?"

Sebastian's confident expression turned sheepish. "The only place a man like me can meet a girl like her—in church." He looked as if he expected the priest to be shocked.

Padre Junipero gave him a reluctant smile. "Would it surprise you that I was a man before I was a priest? I know about such approaches. Please tell me more."

The actor leaned forward again. "It was shortly after I arrived in Potosí, on the feast of the Epiphany. In the cathedral. I saw Inez enter with her mother. Actually, it was the mother who first attracted my attention. An extraordinarily beautiful woman. And she wore one red glove, the other white. I thought it was a fashion. Indeed, I admired the idea, until I saw the daughter was sullen and mortified and realized the mother was... shall we say, under the spell of Bacchus?"

"Doña Ana is a very troubled lady," the priest said diffidently.

Sebastián smiled with an easy amiability that further annoyed the priest. "I would say that is putting it mildly, Padre. Anyway, the ladies de la Morada found two other women in the seats they normally occupy. Doña Ana walked up and slapped the face of one of the other ladies—a Basque woman, I believe."

"Yes," the priest said. "I remember hearing about this. It was Doña Inmaculada de Aguirreya. There is a certain animosity between the Basques and the other Spaniards in this city."

"You *are* given to understatement, Father. Animosity? It is pure hatred."

"They fought a civil war. With many battles and many dead. About twenty-five years ago. The enmity goes on. Please finish your story."

"Another Basque—a man—came to the slapped lady's rescue."

"Don Luis de Medina."

The actor shrugged. "Whoever. A great outcry ensued. Priests came out to stop the shouting and jostling. In the melee, I saw that Inez was distressed over her mother's behavior. I offered my services to escort her home."

"And she accepted." The priest saw how it must have been. "And then you took advantage of her."

Sebastian lifted his head. "She was a very willing participant. She fell in love with me." The actor pointed to the mirror that hung on the wall behind the priest. "She gave me that looking glass from Flanders as a gift. She wanted me very much."

Bile rose in the padre's throat. How dare this handsome, careless wastrel speak so about a dead girl! "Do not try to shift the blame to her. You seduced her." The priest knew too well the guilt Vázquez should feel.

"It is an actor's prerogative." He said it as if it were a joke.

Padre Junipero leapt to his feet and shook his fist. "To despoil virgins?" He fought to control his rage.

"Oh, come now, Father. It is well-known that you priests seldom sleep within the walls of your monasteries. Perhaps you'd do better to repent for your own sins rather than scolding me for mine."

The padre poked his chin up sideways. "I am not that sort of priest."

"Ah, yes, Inez told me what a holy man you are."

His muscles rigid with rage, the priest stood over the seated larger man. "Inez never confessed the sin you led her into. She went to her death soiled with it." It took all of his strength not to pummel the actor's golden head.

"Dead? Is she dead?" The actor gazed up at Padre Junipero with incredulous eyes.

"Yes. She is dead."

The man sank back against the wall. "How? She was so young. So healthy."

The priest lowered his fists but kept them clenched. "That is what I am trying to find out. What do you know about her death?"

Sebastian's eyes went blank. "Nothing."

"What do you mean, nothing? You have admitted you were her lover."

Now Sebastian rose to his feet. He flattened himself against the wall and was silent for a second. Fear filled his eyes. Then he stood up tall. "We planned to marry."

The priest snorted derisively. "Ridiculous. You? A penniless bastard? Her father would never allow that."

"She said she could make him agree. I believed her. She was very persuasive."

The priest shook his head, but in his heart he too believed she might have convinced Morada. The Alcalde denied her nothing.

"Instead, she got into an enormous argument with him. About some papers or something."

"Does her father know about you? Who you are?"

Guilt and fear intensified in the actor's face. He did not answer.

"If her father knows you seduced his virgin daughter, he will surely kill you." A glimmer of another idea was beginning to dawn on the horizon of Padre Junipero's mind.

The actor eclipsed it. "She was not a virgin when she came to me."

"What?"

"You heard me, Padre."

"I do not believe you!" the priest shouted, but he knew he would not have protested so loudly had he been perfectly sure. Then suddenly the cause of the actor's fear dawned on him. "You killed her," he blurted out. And having said it, he was sure it was true. "You murdered her because you were afraid she would reveal your identity to the Alcalde and cost you your life." The priest stood up to the actor, certain he had him.

The handsome face contorted. His mouth opened and closed. His breath quickened. He raised his powerful arms.

The priest saw the blow coming but did not have time to avoid it before everything went black.

CHAPTER

12

Alone in the infirmary for the first time since Sor Elena fell ill, Sor Monica peered into the vial she had confiscated from Juana's trunk. She poked at the brown mass with a long needle. If the substance were hard, she might have thought it was a bezoar stone. It was the right color and size. Though where Juana would have gotten the money to afford such a thing, the nun could not imagine. Bezoar stones were found in the entrails of llamas and vicuñas and used as powerful medicine for the heart and as an antidote for snakebite. They were so rare that one of this size would have cost many months of Juana's salary. She could never have afforded it. Besides, this stuff was soft and sticky, not hard like a bezoar stone.

Sor Monica did not want to feed it to the cat.

It probably wasn't poison any more than the water in Inez's carafe had been.

She would taste it herself. Perhaps just a little to see if it had any effect.

It was probably just another Indian herb—like coca or the

gum of that tree that took away pain. Perhaps it was an intoxicant, like *chicha* or wine, but stronger.

If she tasted it, she might become intoxicated herself, and that was against the rules.

If she tasted it, she might die.

She put it aside. Vitallina had gone out to gather the last of the garlic, onions, balm, and mint from the garden in the cloister. Monica did not want to risk dying alone.

Tomorrow was Easter Sunday. In thirty-six hours, the Visitor General and the Inquisitor would arrive in Potosí. At dusk, the crier had called out that there was snow in the mountain passes. Perhaps Visitador Nestares and his entourage would be delayed. Perhaps the day of reckoning for Mother Maria would be postponed.

Sor Monica spooned some yerba maté into a gourd and ladled in some boiling water. Even if the snow slowed their arrival, it would not stop it. Even if Nestares and the Inquisitor had to wait for spring, they would still come to bring the city to justice for the false money and to arrest the Mother Abbess. Sor Monica had heard of prisoners of the Holy Tribunal being kept for six, eleven, even thirteen years before they were brought to trial.

She put a silver straw with a small strainer on the end into the gourd and swirled the yerba tea.

She took a taper and lit three candles against the gathering gloom. They treated candles as if they were nothing in this city. Tomorrow for Easter, more wax would be burned here in a day than they burned in her home church in Sevilla in a year.

She held up Juana's vial to the light. She took her notebook from the shelf and a quill and ink. On a blank page, she scratched a description of the sticky brown mass. She pulled the cup of maté toward her.

If the Inquisition indicted Maria Santa Hilda, might they also take her? As a woman, she could be accused of sorcery for curing diseases. They might confiscate the notebooks in which she had recorded the actions of almost three hundred herbs. She had found many that were useful. With what she had learned, she could cure rheumatism, gallbladder, colds, and diarrhea. Her herbs were powerless against hereditary diseases, like sickness of the heart, or diseases that had become too advanced. Still, if DaTriesta wanted to, he could make a case against her. There might even be substances on her shelves that, unknown to her, were illegal. Ordinary coca, as common as bread in Potosí, was banned in Lima. People could be excommunicated for using it.

She dipped the pen and wrote out her own state of health and age. "Strong. A virgin. Thirty-one."

If the Inquisition took her, they would strip her, lash her, try to make her confess to witchcraft for the medicine she practiced. Many times she had asked Padre Junipero if it was a sin for a woman to do what she did. He always said it was not.

Still, the Holy Tribunal had its own ideas. They might arrest her. And keep her forever. Some men were allowed to escape the Inquisition. They paid handsomely for it. They gave up all their wealth, even their identities, and became fugitives. They were allowed to disappear from the cells and then were declared dead and burned in effigy. But she had never heard of a woman doing such a thing. Where could a woman go without an identity?

People in Spain said that the discovery of silver in Potosí was the most important event since the birth of Christ. When she came to the New World, she felt she was participating in history. Now, her role might be recorded in the annals of the Inquisition.

She stirred the tea again to make it strong. She had used it many times to help people cast up whatever incommoded their stomachs. But would it bring up poison? Would it bring it up fast enough? If she vomited the stuff too soon, would she falsely conclude that it was not poison?

She ought to have someone with her when she did this, to testify about the poison if she died. Inez had died very quickly, she was certain of that. She had not thrashed about. She had fallen dead in a second.

Monica took up the quill again and wrote what she was about to do, as a record for those who might find her. She could not have anyone with her in this, because no one would permit her to do what she intended. They would make her kill the cat. But trying the poison on the cat would not tell the story. Many substances acted differently on animals than they did on human beings.

She uncorked the vial. If she ate this substance, would her soul be condemned forever for suicide? She wanted only to help her Abbess. To save the life of the holiest, most intelligent, most useful person she knew. Christ willingly gave His life. Wasn't this similar?

She blessed herself, hoping that it was not a sin to compare her sacrifice to the Lord's. "God have mercy on my soul," she wrote at the bottom of the page. She inserted a glass rod in the vial, took a bit of the substance, as much as might fill the end of a small spoon. She grasped the gourd of maté with her left hand, and with her right, she raised the glass rod and put it in her mouth.

At that same hour on the eve of Easter, Maria Santa Hilda found herself pacing the halls of the convent, waiting for the tolling of the Vesper bell. In less than thirty-six hours, Visitador Nestares would enter the city and receive a hero's welcome, despite the dread the citizens had of him. Fear consumed the Abbess. Fear and guilt.

She had spent the holiest days of the year trying to find a defense for herself against Commissioner DaTriesta's accusations. She had discovered nothing to ward off his threat, but in the process she had caused the women in her care to give evidence against one another—perhaps false evidence. And she had neglected all the other duties of her office. No texts were chosen for reading aloud at meals during the Easter season. No arrangements were made to transport the winter supply of charcoal from Cochabamba.

From the arched upper story of the rear cloister, she watched the Cerro change colors in the sunset and finally darken in the gathering twilight. She had not given a thought to the damage devaluation of the currency would wreak on the convent's finances. Less than a week ago, she had been worried about Captain Morada withdrawing his support from the missions. Now, the convent itself faced potential financial crisis. The Abbess's life before she took her vows had never required her to pay the slightest attention to how one managed in the face of want. She ought to be planning how to continue the convent's charities and the hospital even if the money lost its value. More important, she ought to be examining her soul for taints of the sins of which DaTriesta would accuse her. Perhaps she was guilty. Perhaps there was no explanation for Inez's death, except that God was testing the Abbess. Evil dwelled within her walls, of that she was certain. The convent's aura of holiness was a sham, like the decoration in the chapel that was painted to look like carved wood but was gesso underneath.

The sun had set. When it rose again, it would be Easter morning—a day for the greatest rejoicing of the year. But what joy could there be here, with a dead girl moldering beneath the choir floor and the taint of the demon in the air?

Vespers finally rang, and she started toward the chapel. A commotion below slowed her steps. She leaned over the balustrade to see the normally lazy maid Luisa running along the corridor, black braids flying behind her. The girl looked up, saw the Abbess, and let out a wail. "Ayeee! Oh, Mother, we are all doomed. Ayee! Ayee! She is dead. She is dead!"

The Abbess grasped her skirts and took the stairs at a full run. She caught Luisa. The girl's round face was twisted with terror. Her eyes were wild. She sobbed hysterically. The Abbess shook her. "Stop. Luisa. Tell me what you found."

"Dead!" Luisa screamed. "We must run away. Dead! She is dead, just the way Inez was dead. I found her. I saw her lying there. She was blue, just like Inez. Only she was not naked. But she is dead. We must run away." The girl struggled to pull free of Maria Santa Hilda's grip, but the Abbess held her fast.

"Who? Who is dead?" Others had come. They all stared at the terrified Luisa.

"Hippolyta!" she screamed. "Hippolyta is dead!"

The Abbess reeled with shock. She let go of the maid, lifted her skirts, and ran to Hippolyta's cell. The door was open. The girl lay sprawled half on and half off her bed. Her habit was undone in the back. Her rosy, soft shoulders were pierced here and there with marks of the flail she still held in her right hand. Her large, dark eyes so soft in life stared and gleamed like polished coal.

A moan escaped Maria Santa Hilda. She moved to lift the girl.

"Stop. Don't touch her yet." Sor Monica was pushing her way through the crowd at the door. "I want to examine her first."

The Sister Herbalist held out her arms to keep the others at bay. She scrutinized the body without touching it. Sniffed the air. Looked carefully at the items on the table beside the bed. Opened the *armario*. Checked the brazier. "Cold," she said absentmindedly. She asked the sobbing and shaking Luisa if Hippolyta's door had been locked.

"No," the girl managed to choke out.

Only then did Sor Monica begin to inspect the body. She peered closely at Hippolyta's back. She bent her limbs, parted her lips, and poked at her tongue, looked again at the marks on her back. The Abbess saw nothing unusual. Hippolyta had used the flail she held in her right hand. There seemed to be no excess in the self-inflicted wounds. They looked like the normal results of the penance all the sisters did from time to time.

Maria Santa Hilda had always been careful to guard against her sisters becoming overly abusive in their self-discipline. She instructed them to use the flail only twice a week while they were saying the Miserere. She never left this part of their instruction to Sor Olga, the Mistress of Novices, who ordinarily would address such issues. Olga often wore, under her habit, a blouse embroidered with sharp wire prongs that stuck into her flesh. She had asked the Abbess's permission to have the thing made. Maria Santa Hilda had reluctantly allowed it only on the condition that the Mistress of Novices would not foster the practice in her charges. The Abbess had discussed the issue with Padre Junipero many times. They agreed that for the sisters in the convent, self-flagellation should be a symbol of penance, not so harsh that suffering became an end in itself. "Remember," she always told the novices, "too much is just as bad as not enough."

Luisa continued to sob. The Abbess put an arm around her shaking shoulders. "Sor Dolores," she called out. When the nun appeared, Maria Santa Hilda handed the terrified maid into her care.

Monica beckoned to Sor Eustacia. "Please go out to the cloister garden and bring Vitallina here."

Eustacia, her face grim with grief, bowed her head and left.

"The rest of you," the Abbess announced to the crowd at the door and in the hall, "go to the chapel. Sor Olga, in place of Vespers, please lead the prayers for the repose of Hippolyta's soul." She said nothing of the poor baby who had died within its child mother.

As the sisters moved off toward the chapel, Beatriz Tovar pushed her way through toward the Abbess. She looked pleadingly into Mother Maria Santa Hilda's eyes. "Please, Mother," she said haltingly, "I want to go home to my parents."

The Abbess shook her head. "Not now," she said sharply. "You may not leave now."

"But—" Beatriz protested.

The Abbess held up her hand in command. "Do not question me, child. Go to the chapel."

The girl curtsied and opened the door. As she exited, Sor Eustacia and Vitallina arrived. The African woman's handsome face betrayed no shock. She looked at the dead girl and back at Sor Monica and said not a word.

"Take her, please," Monica said. "I will meet you in the infirmary in a few minutes."

The tall Negress lifted the body and carried it out.

The Abbess drew Monica and Eustacia out into the gloomy cloister. "What is happening?" she demanded. "Why have two young women died here?"

"I do not know," they answered, practically in unison.

"What can you tell me?" the Abbess asked of Sor Monica.

"Nothing useful. Like Inez, until she died, Hippolyta seemed in perfect health."

"Could she have died from being upset by a great guilt?" The Abbess eyed Eustacia but could not see her clearly in the gathering darkness.

Monica clenched her hands together. "It is true that strong emotion can upset the balance of the body's humors and set a person out of harmony, but in such a case, sickness slowly takes over. One does not see sudden death." She opened and closed her hands in a gesture of frustration, and they showed white and ghostly beneath the black sleeves of her habit.

"We know no more than that?"

The spirit hands fell to Sor Monica's sides. "I am quite certain that whatever killed Inez also killed Hippolyta. She seems to have died instantly. Her lips were blue."

Sor Eustacia lifted her head. "What about the substance we found among Juana's things?"

"A person can eat it without harm," Monica said.

"A person, Sister?" The Abbess was horrified.

"A person or a cat," Monica whispered, and bowed her head.

"I never want to hear that you are putting yourself in danger," the Abbess scolded.

"No, Mother." Monica did not raise her head.

"Can you learn anything more from examining the body?"

"I will try."

"Go, then, and do it now. I excuse you from chapel."

Monica walked away down the arcaded cloister walk, close to the wall, with her hands folded in her sleeves, in the humble way of any mere postulant.

The Abbess turned to Eustacia. "Let us go and pray now, but I want to talk to you in my office before the Compline bell rings tonight."

CHAPTER 13

Pilar Tovar stood in the corridor outside her husband's study and listened at the door. Muffled, angry voices of Antonio and his *mayordomo*, Domingo Barco, came through. This was not the moment to approach.

Because it was the eve of Easter, the mill beyond the wall was quiet. The only sound out there was the thudding of a maid beating a carpet. It could have been the pounding of Pilar's heart. What she intended to say to Antonio would destroy their life together.

She took a few steps away and stopped. If only she had Beatriz's determination and fearlessness. It must be the air of this New World where her Criolla daughter was born that gave females such courage. Even the temperate valley by the lake of Tarapaya where she had gone to birth Beatriz seemed to infuse infant girls with a force of will unknown to women born in Spain. Spanish women feared their husbands and fathers too much to defy them. Pilar had caressed and kissed every part of Antonio's body. In bed, she matched his passion. He encouraged that. But in the light of day, he expected her to be timid. And she was. She told herself she had no choice. But—

She returned to the office door and burst into the room.

Barco and the Captain were seated across the writing table from each other. They leapt to their feet. "What?" Antonio snapped.

Pilar stiffened her neck the way she had seen her daughter do when she was being willful and barked back at him, "I must speak to you at once." She felt her voice shake, but only slightly, and wondered if they heard it.

The handsome Barco's glistening eyes stared at her for a moment and then closed. He scooped up his plumed hat from the floor beside his chair, bowed low, and left the room without a word.

Her husband glowered. "Woman, have you lost your mind?

"She shivered inside her fur wrap. "I have a grave matter to discuss." She sat in the chair Barco had just vacated. Her husband did not sit down. He turned and looked out the window. She rose and went to his side. Angry heat emanated from his body. Courage failed her. She could not speak the words she had prepared.

Outside, no one stirred within the stout stone walls of the *ingenio*. Since Beatriz had gone away, this fortress that protected her had become a lonely prison. Pale candlelight glowed from the windows of the chapel, where the women were decorating the altar for Easter. What would the feast be without Beatriz to cheer her?

Thin plumes of smoke rose from the cooking fires of the Indians. The smelting furnaces were cold and the waterwheels still. White frost fringed the rivulet that flowed through the aqueduct. Pilar wondered where the water went when it left the city. Did it find its way down from the Altiplano, through the passes and valleys? Did it find the ocean? If she wrote her heartaches on pieces of paper and floated them on the water—

"That bastard Morada is a Portuguese and a Jew." Her husband's words were guttural and ugly.

"Oh, Antonio, you know that is not true." Whatever troubled him in his work or in the administration of the city, he blamed on Morada.

"He was just a rural magistrate when he put my brother to death without a priest."

Pilar placed a hand on her husband's shoulder.

He shrugged her off. "Miners used to dominate this city. If justice prevailed, we still would. We take all the risks to produce the silver." It was a story she had heard at every meal this week. How, many years ago, the Basques had taken control of the Cerro in the sure knowledge that it was the source of all power in Potosí. How now the worm had turned, and they were enthralled to Andalusian silver dealers and the moneylenders not of their brotherhood. How their petitions to the King and the Council of the Indies all fell on deaf ears.

Antonio flopped into the carved wooden chair next to the desk. He leaned forward and held his head in his hands. "The whole city is on the verge of ruin, and those idiots in the Cabildo are planning fancy parties. What folly! How can banquets make up the difference between false money and true?"

She knelt before him, took his hands, and looked up into his face.

"I could hardly keep up with my debts before." He took her hand. "Those bastards are going to make me a failure."

The word stunned her. Her fist started toward her mouth but stopped halfway. "What about the silver you sent to Spain on account?"

"It was taken by the King."

"Taken?"

"They gave me bonds in its place. Bonds that I cannot redeem."

"Good God! Then the King is a thief."

In a swift gesture, he put his fingers to her lips. "Do not speak treason." He went to the window and then, on tiptoe, to the door, which he opened softly and, after seeing no one outside, closed again.

She bit her lip. Any remark, even one uttered in vexation, could be punished. "If Nestares catches the people responsible for the false money, won't that be the end of it?"

"You are naïve."

She affected Beatriz's bravado. "I am. But I am not stupid."

He sighed. It was the closest thing to agreement she would get from him on that subject. "Spanish money has been the strongest in the world. Spain cannot afford to be passing false currency. The city's punishment must be harsh."

"We cannot avoid poverty, then?"

"I know no other honest occupation." He looked into her eyes and let her see his terrifying, heart-stinging humiliation. "I could become a smuggler, I suppose."

She rose half out of her chair. "Too dangerous! You could go to jail."

"I could go to jail for what I owe the King for the mercury I am forced to buy at inflated prices."

"The King is not fair," she nearly shouted.

He glared at her.

She lowered her voice to a whisper. "You are not allowed to lend money to the Indians and keep them in peonage, but the King does to you what he forbids you to do to them. Why do we have to treat the Indians better than the King treats us?"

He flashed her a bitter smile. "You are losing your innocence, Doña Pilar."

A soft knock at the door interrupted him. He strode across the room and opened it. The maid Mariza ushered in a thin, serious Mestizo lad. "This boy brings a note."

Silently, the boy put a paper in Antonio's hand. Antonio took a coin from his pocket and handed it to the child, who bowed low and backed out with Mariza. Antonio opened the letter and read. His face contorted with pain. He made a low noise, half groan, half sob.

Pilar rose. "What is it?"

"It is from the convent. In Beatriz's hand." He read in a halting, disbelieving voice, " 'Gentle Mother and Father, I kiss your hands and send you the greetings of my heart. It pains me to give you the grave news that Hippolyta de Escobedo met with the same fate that took Inez de la Morada. Some force is taking the postulants of this convent. I pray you to relent. Let me come home and marry Domingo. I am afraid to remain here. Your loving daughter, Beatriz.' "

Though she could not read, Pilar ripped the letter from his hands. She crushed it between hers. Hippolyta dead? "Antonio?" Her own voice sounded like a ghost's. "We must give in."

"I have told you it is out of the question."

She would not be deterred. "You are afraid for her, too. I hear it in your voice, see it in your face." Surely he would relent now.

"What I fear is for the soul of this girl who has the audacity to use another girl's death as a weapon against her own parents."

Pilar gulped. "That is unfair." She could not bear it when Antonio criticized the girl. Not even when he was right.

His broad chest heaved a sigh. "Beatriz is willful, opinionated, and stubborn."

Pilar's fists went to her hips. "She is also energetic, and brave, and confident. Her faults are your faults, Antonio, just as her virtues are your virtues."

He grimaced and turned away.

Without his eyes on her, she let flow the argument she had prepared for him and had been unable to deliver before. "My husband, I have told you I cannot, I will not, allow my child to languish in that convent. I brought myself here to this desolate land to be with you. I left my mother and sisters forever. I came here to the mine you started with the money from my dowry. But I will not remain without Beatriz. I—I will leave you and go into the convent to be with her." She trembled at the thought.

He turned back to her. His dark eyes were on fire. "You are my wife. You will stay right here, as I tell you."

She had prepared herself for this. "You will not keep me. I will find a moment to escape. I will lie to the sisters about your treatment of me. The Abbess will give me sanctuary. Even if it means giving you up, I will have the company of my daughter." She gazed right into his face and prayed to keep her resolve.

The jagged scar on his left cheek—from a wound of a pike in the war—burned a reddish purple with his anger. "You would make such an unspeakable threat to me?"

"I would." She tried to draw up her head, but it sank. "Oh, Antonio. Listen to me. Barco will take Beatriz without a dowry. Use the dowry to pay down some of your debts. Your profits will return. I do not care that Barco is Mestizo. He eats at our table. He is handsome and kind. I think he loves her, too. He has always been so affectionate to her. In the course of time, when you have the money, you will buy a royal *cédula* declaring him white. Please, Antonio, I went to see her yesterday. I tried to persuade her to marry Rodrigo. I told her we would not relent. She called me a traitor. She will never give up."

His mouth softened for a moment as if he would give in, then it hardened again. He uttered a phrase she did not hear but that shook his body as it escaped him.

"What?" she said, trembling.

"I said," he enunciated slowly, "that Barco is my son. Beatriz cannot marry him. He is her brother."

The aroma of beef, meat the padre had not eaten for months: The hunger for it made his temples throb. He inhaled it and other, strange smells. Musty clothing. Dust. Boot polish. A woman's perfume.

Padre Junipero sat up and shook himself. "Stop." He tried to shout, but his voice was weak. The door to the hall was open, and the actor was nowhere in sight.

The priest rose unsteadily to his feet and peered down the corridor. He brushed off his cassock and cloak and found his flat, wide-brimmed hat among the baskets and costumes strewn on the floor. He made his way back to the auditorium, where the rehearsal was still in progress. Not surprisingly, Sebastián Vázquez was absent from the company. The priest demanded to know his whereabouts. At first, no one admitted knowing where he had gone. Then General Velarde left the company of his actress friends and whispered to the priest that the young man had gone to the monastery of San Augustín to seek sanctuary. "What has he done?" asked the portly former magistrate.

"I have reason to believe—" The priest caught himself before he gave himself away. Too much could be made of his suspicion. In this city, in an hour, a tiny rumor could surge into a tempest of revenge. If the Alcalde found out that Sebastián had killed his daughter, the actor would not be safe, not even in the sanctuary of San Augustín. Years ago, Morada had dragged a Mestizo miscreant from the Church of San Martín in order to bring him to justice. There would be no telling what he might do to avenge the murder of his beloved Inez. "I am not sure," the priest answered, and quickly left.

Certainly the actor needed to be brought to justice, but not until after his testimony had thwarted DaTriesta's destruction of the Abbess.

The priest hurried through the bitingly cold evening. The streets were thronged with Indian workers who, having collected their wages on Saturday, came into the city from the outlying villages to shop. In the open-air market in the Plaza de la Fruta, goods that had been set out by the Indian women blew about in the violent wind. In the Calle de los Mercaderes, a long pack train goaded by muleteers was just arriving to unload wine, charcoal, sacks of flour, and jars of oil for the feasting that would begin with Easter tomorrow.

Rather than plow through the milling, shouting confusion, the priest doubled back to the Plaza Mayor and along the east wall of the Mint to the monastery of the Augustinians. He rang and was let in by the Brother Porter. "I must speak to Fray Vincente. It is urgent."

The Brother Porter left Padre Junípero to wait in a room bare except for a long wooden bench and a statue covered with purple muslin. After just a few minutes, the tall and powerfully built Vincente came rushing into the room and embraced his friend. "Junipero, tell me why you honor me with this visit." There was considerable bulk beneath Vincente's cassock of coarse-woven gray cloth. Never slender, he had gained weight. He was too fond by half of the pleasures of the table. If he continued, he would soon be totally unfit for the strenuous life at this altitude.

"I am sure you already know," Padre Junipero said. Vincente was a good priest and one Padre Junipero knew he could trust. "Within the past hour, a young Castillian nobleman presented himself here and asked for sanctuary. Knowing you, I am sure you have encouraged him to confess—"

Vincente held up his hand in protest, as if he believed the padre were about to ask him to divulge some secret.

Padre Junipero dismissed such worries with a wave of his hand. "I do not want to know what he told you. I just want you to hand him over to me."

The Augustinian took Padre Junipero by the shoulders and drew him to the bench. "Sit down and let me give you the message he sends to you."

Reluctantly, Junipero acquiesced. "I haven't a lot of time."

"What is the great hurry? The whole city has seen you rushing about since Inez de la Morada died." Vincente's eyes gave him a knowing, pitying glance that said he remembered the conversation the padre hoped he had forgotten, which had revealed Junipero's hopes for Inez. Vincente had counseled him then to draw away from the girl, that perhaps he was becoming too attached to her. Junipero had ignored the warning, knowing in his own heart that after that grave sin of his youth, he would never, never again be able to be with any woman.

He explained to Vincente the circumstances of Inez's death and DaTriesta's threat against the Abbess.

"And how do you know she didn't take her own life?"

Junipero looked directly into his friend's eyes and let him see into his heart. "I know."

Vincente sighed. "You have convinced yourself, but your personal conviction will not save Maria Santa Hilda."

Junipero gripped his friend's arm. "But the man you have here, Sebastián Vázquez, can. I have reason to believe he murdered Inez de la Morada."

Vincente looked amazed. "How could he when she was in the convent? You yourself just told me she was locked in a room, and no one could have gotten in or out."

"He would have had to have an accomplice. The way he acted when I questioned him revealed his guilt."

Vincente shook his large head. He lifted his skullcap, scratched under it, and replaced it. "It is not what he told me. He did not ask for the sacrament of confession. He merely talked to me."

"And?"

"He gave me permission to tell you the truth. For one thing, he is Portuguese—"

"Castillian," Padre Junipero objected.

"No. He has been posing as a Castillian, but he is not."

They both knew that while many would imitate a Castillian for the social advantages of being of the highest class of Spaniards, no one in Perú would say he was Portuguese unless he really was. All Portuguese were suspected of being Jews. Portugal had exiled all her Jews, and many had made their way across the Atlantic to Brazil and thence by smugglers' routes to the rest of Spanish America. Jews had three choices: to lie about who they were, to renounce their religion, or to die in the flames of the Inquisition.

"His accent is perfect. His blond hair. It's difficult to believe. Still, he would be condemned as quickly as a Jew or as a murderer. It must be the truth."

Vincente nodded gravely. "Of course he did not openly admit religion, but he knew what we would conclude."

"Tell me exactly what he said."

Vincente's benign face took on an indignant edge. "You must promise me first that you will not denounce him to DaTriesta. I will not be party to a man's death." A glint of insistence hardened his kind, dark eyes.

Like Junipero, this monk had devoted himself to lifelong repentance for a sin of his youth. Vincente's was the wrongful death of his own brother. A few years ago, the two friends had confessed to each other their deeply buried grievous deeds. Though they never spoke again of their shared torment of guilt, they continued as friends in the strangely comforting knowledge that there was one other person in the city who knew and loved anyway. "I will not reveal him," Padre Junipero promised. "Now, tell me what the Portuguese said."

"At first, he thought you were the agent of Inez, someone come to tell him when and how they would meet and marry."

"Like a priest in a play." Padre Junipero shook his head in sad amusement.

Vincente smiled. "He is an actor, after all." The smile faded. "When you told him Inez was dead, he was horrified. He thought you might be Morada's agent, come to kill him for defiling his daughter."

"So, he thinks the Alcalde knew about his liaison with Inez?"

"He wasn't sure. He said she would have done anything to get her father to give her what she wanted."

"The Alcalde would have given her anything."

"Perhaps not marriage to a Jew."

Junipero threw up his hands. "Inez was far from stupid. Even if she knew the actor was a Jew, which I doubt, why would she have told her father?"

Vincente shrugged. "All I know is that Inez said her going into the convent had something to do with getting money to marry him. It had something to do with some documents. He didn't really understand what she meant by that."

Documents again. Pilar Tovar claimed that her husband's *barretero* was killed over documents. But he couldn't go off on that tangent. "So the actor claims, but perhaps when she got to Santa Isabella she changed her mind about marrying him. Perhaps she succumbed to God's grace and jilted him. He might have killed her for that."

"I suppose." Vincente's doubt clouded his eyes.

"Or perhaps he was afraid she would reveal his identity to her father. The Alcalde would certainly kill him. Yes. Yes. The Portuguese could have killed her to protect his own identity."

Vincente grasped him by the shoulders. "You are letting your imagination run away with you, Junipero. You should not be involving yourself so passionately in this. That girl was a temptation to you in life. Don't let her endanger you in death as well."

"I told you. I am trying to save the Abbess from the auto-da-fé."

"Can the Abbess not appeal to the Bishop?"

"The Bishop is siding with DaTriesta."

Vincente looked dubious. Bishops resisted the Holy Tribunal since it sapped their episcopal power. "Is there no way the Bishop can turn a profit by protecting the Abbess?" They both knew silver, and not much else, motivated His Grace.

The padre shook his head. "Perhaps the Commissioner has something in his Sumaria about the Bishop."

"If you can open a rift between the Bishop and the Commissioner, perhaps you can save the Abbess that way."

Padre Junipero rose. "I am going to find out if the Alcalde knew about Inez's liaison with the actor. Please keep him here and guard him well."

Fear blazed in Vincente's eyes. "How can you ask questions of the Alcalde? You would have to reveal too much. If he finds out, he will come here and take the actor by force."

"I have another source of information." The padre embraced his friend and quickly left.

The bitter cold streets were still crowded with Indians, many addled with strong drink. God give him grace, the priest did not blame them for their excesses on Saturday night. No white man could do the work they did at this altitude without dying of fatigue.

Junipero stopped at a *pulperia* in the corner of the Plaza de la Merced and ate a piece of hard bread and a bit of strong yellow cheese. He allowed himself a glass of wine to ward off the chill. As he chewed the first salty bites, he realized he had not eaten all day. A fast at the end of Lent. Perhaps he should have forgone even this. He drained the wineglass and left the counter.

He made his way quickly to the Casa de la Morada.

The inner courtyard was jammed with people, including Ramirez, the Tester of the Currency. Strange that a nobleman would be left to wait with the rabble.

Perhaps because he was piqued about being snubbed by Morada, on seeing the priest, Ramirez grasped his sword hilt and grumbled something hostile but unintelligible. Junipero pretended not to notice and quickly moved away. He wanted no noisy confrontations.

Also among the crowd, the padre saw Juana, one of the maids from the convent, sitting on a bench with her back against the wall, asleep. He had heard that she was trying to save her brother from the mine—that mouth of hell that consumed the poor, peaceful Indians in their thousands every year. What the galleons carried to Spain was not silver, but the sweat and blood of innocents.

"The Alcalde is not here," the guard at the inner door told him before he had a chance to say a word.

"I have not come to see the Alcalde," Padre Junipero said. "I want to see his daughter Gemita." The soldier rightly raised his eyebrow. It was highly irregular to visit the girl after dark, but with less than two days left before the Grand Inquisitor arrived, the priest had no choice. "Please ask her mother if it is permitted."

The burly guard received the priest's request with a sniff, opened the door, and escorted the padre into a sitting room that overlooked the mountain. The Cerro rose, multihued in the silver moonlight. The night sky was clearer at this altitude than anywhere else on earth.

Within a couple of minutes, Inez's sweeter but not as beautiful or intelligent younger sister entered the room, accompanied by her mother's African maid. The liveried servant was dressed more richly than her little mistress.

"May I offer you some Paraguayan tea, Father?" It was what an adult would have said, and it touched him that she tried to act the grown-up.

"No, thank you."

Gemita eyed the maid askance, and the padre saw she was looking for a way to get Bernardina out of the room.

"On second thought," he said, "yes, I would."

Once the maid was gone, he came quickly to the point. "Does your father know that your sister, Inez, had a lover?"

The girl showed no shock. She put her small hands behind her and paced to the window. Her frock was spring green, a curiously bright color for a girl who had just lost her sister. "My mother says it is not right to speak ill of the dead. That they will get revenge on you."

"God's Blessed Mother will protect you if you tell the truth."

The girl hesitated only a few seconds more. "I am not sure my father knew about the actor," she said as innocently as if she were talking about her dolls. "But he did know about Domingo Barco."

The priest's thoughts froze. "Domingo Barco?"

"He was her lover before Sebastián Vázquez."

"Impossible." Barco was the *mayordomo* of Morada's chief enemy—Antonio Tovar. And a Mestizo to boot.

"Being alone with him was easy for Inez. His mother is our cook. When he came here to visit, Inez dressed him as a maid and sneaked him into her room."

The priest suppressed a gasp of shock. Scandalous, how this seemingly innocent girl matter-of-factly described her sister's debauchery. He would have preferred to disbelieve her, to imagine Gemita was inventing this story out of some sisterly jealousy. But he had already invented every defense for Inez his mind could produce. And they had all fallen before the onslaught of her history. His dream of what Inez had been, what she might have become, blackened and burned in his heart.

The girl went on blithely. "When she took up with the actor, she had to get out of the house alone." A hint of glee glinted in Gemita's round, dark eyes. "Then she invented a million deceits. Once she stole a key from the maid who carries in water from the fountain in the plaza. After everyone was asleep, she dressed herself in robes so that only her eyes showed. She let herself out by the kitchen door. Another time, when my father and his men were not here, Inez even pretended she heard people shouting a warning in the street that the Caricari dam had broken again." The girl was speaking rapidly now. Recounting the story with relish, as if it were an adventure from a chronicle. "Mother started screaming that we would all be washed away. She pushed us and the maids out the door into the street, shouting, 'Run. Run towards the Mercaderes.' Inez ran, but toward the theater. And another time…"

While the girl rattled on, the priest went back over the facts. Barco. She had jilted Barco. He could have killed her, then. Beatriz Tovar. The Abbess said Beatriz fancied herself desperately in love with her father's *mayordomo*. Spanish girls were notoriously jealous. Beatriz could have—

By the time the maid's bracelets clanked outside as she turned the door latch, he was on his feet, pacing. He had a vague recollection of the Alcalde's cook—a wiry woman, handsome despite her pockmarked face, who had once sent her Mestizo son to learn reading and mathematics at a small school run by the Mercedarian order. Evalin, her name was. That boy must have been Domingo Barco. The priest had never put the two together.

Junipero gestured away the gourd of maté the maid offered. "I must speak to the cook."

Bernardina peered at the tea and frowned. "Is something wrong with it?"

Gemita and the priest left her in the salon holding the tray. The padre followed the child across the family's central patio to the rear of the house and a small, messy courtyard filled with buckets, mops, and empty crates. A scrawny black-and-orange cat poked listlessly among the trash.

They entered a cluttered kitchen that smelled of good soup.

Gemita presented the priest to the wary cook and took a place near a great stone fireplace in which a cauldron simmered over a charcoal fire. There were bowls of grapes and olives on the table in the center of the room.

"Thank you for escorting me here, Gemita." The padre gave her his most charming smile. "I think I need to speak to this lady in private." He purposely confused the girl by calling her cook a lady.

Gemita folded her arms across her burgeoning breasts. "Everyone treats me like a baby when I know more than anyone."

The priest gestured her toward the door. "Nevertheless, you must leave us alone." He waited silently the few moments it took her to acquiesce. She twisted her mouth and stomped out.

"What do you want with me, Padre?" Evalin demanded unceremoniously. Though there were two plain wooden chairs in the room, she did not invite him to sit down.

He remained standing with her as if she were the lady he had called her, and he addressed her in Aymara. "Is Domingo Barco your son?"

"Yes." The woman's black eyes hardened.

The priest waited, but she offered no further information. "Does the Alcalde know this?"

She wiped her hands on the long sleeves of her rough cotton dress. It was the color of river mud. She never took her sharp black eyes off his. "Yes."

"Does Antonio Tovar know that his *mayordomo* visits you in the house of his enemy?"

Her thin lips curled. If there had been any joy in the expression, he might have called it a smile. "Yes."

"And does—"

She held up two brown, callused hands. "Let us just say that both gentlemen have reason to believe I am loyal to them and that the information that passes between me and my son is useful to both."

"And to whom are you loyal?"

The cold smile broadened. "To my son. And myself."

He could not fault her for that. He knew better than to underestimate her intelligence. Many Spaniards thought the Indians simple because they spoke Spanish with thick accents and believed in pagan gods. But this woman came from a race that had a complex civilization here before the Conquistadores arrived. She had borne a son by some Spaniard, who probably got her with child and abandoned her. It was against the law for a Spanish man to violate an Indian woman, but if caught, the man paid only four pesos and nine reales, a fine for the public Treasury. No more than he would have given a prostitute. Unlike a whore, the Indian woman got nothing for her trouble. But, perhaps, a child. A child who might become everything to her. "Do you know that your son seduced Inez de la Morada?"

Evalin snorted. It was a masculine sound. "You have it the wrong way round, Padre. My poor boy succumbed to her wiles."

He was speechless.

She laughed the louder. "And so did you, I see. Well, she is dead now. I do not care. She endangered my son. I only hope that love is like the pox. That if you have had it once and survived, you cannot catch it again." Her hard eyes were dubious, as if she knew, with her son, such hopes were in vain.

Yet another suspicion flickered. "Endangered Domingo?"

"Yes, by putting him in the way of the Alcalde's wrath." Her tone said he was a fool not to see it. He was a fool not to see so many things.

The priest sought a sign of guilt in her. She could have murdered Inez. Anyone could be guilty. People were not as good as he wanted them to be. Or so much better than he, as he thought they must be. Anyone could be guilty. Barco. He could have—if he knew about Sebastian and was jealous. "She had another lover."

"I knew that, but my son did not. I kept it from him to protect his heart. But it broke anyway, when she went into the convent."

"Did the Alcalde know of her liaison with your son?"

"No," she said too quickly.

He looked at her and waited. She would never give evidence against her son. If he was accused, this woman would confess to the crime herself to save him.

She held the priest's stare.

"If I tell the Alcalde, he will kill your son. He will have to if the word gets out that Domingo defiled his daughter."

She gripped the edge of the table. "The Alcalde knows. His bitch of a daughter told him herself."

But Barco lived.

"She blackmailed her own father." The tiny woman's eyes dared him not to believe it.

The priest was beyond astonishment. "Tell me."

"She had letters of her father's. Letters that could cost the Alcalde his life. She entrusted them to my son. I took one and kept it."

The priest doubted her.

She raised an eyebrow. "Yes," she said. "I can read. My son taught me. I took the damning letter, and then I made a pact with Morada. The letter I stole is in the hands of a secret person. If any harm comes to my son or to me, no matter how innocent the Alcalde seems, the letter will be revealed, and Morada will be ruined."

"Treason? What does the letter say?"

"If I tell anyone that, Morada will kill my son."

A quarter of an hour later, on his way back to his monastery, Padre Junipero passed Don Jerónimo Taboada and Don Juan Téllez, Morada's closest allies on the Cabildo, with a group of young thugs, lounging against the carved stone facade of his chapter's church. As he approached them, to his utter astonishment, they drew their swords.

CHAPTER

14

The Abbess clenched her fists. "What was Inez to you?" she asked. She tried not to turn away from Sor Eustacia's smoldering gaze. In the end, she gave up and looked up at the high, dark window.

"You have always been the holiest person I knew." The younger woman's voice shook. Her vow of humility evaporated in the crucible of her anger. "The threat of the Inquisition has turned you into an Inquisitor yourself. I would perish in the flames in your stead, yet you ask me such a question?"

Maria Santa Hilda sat straight in her hard wooden chair and gripped her hands together to stop their trembling. The naturally dulcet Eustacia's assertion stung and terrified her. The Abbess, who had the habit of command, had no words of defense. All she could do was repeat the offensive question: "I must know what your relationship was with Inez." She prayed Eustacia would have a response to erase Hippolyta's disgusting accusation.

Like some great mythic bird-woman come to life, Eustacia leaned forward and grasped the edge of the table, looking as if she would fly across it at the Abbess and tear her apart. "You think I killed her."

Maria Santa Hilda's stomach trembled under her heart. At this moment, Eustacia seemed capable of it. "Did you have reason to?"

The younger woman's powerful grip on the table tightened. The heavy table moved. Hate, then fear, then despair, paraded in full sight on Eustacia's lovely face. At last, she dropped back into her chair and bent over, gripping the sides of her head. "I have borne everything," she sobbed. "I can bear this, too." She lifted her head. Her eyes were defeated. "I was her lover. For only one night." She paused, and in the silence, torture passed over her countenance. She stared back at the Abbess, her soft eyes filled with guilt. "For only one night, but I did it. And I have been in hell ever since."

Waves of horror and shock, of pity and suspicion, crashed over Maria Santa Hilda. "Speak to me, Eustacia," was all she could say.

"I came to this convent to be worthy, to try to be truly holy. Since I entered the order, I have not taken a glass of water without permission. I have accepted this slow, monotonous life, of obeying the bells, of endless repetitions. I thought it would bring me solace."

"But it has not."

Eustacia held up her head. "Before I became a nun, I had wealth, you know."

Maria Santa Hilda nodded, but she had not known. Eustacia was noble; otherwise the order would never have accepted her. But many noblewomen had only a scant dowry, enough for the order but not for a suitable husband.

"I was not some English spinster—the victim of primogeniture. My mother was a widow, I her only child. A man came to ask for my hand, and my mother consented. In the chapel of our villa in Andalusia, he swore with the missal and the crucifix in his hands that he would be my husband. He begged my mother a moment, there in the chapel, to be alone with me. When she left, he seized and raped me. When I tried to scream for my mother, he beat me. At the point of his dagger, he molested me. And he threatened to stab me to death if I told anyone or tried to get justice from the King or the Church. After that he came to my house whenever he wanted and abused me. When, in desperation, I finally told my confessor, the old priest offered me the only remedy available. That we force the man to marry me immediately."

She straightened now and looked directly at the Abbess with eyes demanding justice that did not exist in this world. "My own mother, even after she found out about his brutality, tried to force me to go ahead with the marriage. No matter how I screamed and cried, no matter how many times I tried to lock my door against him. She became his ally. How can a mother subject her daughter to such a fate? Married to him, every night of my life would have been another rape. My mother told me no one would marry a girl who had lost her virginity. Marriage to him was my only hope for a normal life." Eustacia laughed the laugh of a madwoman. "Normal life." She leaned forward now like a supplicant in a painting of the Virgin. "I told her if she forced me to marry him, I would kill him. So she sent me to the convent."

"*Deo Gratias.*" The words escaped the Abbess.

"I told myself I would be a good nun."

"You were a good nun," the Abbess said, for so the mild Eustacia had seemed—until Inez. "Weren't you?" She realized she was speaking in the past tense.

"I have broken many rules."

"How?" The Abbess heard the apprehension in her own voice. These were the things she had not wanted to know.

Eustacia smiled indulgently, as if she were about to tell the harsh truth to a child.

Maria Santa Hilda's back stiffened. "Tell me everything."

"You are so good that you do not see how evil is the world around you."

"That is not true." The denial came out too loud. "I know the greed that grips this city. I know about the brothels, where men fight to the death over the favors of whores." She knew another, personal evil, but she must not think about it.

Eustacia's face was now inches from hers. "You know evil from arm's length. You pray for sinners in the abstract. I know evil firsthand."

The Abbess unclenched her hands and reclaimed her calm. "So you have only now told me. But almost everyone who comes to this convent carries heavy troubles." She had taken in hysterical, scrupulous girls who saw this as the only place to hide from temptation. Despairing daughters of widows whose dowries were not sufficient to entice anyone to take on responsibility for their mothers as well as themselves. Rejected girls who came here rather than feel like failures in the outside world.

"Yes, and when they enter your care, you encourage them to forget. You expect that spirituality and scholarship will scrub their souls clean."

"I thought those comforts satisfied you, that you were serene in your silence."

"The stains of my old life remain."

The Abbess knew this was true of herself also. As long as she had been a nun, hardly a day passed that she did not think of the pain of losing her mother, of the ill will she bore her father.

"In the night, I have been meeting with the newcomers."

The Abbess could not suppress a grimace. "For what purpose?" she demanded indignantly.

Eustacia threw her a dagger glance. "Just to talk. To get them to tell me if they were troubled, what troubled them."

"They are supposed to confess to the padre, not to you."

"The sacrament takes away the sin, but not its scars."

"Those scars are between a soul and God."

"Those scars torment."

"Pain that can be offered to God."

"Pain that can be relieved. Sor Monica seeks to take away the pain of the body. I have sought to unburden the spirit. I talk to the young ones. Mostly I listen to what they tell me."

"In their beds?" the Abbess asked. It was a cruel barb. And

wrong to have said. Worthy of Sor Olga or DaTriesta. She had lost control of the conversation. Of herself.

Eustacia winced. "No," she whispered, and turned away her gaze.

The habit of silence descended on them, and neither seemed willing to break it. The Abbess knew she must take control, but her heart was too sunk in confusion to choose her words.

Finally, Eustacia rose and went to the door. With her hand on the latch, she spoke again: "Do you know who was the father of Hippolyta's child?"

The Abbess stroked the smooth edge of the table. "Her father's page. Don Diego killed the boy."

Eustacia shook her head. "It was her father himself."

Maria Santa Hilda's jaw dropped.

"Yes," Eustacia said quietly but vehemently. "He started on her when she was only ten years old. He used her. And then when he had made his own child pregnant, he murdered that poor Mestizo boy and sent his poor children here, the one within the other."

The Abbess blessed herself and grabbed for the rosary that hung from her belt. In its impossibility, she knew it must be true. Her fast-starved stomach churned with disgust. "God forgive him." God forgive her for being so ignorant.

"I don't know if I could love a God who would forgive such a thing."

"Please do not blaspheme."

"Poor Hippolyta felt guilty. Her father told her it was her own fault. And she believed him."

The Abbess's belly heaved.

"Well might you retch," Eustacia said. "And you are a virgin. You cannot truly imagine the horror of such a thing."

The Abbess bit hard on the knuckles of her right hand. Eustacia was wrong, but she could not protest. She composed herself. "Eustacia, you speak of the horrors of others, but what of your own? What about Inez?"

The younger woman, who now seemed to the Abbess

suddenly older, looked away. "She seduced me." She let go of the latch and dropped to her knees, bent over with anguish. "It does not wash away my guilt, I know, but she was beautiful. And—and skillful." The last word slipped out of her, like a tear.

The Abbess's face burned. Shame, guilt, and outrage seared into her bone marrow.

Eustacia's broad, beautiful face twisted with pain and frustration. "I longed to be one of those mystical women who loses herself in Christ. But I cannot. If a surgeon opened my chest, I wonder if he would see the scars on my heart."

Maria Santa Hilda thought to ask directly if Eustacia had killed Inez. But she did not. She had no way to judge the truth of Eustacia's replies. Beata Sor Elena would have known how to help her. But her old confidante was dead and under the boards of the choir, buried there along with Inez.

The Abbess hardened her will. "You had better tell me all you know."

Eustacia rose and took the chair opposite the Abbess. "When Inez came to the convent, she was not truly repentant. She tried to convince me that she was, but I saw through her fabrication. Her secrets came out too easily, too well formed. If they are truly afraid or guilty, they cannot tell the truth so facilely. Often they do not admit the truth to themselves."

Mother Maria saw the logic of that.

Eustacia folded her hands into her sleeves. "I was able to bring out one thing that sincerely troubled her."

"Which was?"

"Her father killed an Indian over some secret documents and had somehow made her feel guilty about it. I think that almost everything she said to me was a lie, but not that. She said that if it hadn't been for her, that Indian would still be alive." Eustacia placed her hands over her mouth, as if suddenly she had thought of something unthinkable. "Perhaps her father killed her because she knew about his murder of the Indian."

The Abbess threw up her hands. "That is absurd. The

Alcalde must have killed many Indians in his life. He hunts down all manner of fugitives. How could his killing one more Indian make such a difference? Besides, Captain de la Morada is the very last person who would have harmed his daughter."

"I agree," Eustacia said. "She loved him, too. Of that I am also certain. She mourned the loss of his company."

"She told me she came here to escape his influence for a while."

"Nevertheless…" Eustacia's voice trailed off. "I think Inez seldom told the truth."

Considering the surprises and shocks Eustacia had revealed today, Maria Santa Hilda wondered how often she had hidden the truth.

"Inez was very troubled," Eustacia said. "I have come to believe that harboring secrets unbalances the mind. And Inez harbored many secrets." Her eyes turned furtive. "Perhaps we should return to the theory that Inez took her own life."

The Abbess saw how wrong that was. "More than ever, I doubt it. All her cleverness and greed for power could not reside with despair. Inez wanted something too much to give up her life before she got it." The actor, she thought. He must have something to do with why she died.

"Murderer!" Taboada growled. His powerful fingers dug into Padre Junipero's arms.

The stunned priest felt himself lifted and tossed like a sack of maize against the façade of the Compañia de Jesus. His breath left him, and before he could get it back, they were on him.

"You killed her. I heard the Alcalde say so." Ramirez spat the words at him. "You priests claim to be holy, but everyone knows priests carried Toledo steel and used it in Cortez's army."

The padre opened his mouth to object. A big, gnarled hand gripped his throat. He gasped for air. Thudding, crushing blows, on his chest, his shoulders, his back. He crumpled to the pavement. He tried to cover his head. A hand wrenched his arm back. His shoulder screamed in pain, but he could not utter a sound. A cracking kick knocked a searing pain down his spine. Sprawled and heaving for breath, he could only pray: Make them stop, Lord. Make them stop. His eyes would not focus.

Ramirez drew a sword. Raised by strong arms and backed to the wall, the padre squirmed and darted and managed to maneuver to the portal. He clung to the slender column that guarded the front door of the chapter house. "Please." He humiliated himself. "You are mistaken. I swear by the soul of Santiago."

"I heard the Alcalde accuse you," Ramirez said. "Through the door, on the night you told him of her death. He said you killed her."

"If I had, would not the Alcalde have killed me himself?" The priest raised his hands over his head, like a condemned man before a firing squad. "Why did he not arrest me? Why did he not avenge himself on me?"

Ramirez's sword prodded his throat and stopped his heart. "The Alcalde could have been too overcome with grief to act." Ramirez said. "Now I am here to do it for him."

The priest folded his hands in front of him. "Please," he said, "ask him again. If he says he is convinced that I killed her, I will submit to your swords. But in the meantime, do not slay me unshriven."

Juan Téllez, the third of the group, a man the padre knew was devoted to the Blessed Mother, crossed himself and grasped Ramirez's sword arm. "Give him a chance to confess before he dies, Felipe," Téllez said to Ramirez. He turned to Junipero. "The logic of your famous mind has saved you this time, but it will not the next."

Ramirez lowered his weapon. "Do you have sins to confess? Shame on you, priest." He spat out the last word as an insult.

"God help me," Padre Junipero whispered.

Jerónimo Taboada grasped the front of the padre's cassock. He brought his face close. He smelled of stale wine. "Go and confess," he said in a hoarse whisper. "We will find you when we want you." He reached around the priest's trembling body, opened the monastery door, and tossed the padre into the dark entry.

The Bishop was disquieted. Perhaps because the weather had been so violent in the wee hours. Hailstones as large as dove's eggs had fallen on the town and awakened him even earlier than the dawn Easter ritual required. The noise in the night had sounded like a volcano erupting out in the cordillera.

Soon the snow would pile up in the plazas and cold wind would torture him. In this comfortless city, with only coal to burn, noxious fumes could any moment cut off his life. He had endured three such winters, and he would endure another. The only alternative was to travel to Lima—mule sore and sickened by horrid meals along the way—and to be greeted by great expense when he got there.

Ordinarily, a ceremony such as this morning's welcoming of the Easter sunrise satisfied his Spanish soul. Even on this treeless plain, the grandeur of the ritual matched anything they were capable of in Sevilla or Naples. At three in the morning, he rose and, over his warmest silk-and-vicuña undersuit, donned silver-and-gold-brocaded garments befitting the most joyous day of the Church year. He was met at his front door by eight priests, who rode with him on mule back, as Christ had triumphantly entered Jerusalem before his death. Worshippers, resplendent in furs and silk finery, streamed with them out of the center of the city, to the foot of the Cerro, where on a high promontory they faced the brightening eastern sky and awaited the first rays of the rising sun.

Nothing consoled the Bishop. Not even his entourage of great families with their trains of servants, all decked out in gorgeous clothes and jewels—many purchased within the last few days in anticipation of the coming devaluation. He himself had wished to convert his soon-to-be-diminished fortune of silver into precious stones. But during Holy Week, the head of the Church could not be seen, even through his agents, to be trading rather than praying. So the Bishop took no comfort from being surrounded by the wealthy in full plumage or from the Indians in their native regalia, ready to perform ritual dances to welcome the Risen Christ. His Grace's mood was set by the thin, icy air, the shrieking wind, the brooding isolation of the vast Altiplano stretching before him, and the snapping of frost-cracked rocks.

On the horizon, the first light exploded forth—impossibly bright here where no mist obscured it. The Alcalde Morada touched his torch to the great bonfire prepared for the occasion. At once, the sextons of the ninety-odd churches in the town tolled their bells in a glorious cacophony of joy. The crowd of thousands on the mountainside sang out an Alleluia, their voices rich and fervent, but with a shrill brightness of desperation.

Within minutes, candles were lit everywhere. Shielded from the wind in glass globes, they were carried by the splendidly liveried pages of the wealthy families and glowed in the windows and on the balconies along the route of the holy procession. A canopy was unfurled to be carried over the Bishop's head, but the wind whipped it so strongly that the men could not hold it and had to put it away. The members of the Cabildo struggled to keep hold of the platforms on which they bore statues of the saints. Led by the *azogueros*, who—because they were the ones who produced the silver—since the founding of the town had the honor of leading the Easter procession, the faithful descended quickly toward the shelter of the cathedral. Tall, exquisitely handsome Antonio Tovar was at the head, resplendent in a red cape worked with gold, riding a proud black Chilean horse shod and caparisoned with silver. The other miners followed, and their wives traveled behind them in calashes drawn by mules. Their Indian *pongos* and the *caci-*

ques of all the surrounding Indian villages followed after, their ostrich-feather umbrellas torn apart by the fierce wind.

Don José de Aureliano, who earned this honor by making a large donation to the Bishop's private fund for his burial mausoleum, took the layman's place of greatest prestige, carrying the cross before the Bishop. Don José held the city license to manufacture playing cards, an extraordinarily lucrative business despite the fact that he had to share his revenue with the Crown.

On foot now, to the beat of the savages' drums and their strumming *vihuelas*, the Bishop kept an appropriately stately pace down the cursed rocky trail. By the time he reached the stone-paved streets, his gout-punished left toes throbbed and his stomach growled from the forty-day fast that would blessedly end after this morning's Mass. Longing for a sumptuous lunch plagued him almost as much as his burning foot.

When the classical façade of La Matriz, the cathedral, was finally in sight, he allowed his pace to quicken across the Plaza Mayor. Inside, the nave was suffused with gentle candlelight and sonorous chanting of the monks in the choir. The Bishop ascended the altar and commenced the Mass of the Resurrection.

During the Offertory, he sat on his golden throne and sighed with, he feared, a too audible relief from the pain in his foot. He received the faithful who came forward on this joyous day to make their petitions to the Church. He himself had inaugurated this ritual to give the subjects of Spain, so far from their King, an opportunity to beg favors.

A couple of destitute priests from the outlying districts entreated better assignments, but they knew as well as he did that ecclesiastical patronage belonged to the King and that their Bishop could appoint only those the Council of the Indies had chosen. He did not hide his annoyance at these ragtag clerics for reminding him of his lack of real power. They bowed and backed away, already mouthing the usual antigovernment grumbling.

More than twenty women came forward who wished, by claiming brutality, to avoid living with their legal husbands. He refused, as he always did, to involve himself. He did not wish to appear arbitrary, but he was—unlike so many of the low-class ruffians they sent to be priests in the New World—a nobleman and completely celibate. What could he know of marital matters? The disappointed ladies returned to their pews. One of them had the gall to weep openly.

To his enormous consternation, the Abbess of Los Milagros came forward to beg him to protect her from the Inquisition. Given her elegant approach and regal bearing, he rather wished to grant her petition. He was a bishop, a prince of the Church. It rankled that the Holy Tribunal had the power to overrule him. The Inquisitors divided the Church's power—a danger in these times of growing Protestant strength. They collected fines, used the money for their own ends. No one, not even a bishop, could defy them.

Behind the Abbess stood the last petitioner in the line—the impenetrably obstinate Fray Ubaldo DaTriesta, a man who worshipped the Virgin and his own mother but despised all other women. "I can do nothing for you, Lady Abbess," the Bishop whispered as she knelt to kiss his ring. "Tomorrow, when Visitador Nestares arrives, he will become the principal director of the King's affairs—and of your fate. You might appeal to him, but since he and the Grand Inquisitor are coming together, your entreaty would likely fall on deaf ears." He raised his hand to bless her. She crossed herself, rose, and walked away with an elegant carriage and serene, noble countenance that made her look as if she had triumphed in the dearest wish of her heart.

The upstart DaTriesta began, in his typical rude fashion without any greeting or deferential preamble. "I have heard some very bad news from the Tester of the Currency, Felipe Ramirez. It is time we drew Padre Junipero into the noose."

The Bishop was amazed that the Commissioner saw fit to begin this conversation here at Mass. "What did he do?"

"Let us just say that he has committed many acts that make him unworthy of his priesthood. We both know that the Jesuits are too liberal, almost Protestant. Our Padre Junipero cannot seem to comprehend—for all his supposed incisive intelligence—

that there will always be injustice and unhappiness in this world. The majority of people have never known happiness before, therefore would never miss it."

The Bishop sighed. He had no idea what DaTriesta was going on about. "Very well," he said wearily, beginning to think of the great feast that would await him and his guests after Mass this morning. "Arrest him, too, if you must."

CHAPTER 15

On that strange Easter Sunday, more Potosinos were engaged in preparations to welcome Visitador Nestares than in the usual feasting and singing of glorious hymns. Though it was the holiest day of the year, many labored. Far into the following night, work ran at fever pitch. Cloth was draped. Colorful feathers were arranged. Children who had been scrubbed the night before for Easter were scrubbed again. Wrinkles were steamed out of heavy satins and brocades. *Vihuelas*, violins, and guitars were tuned.

Into the dark, deep silence of the cloister of Santa Isabella de los Santos Milagros, where, like a knight in the court of the Cid, the Abbess kept vigil, sounds from the street—hammering and shouting and heavy things being dragged—penetrated and distracted her from her prayers.

If the truth were known, she could not bring herself to bother God with the same repeated requests. She looked blankly up at the image that hung on her cell wall of the Virgin of Carmen and her baby son. Their skin, white as wax, glowed in the candlelight. The eyes of the mother and child were starry with love for each other. Maria Santa Hilda had seen that sort of adoration in the eyes of the Indian children when she brought them bread and warm clothing. In her best moments, she felt that kind of love for God.

She rose from her chair and paced. After such a cheerless Easter Sunday, all she felt was desperate homesickness for the Spain she would never see again. For the steep streets of Guadaloupe, for the awe-inspiring music in the monastery church where the pilgrims came and went on their travels to Rome and the Holy Land. For the taste of real fruit and real wine.

She sat again and, exhausted as she was, tried to force her heart to the problems of here and now. Dawn would soon come and then, at noon, the procession to welcome Nestares. Some time after that, only the Lord knew how long, the officers of the Inquisition would come for her. Perhaps tomorrow. Perhaps they would give her a few extra days to pray. But for what?

She sank to her knees at her prie-dieu. She tried to pray, but her thoughts went again to the mystery of Inez's death. Her investigations had uncovered no useful defense against the Holy Tribunal. What she had learned only incriminated her more. By rights, she should spend whatever time remained preparing her community for her arrest. She had already begun. She still had much to do. Forcing her eyes to stay open, she went over again her decisions, like a litany: Sor Monica would take over the management of the kitchens and the work of the missions. Lord, have mercy. Sor Barbara would look after the children who came for lessons. Lord, have mercy. Sor Olga would…

Chains. They weighed on her arms. She had to get away. To go to the Royal Audencia. A priest would be unjustly removed from office. She wanted to run, but she could not free herself from the chains. They bound her to the tree in the square outside her grandmother's house. In front of a workshop nearby, an ugly old man sat and painted clay pots. She slammed the chains back and forth, trying to tear them loose. They clanked and rattled, but they would not release. The bell of the church across the square began to ring. Her grandmother stood in the door of the church and called for her, did not see her, though she was right there. The pot dropped from the old man's hands and smashed on the paving stones...

"Mother... Mother..." Sor Eustacia's voice called over the rapping from the outside door and the ringing of the bell.

The Abbess was on her feet before she realized she had been asleep. "A moment," she called out.

"Mother," Eustacia said in a loud stage whisper, "it is Fray de la Gasca at our door. He has come."

The Abbess's heart thudded twice and turned to stone. Pedro de la Gasca, the Grand Inquisitor, was one of the most famous men in Perú. She had expected his officers. DaTriesta. Perhaps a guard of soldiers. But not the Inquisitor himself. His reputation made him the more fearsome. Brilliant, they said. At military matters as well as theology. He had defeated a group of heretics in Spain and come to the New World with full ambassadorial powers. He had put down an uprising of colonists against the King. Yet his humility was his most talked-of virtue. He conducted his affairs with little pomp, traveled with but a small retinue.

The banging on the outside door came again.

"Mother, we must answer," Eustacia insisted.

The Abbess blessed herself with holy water from her chapel font and went out into the hall. With Eustacia at her side, she unlocked the front door herself and faced, in the eerie, predawn light, a tall, handsome priest in severe, plain black, who bowed and said, "God's blessing on you, Lady Abbess," in a perfect Castillian accent.

She bowed. "And on you, Father." There were others with him. Three wearing priestly collars and metal breastplates, with swords at their sides. And behind them, in the shadows, DaTriesta.

"Forgive me for arriving at this hour, Mother," de la Gasca said, "but I was unable to sleep and thought it was time to be about God's business."

"It is always time to be about God's business," she said. And bit the tongue that so often betrayed her with sarcastic, rebellious words. "I hope," she said sweetly, "that Your Excellency is not ill."

"Merely light-headed from the altitude," he said.

She bowed again. "Won't you enter my humble convent and allow me to offer you an elixir to relieve you." She stepped back, and they entered. DaTriesta gave her one of his disgusted sniffs but did not look into her face.

She and Sor Eustacia conducted them to the patio of the outer cloister, where in the days before the new theater was built, passion plays and religious masques had been staged. Other sisters, who must have heard the uproar and come to eavesdrop in the dark recesses, retreated to the rear cloister as soon as the men entered.

The Abbess drew Eustacia aside. "Have Sor Monica prepare her infusion of coca and tree bark, but tell her to put honey in it. We do not want him to think we are drugging him."

Eustacia bowed and left in silence. With the help of the maids and Sor Barbara, the Abbess made de la Gasca comfortable with a chair and table. Though chairs were provided for the others, they remained standing.

After the elixir had arrived and he had taken a few sips, the Inquisitor looked around him. He stroked the scrolls and leaves carved in low but clear relief on the slender column next to his chair. "I can see that, isolated here together, the Spanish and Indian arts are uniting into something new." He sounded as if he were talking to himself.

He put down his gourd with a thump and turned to Eustacia, who stood beside her Abbess like a guardian angel. "Please call the Mistress of Novices, the postulant Beatriz Tovar, and the Sister Herbalist to testify."

Eustacia hurried away.

Testify? The word turned Maria Santa Hilda's veins to burning ice. Testify? Surely they would not conduct an official hearing here on her patio, at this hour. The Inquisition was formal. It followed rules and protocols. Her frozen heart began to thud.

When they were all gathered, de la Gasca motioned to one of his men, who set a large black book, ink, and quills on the table before the Inquisitor.

Panic seized the Abbess. Her legs shook. Her breath stopped. De la Gasca folded his elegant hands on the still closed book. "Our chief occupation here today is to find facts. Discipline and moral rectitude should be our bywords. Submit to our authority, my daughter, and you will be pardoned."

Without thinking, the Abbess blessed herself and bowed. The hospital. The orphanage. The convent. Her mind screamed out the ways in which she had labored for the glory of God. But her silent mouth would not protest. She knew too well that a woman's accomplishments meant nothing to the men of the Inquisition. Good works were credited to God's Grace and inspiration. Only evil redounded to the individual woman.

While her insides screeched with outrage, de la Gasca sat with that placid exterior of calm, even-humored masculinity she had learned to despise in her father. To complete her purgatory, DaTriesta stepped forward, moistened his cruel lips, and spoke. "With your permission, Your Excellency, I will begin."

Already tall, he stood with his head up, nearly leaning backward, emphasizing his hateful superiority. "We know, Your Excellency, how easy it is for convents to become depraved. Being insufficiently attractive to bind some man to their maintenance, women in such a place as this can easily sink into sin. Since her deceits and guile have not worked in the outside world, I will prove that this woman, the Abbess Maria Santa Hilda, has turned her cloistered domain, which should be a wellspring of grace for the community, into a university of evil that instructs the young in diabolical arts."

The Abbess remained stupefied. Shock and shame froze her deeper into inaction.

"What witnesses do you offer?" de la Gasca asked in his maddeningly calm, nearly bored voice.

"I call the postulant Beatriz Tovar." With a gesture, he signaled her forward.

Poor little Beatriz, silly romantic girl, stepped out of the shadows. The smooth skin of her face was still lined with the impression of her pillow. Her white postulant's veil was askew. Her dark eyes were huge with awe and fear. She smiled awkwardly at the severe man in the chair. "Do not be afraid, my child," he said in a kindly voice.

But be careful what you say. Oh, be careful. Silently the Abbess prayed to her young charge as if she were a saint in a painting.

DaTriesta did not look at the lovely girl. "Tell us what you know about the sinful practices of this place," he said. "If you but tell the truth, you will be saved."

Beatriz gazed at the tall, ugly priest standing behind the table, at the Abbess, and back at the elegant, seated priest. Who were these men? The ugly standing one who asked her the question wanted her to say awful things. She could tell. He looked at her the way her father did when he expected her to confess some sin. But her father was a chirimoya pear—hard on the outside, but soft and sweet underneath. This tall priest standing so proudly was like an ear of old maize—hard and dry all the way through. Being near him made the damp and cold feel worse. He wanted her to say bad things. She shivered and gazed up at the sky. She would not. Not to this ugly one. The moon was still visible, even though the sky was light.

"Again I ask you," the ear of maize said in a low, nasty voice, "make a full confession or we have ways to make you talk."

She stepped back, confused.

The handsome priest at the table held up his hand. He wore an elegant ring and looked very noble in his plain clothing. "There is no need to threaten her yet." He turned to her and smiled. "Please, my child, tell us what you know." His accent was beautiful, making the words sound like a lovely song. He was an avocado—a layer of soft sweetness over a huge hard stone.

Beatriz's sleepy brain flashed into wakefulness. Threaten? Ways to make her talk? This was the Inquisitor! Oh, God! These men had come to take Mother Maria away. She could not let them. She folded her hands in front of her, the way Inez used to do when she was about to tell a lie and wanted to be believed. "Evil, Father? I know of no evil here. We pray. We only pray for the repose of the souls of the dead, for God's grace on Holy Mother Church. This is a good place. The very best place in this city." She opened her eyes wide and smiled right into the faces of the two men, the way Inez would have. She looked at the Abbess, who did not meet her gaze. Beatriz pressed her clenched hands beneath her breasts. A screaming child in a nightmare in her heart insisted she should have told the truth. But that little coward was wrong.

"What do you know about the way Inez Rojas de la Morada died?" asked the seated priest.

"Nothing," Beatriz answered. "Mother Maria is a good and holy woman."

The corncob came near her. He smelled like dead flowers. "What about midnight meetings of coveys?"

Beatriz tried hard not to wrinkle her nose. Inez would not have wrinkled her nose no matter how he stank. "I have never heard of such a thing. We only pray and chant." She tried to smile beguilingly at him, but he would not look at her.

"I have heard a rumor about women having illicit relations with other women?"

Beatriz widened her eyes. "Here, Padre? That never happens here."

He smiled at her, and her breath halted. His eyes had turned cold and triumphant. What had she said? She hadn't said anything to hurt Mother Maria. His big, pink tongue darted at the corner of his mouth. He turned to the avocado, who sat sipping maté from a gourd. "You see. This child shows no shock, no confusion, at the mention of such depravity. She knows of such liaisons. How else could she, but that she learned about them here? May even have been taught to participate in them."

The panicked child in Beatriz's nightmare escaped. "No! That is not true. No bad things ever happen here. None. Mother Maria is good. She is very good."

"You are endangering your soul and your body by lying," the corncob rasped at her.

Beatriz could hardly breathe. "All I know is that Mother Maria is the holiest woman I know."

He dismissed her with a wave. "You see, Your Excellency, how well trained they are. There is no guile or deceit they do not practice and teach the young."

The avocado took up his pen and wrote something slowly and carefully in the big black book on the table in front of him.

"No. I am not lying!" Beatriz shouted. She tried to look in the face of the Abbess, but Mother's head was lowered and her eyes closed, as if she already knew herself to be dead. Beatriz bit her lip until it bled. If they asked her another question, she would not say another word.

But they did not ask.

Eustacia seethed with indignation. When DaTriesta asked her the same sanctimonious questions he had asked poor, well-meaning Beatriz, she could not hold her pounding anger. It boiled over like milk left too long on the fire. "How can you waste time investigating this holy woman? You are committing an outrage against a saint!"

Maria Santa Hilda shook her head vehemently. Her eyes pleaded with Eustacia to desist.

Eustacia could not comply. "Yes," she insisted, addressing the Abbess rather than the Inquisitor. "You are. Especially compared to the evils they impute to you." She glared at de la Gasca and DaTriesta. "There are real evils in this city. You should be striving to deal with them. Bigamists, for instance. Half the Spaniards have left wives in Spain and taken new ones here. Men abuse their own daughters. Get them with children. But then it is women you want to torture, isn't it? Not men."

The sisters around her all gasped. Shock registered even

in the Inquisitor's placid face. She bit her lip. She was insane, really insane to have said such things. She saw it herself. A cry of anguish escaped her.

DaTriesta shook his large, beastlike head. "Women, as you are all amply proving by your unconsidered words, are prone to spread evil. You poison God's creation with your sins." He turned in disgust to de la Gasca. "I think we have enough proof to take them."

Eustacia abandoned any attempt at self-control. "Women were bishops in the early Church. They administered the Sacraments. There are Greek texts that prove this."

De la Gasca, who toyed with his pen but wrote nothing, gave her a supercilious stare. "I would not mention the Greeks if I were you, Sister."

Her veins burned with embarrassment and anger. "I? You think I am worthy of your notice? If you must torture a woman, torture one who deserves your wrath. Do you know there is an old woman in this city who used to be a wet nurse? Do you know that now that she can no longer give suck to children, she sucks them, but in a different place? She is harming them. In a way that can never be fixed. I know. I have talked to her victims. If you are looking for witches, why don't you go and take her?"

They looked at her, dumbstruck. Even the soldier-priests standing against the wall stared in disbelief.

Eustacia fell at Mother Maria's feet. "Forgive me, Mother. Forgive me." She wished she could take her own life. She did not care what happened to her. At that moment, she wanted them to take her away and burn her.

Monica rushed to Eustacia and tried to lift her from the ground. Mother Maria stood as still and hard as the columns of the cloister. She would not or could not move. Too small to lift Eustacia, Monica bent by her side. "She is ill," the Sister Herbalist told the priests of the Inquisition. "Her humors have been out of balance. She has had a cold. Too much intensity. You must not take what she says to heart."

But de la Gasca was already writing in his book. And once written, his words could not be canceled.

"We will deal with you in a moment, Sister Herbalist," DaTriesta said. "We have particular questions to ask of you."

De la Gasca held up his hand. "In the meantime, Sister," he said softly, "would you bring me some more of your excellent elixir?"

She tore herself away from the sobbing, prostrate Eustacia and took the maté gourd from the table. She bowed and, marshaling all her strength, managed to walk slowly out of their sight. Then she ran. She did not want to miss a word of what transpired. She had to be there to hear any chink in their arguments, any false turn of logic that could be counterargued to save Mother Maria.

When she got to the infirmary, she refilled the gourd with Vitallina's help and ran back.

She had to push her way through a crowd of sisters eavesdropping from around the corner. "Pray. Pray with all your might," she whispered to them as she pushed past.

Olga was speaking. Monica placed the maté on the table where de la Gasca was writing furiously. She bowed and took a place in the shadows.

Olga stood before de la Gasca, her thin, wrinkled face glowing with righteous joy. "—buried in our sacred vaults, when she so obviously took her own life. This Abbess has tolerated illicit love between women. She espouses dangerous notions about the rights of women. And"—Olga paused and looked defiantly into Monica's stunned eyes—"she has condoned sorcery involving a cat."

Monica began to shake. She backed against the wall and dug her fingernails into the bricks. Her neck, her jaw, were rigid. "No. Dear Blessed Mother," she mumbled.

DaTriesta came toward her.

She clasped her hands in front of her and bit her fingers.

"Obviously," the Commissioner said, "Sor Olga's accusations have struck a chord with the Sister Herbalist. Come forward, Sister, and speak."

Monica took a tentative step away from the wall and

stopped. "I—I—" She wanted to say she knew nothing, but that was not the truth. So she told them all the facts—the circumstances of Inez's death, about Hippolyta, about the cat, about the noises in the night. As God was her witness, every answer she gave was the truth, but she was certain that the sum of what de la Gasca wrote in his awful book was not the truth. He did not begin to understand. He did not even seem to want to. Despair fell on her like a pall.

"I say we take the four—the Abbess, the practitioner of perverted sex, that sorceress of an herbalist, and the lying postulant," DaTriesta declared.

De la Gasca fingered the now empty gourd on the table beside him.

Oh, God, must I burn? Monica did not know whether her thoughts were a prayer or a curse.

"Not the herbalist. Not the postulant," de la Gasca said. He began to rise from his chair. "By the authority of the Council of the—"

Suddenly, the stone Abbess raised her hand. She drew herself up to her full stature.

De la Gasca continued to rise but not to speak.

For the first time since she took her vows, Maria Santa Hilda allowed all of the pride she was taught to take in her bloodline to show in her face. A long-closed door had flown open in her heart. She was suddenly the daughter her father had always insisted she be. "A moment, please, Your Grace." She addressed him as the Marqués he would have been had he been born a first son and inherited his father's title, instead of a second son automatically dedicated to the Church.

His impassive aspect turned slightly wary.

"I believe," she said, taking a tone of refined dinner table conversation, "that given..." She hesitated. Should she plead for time before her trial to put her convent's affairs in order? Should she appeal to his gallantry, on the grounds of harm to her order?

"Yes?" He faced her squarely across the table.

"I believe, Your Grace, that, like myself, you are a cousin to

His Royal Majesty." Her kinship with the King was closer than his, counted for much more.

One of his eyebrows bounced. "Yes, that is true. Through my mother, as you are through yours."

"I think, then," she said, as if she were going to ask to borrow his carriage to take her home from a ball, "that you will want to allow me time to put my affairs here in order."

DaTriesta fairly leapt forward. His stench came with him. "They must be taken at once. We must remove them and their sinful influence from this place today."

De la Gasca eyed his local Commissioner but continued to face his distant cousin, the King's near relation.

The Abbess smiled at him. The humility she had nurtured for twenty years seemed to have evaporated. She knew her own power. It could not save her from the stake, but it could buy her the time to try with logic to save herself.

DaTriesta stepped closer. "As long as she stays here, the debauchery will continue."

The Abbess did not take her eyes from de la Gasca's. "I have been accused, but not tried and not found guilty."

"You will not leave your convent," de la Gasca said at last. "You will not communicate with anyone outside these walls for any reason."

"My confessor?"

"We will appoint a suitable priest."

"This must not be," DaTriesta sputtered. "We all know she vowed never to appeal to her lineage. She is breaking another vow. You cannot..." His voice trailed off. He must have finally grasped the futility of trying to overcome blood ties with argument.

"We grant a short time, a matter of a day or two." De la Gasca reached down and slammed the book shut.

CHAPTER 16

No one at the grand entrance parade of Nestares into the Villa Imperial of Potosí noticed that a lock of hair showing from under one of the elaborate Indian headdresses was a shade of light brown never found on an Inca head. Or that the eyes that looked out from the man's feathered mask were blue.

Such small details were lost in the outpouring of pomp and grandeur. The world-famous spectacle of a royal emissary's grand entrance into the Silver City mesmerized even its own citizens. The "white Indian" in the condor costume himself wondered at this reception—fit more for a viceroy than for a prosecutor.

A sudden clamor in the street ahead seemed to signal the Visitador's arrival. *"Ahora,"* an Indian leader called, and the drums began. The troupe of forty gaudily clad men began to dance. The condor man moved his arms and legs in the compli- cated pattern he had hastily learned at dawn that day, all the while alert, scanning the crowd that lined the Calle de Santo Domingo. Death was ready to strike. He had a plan. He was ready. Even here. Even now.

The wave of breathless anticipation that stirred the crowd near the Dominican monastery turned out to be one of the many false alarms of the morning. Though Dr. Francisco de Nestares had started out before dawn, he would not arrive for another hour.

In darkness, a ceremonial squadron mounted on fine steeds had met him at his hospice six leagues from the city. Don Fernando de Almanza, the Viceroy's nephew, led the group of three hundred nobles who represented all the various provinces of Spain and tribes of Peruvians. They had found the Visitador not quite ready. Most of his entourage, including the priests of the Holy Tribunal, had gone ahead the evening before, slipping quietly into the city. In order to enter with proper pomp, he, plagued by headache, breathless in the thin air, and exhausted, had spent one more night—his twenty-fifth—on the road.

Eschewing an effeminate man-carried litter, he had bumped along the rough trails for weeks, hours each day, in an ox-drawn cart or jogged on a cantankerous mule to saddle-sore exhaustion. Blessedly, the *tambas* along the route were placed close enough together so that he, if not all of his retainers, had passed nearly every night in a decent bed.

This morning, he saw in his looking glass a travel-weary man, his long, regal face drawn and pale, his eyes vacant and smudged beneath with exhaustion, his lips white from the lack of good meat. He called his barber to trim his hair and beard and tint his wan, chilled cheeks with pomegranate juice. He donned court dress and a gold chain bearing the jewels of his office. In the pink light of dawn, he greeted his honor guard and mounted a beautiful black Chilean horse they had brought for him. The magnificent beast was caparisoned with gold-plated silver and bristled with energy even in this killing climate. Nestares patted the horse's neck and drew in its warmth, soothing in the chill air.

Up at the summit of the conical Cerro Rico—whose shape was unmistakable to him as it would have been to any educated person in the Spanish Empire—huge flags had been unfurled to greet him. They whipped in the harsh wind that looked as if it would tear the banners off their slender poles. The King's envoy nodded to a cavalier carrying the mace, his symbol of authority, to lead on.

Maria Santa Hilda signed and folded her letter to Padre Junipero. She would give it to Beatriz Tovar to deliver. In defiance of the Grand Inquisitor, she had sent him one message already—by the boy who waited in the *plazuela*. In return, she had received only a cryptic note. It lay on her desk now: "I am in danger from Morada's men, who think I killed Inez. I must conceal myself, but I am going to continue on a path that I am sure will lead us to the truth."

He was in harm's way because of her. And the note she was about to send him would intensify that danger. She pushed down the guilt that rose in her gullet. She had broken so many promises she had made to herself, and to God. She could not fathom what the implications might be for the future of her heart. Who was she that she could put other people's lives in danger? She did not know herself anymore.

The events of the past few days had ripped from her soul a raiment that had felt like shining gold. What lay beneath it was dross. Her bones felt as if chunks of flesh had been torn away with her illusions.

Yet as if a veil had also been removed from her eyes, she saw at once the power of her person—a power she had always ascribed to the Lord, to the inspiration of the Holy Spirit. If it was God's power that worked in her, it worked in her in a particular way because she was who she was. No matter what happened, no matter the verdict of the Inquisition, she would never diminish herself again.

Her guilt and her new awareness of herself warred within her, and even still she saw everyone and everything more clearly now. All the unexplained facts she had learned so far must fit together in some way. Drop by drop, the truth trickled into her consciousness.

Inez had said she was threatened by knowledge of a secret. What information so dangerous could a mere girl know? But

Inez was not an ordinary girl. She had been her father's confidante. The Abbess herself and the padre both worried that her father had involved her in his worldly affairs to the detriment of her immortal soul. Inez had told her sister, Gemita, about some documents that could protect a person's life. Could not letters that would save a life also take a life?

The Alcalde's silver was in the convent vault. Everyone knew he had been hiding it, they thought out on the Altiplano. But it lay here, under the floorboards of the convent's vault. Why had he decided to hide it in the first place?

The currency had been falsified. Ramirez was the Tester of the Currency. Could false money have been minted without his knowing? He was the Alcalde's most loyal and closest supporter. Could Ramirez have tampered with the currency without Morada's knowledge?

These events and Inez's death must have something to do with one another. She could not prove it, but she was sure that the explanation of the one crime would also explain the other.

She had already charged Sor Monica with discovering who had carried out Inez's murder and how. She was certain that all the parts of that puzzle of how were still here in the convent. Only by finding out who in the convent had committed the actual murder could they understand the motivation behind it.

The note she had just written charged the padre to find and recover the letters that Inez had talked of to Gemita. Somewhere in them lay the explanation.

This would all take time. De la Gasca had given her only a day or two, but he was unwell with altitude sickness. That could buy her an extra day.

Rather than waiting for Beatriz to be brought to her, she took her letter for Padre Junipero and went in search of the girl.

Francisco Rojas de la Morada waited on horseback for Nestares and his honor guard to appear at the entrance to the city. He was certain this expensive charade would not save them. Nevertheless, he had attended—since Inez's burial—to every detail, for he knew that given the fame of Potosí's magnificent welcomes of royal envoys, the city could not slight Nestares by stinting today. Though a perfect ceremony would not ameliorate their situation, any misstep, any insult, however unintended, could bring harsher and speedier punishment.

Morada scanned the crowd for Taboada. His bone marrow told him Don Jerónimo was more dangerous as a friend than another man would be as an enemy. Taboada had hinted he would surprise the Alcalde today with yet another proof of his loyalty and friendship. The glint in his eye foretold murder. Morada had admonished him that nothing must happen to the Visitador General once he entered the city. Taboada had smiled and said the surprise he had in mind would free the Alcalde's heart from a great burden. Morada again ordered Taboada not to harm Nestares. Taboada had a faithful soul, but his desire to please overruled his judgment. And there was no way any of them could survive a mistake now.

The cortege leading Nestares rounded the bend. Morada signaled the ceremonial bearers, who unfurled a canopy of crimson embroidered in gold with the arms of Spain and supported by stout staves of solid silver. The Chief Constable, the Public Trustee, the Inspector of Weights and Measures, and the Collector of Judicial Fines made ready to carry the canopy over Nestares's head until he reached the first of the triumphal arches erected in his honor. Don Diego de Ibarbarú, Don Baltasor de Salamanca y Lerma, Don Francisco de Sagardia, and Don Juan Bravo, the Count of Portillo—all carrying their glittering wands of office—the corregidors of the surrounding provinces, venerable members of the clergy, doctors and masters of the city, and priests of the nearby towns placed themselves in formation along the Calle Lima, the main street leading to the center of the city.

The cortege accompanying Nestares neared. At the Visitador's side, a young nobleman carried in the crook of his right arm a gold-and-silver mace encrusted with rubies, diamonds, and emeralds. This emblem announced that Nestares came on the King's business, with full authority of life and death. Behind him rode the honor guard uniformed with blue hose and red doublets, gorgeously and profusely ornamented with gold braid.

A detachment of soldiers formed to the rear of the cortege. They carried harquebuses and held their heads up—to a man, maintaining a fierce expression. Safe in the powerful impression of his symbols of authority, Nestares himself affected a kindly aspect and a calm, steady gaze.

"His Majesty's subjects of the Villa Imperial de Potosí welcome you, Dr. Francisco de Nestares, Visitador General, emissary of our Sovereign." Morada pronounced the words with what he hoped was a thoroughly charming smile. At his signal, the squadron of nobles that had met Nestares that morning spread out into the field of San Martín, offered a volley, and then preceded the Visitador into the town.

As soon as Nestares began to move down the Calle de Contería, the form of the festival welcome took on a life of its own, and celebration of Nestares's entry ruled the day.

At the first triumphal arch, the remaining members of the Cabildo, attired in court dress, waited under a canopy of pearl-colored cloth. Nestares nodded benignly to all.

The white Indian in the condor mask remained unconvinced by that beneficent smile. He saw in the Visitador's severe pointed collar the real indication of his character. In fact, everything about him was pointed—his chin, his nose, his gaze. And the condor man had heard from an unimpeachable source that whatever aspect the emissary from the King portrayed, he was arbitrary, irritable, and above all suspicious.

The band of dancing Indians followed Nestares as he passed down the cobbled street between the whitewashed brick-and-stone buildings. Cheering crowds filled every space. Thanks to the generosity of the Cabildo, even the poorest in the city were decked out in silk. The rich found they could afford to dress the destitute in vanities today.

Flags flying from the belfries whipped in the stiff breeze. The pealing of bells of every church and convent made an almost deafening din. The Alcalde and his friends bore all the cost of this pageantry. The members of the Cabildo, fearing for its power and prestige, had decided they must give their own money rather than tax the less fortunate. It was not charity that moved them. Devaluation, they knew, would punish the poor more than anyone. Poverty, if it became desperate, became dangerous.

Everywhere along the route of the march, the buildings were hung with inscriptions, symbols and devices, and emblems of the King. Nestares rode triumphant to the music of drums, horns, trumpets, timbrels, pipes, and flutes. The Mestizo musicians were dressed all alike in sandals and belts of silk and gold worked with pearls and rubies, shirts and jackets of fine brocade, and, as was their wont, many heavy chains and pendants of gold. Women and girls in brilliantly colored, fur-lined silk cloaks jammed the wooden balconies overlooking the narrow streets. In this climate where no plants grew, they strewed Nestares's path with flowers made of feathers.

The priest disguised as a dancing Indian despaired that all these tributes would not influence Nestares at all. Not the three triumphal arches that graced the Visitador's route to the Plaza Mayor, not even the eight hundred silver ingots that had been paved into the street along which he passed. Since there had not been time to paint simulated jasper and marble, the constructions were draped with precious stuffs, costly embroideries, and rich silks. The first spanned the small plaza near the Church of San Martín, close to the eastern limits of the city. The second, and more magnificent, in the Plaza la Merced was constructed of Ionic, Corinthian, Doric, and Tuscan columns. Its architrave was decorated with mirrors, ribbons, and, on top, statues— some enameled, some dressed in fine cloth—that signified the moral virtues.

The irony of those virtues gazing down on this city was lost neither on the Visitador General nor on the priest dressed in feathers, so intent on his mission, so incapable of completing it with dispatch. How could a man save a life if he had to dance in a vain parade just to cross the town and speak to someone? And there was DaTriesta's face in the watching crowd to remind him of the urgency of his task and the snail's pace of his progress.

DaTriesta took no notice of the dancing Indians. He was focused on the triumphant expression on the face of Nestares. His own triumph had been postponed. The Abbess and her perverted sister were still in the convent, when by rights they should be chained to the stone walls of the keeping room in the rear of his house. Standing on the steps of the Church of the Mercedarians, he felt himself completely at odds with the shouts of the joyous crowd as Nestares stopped under the arch. Just as His Excellency entered underneath, a folded cloud opened and disclosed a tiara, which dropped a good distance through the air and stopped a few inches above his head and hung there. At that moment, the girls on the surrounding balconies showered the Visitador with beaten gold and silver that glistened in the blinding sunlight.

Enormously proud of their city, the citizens had, for the while, forgotten their worries and lost themselves in the spectacle and celebration.

Nestares went on to pass under the largest arch, at the entrance of the main square, twenty-five yards high and ten yards wide, its top tier surmounted by a handsome throne in the form of a cedar-wood pedestal all carved with curious moldings and covered with shining gold. On the throne sat an image of His Majesty Felipe IV of Spain and beside it Gemita, the daughter of the Alcalde, representing Fame. She was dressed in a tunic covered with flowers made of silk and feathers, girdled with a richly embroidered sash. A yellow banner flew from her hand. Though she affected a brave smile, the condor man came close enough to see she was sad and frightened.

The other Indians in the band saw this, too. "The height of her perch and the stares of the crowd frighten that poor girl," one of them remarked. But the white Indian knew better what her fear was made of.

The procession moved toward the cathedral, where a "Te Deum" was sung and the Bishop offered a prayer more or less in Latin. The honored guests moved out again to the Plaza Mayor, where on a platform erected for the occasion, a chair and cushion awaited His Excellency. Two children, representing Urbanity and Generosity, guarded this place of honor.

The cavalier who carried the mace mounted the platform and proclaimed an amnesty for all past offenses by the inmates of the city's jail.

While the crowd of Indians around the Visitador cheered the amnesty, the condor man shook his elaborately dressed head. The announcement was not motivated by compassion. The intention, he was sure, was to clear the jail cells for the people Nestares himself would put there.

No sooner had the Visitador taken his seat than trumpets blared. In the four corners of the square stood four pyramids decked with silver work. Multicolored pennons flew from their summits. At a signal from the Alcalde, who stood beside Nestares, companies of cavaliers rode in, one from behind each pyramid, and executed four charges in close-order drill, all very showy and greatly admired by the ladies who observed from the balconies.

The Alcalde then gave a short, formal speech of welcome and announced a composition in Nestares's honor by the Reverend Maestro Padre Fray Juan de la Torre, sung by a chorus of Indians.

When the music stopped, Nestares stood to speak. Despite the urgency of the white Indian's task, he stopped to hear the man who could visit devastation on the city. Suddenly, after all the din of the cheering, the square went still. In the hush of the crowd's collective fear, only the horses and the snapping banners dared make a sound.

But Nestares spoke no evil. He made reference to the hard mule ride, to his twenty-five-day journey. Finally he waved and said, "Thank you for this glorious welcome, for this outpouring of goodwill. I offer you my goodwill in return."

The citizens who heard him stared in wonder. Perhaps they were safe. Perhaps with this great show of their respect, they had convinced Nestares to blink at human foibles, show kindness to ill doers.

The white condor man had mounted the steps of the Alcaldía to pass to the other side so he could continue on to the river and across. Suddenly, a hand grabbed his shoulder. "What are you doing here?" a voice growled.

The condor man trembled. Morada's men, bent on vengeance, had found him. How? He had been betrayed. He opened his mouth to defend himself, moved his hand to remove his Indian garb.

A powerful grip stayed his arms. "Away, Inca." It was a soldier of the guard. He smelled of *chicha* and slurred his words. "Get off these steps. This is a place for white people."

While Nestares was entertained by more close-order drill, the condor man ran from the center of the festivities, down the Calle Lanza. The drunken guard pursued him and caught him by the arm. The white man in the Indian costume shook with fear. He bowed and apologized in Aymara and broken Spanish, like a properly subjugated slave. His humility seemed to further enrage the guard, who drew his sword and ripped off the Indian's headgear to reveal Padre Junipero of the Compañia de Jesus.

The astonished guardsman drew back.

The priest knew he could not explain himself. He turned and sped off, praying the drunk would be too stupefied to follow.

Half a block away, he allowed himself a glance over his left shoulder to see. The guard was holding his head and vomiting in the street.

When the priest turned to continue on his way, a sword pointed at his throat stopped him in his tracks.

"Interesting garb for a priest," Don Jerónimo Taboada sneered.

The terrified, confused padre looked around for anyone who might help him. The street behind him was deserted. He folded his hands at his chest in a gesture of prayer—to his attacker, to God. He did not know.

"It is time for you to pay for the murder of the Alcalde's daughter." The sword drew closer to his eye. Taboada gripped his arm and began to drag him toward the deserted lanes near the Ribera. In the dark corner of an *ingenio* entrance, Taboada pressed the padre to a wall.

"I did not kill her," the priest barely choked out.

"He told me himself that you did." Taboada's powerful grip tightened. His sword grazed the hair that had fallen into the priest's eyes. "And I intend you to die for it."

"It is a lie." The priest prayed for the courage to fight back.

"Why would the Alcalde lie about such a thing?"

Terror blotted out all reason. "I—I—" The priest groped his stricken mind for any answer.

A red cape flashed to his left. Before he could turn his head, the man in red shouted, "Halt, whoremaster."

Taboada spun around, still gripping the priest in the feather costume.

Domingo Barco, sword drawn, charged them. With one gesture, he threw off his cape and smashed his weapon into Taboada's. The priest was pitched to the ground. Clanging steel echoed from the buildings of the narrow street. Padre Junipero crawled into a doorway.

Taboada bellowed and attacked mercilessly, but the Mestizo, with great agility and grace, parried the powerful blows and returned them.

With his left hand, Taboada fumbled with the ornate clasp of his heavy ceremonial cloak. *"Mierda,"* he growled.

Barco seized the moment and charged. With shattering two-handed blows, left and right, he smashed Taboada's sword from his hand. It clattered across the paving stones to the priest's feet. Still gripping his weapon with both hands, Barco held its tip to his opponent's throat. "Pick it up, Padre. You finish him off."

Beneath the ice crust of fear, rage seethed in the priest. He began to move toward the hilt of Taboada's weapon. His vow stopped him. Never. He had promised God never to touch such a thing again. He stood and withdrew again into the doorway.

Barco spat in disgust. Then, smiling malevolently, he swung his weapon back and spun forward with it, smashing Taboada's chest with the hilt. The blow lifted the vanquished man from his feet and sent him sailing several feet before he landed, unconscious, against the wall across the street.

Only then did Padre Junipero take up Taboada's sword. "Thank you, my son." He offered the weapon to Barco.

Barco took it and slung it toward Taboada's inert body.

"I truly owe you my life," the priest said.

Without putting up his sword, Barco scooped up his red cape and threw it over the priest's head. "Perhaps I will take the life you owe me," he said coldly, and at the point of his sword, he marched the padre through the now dispersing crowd.

No one took any special note of Don Antonio Tovar's *mayordomo* marching an apparently drunken Indian dancer toward the Mint. The crowd expected such an aftermath of the ceremony they had just witnessed.

Nestares himself was being ushered much more ceremoniously in another direction, to the mansion of His Grace Bishop Don Fray Faustino Piñelo de Ondegardo.

After breakfast with the Bishop, the Visitador rested only briefly before the guild of amalgamators escorted him to the performance of Mareto's *Trampa Adelante*. The Visitador remarked at finding such an opulent and modern theater in such a remote place. The citizens smiled and accepted his compliment, though inwardly they were insulted and disheartened that Nestares did not seem to understand that Potosí was the most important city on earth. After the play, the weary Nestares dined with the Alcalde Morada and the members of the Cabildo at a state banquet, where the table was set with vessels and plates of gold-plated silver adorned with diamonds, pearls, and rubies. As if he weren't totally exhausted already, his hosts promised him three days of bullfighting sponsored by the officials and silver traders, banquets and fireworks every night in the major plazas, and daily tournaments of jousts.

He wished they would just stop.

17

Behind the walls of the cloister of Los Milagros, a thin edge of chaos had wedged into the calm. Mother Maria would very soon be taken away. The small planets that had circled that sun would be left wandering in space.

Sor Monica, though racked with remorse, fought to carry out—amid the confusion around her—the instructions of her Abbess. Her own words about the Abbess to the Grand Inquisitor de la Gasca had sealed Mother Maria's fate. She had no choice but to prove herself instead the instrument of the Abbess's salvation. That meant assuming a posture of command that terrified her.

"It is an act of pride…well, perhaps it is an act of pride," she told Vitallina, "but I will die before I see Mother Maria burn. She is innocent."

"You are all innocent," Vitallina muttered with that cynical edge she gave nearly all her words, as if they meant less or much more than they seemed.

Monica studied the tall, stately Vitallina but could not

fathom her. Her neat, graying hair was pulled back in a tight chignon. Her broad mahogany face was impassive, like the face of a woman carved on the prow of a ship, whose features never changed no matter how storms raged and waves crashed, not even when the souls of her sailors sank to hell.

Monica shook off images of damnation. "I will do it. I will prove that Inez did not take her own life."

Vitallina seemed to be laughing at her. "To do that, you need to imagine how the devil thinks. You have to have some of the devil in you."

A chill crept up Monica's spine. "I know he may be here in this convent."

Vitallina smirked. "But do you have the heart to find him? Can you look him in the face?"

Sor Monica sniffed. "You are being impertinent." She sounded like Sor Olga.

Vitallina lifted her strong arms and let them drop to her sides.

Monica knew it was a mistake to allow the Negress too much familiarity. But she needed her. The Sister Herbalist fixed her features in what she hoped was a stern, superior look but said nothing.

Vitallina smiled. "Can you imagine, for instance, that the child who died was a murderer herself?"

"Inez?" What sense could such a theory make?

"I do not mean Inez. Inez was no child. I think perhaps she was never a child."

Monica shunned the bright light of an unthinkable thought. "Then—"

"Hippolyta," Vitallina said, as if the idea were tenable. "Suppose she killed Inez and then killed herself out of remorse."

The notion staggered Monica. She stepped back and sat on the edge of the pallet where Sor Elena had died. She touched the pillow where her wise old friend's head had lain. Oh, if Elena were only here, with her capacity for transcendent prayer, to help her friend look in the eye of Satan. "Hippolyta could have…" Her voice wavered. She made it stronger. "She could have offered Inez a sweetmeat." Monica pressed her mind forward. She was determined. The less she wanted to think a thought, the more she must force herself to think it. "She could have despaired over having committed such a sin and then eaten some poison herself."

Vitallina nodded.

"But why? Why would she have wanted Inez dead? How could she have done such a thing? She was so timid and pliable."

Vitallina's hard black eyes waited.

Was not the weak Hippolyta precisely the instrument the devil would have chosen to do his works? Monica leapt up and raced toward Hippolyta's cell.

She had found sweetmeats hidden in the folds of Hippolyta's undergarments when Mother Maria ordered the search. The candies had seemed then like a girl's small indulgence. Could they have been a weapon of murder?

As Monica and Vitallina crossed the cloister, the door to Hippolyta's cell opened and quickly closed again.

Vitallina sped ahead and flung open the door. When Monica entered the room, Vitallina had the maid Juana by the shoulders. The tiny Indian woman's toes barely touched the ground. "I came in to clean. It is my work," Juana protested. Vitallina did not let go.

Monica's eyes scanned the room. "Let her down, please," she said distractedly to Vitallina. She glanced over the sparse furnishings, the rough wooden cot, the primitive table. Look Satan in the face, she told herself. Believe Hippolyta's sweet, round, dimpled face was the mask of the Evil One. Believe that her sad eyes saw such debauchery.

Her gaze lit on the *armario*. "Wait," she said involuntarily. She opened the door and touched Hippolyta's neatly folded woolen undergarments. "No sweetmeat could have killed Hippolyta. True, we found some here, but I threw them in the trash myself hours before Hippolyta died."

Juana started quietly for the door. Vitallina blocked her way. "Perhaps the girl had others, more carefully hidden."

"Nothing escaped our search. Whatever killed Inez also killed Hippolyta. But it wasn't sweetmeats hidden in this room."

Juana listened but said nothing.

Once again, the Sister Herbalist's eyes surveyed the room. "Go and fetch Beatriz Tovar," she commanded Vitallina. "She should be in the postulants' refectory." Vitallina went out, and Juana made to follow her.

"One moment, please, Juana. I want you to stay here." The maid stopped but did not turn around.

Monica went to the foot of the bed and picked up a flail. The instrument's silver handle was heavy and richly ornamented, with four light chains each carrying a steel barb fashioned like a thorn of Christ's crown—the means to remind oneself of how He suffered for the sins of man. She went to the bedside table and picked up a second, almost identical flail. She looked at Juana. "What do you know about this?"

"Nothing. I came in to clean. The others left the room dirty after the girl died. They are afraid. They think it is haunted with evil spirits. But I know Our Lady of the Rosary will protect me." She lowered her eyes.

"May she protect us all," Monica responded. Her mind clicked. The room had been left undisturbed until now.

Vitallina entered with Beatriz. The girl's pretty face was drawn and dark under eyes big with fear. "Come here, my child," Monica said gently. She showed the girl the silver handles of the two flails. Both were the unmistakable work of the same silversmith in the Calle de los Mercaderes. "Beatriz," Monica said softly, "do you know which of these belonged to Hippolyta, and to whom the other might have belonged?"

"That one with the crest on the end of the handle was Hippolyta's," Beatriz said, indicating the one Monica had found on the table. "The other belonged to Inez. Inez showed them to me. She had them both made from bracelets she was wearing

when she came here. She gave one to Hippolyta as a gift. But…"
Beatriz's soft eyes searched Monica's. "Why are they both here?"

The Sister Herbalist shrugged. "I just discovered that there were two here. I do not know why."

Sor Diogene, the Sister Porter, came to the door. "The sedan chair has come to take you home to your parents," she said to Beatriz.

"Go at once," Sor Monica told her, and they rushed out.

Juana gazed at them, taking it all in—looking for gossip, as all the maids did. "Juana, you may go."

The maid too went out.

Monica took the flails and returned to her infirmary and to her confusion. The more she learned, the less she really knew.

As Sor Monica prepared to examine the two flails, Beatriz was being carried from the convent in a sedan chair. She was trying frantically to think of a way to force her parents to let her marry Domingo Barco. At that same moment, the object of the girl's desire was forcing Padre Junipero, at sword point, through the door of his humble quarters in a corner of the Ingenio Tovar.

Between the Calle de la Paz and here, no one had asked Barco why he was marching a costumed Indian with a cape over his head through the streets. No one would. The *mayordomo* of a refinery would have charge of many Indians. He had a right.

The priest had thought to call out for help to passersby whose voices he had heard but whose faces he could not see. But how could he know they were not Morada's men? With Barco he might talk his way out of danger. Téllez or Taboada would run him through without allowing him to utter even a final prayer.

When the cape was removed from the priest's head, he found himself in a low-ceilinged room with a packed-earth floor. In one corner, a narrow cot was neatly made up with rough homespun blankets. Above it on the whitewashed stone wall hung an oversize cross bearing a silver body of the dead Christ. The room contained a table and small bench and a shelf with an astonishing number of books—at least twenty, with worn leather bindings. A book lay open on the table.

Terrified as he was, the sight of the volumes arrested the priest's gaze. Nowhere in the city outside the monasteries and convents had he seen so many books. Not even the Bishop owned a library so extensive.

Barco was eyeing him with a raised eyebrow. "They surprise you, I see. My father taught me to read, and I am somehow compelled to do it, though it only reminds me of what a Mestizo bastard like me cannot have."

The words echoed in Junipero's brain—it was exactly Sebastian the actor's complaint. Twice Inez, the girl who had everything, had attracted illegitimate sons who longed for what they did not have. And she had loved them. Or wanted them. Or used them. She had certainly used Barco. "You knew your father?"

"And know him still." The words carried an ominous ring.

"Who?" the priest asked before he realized it was the wrong question.

The sword rose to his throat. "That is not the business we have to discuss."

"No," the priest said, panting. The weapon was within a hair's breadth of piercing him. "But I believe you have something on your conscience, my son. Come, unburden yourself to me."

With one powerful hand, Barco wrenched the priest's arm and shoved him onto the bed. The Mestizo did not lower his sword. "What were you doing snooping around my mother, asking questions about me?"

Padre Junipero held an empty, completely vulnerable hand between his heart and Barco's weapon. "I was looking for a way to save the Abbess of Los Milagros from the auto-da-fé." His skin burned inside his suit of bright feathers.

Doubt clouded Barco's eyes, but he did not speak.

The priest explained about Mother Maria's impending arrest. At the mention of Inez's possible suicide, Barco sank back and sat on the stool near the desk. His dark, handsome face contorted with anguish. "She is dead, and I will avenge her."

The priest stood up and leaned toward him. "Please," he begged, "for the love of the Almighty, tell me what you know."

Barco's tear-filled eyes became wary again. "I know little."

"How can you hold back when a holy woman's life hangs in the balance? Inez is gone. If there is anything…" The proper argument finally blared into the priest's struggling mind. He put a steadying hand on Barco's shoulder. "Domingo, my son, you alone may have the key that proves Inez did not take her own life, that her soul is not in hell. By the love you still bear her, help me prove her innocent of taking her own life. Otherwise, the Tribunal will remove her body to unconsecrated ground."

Barco worked his lips. "They would do that?" His voice was hollow.

The priest nodded.

Barco looked at him for a long time. "My mother—" He broke off. The sword clattered to the floor.

Padre Junipero held every cell of his body still, burying his own horror at inveigling a man to betray his own mother.

"My mother says that Doña Ana did it."

A groan escaped the padre. "Do you really believe she could have?"

"Doña Ana is capable of anything if she thinks it will hurt the Alcalde."

A frost hit the priest's skin under his suit of feathers. "Tell me what you mean." They were the words and tone he ordinarily used only in the confessional.

Barco's eyes dared the priest to believe him. "Her mother… She… Doña Ana found out that Inez was seeing that actor. She began to help her meet her lover. My mother said Doña Ana even let the man into the house. She gloried in the fact that their daughter was dishonoring the Alcalde. She laughed about the day she would reveal it to him. She would do anything to hurt him."

"Did she reveal it? Did Doña Ana tell the Alcalde?"

"I don't know. Once Inez took up with the actor, I only saw her once. The actor might know, but I do not."

"I must speak to him again." The priest knew he must go back out into the town, whatever the risk. He eyed Barco's sword on the floor. "I need your help."

18

Beatriz Tovar peered through the green baize curtains of the sedan chair her father had sent with bearers to carry her home. She wondered at the scene surrounding her. Even within the convent walls, she had heard that someone important had come to Potosí. The maids had talked of some festival for some special envoy from the King. But this! The streets were absolutely filled with the sounds of drums and cheering crowds. So little happened in this remote city, and she had been buried behind those walls and missed the best part of the biggest festival of her life.

Well, she was out now. All she had to do was get the Abbess's letter to Padre Junipero. And then summon the courage to run away with her Domingo. He would be so thrilled to see her again. Perhaps he was nearby now, among the reveling throngs.

She pressed back against the blue velvet quilted headrest and scanned the crowd, trying to see without being seen. There in the Plazuela Campero was a circus with as many different kinds of animals as Noah's ark and a fountain that simultaneously spouted wine, water, and *chicha*.

Ahead, an Indian company blocked the street with their improvisations and dances. All about her were crowds of men on horseback and donkeys, and toreadors ready to enter the Plaza Mayor on foot, dressed in wild colors, accompanied by kettle-drummers and mules covered with rich trappings and laden with spears and lances. Pages in splendid livery walked behind their masters. One of the boys—obviously drunk—pushed back the curtain and leered at her. She slapped him and screamed, but the din of the drums drowned the sound. He pulled open the door. The chair rocked as if it would fall. It was set down. The bearers, she thought, would chase the boy away, but he fell on her, pulled open her vicuña cloak, and pawed at the bodice of the plain muslin dress Sor Monica had given her to wear home. She shoved at him, but he just smiled. She put her hands against his face and pushed with all her might. Spittle drooled from his mouth onto her hands. She shuddered in disgust, kicked, and screamed.

Suddenly, he was pulled away. Panting, she slumped back against her velvet seat and then peeked out to see the drunken boy slapped in the face and passed to a large man in a tawny cape. The man grabbed him by the neck of his shirt and dragged him away.

A handsome face appeared at the door. "Señorita?" The man showed a beautiful smile. "Allow me to—"

"No," she commanded. "Do not speak to me. Do not touch me."

He drew back a little. She sat up straight, taking charge of her tiny domain.

The handsome smile disappeared. "I must accompany you home. You have—"

"No! Carriers, take me home. Where are my bearers? How could they have let this happen to me? They must take me home immediately."

"They are here, but they are unarmed. Please," the man pleaded, "I offer you only protection."

"I don't know you. Go away. Carriers, take me home. Now."

The handsome head withdrew. A gauntleted hand closed the door. "Take her immediately across the Ribera to the Ingenio Tovar." His voice was commanding and clear. He knew who she was, though she was sure she had never seen him before. She would not have forgotten if she had.

However beautiful his face and bearing, however intriguing the sights of the celebration, she wanted only to get away. He had offered escort, but she would not risk the unwanted attentions of some unknown blackguard who thought he could take advantage of her just because he had saved her from that slobbering boy. Who knows what he himself would have tried once he was alone with her in the deserted quarter across the river. In the convent, she had come to know a mother and daughter who were raped by a merchant in a shop. Both escaped with their lives but would pass the rest of their days condemned to the convent for their shame. Beatriz would never go back there. No one would put her in that position.

Once across the Bridge of Santiago, she looked out to make sure he was not following, though she did not know what she would do if he was. The street was empty except for a couple of old Indian women sitting before their doorway, mending sandals. A shaggy llama stood near them and inserted its head between them as if to join in their conversation.

When her bearers set down the chair and knocked at the gate of the Ingenio Tovar, her heart stopped. Perhaps Domingo would swing open the tall green doors. She patted her hair and alighted, not waiting, as a lady should, to be well inside before showing herself. The bolt opened. She smiled like the sun face carved into the center of the stone lintel. She touched the beautiful scrollwork of the door surround. She was home.

It was not Domingo who opened. Rosa Yana, the widow of that Indian who had died in the mine, greeted her. The outer patio was completely quiet. The door between it and the *ingenio* yard stood wide open, but even the yard was silent. No Indians stirred amalgam. The waterwheel was still. Hides under which the mercury and silver united were tied down against the constant wind. Cones of amalgam—lined in perfect formation—awaited the purifying ovens. By contrast, the canvas bags they used to filter out the mercury lay in jumbled piles.

Rosa unlocked the inner patio door, and Beatriz ran inside. She looked up, thinking to find her mother watching for her from the second-story gallery. In the arches, ferns in clay pots waved in the breeze, but no one was about. *"Madre?"* she called tentatively. She went into the lower hallway and was blinded by the sudden dimness after the glare of the sun outside. Down the hall from the kitchen came the smell of baking bread—made from wheaten flour according to the method brought by her mother from the home of that sweet grandmother in Spain whose letters Beatriz had read but whom she would never know.

Her eyes began to adjust to the light, and she started for the stairs to the upper story. She heard her father's voice from behind his office door. She put her ear to it and listened to her father's words.

"The King ordered him to punish the counterfeiters, although taking pity on them and not creating any scandals. Everything is left to his prudence and discretion." He sounded sad. She wanted to see him, to make him smile.

"Will he be prudent and discreet?" It was her mother! Mother never went into this room that was reserved for manly matters. She strained to hear every word.

Her father spoke low, growled a word Beatriz could not make out. It sounded like a curse.

She knocked gently.

"Come," her father commanded.

She opened the door tentatively.

As soon as her mother saw her, she rushed and enveloped her in a warm embrace. "My darling girl. My darling girl," she repeated over and over, kissing Beatriz's hair and hands.

Her father's face—dark and angry as she entered—turned indulgent, with a hint of triumph that chilled Beatriz's joy. He came and embraced her. "I am glad to know you have learned your lesson," was all he said.

Her body stiffened in his arms. She pulled her cheek away from his kiss. "Where is Domingo?" she countered brazenly. Her father made her so angry. He did not care for her at all, only for his will, that it be done. She looked right into his bright, black eyes and held them despite the terror his anger evoked in her. "I came home only to save Mother Maria from the pyre. I never intended to do what you say. I lied about marrying your Rodrigo. I just wanted to get out of the convent. I will run away. I will run away the first chance I get."

He gripped her shoulders hard and held her at arm's length. "You are as stubborn as a llama."

"I take after you!"

He shook her. Her mother moaned. And she screamed, "I hate you!"

"This is your doing," he said to her mother. He turned back to her, his stormy face inches from hers. "You will never leave this house. I will lock you up here for the rest of your life. You will not go out, not even to go to Mass. You can hear Mass in the chapel with the workers. You will never see another soul except your mother until you learn respect and obedience. Go to your room and stay there. Take her away, Pilar. Get her out of my sight."

Her mother took her in her arms and led her down the hall. By the time they arrived at her room, Beatriz was sobbing. She threw herself on the recamier near the windows—where she had lain so often, dreaming of being loved by Domingo. "I hate my father." She could hear the stubbornness in her own voice. "I hate him." Her heart seared with humiliation and shame.

"He wants only the best for you." Her mother stroked her back.

She shrugged off the touch. Her mother was on her father's side. She had no one, no one who cared what was in her heart.

Her mother got up and went to the wardrobe. "Come, Beatriz, change into one of your own dresses. Let me have Rosa

Yana bring you some tea and fresh bread and honey." She rang
for the maid and ordered a tray.

"You can't bribe me with finery anymore," she said, and
looked away.

Dresses rustled softly as her mother rummaged in the wardrobe. Beatriz fingered the plain muslin front of her convent-made
dress. She had to find Domingo. She would declare herself to
him. It was the only way. There was no point in waiting for him
to come to her. She was his master's daughter. It would be impossible for him to declare himself to her. She had to speak first. She
smoothed the rough front of her dress. She wanted to look beautiful when he saw her.

Trying to look reluctant, she stood and let her mother undo
the modest muslin frock. She ran her hands over the dresses
on the shelves—bodices laced with gold and silver, broad open
sleeves of Holland and fine Calabrian linen. She smiled at them
in spite of herself. She was vain. She knew it, but she couldn't help
it. Mother Maria had tried often—

"Mother Maria!" she exclaimed. What had she been
thinking? Mother Maria relied on her. Only her. And she was
here fussing with dresses, like a silly, shallow girl, when she had
sworn to Mother Maria that she would carry out her mission like
the Cid's own page. "I must find Padre Junipero. I must go to
him right now!"

Her mother continued to finger the dresses. "Do you want
to confess?"

"No! I told you before in the office. No one listened. No
one ever listens to me. I must get word to Padre Junipero. He is
needed at—"

A sudden banging at the door stopped her words. "My
lady!" Her father's voice was urgent, even tinged with fear.

Her mother ran to the door. "What is it, Captain?" She
opened, even though Beatriz was standing there in only her
chemise and petticoats.

Her father did not even glance at her. "A cave in at the mine
of Prudencio in the Corpus Christi lode. I must go at once. They

said they heard the noise of several explosions from collapsing works."

Her mother crossed herself. *"Dios mío,* help us, dear Lord."

"There could be more than thirty or forty men in there. We must attempt a rescue," her father said, and disappeared.

"I thought—" her mother started to say to her father's disappearing back. He was gone, but she finished her thought. "I thought the mine was supposed to be closed for the festival." She stood for a moment as if transfixed, then closed the door and slumped back against it. *"Madre de Dios,* help us. Holy Mother Mary, protect them." She clasped her hands before her breasts.

Beatriz moved toward her. "How can this be, Mother, if the mine was closed?"

"The workers go into the mine when it is closed, to take silver for themselves."

"Steal it?"

"Not really. It is a custom. It has been that way for a hundred years. The mine owners turn their heads and pretend to ignore it. I think they allow it because despite whatever else they say, they know it maintains some sort of balance between what the Indians get and what they give."

Outside her bedroom window, there was a sudden commotion in the *ingenio* yard—*barreteros* and *pongos* scrambling to assemble tools. Her father shouting brusque orders. In minutes, they all galloped off.

When the yard was quiet again, a thought dawned that chilled Beatriz's heart. "Domingo? Mother, could Domingo have been in the mine?"

Her mother sank to the window seat and looked up at her, her face full of a strange mixture of exasperation and pity. "No, darling. Domingo certainly was not there."

Beatriz fell to her knees and took her mother's hands. "How can you be sure?"

"I am sure. Now tell me what you were going to say about Mother Maria."

"Oh, Mama, she will be taken any minute by the Inquisition. They came to the convent and questioned us. I am sure that things I said made them think they should burn Mother Maria at the stake. I must try to help her. I must."

Her mother took her hand. "Oh no, dear. That cannot be. How can anything you said be so harmful?"

"It was. I know it was. Listen to me. For once, listen to what I am saying." As she explained the events at the convent, her mother's grip tightened on her fingers.

"This is horrifying," her mother said.

"Mother Maria said her only hope is for me to find Padre Junipero. Why don't we go to the Compañia de Jesus? We can send Padre Junipero to the convent and stay to pray for the trapped miners."

Her mother gave her a sad smile. "I cannot take you out. Your father has forbidden it."

Beatriz stared in disbelief. "I have just told you. Mother Maria's life hangs in the balance."

"I will send the maids out," her mother said gently. "They will look all over the city. They can go places we would never be able to go. They will find the padre for you. In the meantime, you must stay here. I cannot go against your father."

A sigh of exasperation escaped Beatriz, but she kept her face soft. There was no arguing against her mother's total obedience to her father. "Then let's send the maids right now. All of them. We must find Padre Junipero immediately."

At least her mother readily agreed to that. Once they had dispatched the maids, she and her mother went back to her room, and she changed into one of her own dresses, not caring which one. Her nerves jangled with anxiety.

Her mother dressed her as if she were a doll. "Shall we say an *Ave* for the safety of the miners?"

Beatriz lifted her arms and let her mother do up the laces of her bodice. "How can we be sure that Domingo was not in the mine?"

Her mother took her hands, softly now, and looked into her

face with an intensity that was almost frightening. "I must tell you something about Domingo that I am afraid will shock you, my child."

At that moment, when all thought of her duty to the Abbess was being driven from Beatriz's mind, a solemn function was beginning in the cathedral. His Grace the Bishop officially acknowledged the Tribunal. The Inquisitor de la Gasca asserted his authority by reading an Edict of Faith that called upon every Potosino to denounce all offenders against the laws of the Church.

Fray DaTriesta, the local Commissioner, stood before the gold-leafed altar, stretched out his long, skinny arms in the shape of Christ on the cross, and reminded those present that it was April 10, the anniversary of the founding of the Silver City. "Here in this harsh and restless landscape," he intoned, "full of jagged rocky hills, fantastic in the sharp light of the overhead sun and the weird perspective of this altitude, one hundred and five years ago, brave knights found this source of wealth, to strengthen our Catholic monarch, to make Spain mighty in defense of the Faith. We must be no less harsh on offenders against the purity of our beliefs. No less restless in our pursuit of blasphemers. No less sharp in our vigilance. No less brave and mighty in our battle against the works of the Evil One." On his last words, he raised his bony arms slightly and let them drop to his sides.

The Bishop on his gilded throne thought he would puke. That such a worm—so common and so ugly—should speak such words, as if DaTriesta's ancestors hadn't been groveling in some rocky mountain field in northern Spain at the time Potosí was founded. It was disgraceful how, merely by coming to the New World, a lowly peasant's son could improve his condition nearly to that of a nobleman.

De la Gasca, the Inquisitor, then rose and, aristocratic as he was, offended the Bishop even more deeply by declaring the first monetary fine of the Tribunal's campaign in Potosí. Two royal officials were to pay eighty ducats for some minor offense involving supplying food for poor prisoners. The guilty men, resplendent in the finery of their position and wealth, marched up the center aisle of the great church and laid their pieces of silver on two gold plates set out on the steps of the altar. A great, boring show was made of their repentance and their forgiveness.

The Bishop suffered seeing the money placed into the black velvet bag carried by one of de la Gasca's lieutenants, and without a word—other than the final blessing of the congregation—His Grace made his way to his carriage and to his study, where he poured himself a glass of the strongest drink in his house.

Chicha, made by the Indians out of maize, was disagreeable to the Bishop's sight and worse to his taste. But smoky and brown as it was, he preferred it to the harsh and hardly intoxicating wine they made in this benighted region, where they harvested grapes exactly at the time when in Spain they were just pruning the vines. He drained the glass and poured himself another.

Ocampo, his cook, entered with a tray of cold meat pie and boiled potatoes. His Grace nibbled at the food disconsolately. After forty days of eating almost nothing but dried eels from the coast that were the closest thing to fresh fish in this dreadful country, he could now not even enjoy his Easter meat—what with all this nonsense of DaTriesta's.

A shout in the plaza outside drew him to the window. One of the endless bullfights that were being staged every afternoon in celebration of Nestares was in progress. Yesterday, one of the city's halberdiers, who was posted at the door of the Alcaldía across the square, had been fatally gored. Today, the spectators were tense and excited in expectation of more blood.

The Bishop drew aside his curtain the better to see. A huge black bull pawed the earth that had been scattered over the paving stones for the occasion. A tall, lithe toreador on a beautiful white Chilean horse pointed his silver-tipped lance. The crowd clamored for the bull's life. The Bishop was just becoming sufficiently engrossed to have nearly forgotten the fortune the Inquisition would collect, which he would never see, when a knock at his study door forced him away from the window. He groaned. DaTriesta, no doubt, come to gloat and fish for compliments about his words in the cathedral. "Come."

It was José, the sacristan of the church, who doubled as his serving man. He carried a letter on a silver tray.

The Bishop tore open the seal, In the Abbess's fine, ladylike script, the letter read, "To His Excellency Don Fray Faustino Piñelo de Ondegardo, by the Grace of God Bishop of Potosí—" He cut to the second paragraph. "I appeal to you as my Bishop and as my fellow nobleman to intercede for me and my poor companion, of stock as noble as mine, who has become seriously ill from the shock of these proceedings. In the name of my ancient and aristocratic family, I implore you…"

"Dear God," the Bishop murmured, "what have I done to deserve this new cross?" If he interceded for that troublesome woman, he might fail anyway. Defending a blasphemer, he might himself be accused of blasphemy. He looked again at the fine, graceful script of the Abbess's hand. She was of the highest birth. The true son of his father would help her. Were he a knight… But he was not a knight. He was a priest. For him, prayer must be the answer. "I will pray for her," he said to the empty room. He dropped the letter onto the coals burning in the brazier and went immediately to kneel before the statue of the Holy Infant that stood on a pedestal in the corner. He bowed his head.

As the Bishop prayed, three priests in armor and carrying swords pounded on the door of the Convent of Santa Isabella de los Santos Milagros. When the Abbess and Sor Eustacia were brought to them, a man with a large beak of a nose and a powerful gaze of hate spoke. "By the authority of the Council of the Indies, I arrest you, Maria Santa Hilda, for having knowingly placed the corpse of a suicide in sacred ground. And you, Eustacia, for falsely administering the sacrament of confession. May God have mercy on your souls."

Maria Santa Hilda stood impassive and repeated the creed to herself to keep her mind blank and her mouth silent while the soldier-priests drew from under their capes two saffron robes. They placed one over her head, the other over Eustacia's. The stouter of the priests hung a chain around each of their necks.

Monica arrived at an unseemly run. She went and embraced them. "We will save you. We will." She embraced Maria Santa Hilda a second time. "If they take you to the stake," she whispered, "confess at the last moment, and they will strangle you and spare you the pain. God will forgive such a small lie."

Maria Santa Hilda kissed her and whispered in return, "Complete the work you have started. And pray with all your might."

Flanked by the stern soldier-priests, the Abbess walked through the cold morning, not knowing where they were taking her. There were rumors about a secret prison in DaTriesta's house.

Bells began to ring all around them, bells that signaled yet another celebration for Nestares. The streets about them were deserted. The citizens were gathered at whatever meaningless event was taking place.

Suddenly they came upon Juana, the maid, walking swiftly toward the convent. The small, sturdy woman did not seem to recognize the two women in the saffron robes.

The Abbess thought to shout for help, as if Juana could know something to save them. But Maria Santa Hilda knew there was very little chance that anyone could save them now. She kept her silence. Despair had begun to leak into her heart.

The Inquisition went on to hear scores of secret informants, to collect information about many of the King's subjects, to levy fines, and to make arrests. From Taropalca—a nearby town of Christian Indians—they took Doña Angela Carranza, revered as a mystic. DaTriesta and de la Gasca dubbed her an impostor and dragged her off to prison, where she could consider her ugly dilemma: Should she confess to the sin of heresy and seek absolution before she was burned or insist on her own saintliness and die anyway, but in defiance? In the first case, her detractors would think her saved and her followers would feel she had betrayed them. In the second, her accusers would think her in hell, but her faithful would revere her as a martyr.

In the Convent of Santa Isabella de los Santos Milagros, none of the holy sisters had ever heard of Doña Angela, but Vitallina, who had long put her faith in La Carranza's mystical powers, trudged around the halls in a pair of the famous Indian woman's old shoes, convinced they would protect her from those terrible headaches that had plagued her since her womanly flux had begun to wane.

She shuffled into the infirmary to find Sor Monica bent over some vials.

The scraping of the shoes on the tile floor frazzled the Sister Herbalist's already overheated nerves. "Must you wear those things? They hardly fit over your toes, they are so small. I told you I would buy you any pair of shoes in the market."

"I prefer these, thank you, Sister." Vitallina proceeded to the cauldron over the fire and ladled hot water into a wash bowl. She then, seemingly making as much noise as possible, washed the crockery.

Sor Monica poked at the mysterious substance in the vial in front of her and tried to concentrate. Potosí was a place where, for a price, one could buy anything. Endless shiploads of forbidden wares were unloaded at Rio de Janeiro, Montevideo, and Buenos Aires, made their way up the river system, through the lowland forests and rising highlands, and finally emerged on the high broken tablelands of the Altiplano. Along the way, products of local manufacture were stowed away among the contraband parcels. Eastern Indians were clever at many things, especially poisons.

Vitallina peered over her shoulder. "What is that?"

"Nothing," Monica said. "I found it when we searched. And I ate some. It is harmless, whatever it is."

"Why didn't you show it to me?" The big black woman tried to take the vial from her hand.

Monica pulled it away. "I did not want to." She meant her words to sound commanding, but they seemed to come from the mouth of a disobedient child.

Vitallina kicked off her silly shoes and ran barefoot out of the room.

Monica sighed. Now her assistant had gone off in a huff and left her to puzzle out this mystery alone while the Inquisitors marched the Abbess away. Maria Santa Hilda could spend years in prison. Even if she was acquitted, the Tribunal would not necessarily release her immediately. She could die of some disease while living in such conditions in this dreadful climate. Monica whispered a prayer for the Abbess's and Eustacia's protection.

She could not give up the idea that this mysterious substance had something to do with the death of those girls. The two flails lay on the counter beside the vial. It also seemed clear to her that Hippolyta had taken Inez's flail and used it to punish herself. Was that just an act of self-mortification offered for the repose of her friend's soul? Or was it an act of penance for the sin of murder?

Monica held her head in her hands. Try as she might, she could not accept that Hippolyta had killed Inez. If that child had committed such a sin, then perhaps this substance had nothing to do with the deaths. It belonged to Juana. And what could Juana, so beloved of the young girls, have to do with any of this?

Monica racked her brain to remember some piece of gossip Vitallina had been blabbering. Something about Juana having given her brother the money to pay instead of taking his place in the mine. They called it making an Indian in silver. Monica ordinarily ignored convent gossip, but Juana's problem had interested her. The sturdy, dependable maid was a good sort, and the dangers of the mine were legendary. People said that Indian women maimed their male babies so they would not have to serve in the mine. And because the smallpox plagues had killed so many natives, fewer and fewer men came to work. The ones who did were forced to labor harder and harder. Padre Junipero said the *azogueros* sometimes made the workers stay underground for two days at a time, even sleep there. Cutting rock with bars weighing thirty pounds, crawling along like snakes, burdened with ore, they sweated blood. They were whipped and lashed. The King had sworn to protect the Indians. There were judges specially appointed to hear their suits, but still they suffered miserably.

Vitallina appeared at the door, carrying the cat.

"What was it, Vitallina, that you told me about Juana's brother?"

"That Juana had given him money to buy his way out of service, but that a card trickster cheated him out of it."

"I want you to—"

Vitallina turned and took the cat to the counter against the wall. She held the struggling animal in one hand, spilled the gummy substance from the vial onto the counter, poked the point of a knife into it, and thrust the knife into the cat's paw. Its limbs went immediately stiff; it made one small, desperate gasp and died.

Monica gasped, too. At the suddenness. She gripped her arms across her chest. One hand went to her throat. "But— What—"

"It is called curare. The Indians along the great Brazilian river make it. For hunting."

The hand on Monica's throat tightened. "But I ate some."

"It does not kill that way. Only on the tip of a knife or a dart."

Monica stared at the flails. Those barbs. "Come with me. We must find Juana."

"Most of the maids are in the choir for a service."

Monica scooped the poison back into the vial and took it with her. They hurried across the rear cloister and up the narrow stairs. Monica pulled her veil over her face as she reached the top. Unlike the old thick-walled churches with their single narrow nave and octagonal altars, this new church was in the form of a cross, with a dome over the altar. The convent choir overlooked one of the arms of the cross. The heavily decorated dome soared gold and gorgeous above them. The great stone arches echoed with a "Dies Irae" being sung for Hippolyta by her father's Indians. The girl's funeral was to take place the following morning.

The maids of the convent chanted with them. One, no more than a child, sobbed softly as she tried to sing. Monica touched her shoulder as she scanned their bowed heads.

Juana was not there.

They found her in the maids' dormitory, spinning vicuña yarn with a drop spindle. Piles of wool, pale yellowish brown, gray, black, lay on the floor near her feet.

Confronted with a murderer, Monica could not speak. Her racing mind stumbled. She held up the vial with the poison wad at the bottom.

The arm with the spindle dropped to Juana's side. Her eyes glanced toward the box under her bed. Recognition dawned in her bright, black eyes. Vitallina's powerful hands closed on her shoulders.

"We know," Monica said simply. "Tell me how this came to be."

"There is a snake," Juana said, "a huge black snake in the mountain. It has a flat head and fiery eyes, and it causes the earth to shake and cave in."

It was as if Juana had started to speak a language Monica did not understand. She pulled Vitallina's arms away and backed Juana into the corner. "What are you talking about? What does this have to do with those poor dead girls?"

Juana sank to the floor and sobbed, "Pachamama, now the Spanish will kill me."

"You can have sanctuary here," Vitallina murmured consolingly. "Just tell us what you know. Help us help the Abbess."

The anguish fled from Juana's face. "Sanctuary. Will you grant me sanctuary?"

"Yes," Monica said. The Abbess would say yes. She was sure of that. "Tell me. Tell me quickly what you have done."

"I put the poison on the flail."

"But why? Why would you kill those girls?"

Juana stared at them for a long time, but she did not answer.

"Tell me, and I will do anything I can to save your life." Monica was not sure she could keep such a promise or that she really wanted to. This woman had murdered Inez and Hippolyta. Monica had to extract the information she needed.

Juana stammered and finally said, "I killed Inez because of what she did to Sor Eustacia."

"What do you mean?" Monica demanded.

Vitallina put out her hand. "The maids have all known that Inez seduced Eustacia. The maids know everything."

Monica's mouth gaped. Her hand rose as if to slap Juana but stopped in midair.

Juana cowered. "She ruined the life of the kindest sister in the convent. I put the poison on the flail because I knew she would use it and kill herself. She loved the flail. She was evil."

"Did you punish Hippolyta, too?" Monica asked. "Why did she have to die?"

"I did not mean for her to die," the Indian woman said. "I did not know she would take Inez's flail and use it on herself."

"Do not leave this room," Monica said. "I will be back. Vitallina, stay here and make sure she does not leave. But first, I must speak to you in the corridor."

When they were out of earshot of the maid, Monica asked, "Do you believe that she did this?"

"Oh yes," Vitallina said. "I believe that she meant to kill Inez, but I do not believe her reason."

"Neither do I."

P adre Junipero stood in the reception parlor of the monastery of San Augustín, gazing up at the statue by Gaspar de la Cueva of Christ bound to the column. It seemed sculpted by angelic rather than human hands—the kind of statue that might perform miracles. Perform one for me, he prayed to it. Help me save the Abbess.

Fray Vincente entered the room and embraced him. "I have seen the Abbess. She has been taken by the Tribunal."

"I know. It is the gossip on every street corner."

"She asked for me to go and confess her, but instead she gave me messages. She told me to tell you to go to the Alcalde and to—"

"I cannot," Junipero said. "The Alcalde's friends are trying to kill me."

Vincente's eyes clouded over.

"I must speak to the actor Sebastian," Junipero said.

The portly man frowned. "I am sorry, my friend, but he is not here."

"Not here? You let him go?" Vincente had the soul of a saint and the intelligence of a wood-and-gesso statue.

"He told me you were finished with him. He was truthful about his origins. Why would he lie about that?"

"Do you know where he went?"

"He promised that if I did not denounce him to the Inquisition, he would leave Potosí and go east to Brazil. But I doubt he has left yet. He was going to try to find a smuggler to travel with."

Junipero's fingers went to his lips. "I have to see him before he leaves. I must hurry. But listen. I have an idea what the Abbess suspects. You must go to find Gemita de la Morada and tell her that I said she may be in danger. Tell her to go to the house of Tovar. I will find her there." He turned to the door immediately.

Vincente put a hand on his shoulder. "I am sorry to tell you, my friend, but the Tribunal has put out an order for your arrest. They charge you with blasphemy for burying the Morada girl in a consecrated place."

Junipero looked into Vincente's eyes, showing the monk his desperation, reading his friend's compassion.

Vincente removed his hand. "Be careful, *amigo*. There are many others who would hand you over to the Inquisition without muttering a Miserere."

Without another word, fearing speech would break the spell, Junipero covered himself with the motley cloak and black felt hat Barco had given him to disguise his identity and ducked through the monastery's side door to the street.

Feigning the ambling gait of a bowlegged muleteer, he hurried along the Calle Quijarro, which zigzagged to break the impact of the wind gusts. The street led to that raucous quarter where miners and transients went in search of recreation. Impassive Indian women sat on the curbs, selling medals and holy images, but the priest knew sin was rampant here.

Where would one begin to search for one man in all this chaos? There were more than a dozen dance halls, but somehow the priest felt Sebastián would not look for lewd entertainment.

The actor would want a place where he could meet smugglers and other desperadoes, not women.

Junipero entered one of the two score gambling houses that lined the side streets of the district. In a low, dark room that stank of men who had sat too long on mules, he had no sooner begun to describe Sebastian to the barman when three officers of the Inquisition burst in. The soldiers, dressed in black with shining steel breastplates and long swords at their sides, stopped all conversation.

In terror, expecting instant arrest, the priest forgot his disguise of a Mestizo in search of easy money and blessed himself and prayed.

"Sinners, repent," announced one of the officers. He proceeded in a loud voice to denounce the gambling that was almost universal in the city. It was a mortal sin, he said, and then gave the familiar laundry list of how gamblers, their families, and Almighty God suffered because of it.

Weak light from candle stubs on the tables glinted off the soldier-priest's shining armor. A scruffy llama driver near Junipero rose, doffed his cap, and, after expressing disgust at his own weakness, publicly swore he would never play at cards again.

"What will you forfeit if you sin again?" demanded the soldier who had preached.

"One hundred pesos in pure silver," the penitent croaked out.

It was a fortune for the man. And if he was anything like the thousands of others who had made the pledge before him, he would inevitably backslide and forfeit his fine to the pious uses of the Inquisition.

A few more wretches were cajoled into similar vows while Padre Junipero sweated under his coarsely woven cloak and tried to be invisible.

When the black-and-steel envoys of the Wrath of God finally departed, Junipero cautiously got up to leave. A stranger to his right stopped him.

His heart thudded while he turned to face the man.

"The transient you asked after," the tall, thin stranger said in a heavy Italian accent. "For ten reales, I might tell you where he is."

The padre eyed the man. His clothing was of good cut and fabric but worn and dirty. The priest grasped his own grimy cape. "How could a beggar like myself produce such a sum?"

"It was worth a try," the Italian said with a twinkle.

"Do you know something? For the love of God, tell me. It could save a dear friend's life."

The man shrugged. "Since you put it that way, why not? It may not even be him, but a man who looks as you described is staying at the Tambo Lo Caliente."

Junipero bowed to his informant and beat a hasty path down the street and around the corner to the inn. It was a reputable-looking place and smelled of good, spicy chicken stew.

Determined not to let his haste draw anyone's suspicions, the padre first took a seat at a table in the outer courtyard and ordered a cup of *chicha*. About him, traders in everything from Persian rugs to English and French furniture gossiped about what devaluation would do to business.

He ran his hand over the name *Juan Ulloa* scratched into the table in front of him. Every table or bench in every public room in Potosí was carved like this—with first and last names, often with dates. What did they hope to accomplish by inscribing their names here? In olden times, pilgrims to Rome or the Holy Land put their names on the walls of hostelries to give notice of their route to anyone who might be searching for them along the royal road. Now, with no apparent usefulness, the practice had become so common in New Spain that every inn and drinking place was adorned with names and obscene words. Thus, the priest supposed, the common man hoped to leave his mark.

At the next table, a man who dealt in purple satin from Florence was refusing the coin of the city and demanding gold for his goods.

When the skinny, sour-faced innkeeper brought the drink, the priest asked if anyone answering to Sebastian's description was at the inn.

"He came in a few hours ago. He said he is here to transport clothing to France to be cleaned. He was talking to another carter about going by mule or llama to the coast." The skinny man leaned closer. He smelled of onions and hair pomade. "Don't tell the priests," he whispered to the man he thought a Mestizo trader, "but I think your handsome blond might be a Jew. I gave him bacon for his dinner, and he didn't eat it."

The priest grunted noncommittally and then followed the innkeeper's directions to a room that opened onto an inner courtyard. A sign on the wall declared, "It is forbidden to cook or bring horses into these rooms."

Before the priest could knock, a weathered wooden door beneath the sign opened and the actor came out carrying a red sack. He smiled until the priest doffed his hat and revealed himself. "Padre... Padre..." He eyed the corridor that led toward the street.

"Stay, my son. The first time we met, you left me unconscious. This time I beg you, give me the information I require. I will not ask you to testify before the Tribunal. I will not reveal who and what you are."

The actor backed into the room, pulled the priest in with a rough jerk, and silently closed the door. "Make your threats more quietly, Padre," he whispered, "or I'll be carted off to the dungeons before I can tell you anything." He gave the priest the only chair and sat cross-legged on the bed.

Guilt tightened Junipero's throat. He loathed threatening the young man with the same odious fate the Abbess faced, but he knew no other way. "Tell me or I will have no choice but to identify you to Grand Inquisitor de la Gasca's men."

"If I tell, you will betray me anyway." In sadness, the actor's face was even more beautiful than when he smiled. A sculptor would model John the Baptist after him. "Perhaps I should give myself up and accept my father's fate as my own."

"Your father's?"

"I almost prefer it to this life of constant fear." His eyes searched the priest's. "My father was Francisco Maldonado de Silva."

Junipero drew a breath of amazement. Everyone knew de Silva's story. The Inquisition made sure everyone heard it as an object lesson in its own inexorable tenacity to convert the wicked or destroy them. Sebastián's father was a surgeon of high repute in Concepción de Chile, the son of a Portuguese who had been arrested as a Jew, been reconciled, and brought up his children— two girls and a boy—as Christians. The boy, Francisco, was a good Catholic until the age of eighteen, when he chanced to read the *Scrutinium Scripturarum* of Pablo de Santa Maria, Archbishop of Burgos, who had been the Rabbi Solomon ha-Levi. Converted in 1390, ha-Levi had risen to be Regent of Spain in the minority of Juan II and later a papal legate and a bishop.

Instead of confirming Francisco's faith, the book raised doubts. He consulted his father, who, he found, still secretly practiced his ancient faith. Francisco became an ardent convert to Judaism, but he kept his secret from his mother and two sisters and from his wife. Eventually, though, he revealed his beliefs to his sister Isabel and tried to convert her, but in vain. Though she loved her brother and he was, by then, the sole support of her, her mother, and her sister, she loved God more. She denounced Francisco to the Inquisition. For this, she was extolled from the pulpits as a brave defender of the Faith. Padre Junipero tried not to despise her as a traitor. His own sister had protected him from the consequences of his sin, helped him escape to the monastery.

After Francisco's arrest, the priests of Concepción, Santiago, and Lima made many attempts to convert him, but he was resolved to die in the faith of his ancestors. He was brought out in the great auto-da-fé at Lima in 1639.

"I wish I had his courage," Sebastian said. "When my mother was away, before I was born, he circumcised himself. Can you imagine it?"A chill hit the priest's crotch and ran up his back like a bolt of cold lightning. He drew a gasping breath at the very thought.

"When they read his sentence in the square, a sudden whirl-wind tore away the awning under which he stood before the Inquisitor. He looked up and cried out, 'The God of Israel does this to look upon me face-to-face.' That was the last thing he said before they burnt him alive."

The sermonizers left these last facts untold, but the young man had the air of one telling the truth, and the priest was inclined to believe him.

"You can get at least small revenge," Junipero said. "They killed your father, but at least you can thwart them now. You can save the Abbess from them."

Sebastian smiled and shook his head. "A point, Father, but a weak one."

Junipero considered the actor's countenance. That smile had beguiled Inez. Suppose Sebastian's story was all a fairy tale. Suppose he was not the son of Francisco de Silva but merely a wastrel plying his actor's trade to foil a sympathetic priest? The youth had fooled him before with his perfect Castillian accent and his aristocratic manners. Why not with this story?

The courtyard outside was now in shadow. The room had grown so dim, it was difficult to read the man's eyes. Why would a man who was not a Jew claim to be one? More than trusting the actor, the priest knew he must win his trust. There was only one way to do that—to prove he trusted him.

"I will tell you a story in return. My real name is Diego Cortéz de Aragón," the priest said. And in response to a quizzical grunt from the actor, "Oh, yes, I am a real priest. But I am also a notorious felon. I was born in Hispaniola of Spanish parents and sent to Madrid at a young age to live with an uncle and be educated. There in the company of other wild boys, I raped a great nobleman's daughter. I escaped to Sevilla before her father caught me. I changed my identity and, unrepentant, spent my time in seduction."

The actor snorted and eyed Junipero's emaciated form.

The priest smiled despite the guilt that ground at his heart. "I know I do not look the part now, but I have not always had the physique of a penitent." He remembered his youthful beauty only with remorse. "After years of debauchery, I suddenly became ill. I could not eat. I vomited everything. My sister visited me and asked if I had finally become disgusted with myself. I entered the Jesuits and was, by the Grace of God, received into holy orders, but my crime was notorious. If my real identity was ever made known, I would be disgraced. Now, Sebastian, you have information sufficient to threaten me as I might threaten you. Please. Trust me. Tell me what you know."

"If you protect me and they find you out, you'll be sent to the galleys for life, priest or no priest."

"I am doomed anyway, to tell the truth," the priest said. "Morada's men are trying to find me to kill me, and the Tribunal is after me for burying Inez in a consecrated place. I only want to save a holy woman before I die."

Sebastián moved from the bed and sat on the floor close to him. "I did not want Inez to die," he whispered, the way men did in the confessional. "I wanted her to come away, to join the troupe. She would have made a great actress. You saw how she beguiled everyone. She was a natural."

The priest nodded. "And now she is dead. Tell me how, why."

The actor opened his hands and shrugged. "All I know is that she was blackmailing her father. She said she had the means to ruin him. She wanted money for us to go away together, lots of money, so she could live like the princess she had been. She was using what she knew about him to get the money and to protect me. Once he killed her, I knew I was a dead man. I am a dead man. She told her father about her love affair with me, though I warned her not to."

Padre Junipero shook his head. This was madness. The man could not be telling the truth. In confession, Inez had revealed none of this. "Why would she have told her father? Did she tell him you are a Jew?"

"She did not know that. I am not circumcised."

"Nevertheless, I simply do not believe you." He made as if to go.

Sebastian rose to the bait. He held up his hand. "Wait. I will show you. I have a letter from her." He rifled through his red sack and handed a piece of paper to the priest. The room was too dark now to read. Junipero went to the small unglazed window and held out the paper in the scant light. The words were scrawled in a hasty script, but unmistakably in Inez's hand: "You were right, my darling. I have overstretched my father's love. He has taken back the evidence I had against him. I have threatened to testify against him myself. But I am afraid. Since I am lost to him, I fear he does not care if I live. He loves me only if he can control me, and he loves his honor more.

"I am going to the convent where he will not be able to harm me. From the safety of that sanctuary, I will force him to give me the money we need to go to Buenos Aires and establish ourselves there. You will see. We will become great in that city. My father will pay for my silence. Then we will be richer than your wildest dreams.

"I kiss your sex and long for the day you kiss mine again. Inez."

The final words sent a shudder through the priest, of disgust and arousal.

"She could create a paradise for a man, Father." The actor had come to Junipero's side and was reading over his shoulder.

"How can you say such a thing about a dead girl?"

"Inez was no innocent victim, Padre. She charmed and vamped everyone, including her father and the Abbess." He regarded the priest knowingly. "Including you, evidently. Her mother and her baby sister were the only ones who saw through her."

"And yet you loved her."

"Loved her? I don't know. She loved me. I could have had a pleasurable and interesting life with her."

The priest handed the letter back to the young man.

"Don't you want to keep it, Padre? As evidence?"

"I could never show that to the Tribunal. It paints her as a wanton and a blackmailer. They will not want to vindicate her from suicide if they know what a sinner she was. Besides, it does not prove anything. What was the evidence she had against her father?"

"I don't know. She never told me what it was, because she said if I knew, he would certainly kill me. The evidence was letters, documents. That is all I know. Her father kept them to implicate others, so they would keep their common secret. She took them and gave them to someone she trusted. Somehow her father took them back."

"Then I must find those letters."

"Don't do it, Padre. There is nothing you can do against the Tribunal. Come east with me. The smugglers are leaving at nightfall. Save your own life."

"No, I must save the Abbess."

"You have no guarantee that you will succeed at that."

"I know," the priest said, "but I must try."

And then the last of the secret he had held so long in his heart slipped out. He had told it in confession. Vincente knew, but no one else. It was almost as if this young Jew, who had so trusted him, were the only man on earth who would ever truly understand. "Maria Santa Hilda would not be in the convent at all if she had not been raped in her youth. She is not the one I and my comrades defiled, but that girl was so like the Abbess in innocence and station, she could have been her. I cannot undo what I did. But I can try to save the life of another such innocent victim. I would die to save her."

That afternoon, before the light faded, the city's rich and noble Indians presented another splendid and colorful masque in which all the nations of Perú appeared in native costumes, some elegant, some savage. The chiefs rode in richly decorated carriages of state, the last of which was made of silver and drawn by fifty forest dwellers dressed in the skins of different animals. Under sumptuous canopies, mine workers carried images made of feathers representing the great monarchs who had been kings of both Spain and Perú—Carlos I, his son Felipe II, and his grandson Felipe III—and also the Inca King Túpac Amaru, who had received holy baptism.

Beatriz Tovar saw none of this. The maids had still not returned from their search for Padre Junipero. Mother Maria's time was running out. And all Beatriz could do was watch impassively in the mirror while her maid parted her thick dark hair in the middle, braided it with precious silver ribbon, and wound it into circlets over either ear. Her mother attached a chain that crossed the upper part of Beatriz's forehead and carried the word *amor*, but the girl tore it out and threw it on the table. Love was nothing to her anymore. She was devastated...mortified... outraged. How could it be? Domingo was her brother. All those impure thoughts she had had about him. Not only sinful. They were odious, revolting.

The maid was just beginning to apply her makeup when a knock came at the door and her mother entered with Gemita de la Morada. Gemita was carrying a small canvas parcel sloppily sewed up with blue thread. She had a wild look in her eyes, as if at any moment she would begin to scream and would not stop for a long time. But she curtsied courteously and kissed Beatriz's hands and let hers be kissed in turn.

She went to the *estrado*, which ran along under the windows, and sat down and said nothing. When Beatriz asked if she was all right, Gemita eyed Beatriz's mother and remained mute.

"I will bring you some maté," her mother announced, and went out.

When they were alone, Gemita whispered, "I am in danger." Her voice sounded old and dry, like the voices of the ancient Indian women in the market. "I ran away."

Beatriz gasped. Wayward daughters could be killed by their fathers, and Captain Morada was known to be fierce in defense of his honor.

Gemita put the tip of her pudgy little forefinger to her lips. She tiptoed to the door, opened it and looked out, and then came back. "The proof is in here." She still whispered in that raspy voice. She placed the packet in Beatriz's lap. It was the size of an ingot of silver, but not as heavy. "They are letters from my father's *escritorio*. Inez was always stealing them and reading them." Her fingers fumbled, trying to pull out the blue thread. "I read them. I was curious. Only curious. Because Inez said these letters could protect me. I wanted to know what she meant." She began to sob. "Now I know. Letters can kill you." She let out a wail that sounded as if it would split the mountain.

Beatriz's own fingers, trembling, undid the thread. Inside were many letters and papers that bore the red Morada seal and remnants of the seals of many noble families.

Gemita pressed her fists to her mouth. "Read," she choked out. "Read this one." She pointed to one written on folded parchment.

The paper was signed by many of the city's ministers and officials. It carried twelve silver traders' seals. "We agree," it said, "to make coin of alloy—" Beatriz's heart thumped. This was the problem her mother had just explained to her—the danger that faced the city in the person of Visitador Nestares. Beatriz's eyes scanned the page. "...mutual profit...the assayer Ramirez..." According to what was written here, many men had conspired to debase the city's coins, but Francisco de la Morada was the one who had hatched the scheme.

"Look at the date," Gemita said, somewhat recovered now. "The forgery lasted for six years. The coins were only three parts silver, eight parts copper. And read this part."

Fake companies had been set up to conceal the fraud. The recipients of the money formed a partnership, and these papers were drawn up. The missing silver would never show on anyone's ledgers.

"Did you understand this all by yourself?" Beatriz was disbelieving. Gemita had always seemed such an innocent, silly thing.

"Inez was always telling me about it. The secret compartment in his *escritorio*, the one he never revealed to anyone but her. She told me how to open it." Gemita looked down into her lap. "She told me that if I ever needed protection, I should take these from their hiding place." She unfolded another letter. "There are worse ones." She pointed to a phrase written on one page in a thick masculine script. "See? They plan an uprising against the King." She opened another. "And here. The worst. They wrote it just four days ago. They plan to poison the envoy Nestares, and even the Viceroy."

She was becoming hysterical again, opening the pages and strewing them on the floor. "Here. This one. Read this one."

Beatriz felt her blood solidify with terror, but she read on about a plot to bribe Visitador Nestares's black slave woman to poison him. Don Felipe Ramirez had written to Morada that the slave had accepted some silver and a mixture of deadly herbs. When he wanted the deed done, all Morada had to do was send her breakfast on a silver tray. As soon as she received it, she would poison Nestares.

Beatriz's whole body was frozen with fear. "Oh, dearest God. You are right, Gemita. A person could die from knowing this."

"There is a letter from Inez," the terrified little girl said. "Here." She scooped it off the floor.

"Father," it read, "I am going to the convent to keep myself safe from you. I heard you talking to Ramirez about the Visitador the King will send. If I cannot have my way, I intend to send the letters to the King's envoy. You will never find them where they are hidden. And if you do, I will personally reveal your plot against Nestares. Just give me half of your silver, and I will go away forever."

Gemita unfolded another letter. "Here is one he wrote to her, but I guess he never sent it. It wasn't hidden with the packet, just inside his desk with her letter to him. It is in his hand."

In the same script as the document about the forgery, Beatriz read, "My lost darling Inez, By tomorrow night I will have the letters back. Come home and I will forgive you and you will live. Otherwise, know that you cannot escape me, no matter where you hide. If you do not..." The letter was unfinished and dated two days before Inez died.

"He killed her," Gemita rasped out.

"I cannot—" Beatriz began, but she stopped. She was about to say she could not believe such a thing. But she did. "Where is your mother, Gemita? Does Doña Ana know this?"

"My mother went to the lake at Tarapaya."

"And left you?"Gemita nodded.

At that moment, Beatriz's mother came in carrying a tray in her own hands. "I sent the last of the maids to look for the padre. I can't understand why one of them hasn't found him by now." She stared at the papers strewn about the floor and the *estrado*. "What—"

"Oh, Mama," Beatriz cried. "The Alcalde murdered Inez."

The cups rattled on the tray.

"We must get my father," Beatriz said.

Beatriz's mother's eyes were huge with fear. "But he is at the mine. And there is no one here but us—not even one maid."

CHAPTER 20

Sor Monica stood before Sor Olga with Vitallina at her side, holding the dead cat. Words flew out of the Sister Herbalist's mouth like a flock of unruly pigeons. In Sor Olga's eyes, she saw disgust. Her argument was having the same effect the birds would have had. Monica closed her mouth and stopped the flying.

"I must pray for guidance about what to do with this knowledge," the acting Abbess said. She regarded the cat in a way that made Monica's breath come faster and then said precisely what Monica feared: "The sacrificing of animals is pagan and blasphemous."

"Will you at least send for Padre Junipero so that I may tell him what I have discovered?"

"No," Sor Olga said curtly. Her small, wizened face had turned smug.

"He is my confessor. I request an opportunity to receive his spiritual advice."

"Your vow is obedience."

"But—"

"Sister, your spiritual adviser is about to be arrested by the Holy Tribunal for his own sins." Delight replaced disgust in Sor Olga's eyes.

At the dining room table at the Casa de la Morada, the Alcalde shifted in his chair, looking for a position that would not torture his weary back. His closest allies on the Cabildo, men who were bound to one another by pacts of mutual guilt, sat tense in their seats. If one was punished, they all would be. And they sensed the sword over their heads. "My friends," Morada said, "whatever independence and power the Cabildo used to have is long gone. We have all seen it narrowed and weakened for decades."

Taboada raised his hand like a boy in school. "Perhaps if we tried to write again to the King or even to send an envoy to the Council of the Indies. They may not understand the difficulty of mining today. That the shafts now flood because the miners have to dig so deep." His thin voice was pleading. He was the weakest of the conspirators. He had not even been able to find and kill that scrawny, stupid priest. If Don Jerónimo didn't begin to show a little backbone, he too would have to be eliminated.

"Enough." Morada stood and stretched his spine to relieve his pain. "Getting better terms from the King has not been possible in the past. With the debasing of the currency, it is not even an option. Wresting control of the mines and city is our only path now. I send the silver breakfast tray tomorrow. Nestares's death will look like a fever. Once he is gone, we will buy off or kill his guards and do away with the stronger Basques. The city—all of Alto Perú will be ours." He held up the ostrich plume pen and they signed, one by one, and using the flame of the candle on the table dripped some red sealing wax next to each signature. Each man pressed his seal ring into the liquid and held it there until the wax hardened. Ramirez, the last to seal, pressed so hard and held his fist in place so long that the wax broke when he withdrew his ring, and the seal had to be made again.

They had done this before, made documents that incriminated them all, to force them all, under pain of death for treason, to keep faith with one another.

"We will meet in the Plaza Mayor, before the Alcaldía, at dawn," Morada told them, and bade them farewell. It was dark by the time they all left.

He carried the document to his small study for safekeeping. A few candles burned on the table and illuminated the gorgeous ivory face of the Virgin on the shelf in the corner. "My Inez was everything to me," he said aloud to God's Mother. "Why did you not send me a son? Why did Inez have to change? I would have given her anything if she had stayed."

He put the key in the lock of his *escritorio* and twisted it, but it did not turn. His breath stopped. He tried the lid. It was already open. The letter he had left on the slanted surface was gone. He took out the drawer and pulled the latch at the back. The panel under the drawer space popped up. He put his hand into the secret compartment. It was empty! He stashed the parchment he was carrying and ran out, through the dining room, to the balcony surrounding the patio. He flung open the door to Gemita's room. Empty.

He ran to the other bedrooms, to the sitting room. Empty. All empty.

Carlos, the captain of his guard, came running. "I heard a commotion," he said.

"Where is the señorita?" Morada demanded.

"I—I— Isn't she in her room? She went there for siesta."

"No, *cholo*, bastard, she is not. I will kill you as well as her if you let her get out of this house."

They searched the rooms again and did not find her. Morada questioned the servants. Her maid had helped her dress after siesta. That was the last anyone in the house had seen her. Evalin, the cook, was also gone. The convent, Morada thought. Perhaps Gemita had fled there as her sister had. No, she would not have gone there. If she was clever enough to take the documents, Inez must have told her about them. He had killed Inez within the convent walls. Not even Gemita was stupid enough to then seek refuge there. Her only friend was that silly daughter of Tovar. A chill of fear, almost unknown in his life, hit the scalp of Francisco Rojas de la Morada. If his papers fell into the hands of the Basques, he would never be able to buy them back. They would go straight to Nestares. His own supporters would abandon him and throw themselves on the mercy of the Viceroy and the King. He would die in ignominy.

He ordered the captain of his guard to arm his men. Morada strode to the hall and strapped on his own breastplate and took his helmet.

The clock in the tower was striking nine as he and his guard reached the street. If Gemita had left the house after siesta, she would not have found Tovar at home. He would have already gone to the banquet the Basques were hosting for Nestares. The Tovar women would do nothing alone. Gemita and the letters would still be sitting in the Basque's house, waiting for him to return. Tovar would be away for hours yet. Still, with all the Indians in the *ingenio* and perhaps that Mestizo bastard Barco, twelve men would not be enough to storm the house. Certainly if the letters had gotten farther, he would need a sizable band of men. The Alcalde could not call on the other members of the Cabildo. His honor would not allow him to reveal his daughter's betrayal. Nor could he let them know he had allowed the papers to get out of his possession. Yet he needed fighters he could trust.

At that moment when, on the other side of the city, Nestares, in the company of many but not all of the Basque miners, was being served a sweet made with vanilla by a beautiful black slave from the Cape Verde islands, the Alcalde set out quickly to recruit men of force.

It was a simple matter to amass a fierce gang in Potosí. Adventurers who reached the city without a penny expected to become wealthy gentlemen overnight. None did. They could be found easily and bought for a price.

At the bowling court opposite the Jesuit church, where the brawlers always gathered, the Alcalde found seven men, among them Estéfano Curzio, a fearsome Italian who had clashed with and killed five Basques in a rancorous chain of vengeance over the death of a Neapolitan noble youth.

At a billiards parlor, he found six who had been known to kill Biscayans when armed with nothing more than a wooden cue.

He quickly completed his army with the Empedradillo gang, minor traders in illicit goods by day and by night brawlers who could be found on the eastern side of the Plaza del Regocijo, taunting and challenging every armed male who attempted to pass. They were always ready to riot and gleefully joined the Alcalde's ragtag squadron. "Come out with me. We are going to hunt partridges," was all he had to say.

Avoiding the center, where the fiesta wore on, Morada led his small army along the almost deserted Calle de la Paz toward the Ingenio Tovar.

Padre Junipero stumbled out of the Tambo Lo Caliente. Stunned as he was by the actor's revelations, terrified and confused by his need to act quickly and his despair of succeeding, he did not have to work very hard to act drunk. His body lurched along, and he was soon caught up between two groups of reveling miners. The city was lit for a *mascarada nocturna*. Torches burned on the buildings.

Where could he go for help? Except for the nuns in the convent and the Alcalde, his friends in the city had always been among the downtrodden. Indians were not permitted to carry swords or firearms. Without authority or force, with the Inquisition searching for him and Téllez and Taboada trying to murder him, how could he wrest from Morada, the most powerful man in the city, the evidence to save the Abbess?

The throng about him, costumed in rich French tissues,

precious serges, and gorgeously colored brocades, made its way toward the Plaza Mayor. The sight of a handsome young Mestizo decked out in purple satin and sky blue silk brought the priest back from the edge of despair. Barco! The evidence was in the Casa de la Morada. Barco could gain access through his mother.

Against the tide of revelers going toward the cathedral square, a lone figure, heavily cloaked, his black felt hat askew, obscuring his face, took the opposite route, uphill toward the Ingenio Tovar and Barco.

At the *ingenio* that was the objective of so many desperate men, three women gathered up the letters from the floor and refolded them carefully. A cup of maté had calmed Gemita.

Pilar took the papers, arranged them neatly, and tied them with one of Beatriz's ribbons, holding them gingerly, feeling they could burn her if she grasped them.

Beatriz, fists clenched at her sides, paced before the windows. "We will take this information to the Visitador. With it we can save the Abbess."

Her mother's trembling hands went to her cheeks. "We cannot do such a thing. We are just women."

"We must," Beatriz declared in that New World way of hers.

"How do we even know how to find Nestares?" Pilar said. Her daughter's courage shamed her, but she knew nothing of how to act on her own in such circumstances.

"You are wrong, Beatriz," Gemita put in. "It is the Inquisition that took the Abbess, not the Visitador. So we should give the letters to the Grand Inquisitor."

Beatriz's mouth opened and closed again.

Pilar went to her daughter and smoothed her hair. "We need help. We do not know how to proceed. Besides, it would be dangerous for us to charge into the center alone and unprotected, especially with the drunken revelers there." Her mind raced over the possibilities, but her heart had already decided. "I will go to the mine and get the Captain. He will take the letters to the proper authorities." Though her own nerves seared at the idea of going out alone, she feared even more that Beatriz would charge out the door herself. Better for the mother to be endangered than the child.

Admiration shone in the girl's eyes.

"I will go with you," she declared.

Gemita whimpered.

"No," Pilar said, and seeing her daughter's need, gave Beatriz her own heroic role, as if it were the most natural thing in the world for a mother to say to her daughter. "The papers must be kept safe. We cannot take them with us and expose them to theft. You must stay here and guard them while I go to get your father." Pilar prayed the girl would accept the idea, meant only to protect her.

"I will," Beatriz said. "I will keep a sword at my side. Domingo taught me to use one when I was just a child." She leapt to the door. "I will saddle your horse, Mother."

Gemita helped Pilar out of her high-heeled shoes, corset, and exaggerated hoop skirt. She put on a riding habit she had not worn in years and blessed the altitude of Potosí that kept matrons like her as slender as girls. At the last moment, she took one of Antonio's vicuña cloaks and swung it about her.

Beatriz was waiting in the yard with the horse. Pilar mounted and waited while the girls lifted the plank that barred the gate.

"Barricade yourselves in and open for no one but the Captain and myself."

"Go with God, Mother," Beatriz called.

Pilar blessed herself and urged the horse out into the deserted street and uphill, away from the center, in the direction of the mine. She heard the gate shut behind her. The girls would be safe behind the stout stone walls of the *ingenio*, she told herself.

In the clear Andean night, even with the light of the Easter moon, she could barely make her way. She had never ridden out at night in her life. Her pulse beat with fear and excitement. Fortunately, the road was smooth and easy to follow. It led her toward a place she had gone to only once a year—for the ceremony of the blessing—when the Bishop prayed for the mine and the miners and seemed to be praying for wealth, the way the priests at home in Spain prayed for a good harvest.

The maids said the Indians had their own ceremony, that they sacrificed a llama and sprinkled its blood at the mine's entrance to evict evil spirits and ask their gods for a rich vein of silver. Santiago Yana had died there. Rosa said her husband was murdered because of a packet of papers. *"Oh, Dios mío!"* The words were either an oath or a prayer. Pilar did not know which.

She murmured prayers and kicked the poor beast beneath her, urging it go faster and faster until its great flanks heaved with its effort to breathe in the thin, nearly absent air.

21

Beatriz suppressed a laugh. "Not that one," she said. "That's just for ceremonies. It wouldn't cut butter."

Gemita put the sword with the jewel-encrusted hilt back into the cabinet. "I know that. I just wanted to see if you did."

Beatriz took her father's best German saber for herself and handed Gemita a light fencing sword. Certainly they would never have to fight. Surely her father and Domingo would return in time to protect her. Still, she took a perverse pleasure in pretending to Gemita that they would have to defend the house as the Cid might defend a castle. They went up to the second floor, to the balcony overlooking the interior patio. "We'll wait here, where we can see them if they enter and have the advantage of them if they try to come up the stairs."

"Maybe we should go out into the *ingenio* yard to hide among the Indians." Gemita was holding her sword limply, as if it were a flower or a feather.

"The Indians are all gone to the mine—men and women, whoever was here—to help with the rescue."

Gemita's eyes filled with tears. "Then we really are alone. Totally alone."

Beatriz gripped her sword more tightly. "Don't worry. My bro— My father's *mayordomo* taught me to fight when I was a girl."

"But—"

"Shh." Beatriz put her fingers to Gemita's lips. "I heard something out in the street."

They crept through the sitting room to the balcony that overlooked the side street. As quietly as she could, Beatriz went out on hands and knees. She rose slowly and peered over the balustrade. Down in the flickering light of the torches, she saw only a lone, drunken Mestizo, wrapped in a big cape, his black hat askew, staggering toward the corner. She put a hand on Gemita's shoulder. "It's no one," she said, and went back inside.

Padre Junipero rounded the corner, lurched along the *ingenio* wall, and approached the front entrance of the Casa Tovar. Spiraling bands gave the columns on either side of the door a twisted appearance that seemed to writhe in the flickering torchlight. The place was ghostly quiet. The priest glanced up and down the street and saw no one. He was about to ring the bell when whispering voices froze him in his tracks. He backed into the shadows, sweating despite the cold wind.

Down the Calle Cortez, at the end of the street, at least two dozen men were approaching. As they drew closer, the priest saw the Alcalde and his guard and a crowd of motley thugs. Two of them carried the long, thick trunk of a kehuiña tree—the kind of log the town burned in the bonfires in the plazas.

The priest drew breath to call out and raise an alarm in the house, but an iron hand from nowhere covered his mouth. His assailant clamped a burly arm around him and held him fast. Junipero struggled uselessly and watched, helpless, as men came from the rear of the Alcalde's squadron and, after raising two ladders against the low wall of the outer patio, quickly gained entry and opened the postern to let in the others. They were as quiet as nuns in a cloister.

The priest banged his elbows against the hard body that held him. The man smelled of acrid sweat and *chicha*.

New whispers from behind distracted his attacker, who spun them both around to see a small band of noble youths carrying guitars and dressed in capes decorated with ribbons, of the kind young men wore to serenade beneath a lady's balcony. The priest grasped the forearms of his attacker and jerked his own body forward, lifting the man off his feet, and fell forward, crashing them both to the ground. He slipped sideways to elude his attacker's lunge, threw off his hat and cape, and showed himself.

"Help!" he called.

"Priest!" the thug spat out as he rose.

Junipero kicked the man's face with all his might and ran for the serenaders. "In the name of Santiago, help me!"

The thug followed, but two of the young men tripped him and held him down.

"You must help me defend this house, which is under attack," the priest implored.

"How can we, Padre?" said a tall man a little older than the others, a stranger to the priest. He held up a guitar. "We have come armed only with our music."

The drunk out in the street shouted, but before Beatriz could go and have another look, an explosion so loud and sudden that it made her scream came from the outer patio. The sword Gemita was holding clattered to the floor. With the second crash, Beatriz knew. "They are inside the outer wall. They are battering the door of the high inner wall." The crashes came one after the other, and in between, the sounds of men shouting. Still gripping her saber, Beatriz picked up the fencing sword and handed it again to Gemita. "We will have to fight." This has to be fantasy, she thought.

Gemita began to wail. "We cannot. I cannot. How can we fight?"

"The Abbess will die if we do not. We will die." They would die anyway.

The crashing continued. The right-hand door began to move.

"Hide. We have to hide behind the bed curtains." Gemita's voice was now three octaves higher than her normal squeak.

"They will find us."

A huge crash, and the door began to splinter. Gemita dropped her sword again.

"Go," Beatriz commanded. "Get the packet of letters and go to the balcony of the sitting room."

The door cracked with a huge explosion of wood on wood.

"*Now!*" Beatriz screamed. She shoved Gemita in the direction of her room. "Bring that long green silk ribbon. Go. *Go!*"

She picked up Gemita's sword and stood with the saber in one hand and the sword in the other. Her heart and stomach and knees all trembled with each thud. A huge log crashed through the door, and a gauntleted hand reached in. Men came in, wearing armor and helmets bearing the red plume of the Alcalde's guard.

Gemita came screaming down the hall and into the sitting room, trailing the ribbon.

"Up there!" a man shouted from the patio. More men were pouring through the door. Panting, Beatriz waited until the first two were at the bottom of the steps, and then, still holding the swords, with the heels of her hands she launched her mother's stone planters off the balustrade directly on them. They howled.

Without looking to see the damage she had done, she ran into the sitting room and slammed and bolted the door. "Quickly, move the furniture over here." She put down the swords and with Gemita piled five heavy chairs in front of the door.

"To the balcony."

Gemita opened the French door. Beatriz took the packet of letters and strapped them to her body with the ribbon. She took up the swords again as something slammed against the corridor door. "Out."

She followed Gemita onto the balcony. "Jump!" she commanded.

Gemita screamed. "There are men down there."

Beatriz gasped. *"Oh, Dios."* The oath slipped out.

"Jump, Gemita. We will catch you." It was Padre Junipero's voice.

"Thank you, God," Beatriz whispered. Facing the door, a sword in each hand, she glanced back over the balustrade and saw four men holding a cape. Gemita climbed up but hesitated. Beatriz shoved her off. Inside the sitting room, the door was opening.

Beatriz clambered up to the balustrade, still gripping the swords.

"Throw me the weapons," called a tall man standing to the side, next to the priest.

She dropped the saber.

The man leapt aside, covering his head. "Hilt first!" he screamed.

She let the other one go.

The men at the sitting room door crashed through and spilled onto the floor. Beatriz leapt. The hem of her broad skirt caught on something and she found herself upside down, dangling over the open cape. She yanked at the skirt, but it would not come free. Morada's men were on the balcony, grabbing for her. She swung herself away and kicked at their hands. The cloth began to rip at last. She swung harder and slowly, with the ripping of her skirt, fell into the cape. A man above her had climbed onto the balustrade of the balcony and was about to leap into the street.

"Leave the swords and take the girls away from danger," Padre Junipero called to the tall man, who tossed the swords to the others, grabbed Gemita and Beatriz by their hands, and ran down the Calle de la Paz in the direction of the Ribera.

Shouts and clanging of steel echoed behind them. They ran and ran until they reached the Bridge of San Sebastián. Gemita was out of breath and stumbling. The man stopped. "Rest a moment." He put his hand in his doublet and drew out a hand-kerchief and gave it to Gemita.

Beatriz shivered in the wind that whistled down the narrow streets. The man took off his beautiful cloak of double taffeta and wrapped it around both girls. Footsteps pounded on the stones in the dark street behind them. "Come," he said, "we must run."

In the middle of the bridge, a criminal's head had been left on a pike as a warning to others. Gemita looked up at it and began to scream uncontrollably and would not walk past it. Beatriz threw the cloak over her head and dragged her.

A pursuer charged them from behind. Their protector, whoever he was, feinted to avoid the slash of the guardsman's sword and with a lithe and graceful gesture, like the step of a courtly dance, tripped him and pounced on him. The two men rolled over. The assailant's weapon threatened their unarmed protector's throat. Beatriz slipped out from under the cape and charged, kicking at the side of the attacker's head with the sharp heel of her shoe. He groaned, and their protector got the better of him. In seconds, the guardsman was over the side of the bridge and in the water. The tall man had the sword.

"Run. Run!" he commanded.

More footsteps followed, but when they reached the other end of the bridge, the Calle San Benito was crowded with people marching in the *mascarada*. Suddenly, the breathless girls were surrounded by people in colorful disguises and regional costumes. Laughing men and women dressed as historical or mythological characters. Looming next to Gemita was a huge fat man dressed as the infidel Turk. His white, bejeweled turban was askew, and his droopy fake mustache had detached from one side of his face.

"Smile, laugh," their escort said. "Pretend you are here to join the merriment." He glanced often behind him but put his hands on their shoulders and pretended to joke. When they reached the Calle Zarate, he turned them, following a band of revelers to the Plaza del Gato. The heat from a bonfire in the plaza warmed them, and they sat for a moment on one of the

stone benches. Candles burned in the windows and on the balconies. Their guardian watched down the street for their pursuers
and scanned the other entrances to the plaza. "I think we are safe
for the moment," he said.

Beatriz gazed up at him. He was a soldier, she was sure,
well proportioned, with a proud line to his jaw and black hair
that shone in the firelight. There was something about this
man, his voice. She ransacked her memory. His hand still lay
on her shoulder, like the hand of a guardian angel in a painting
in church. Warmth and comfort spread from it and infused her
thoughts, which were so powerful that she thought they must
perfume the air around her. She was certain he sensed them.

"Where are you taking us?"

"To my godmother's house. Let us go." He led them to the
home of the Marquesa de Otavi. He rang the bell and was immediately let into the outer courtyard. "Don't tell my aunt about the
danger," the man whispered as he pulled the bell cord. "I don't
want to worry her. Her health is delicate."

The Marquesa herself came to the door of her palace to give
them welcome and usher them in.

"Aunt, please shelter these young ladies I found in distress. I
will return presently." He took a sword and a heavy cape from a
shelf there in the entryway and quickly left.

The elegant old lady ushered Beatriz and Gemita to a
chamber on the second floor decorated with tapestries from
France and Persian rugs. "You are the Tovar girl," she said to
Beatriz. She touched Gemita's red and puffy eyes. "Lie here on
these couches. My maid will bring you some maté."

In a dank stone cellar, Mother Maria did her best to chant her
prayers. She wanted to calm Eustacia, who like her was chained
to a wall. "*Gloria Patri et Filio—*" Her voice cracked. She waited
for Sor Eustacia's beautiful contralto to respond. Pray. They had
to pray. Prayer was their only hope.

"I cannot stay chained to this wall." Eustacia jerked and beat the heavy iron links against the brick. "I will go mad."

Tears flowed from the Abbess's eyes. Eustacia seemed already mad. *"Et Spiritui Sancto."* She chanted the response herself and went on, focusing her thoughts on the words, words that could drive away all thought.

"Yes," Eustacia moaned. "This is the way it was in the beginning, is now, and ever shall be. Men abusing me. Men torturing me." She continued to beat the chains in an odd bass rhythm to her Abbess's chant.

"Et in saecula saeculorum." Maria Santa Hilda rocked her body. *"Et in saecula saeculorum."* She repeated the words over and over, unable to keep away their piercing truth. World without end. Pain without end. Fear without end. *Saecula saeculorum.* Unending misery. Only death would remove it. Death on the pyre. Death that could lead to the flames of hell. *"Credo in unum Deum,"* she chanted. "I believe in one God."

"I do not believe. Not in a God who allows me to suffer so."

Maria Santa Hilda condemned herself. So renowned for her intelligence, she had let her pride blind her. It had taken her too long to see the truth. Now she knew nothing of how the wheels she had set in motion turned. Had Sor Monica found the evidence inside the convent? Had the padre gotten the letter? She might never know. She struggled to focus on prayer. "Sister, please try to quiet yourself. We may yet be released."

Eustacia, suddenly still, glared at her and then, like a ghost in a nightmare, stood, her arms weighed down by the chains hanging at her sides. She howled, a deep, crushing cry that sounded as if it came from the bowels of the earth.

The long day of festivities wore on for Nestares. Finally, past midnight, his hosts took him to the Calle de Contraste and the home of Don Francisco Gambarte, the finest house in the city.

Its own opulent furnishings had, in the past few days, been augmented with items borrowed from other noble houses of the city six gorgeous settees and a splendid bed hung with scarlet silk.

There, after nineteen hours of continuous adulation, Nestares was finally allowed to retire into the arms of Doña Ilena Nieves, the most beautiful, and skillful, of Potosí's scores of courtesans.

On Easter Monday night of 1650, Doña Ilena's task was the ecstasy of the Visitador, but the exhausted Nestares welcomed her soft body as a source of warmth rather than stimulation. In her naked arms, he fell immediately into a deep, nearly comatose sleep.

In another part of the house, the Cape Verde slave in whose place the beautiful courtesan slept prepared to retire. She thought of the white flesh that yielded to her master and lover. She laid out her best green silk dress for the morning and beside it, in the hopes of the signal from the Alcalde, the packet of deadly herbs she had received from Captain Ramirez.

CHAPTER

22

Well past midnight, in the second-floor hall of the convent, at the only small window that overlooked the field next door, the Sister Herbalist had been more than an hour at difficult work. The other sisters would soon rise for the third Nocturne—the last of the prayers during the night. She had to be gone before they assembled.

She forced her frozen, stinging hands to continue to saw at the lock that she had always thought kept intruders out but that she now realized also kept her in. She pressed her fear into the sawing motion of the rasp, and the lock finally gave way.

"Vitallina," she whispered to the big woman who dozed on the floor at her feet, "wake." She poked her assistant's flank.

Vitallina started. "Yes, Sister." Her voice was thick with sleep.

"Do you have the red pepper?"

"Yes. In the sack with the cat."

Monica herself carried the vial with the poison and the two flails wrapped in many folds of linen to make sure they pricked no one. They were rolled up in the apron of the maid's uniform she wore.

She swung open the iron gate that barred the windows of the upper storage room and looked out on the vacant field behind the rear cloister. Clouds obscured the moon. What little light there was painted a terrifying picture of rocks and shadows and desolation. She climbed out onto the roof.

A tile let go. She lost her footing and slid to the edge. She did not make a sound. "Throw the rope," she whispered to Vitallina. "Dear Mother of God, protect us," she murmured.

Her assistant tied the rope fast to the window grate and dropped it to her. The Sister Herbalist grasped it. "When I reach the bottom, you follow," she whispered. She lowered herself to the ground. "Now."

Just as Vitallina started down, the distant pealing of the convent bell startled them both. "Hurry," the Sister Herbalist urged.

A cracking noise from above stopped Vitallina at the edge of the roof. "It is giving way. The window ledge is rotted," the big woman whimpered. "I cannot do it."

"Close your eyes," Sor Monica whispered. "I will come to help you." She grasped the rope and started to climb. The wood above gave a great crack and sounded as if it would have split if Monica had not dropped immediately to the ground.

"I am going back," Vitallina called. "I cannot do it."

"Please, you must come with me. I hardly know my way around the town. I have never been out alone."

"Forgive me." Vitallina had already climbed back to the window.

As Monica waited bereft at the bottom of the outside wall, the rope was pulled up and then dropped back down. At the end of it was the cloth bag containing the dead cat and a packet of ground red pepper, as if they were the ingredients for a bizarre stew. The window closed.

Monica stood there motionless for the space of a credo. At last, she recovered her own resolve. She took the bag, ran across the Campo del San Clemente, and slipped away into the night.

The Alcalde was relentless. He was the most powerful, the richest man in the richest city on earth. He had amassed a king's ransom. He had tracked the infamous Chocta, found and arrested hundreds of wily Mestizos. No mere silly girls in the company of some effeminate swain would elude him.

That interfering youth's friends—typical of their thin noble blood—ran off once they saw they were outnumbered. The priest might know where the girls had gone, but the Alcalde's guardsmen had come to the point of almost drowning him in the frigid river that powered the mills and still he would not talk. They finally gave up and threw him into the water to certain death.

The Alcalde sent his men to all parts of the city to look for the girls and their protector. In the meanwhile, Morada set out to learn the identities of those young serenaders. They were strangers to him and therefore most likely had entered the city this morning with Nestares.

A place under the Alcalde's heart trembled, a tiny place that seemed like the center of his anger, the source of his rage and power. His essence was evaporating. His life could be over.

But Spanish men did not think such thoughts. The sons of Conquistadores were fearless.

The Alcalde gripped the hilt of the sword at his side and with the captain of his guard, his stalwart Carlos, awaited news of the whereabouts of his daughter and her naughty friend.

He did not have to wait long.

Beatriz and Gemita waited in the upper room where the Marquesa had left them. Beatriz examined the appointments.

The house was all luxury. She ran her fingers across the polished surface of a beautiful Flemish desk. She picked up a Venetian glass bottle and opened it. It held the same perfume from Arabia that scented the tall stranger's beautiful taffeta cloak, which lay now over the couch where Gemita reclined.

"I think this is the antechamber to his bedroom," Beatriz said. She opened the *armario* that stood next to the door. It contained a man's clothing. "Look at this beautiful English hat." She took it out and put it on.

"I wouldn't wear a Protestant hat." Gemita still dabbed at her nose with the stranger's linen-and-lace handkerchief.

Beatriz wished she had been the one to receive it. It would be wrong, but she wanted to keep it, as a token of him. "He must look so dashing in this hat," she said wistfully.

Gemita sat up. "I thought you were in love with Domingo Barco."

"That's silly. Where would you learn such a thing?"

"From Inez. He was her lover. He told her that you fancied yourself in love with him."

Beatriz ignored the flush that rose from her chest to her throat. "That is nonsense." She doffed the hat, swept it across her body, and bowed in the fine gesture of a cavalier. "I would rather be in love with a handsome stranger who smells of perfume from Araby." His voice. In the shadowy streets, she had not seen him clearly, but she knew his voice from somewhere.

Gemita tucked his handkerchief in her sleeve. "What is going to happen to us?"

Beatriz put down the hat. The packet of letters was still tied to her waist with the green ribbon. She undid it. "I don't know. We must get these letters to the Visitador. They are the only proof that the Abbess is innocent." A plan began to form in her mind.

"Do you think the Marquesa's nephew will come back for us," Gemita asked, "and help us take the letters to Nestares?"

"He doesn't know about the letters." A nasty suspicion ambushed Beatriz. Suppose that tall, graceful man owed allegiance to the Alcalde. Suppose he had brought them here to keep them out of the way. They would fall into the same trap they hoped to escape. "We must leave here now, Gemita. It is nearly dawn. We must take these letters and go directly to the Visitador."

"Are you crazy? Two girls cannot go out in the dark alone."

Beatriz took the hat and put it on Gemita's head. "We will not be two girls."

They stripped to their fine linen undergarments and took the stranger's clothing out of the *armario*. Their breasts were already bound according to the fashion of the day to make them appear flat-chested. They put on tunics and Neapolitan hose and shoes, doublets, and mail shirts. Gemita refused the English hat, which Beatriz gladly wore, giving her friend a good Spanish one of white beaver. They took two fine Toledo swords, stout bucklers, and pistols for each, which neither knew how to operate.

"Everything is too big, especially the gloves and shoes," Gemita complained.

"Pull the belt tight, like this. Here." She knotted a sash snugly around Gemita's waist, took a pair of stockings from the *armario* shelf, and shoved them into the toes of the boots. She shoved the packet of letters inside her own coat, then slipped out into the dark corridor. Gemita followed.

The house was silent, but just as they reached the top of the stairs, a sudden pounding sounded at the postern, raising the hall servant, who shouted up the steps, "My lady... my lady. It is the Alcalde and his guard." The Marquesa was nowhere to be seen.

"My father!" Gemita's voice shook.

Beatriz pushed her back through the room where they had dressed and into the adjoining bedchamber. Then she tore a sheet from the bed, tied it to the bedpost, and threw it out the window. While the Alcalde and his henchmen swarmed over the house, the girls they sought slid down the sheet to the roof of a stable and thence to the street.

Once outside, they had no idea where to go. In an hour or so they could go to the Alcaldía to find Nestares. Until then, where could they shelter themselves?

They moved quickly away from the Marquesa's house around to the Calle Zarate. At the deserted corner of the Calle de Santo Domingo, they encountered a cart heaped with skulls, left from the penitential parades of Good Friday.

"We have to go where boys go and pray we are not discovered," Beatriz whispered.

They made their way to the Tianguez, where vendors, scriveners, and sextons gathered during the day and where the bullfighting ring was erected during Christmas. Beatriz had always imagined it was where young men congregated while good girls were safe behind the draperies of their beds.

In the dark of this awful night, the square was deserted. The weak moonlight and the torches burning on the buildings cast grotesque shadows. A shutter flapping in the wind thudded and echoed off the façades of the dark buildings. The girls went to warm themselves near a dying bonfire. They barely spoke. Beatriz patted Gemita's shoulder from time to time while they huddled inside their heavy masculine cloaks and waited.

Suddenly, just as dawn was breaking, three men entered from the Calle de Copacabaña. They drew their weapons and charged toward the two slight young boys who lingered beside the near dead embers in the corner of the square.

CHAPTER

23

At dawn, the bell ringing resumed, continuing the festival to welcome Nestares. The church wardens around the city were taking their turns so that from first light until midnight, the sound of bells could be heard.

Just as the pealing started, stern soldier-priests entered the secret prison near the Augustinian monastery and unchained the Abbess of the Convent of Santa Isabella de los Santos Milagros and her sister accused. They took the two frightened women to join the procession along the Calle Zarate to the Church of Santo Domingo. Though the Inquisitor General de la Gasca was a man of severely simple and elegant tastes, he had approved this pomp and ostentation for the opportunity of making an impression on the popular mind. The faithful must be shown the rewards of goodness and the punishment of evil.

Seven Potosino noblemen led the parade, richly dressed, mounted on white horses, and carrying palms of victory. Behind them were the Inquisitor and the officers of the Tribunal, followed by Commissioner DaTriesta and his prisoners, guarded by armed and armored priests.

Maria Santa Hilda walked beside Sor Eustacia and sought to bear the yellow robe with dignity. She held her head high and forced herself to look at the buildings and into the eyes of the observers as she passed. Blessedly, at this early hour, on the morning after raucous reveling, the streets were nearly empty.

The Abbess gazed up at the Cerro, barely visible against the dark gray sky. When she had first arrived in the City of Silver, that same year, a large earthquake had destroyed almost the entire city of Cuzco and its surroundings. The night of the earthquake, a ball of fire appeared in Potosí, coming from the hills of Caricari and exploding at the summit of the Muynaypata with such force that it shattered all the pines and knocked down the Indian ranches on the bordering hills. If such an event happened now, what would these men who accused her make of it? That God's wrath was warning them that they threatened two innocent women? No. They would see in it more proof that these women were instruments of Satan who placed the faithful on the brink of eternal damnation.

When the marchers reached the church, Maria Santa Hilda took Sor Eustacia to a corner and tried to comfort her. In these past two days, the Abbess had come to believe that Eustacia's silence and devotion, which the Abbess had always admired, covered a reservoir of anger hotter than the ovens that smelted the ore, in danger of exploding, like the volcanic mountains out in the cordillera. The Abbess understood some of the ingredients of Eustacia's boiling cauldron of rage, and she forgave her, but she wondered why, with all that she herself had suffered, she was not mad as well.

Meanwhile, in the main part of the church, the trial of some priests proceeded quickly. From what the Abbess could hear, they were accused of solicitation—the crime of seducing women in the confessional. Presently, five friars left the main church, passed through the vestibule, and exited by the street door. Their hoods covered their faces, and their arms were folded into their sleeves.

The cords that they ordinarily kept about their waists were hung around their necks to indicate their guilt. They seemed strong and young, but they marched gravely behind a solemn friar whose face was also covered but who had the frail step of an old man and wore his cord around his waist.

DaTriesta came to usher the Abbess and Sor Eustacia before the Tribunal. His long arms gestured dramatically, as if he were preparing for the dance of the Moors and the Christians.

The two women entered the main church, where three Inquisitors sat on a dais under a canopy of green velvet lined with blue silk, making it seem as if they were under a perpetually sunny sky. A life-size crucifix hung from the shallow dome above them. The table in front of them was covered with the same green velvet trimmed in blue. Candles burned at either end, and there was a large tome covered in green leather tooled with gold. Except for de la Gasca, who sat in the center, the seated men were strangers to Maria Santa Hilda. The thin, pale ascetic on the right reminded her of her father's confessor—a severe and humorless man. He glanced at her and turned away in disgust, as if she were a plate of mutton that he found greasy and unappetizing. On the left sat a heavy, sweating man with a black stubble of badly shaved beard, jet eyes in his fleshy face. He was probably more interested in his next meal than he was in her guilt or innocence. In the center, the dangerous de la Gasca—perfectly groomed, with his beautiful complexion and an expression completely devoid of emotion. His mind was sharp and precise, like the movements of his thin, immaculate hands as they arranged the pen and inkstand before him. He was a man who saw a straight line between right and wrong, like the perfect seams in the black and white marble squares beneath the Abbess's feet. He looked at the Abbess, and she saw doom in his eyes.

The Tribunal that prepared to judge the Abbess would have immediately arrested Sor Monica for witchcraft had they found her where she hid in the Jesuit cemetery under a cape, with a dead cat and some hot pepper in a bag. The beads she fingered, the prayers on her lips, would have only incriminated her more. Her one hope would have been to be considered mad rather than evil. She was not sure herself.

She had no plan except to get her evidence to the Visitador. She expected the Holy Ghost to guide her to that end.

As dawn broke, she stood and painfully straightened her stiff limbs, smoothed the maid's uniform, and invoked inspiration. *"Veni Creator Spiritus,"* she chanted under her breath as she carried her sack toward the Alcaldía.

Beatriz unsheathed her cutlass. The men who rushed at them stopped but did not seem intimidated.

"Boy," one of them demanded, "have you seen two girls?" He wore several buff waistcoats, and his hair hung limp and dirty around his shoulders. He was missing several teeth.

Beatriz made her voice deep. "No." She tried to sound decisive.

His companions, members of Captain Morada's guard, grabbed Gemita. "And you, young sir?" one of them growled.

Gemita began to wail. She put her hand under her cape and took the pistol and fired. The shot hit one of the guardsmen, broke through his armor, jacket, and jerkin. He fell to the ground.

Gemita shrieked.

With all her might, Beatriz swung her sword at the scruffy thug in front of her. She hit his arm with the flat of it. He looked stunned. She grabbed Gemita, and as the other guardsmen knelt over their comrade, they ran down the twisting, narrow streets of the silversmiths and silk traders to the broad avenue where great mansions towered, with coats of arms over their doors. Footsteps followed them, and Gemita hollered continually, "I killed him… I killed him."

As they reached the Plaza la Merced, one of the men behind them came so close, Beatriz could hear his panting. She glanced back and saw him only a score of paces behind. When he was practically on top of her, she fell to one knee and thrust her sword up at him with all her might. The point went in through the man's throat and came out the back of his neck. He fell dead on the paving stones.

At that moment, the Alcalde's remaining guardsmen entered the Plaza Mayor just as Beatriz and Gemita scrambled down the Calle Real and into the plaza from the other end. A group of men had congregated in front of the Alcaldía. Beatriz went toward them, hoping to find help, and then realized they were members of the Cabildo. She and Gemita barely had time to change direction when the men who pursued them entered the square and began to shout.

"Run away, Gemita!" Beatriz yelled, and she charged one of the guardsmen, swinging her sword with both hands with fierce blows. The guardsman lunged. The blow struck Beatriz but did not hurt her. Then behind the guardsman, a squadron of Visitador Nestares's guard came into the square from the Calle Luizitana.

Immediately, the Cabildo and the Visitador's guard set upon one another from every direction, making such a din with their weapons that it seemed a hundred men were fighting. Sparks of fire leapt from their swords, the blows they exchanged rang, and voices of the cursing men resounded: "Dog of a Jew!" "Scoundrel!" "Indian!"

In the midst of the fray, Beatriz struck back at the guardsman again and again until her arms burned with pain. Gemita called to her, but she could not turn. The guardsman was pressing her so that she was stumbling backward, barely able to fend off his sword. A woman came near her and swung a sack and hit the opponent repeatedly. Beatriz closed her eyes and swung her sword against the side of his head. He howled and drew back. The woman—a maid from the convent—pulled Beatriz out of the fray.

CHAPTER

24

The light of the rising sun changed the rocks of the Cerro from brown to purple to lavender to pink.

When his footman came to his door and woke him just after dawn, Nestares called out his good morning through the locked door and turned to the warm, smooth-skinned Doña Ilena Nieves beside him. After a night of sound sleep, he found himself quite able to do what had been impossible the night before. He did not disappoint her, nor she him. An hour passed before he reluctantly left the scarlet bed where the courtesan lay drowsing behind the draperies. He called his valet, who helped him dress in a black-on-black brocade doublet, a white and well-fitting collar, and a black velvet cape. At his side, he strapped a sword of the Hidalgo. He looked appropriately elegant and severe.

While Nestares waited for his breakfast, he went to the desk near the window to make notes for the pronouncement he would deliver in a short while at the Alcaldía Municipal. He found a supply of the finest Genoa paper.

The Visitador sat and wrote. He would order the coins of Potosí separated into three parts—O, E, and R, respectively, for Ovando, Ergueta, and Ramirez, the three most recent officials of the Mint. In tests at Lima, the coins of the first had proved real. He would leave them at their full value. The second he would lower from eight to six, according to their assay. The Ramirez coins had proven only two parts silver to five parts copper, but here he decided to be merciful. It was more than the bastards deserved, but he would cut the value of these most recent coins only in half. He would throw this bone to stay the dogs' wrath. He dipped the quill and made a characteristic but unconscious gesture—spiraling the pen in the air as he lowered it to the paper.

While the Visitador wrote, many Potosinos, anticipating Nestares's actions, were already packing their mules to flee the city. As in those periods of hysteria over the outbreak of a plague or the pox or fears that the Caricari dam would break again and wash their houses away, many refugees would soon clog the roads in every direction.

To make matters worse, chaos had broken out in the center of the town. Nestares's chamberlain entered the study to inform him that scores of men were fighting in the main square. In this city where a fight could turn into a brawl, a brawl into a battle, and a battle into a war, it was thought best that the Visitador not venture to the Alcaldía while the fighting went on.

While Nestares arranged another, safer venue for his audience of the morning, a servant of Alcalde Francisco Rojas de la Morada appeared at the kitchen door with breakfast on a silver tray. He said it was for the beautiful Cape Verde lady who served the Visitador and was sent by a secret admirer.

Maria Santa Hilda's gaze took in the marble pillars of the altar, the chairs of Brazil wood, the statues of saints richly carved, but she thought only about her defense. They called this a *proceso*, a trial. Presumably, that meant they had not yet decided her fate. Perhaps she could convince her judges of her innocence. But when she thought about it, her glimmer of hope faded quickly. She had already used up whatever leniency Grand Inquisitor de la Gasca would accord on account of their shared nobility. Her early arrest had proved that.

At this moment, Commissioner DaTriesta was citing the accused Abbess's opinions on women as proof of her Protestant tendencies. The arrogant and ruthless-looking men behind the table listened with great interest. Everyone, rich or poor, powerful or impotent, was at their mercy. They levied fines and used them to build more jails for the people they accused.

Yet de la Gasca was not known to be corrupt, as others in his position had been. He was strict, but he was moral. The right argument might win him.

DaTriesta babbled on, accusing her.

Finally, de la Gasca invited her to respond to the charges against her. The best appeal, she thought, would be to their power, to their importance. "You have so many more critical things to think about, bringing to justice Protestants from captured corsairs, bigamists, adulterers. I am a mere woman who tries her best to care for the tortured souls who find their way to solace in an insignificant convent."

"Come now, Lady Abbess." The fat priest to de la Gasca's right spoke for the first time. "Transparent appeals to our vanity will do you no good here." The flesh of his face trembled as he wagged his head with disapproval.

Sor Eustacia tugged at the Abbess's sleeve. "Let me take the blame," she begged. "I don't care what happens to me. I only care that you should live."

Maria Santa Hilda grasped her sister's hand. "I will speak the truth," she said, as much to her accusers as to Eustacia. "We will tell them the truth, and we will rely on God's mercy." And she prepared to say to the men who would judge her that which she knew they did not want to hear.

An Indian smuggling silver he had stolen from the mine of Don Juan de Borea during the night approached the Bridge of Santiago in the pale first light of that cold day, but what he saw in the center of the span stopped him. Three of the Alcaldea guardsmen waited there, near the head of another Indian thief that rotted on a pike. Pachamama, this was no time to be stopped and searched. Instead of crossing, he descended the bank to where the Indians kept balsa logs, which they used—one under each arm—to cross the swift-flowing water out of sight of the Spanish who guarded the bridge.

As the Indian reached the water's edge, he heard gasping. Within seconds, he had pulled from the water the nearly dead body of a priest he knew to be a friend to his people.

When the Indian tried to question Padre Junipero of the Compañia de Jesus, he found the priest witless, the way people became if they stayed too long in the cold.

Beatriz grasped the hand of the woman in the maid's uniform and looked into her face. "Sor Monica!" They had paused under the arch at the entrance to the Plaza Ghatu.

"I have proof that Inez did not kill herself," the Sister Herbalist said. "I am trying to bring it to the Visitador."

Beatriz patted the packet inside her doublet. "We too have proof, that it was the Alcalde himself who had Inez killed."

Sor Monica blessed herself. "God have mercy on his soul."

Gemita pushed back Beatriz's cloak. "You are bleeding!"

Beatriz felt, for the first time, a stinging in her arm just below the short sleeves of the mail shirt that protected her chest and her shoulders. Sor Monica tore open the shirt and with a piece of the sleeve stanched the blood.

A shout behind them raised the hair on the back of Beatriz's neck. The Alcalde, his sword unsheathed, rushed at them like a madman. Beatriz parried his first blow. The second knocked her off her feet. Her sword dropped from her hand. She lay struggling for breath when the Alcalde's foot pinned her. "Run away!" she shouted to the others.

"Here, you dogs," Morada called over his shoulder to his men.

Beatriz caught her breath, pulled the dagger from the sheath at her waist, and stabbed it into Morada's leg. At the same moment, Sor Monica came near and threw something into the Alcalde's eyes.

He howled and drew back.

A large retinue entered the plaza, headed by the Marquesa's nephew. Gemita screamed to them for help.

When the Visitador was finally able to begin his official duties, he was forced by the chaos that had broken out in the streets to hold his audience in the grand salon of the home of General Juan Velarde Treviño.

Potosí's noblemen shuffled nervously while they awaited the announcement about their currency. Finally, when the impatient Nestares gave up waiting for the arrival of Alcalde de la Morada, he took the sheets of fine vellum handed him by his secretary and read out a long royal *cédula* stating the extent of his authority. The end of the document established the totality of his power: "No appeal will be taken from your definitive judgments in these cases. Given at the city of Barcelona on the twentieth day of November in the year of the birth of our Savior Jesus Christ one thousand six hundred and forty-nine. I the King."

Interrupting that dramatic moment, the Visitador's chamberlain suddenly threw open the door of the salon.

Beatriz Tovar, passing under the lintel carved with a cross in low relief, blessed herself. Gemita and Sor Monica did the same.

The Marquesa's nephew, with a gesture of his plumed hat, ushered them toward a tall man in a black-on-black brocade doublet, who eyed them with a penetrating look. Beatriz bent in a low curtsy made awkward by the men's clothing she wore.

"Explain that salute, young man," the Visitador said sternly.

Beatriz was on the point of removing her cape and revealing her identity when a beautiful maid approached Nestares with a silver tray. Without taking his eyes from Beatriz, the Visitador reached for the gourd of maté on the tray.

Beatriz charged the maid, unsheathed her sword, and slammed it against the bottom of the tray, sending its contents flying and setting the maid to screaming. In half a second, Nestares's attendants had grabbed Beatriz and were holding her facedown on the ground. "Poison," she choked out. "I can prove it."

On her insistence, they let her up. "I am Beatriz Tovar," she said, and heard her own voice so loud and clear in the silent room that it seemed not to come from her own body. It frightened her a little, but she looked right into the astonished face of Nestares and told him her tale. Then Sor Monica joined in and laid out before him the evidence she carried. Even Gemita spoke up to explain where she had found the letters.

The Visitador listened almost impassively. In the end, he said gravely, "If those who are supposed to enforce the law flout the law, there can be no justice." He sent the captain of his guard and a large squadron to arrest the Alcalde de la Morada.

Then he turned to the Marquesa's nephew. "We must go to the Tribunal immediately. Come, all of you. Follow me. Ladies. Rodrigo."

"Rodrigo!" The name escaped Beatriz's lips.

The handsome stranger—she knew him now for the one who had rescued her from the slobbering boy the day she left the convent. Could that have been just yesterday?

He bowed low and smiled into her eyes. "I hope very soon

to make your acquaintance properly. Your father has hoped for many months to introduce us. I never imagined a woman as beautiful as you could be as brave."

A blush began down beneath Beatriz's trousers and spread over her belly.

CHAPTER
25

At the lofty stone Church of Santo Domingo, before the dais of the Holy Tribunal, Maria Santa Hilda stood on aching legs and wondered at the slow, meticulous process that marched her relentlessly toward her doom. The cool, painstaking priests at the table went about their work so carefully, listening politely to DaTriesta's accusations, nodding while de la Gasca read out, in a bored voice, from his tome the testimony of Beatriz Tovar, Monica, and Sor Olga. Bit by bit, they built their case that gave facts but no truth. Their underlying method lent an air of calm reason, of well-informed and carefully considered logic, to the violence she knew they wanted to do to her and to Eustacia. They followed rules, observed the laws. They had no cause to doubt what they were doing. No one—not the King, not the Pope, not Almighty God—could fault the way they saw to their duty.

Thoughts tempted her. To condemn, as Eustacia had, the God these men purported to represent on earth. Her sister accused stood beside her, clenching and unclenching her fists, mumbling incoherently. Anyone watching her might have thought she was praying, but standing so near her, the Abbess caught the odd phrase—"wait for you in hell," "spawn of Satan"—that revealed Eustacia's terrified and terrifying thoughts.

With a loud bang and a shout from the guards at the door, de la Gasca stopped reading and looked up; his face lost its bored expression. The Abbess turned to see a large group striding toward them, led by a well-dressed, rather pointy man she had never seen before. He must have been important because two of the three priests seated at the table rose to their feet. De la Gasca remained seated and looked annoyed. As the intruders gathered near the dais, Mother Maria was astonished to realize that two of the lads in the group were really Beatriz Tovar and Gemita de la Morada, dressed in men's clothing and accompanied by one of the maids from the convent. But wait! Not a maid. Dear Lord, it was Monica in a maid's uniform. What madness for her to appear here, before these priests, in that attire.

De la Gasca spoke. "Your Lordship Doctor Nestares, I take it that some tremendously urgent business brings you to this holy sanctuary to interrupt God's work." Still seated, he showed no sign of deference, though the man before him must be the Visitador General.

For a split second, they faced each other—the embodiments of civil and ecclesiastical power, each obviously expecting some honorific from the other. Then the Visitador bowed. "Though you are about God's work, Your Grace," he said, "I must interrupt, for I bring facts before you that I think may alter your verdict in the case of these ladies." He looked into Mother Maria's eyes and bowed again, to her. Through all of this, Eustacia did not move and never desisted from her mumbling.

Nestares approached de la Gasca so that he towered over him. The Visitador motioned to the standing priests to retake their seats, and then he himself presented to the Tribunal the evidence to prove that Inez was murdered and that the Abbess Maria Santa Hilda was innocent of blasphemy.

Before the judges had a moment to digest what they had

heard, Fray DaTriesta stepped forward. "The Abbess is still a heretic and a Protestant," he asserted. "She did not have this proof when she buried the girl. Therefore, regardless of the facts, she sinned and should be punished."

The Abbess in her sinner's robes sought to affect an air of great dignity. "Your Grace," she addressed de la Gasca, "I believe in many things for which I have no proof. This does not make them false nor me foolish."

"Leave us, all of you," de la Gasca commanded.

The accused and their defenders began to file away. DaTriesta remained. "You, too, Fray DaTriesta," de la Gasca murmured.

Pulling Sor Eustacia with her, the Abbess followed them into the vestibule of the church, where Sor Monica began to explain herself. Maria Santa Hilda stayed her words, lest she give the lurking local Commissioner some new accusation with which to torture them.

Inside the church, de la Gasca and his fellow Inquisitors discussed not only the evidence against the Abbess, but also her lengthy and distinguished pedigree. In the end, they exonerated her.

When all had reassembled and the verdict was announced, DaTriesta reacted with pique and disappointment, looking like a diner at a cruel banquet who, when the cover is lifted from his plate, realizes his dish is empty.

"The convent will pay the cost of the trial," de la Gasca pronounced. He turned to the Abbess. "You are released. Misfortune is God's way of bringing us to Himself."

"Your Grace," she addressed de la Gasca, and indicated Sor Eustacia, "I plead for—"

De la Gasca held up an elegant hand. "Her fate is in God's hands," he said with great sanctimony.

"But—"

The raised hand did not move. "Go now," he insisted. "Further defense of her will be taken as heresy."

The Abbess drew herself up, ready to take the risk for her sister.

Eustacia drew near and squeezed the Abbess's hands in her powerful grip. "Go immediately. Remember who I was. Always remember." She dropped to her knees.

"I will do what I can from behind the scenes," the Abbess whispered.

"Just remember who I was."

The Abbess drew Eustacia to her feet and kissed her on both cheeks and blessed her with the sign of the cross. She took the yellow robe from her own shoulders and dropped it to the floor. She walked slowly from the church. No notation of her arrest ever appeared in the annals of the Holy Tribunal.

In the days that followed, Nestares arrested Captain Francisco Rojas de la Morada, Ramirez, the Tester of the Currency, Don Luis de Vila, Don Melchior de Escobedo, and forty other Treasury ministers. He confiscated the account books of Morada's daily transactions. Men who might support or aid Morada in escape or rebellion were disarmed and held under guard in their houses.

Three days after his arrest, Francisco Rojas de la Morada was called to the great Council Hall of the Alcaldía to be sentenced. He strode in, fully resplendent in his best gold-brocaded doublet and crimson-lined cape of Neapolitan silk. He assumed the same posture of command that had been his wont when he presided over this room as Alcalde. At his side, his fellow conspirator Ramirez walked more tentatively, like a man already being led to meet his fate. Neither of them bore a sword. The guard who followed them, however, was fully armed.

Nestares occupied the gold throne at the end of the room—a place that until seven days ago had belonged to Morada. The man who had sat in judgment was here to be judged.

Down the left side of the room, in the chairs normally occupied by his allies on the Cabildo, Morada's enemies had been brought in to gloat over his defeat and disgrace. There near the front of the room, that smug bastard Tovar scowled, as if he saw a spider he meant to squash.

Morada gave him an evil glance that he meant to poison Tovar's heart and then turned and glared into the small, cruel eyes of Nestares. His resolve wavered. His fate was sealed. In truth, he did not wish to escape it. His precious world of wealth and privilege had disintegrated. Inez, his beloved, his beautiful Inez had been the agent of his downfall. Once she had begun to betray him, every step he took to stem the acid that ate away at his crown of perfect power had only heated up and speeded his destruction. On that awful night, he had intercepted the stolen letters, hoping that would stop her. But the virago had run to the convent and threatened him from there. Oh, God, how could she have forced him to do what he had never wanted to do?

The Visitador examined him from foot to forehead, as if measuring him for a coffin. Morada did not move a muscle. He made himself into a statue of a knight. He would take this. His dignity, his honor, were everything.

"Francisco Rojas de la Morada"—the Visitador intoned his name in as loud a voice as if he were calling him from across a valley—"upon examining the evidence, I have decided that you have defrauded the royal Mint of four hundred and seventy-two thousand pesos. I declare you guilty of the crime of treason. You have also been accused of the murder of your daughter Inez de la Morada, but you are exonerated of killing her. Her death was your right, because she dishonored you. This court finds you innocent of any guilt in that matter. I call upon these nobles of the Villa Imperial of Potosí to affirm my judgment and to swear their fealty to King Felipe."

Don Baltazar Andres y Sotomayor, whom Nestares had appointed the next Alcalde, began to rise from his chair at the head of the line along the wall.

Morada, who had willed himself a statue, suddenly burst forward. "Dogs! Bastards!" he shouted at the men along the wall. "The King! You would execute me for what I did to the King. It is for the wrong crime. My child is the one who should be avenged. Not the King. The King takes too much. A mule would be able to see that. We should have taken it all from him. It is ours. We are the ones who suffer living in this godforsaken place. It should be ours. Inez saw that. Even she saw that. Oh, my Inez. You condemn—"

The guard was on him, dragging him away. "Bastards," he raged. "Dogs! Jews! You are condemning me for the wrong crime. Taking my daughter's life. That was my crime." He continued to rage, and his bellowing echoed in the halls of the Alcaldía and the streets of the city until he was locked in a cell under the Mint.

Nine days later, when Morada was brought to justice, his vast fortune in silver was declared to be confiscated, but no one knew where it was, and he went, with his faithful Ramirez, to be garroted refusing to tell.

Many citizens of the City of Silver mourned their Alcalde. He had stolen enough so that he could be generous with those who might have envied him—unlike some poor wretch who does not steal as much and must go to his punishment unloved. In the grip of the people's abhorrence at the death of Morada and the depreciation of their money, they attacked Nestares, and he was forced to flee the city that had welcomed him so grandly.

In the weeks that followed, thousands abandoned Potosí. Freelance miners went to La Plata or to Oruru, where new veins of silver had recently been discovered. These mines were not as rich as those of the Cerro, but they were at a lower altitude where the climate was slightly better and where no threat of disaster hung over the towns. The maid Juana and the brother she had saved from the mine slipped away among the throngs.

Maria Santa Hilda made a vow to pray for the repose of Morada's soul every time she took silver from the cache under the floorboards of her strong room. With those riches, she provided for the poor children of the outlying villages and the broken and damaged women in her care. And she prayed for Inez. She would never know if the girl had repented before she died, but she clung to the hope that the flail that killed Inez had been a means of true repentance.

The Alcalde's widow, Doña Ana, entered the convent and took the name Sor Inez. Her daughter Gemita remained in the care of the Tovar family at the Ingenio de Corpus Christi. The convent assured Don Antonio and Doña Pilar that a substantial dowry would be available for Gemita when the time came for her to marry.

Money changed hands between the Abbess and a certain scribe known to have connections with the lesser officers of the Inquisition, after which Sor Eustacia was released into the care of the Abbess. The record in the gold-tooled, green leather tome said Eustacia was irreparably insane. In the peace of the convent, this eventually proved not to be so.

DaTriesta retired at half pay from his post as Commissioner—the usual punishment for officers of the Holy Tribunal whose offenses were too flagrant to be overlooked or whose personal habits offended the Inquisitor.

For her escapades outside the walls, Sor Monica was ordered by the head of the order in Madrid to return to Spain. Her Abbess mourned her loss, and though Monica would have to endure two consecutive winters and a perilous and horrid journey, she rejoiced that she would arrive in Spain for the following Easter. In the warmth of the Spanish spring, she would plant her herbs. They would flourish, and their blossoms would surround her. "I knew all my prayers would be answered," she told her Abbess. "God has wrought all these miracles through the intercession of His Holy Mother."

How modest they are, thought Doña Ana, now Sor Inez, that they attribute all their accomplishments to God.

Potosí grew poorer, to the great advantage of morals, according to one chronicler who said the citizens stopped burning money and burned wax candles in church instead. The Inquisition went on. The Bishop went on. The injustice went on. But the pleasanter parts of life also went on.

After her adventure in men's clothing, Beatriz Tovar returned home in the company of Rodrigo, the man her father had chosen to be her husband. She found that the prisoners of the cave-in at her father's mine had been released. The *mitayos* had escaped with just a few broken limbs—serious, but not fatal. Rumor spread among the Indians that the curse had been lifted from the Corpus Christi lode.

Domingo Barco confessed to Antonio Tovar and Doña Pilar that he had given the papers to Santiago Yana, when Inez insisted he hide them for her. "I could not keep them myself," he said. "My mother kept one to protect me from the Alcalde. But I knew he would suspect I had them and not hesitate to kill me and my mother. Santiago knew to bring them to Don Tovar if anything happened to me."

"But why Santiago? Why did you give them to him?" Pilar asked.

"Because I knew he had debts, and I could pay him. I thought it would help him. The Alcalde must have followed me that night, when I met Santiago at the inn and sent him to get the papers. Morada must have waited at the mouth of the mine for Santiago to bring up the packet. I should have gone with Santiago and protected him instead of waiting in the town. The Alcalde threw him down the shaft, but Santiago's death is on my soul." His face, bathed in sadness, was handsomer even than when he smiled. So like Antonio's face to Pilar, now that she knew him as her husband's son. She knew too that she would never question Antonio about fathering this son. He had been five years in this New World before their marriage. Antonio—loyal as he had been since she came to Potosí—must be forgiven for this. Much worse her own sin for the son she had lost so many years ago.

The dowry of Beatriz Tovar was only eight thousand pesos, and smitten as the groom was, he did not even ask if the coins were old money or new. The marriage was arranged quickly because winter was setting in. The bridal couple were grateful for the haste because they could not wait to get at each other.

The groom's most noble aunt bought the wedding cake and the bride's gloves and joined with several other godparents to buy the veil.

"Men want their women devout because they enjoy thinking of themselves as bad by comparison," Pilar told her daughter on the eve of her wedding, "but they do not want women to be too intelligent. There is no joy in feeling stupid."

Beatriz was not listening. She was thinking of what her mother had told her earlier and was too busy contemplating the hole in the bridal sheet they would lay over her when she awaited her groom on her wedding night.

All of Potosí society attended the celebration of the marriage—true noblemen, impostors who pretended to be descendants of the Conquistadores, Basques, even some Andalusians.

To his wedding Rodrigo wore a costume so rich, it was valued at eighty hundred thousand pesos, all embroidered with the richest pearls, zircons, rubies, and sapphires and adorned with thirty emeralds of unusual size and also twelve diamonds of great value. In the months and years to come, he would have the cunning goldsmiths of Potosí work these jewels into magnificent adornments for his beloved Beatriz.

The bride wore Italian shoes with high heels studded with silver nails and a green silk mantle lined with lace. She carried a precious handkerchief given to her by her bridesmaid, Gemita. It looked curiously familiar to the groom.

On the morning of their wedding, Rodrigo waited for Beatriz before the gorgeously carved façade of the convent church of Santa Isabella de los Santos Milagros. The music of timbrels and pipes, reed flutes and tambourines, accompanied the bride to meet her groom, who presented her with a bouquet fashioned of feathers to look like fresh roses.

From the hidden choir that overlooked the altar, the nuns of the convent chanted joyous anthems as the couple entered, accompanied by their parents and all the guests. They then sang the glorious Mass of Tomás Luis de Victoria for the nuptials celebrated by Padre Junipero, with his left hand still bandaged from the damage sustained in his torture by Morada's men.

At the feast that followed the wedding Mass, the Indians of the *ingenio* performed the *cueca*, a courting dance, while the company dined on beef and mutton, fowls, venison, raw and preserved fruits, corn, and wine, all of which had been brought from great distance on exhausted mules.

The weather held until after the ceremony, but snow soon closed the mountain passes, keeping the bride and groom in Potosí until spring, to the delight of Pilar Tovar.

The snow also stopped the exodus of miners from the city. The winter proved so brutal that many a day people were forced to remain in their beds for warmth. Some enjoyed this more than others.